# WILD THING

## RUTHLESS PARADISE BOOK 4

### LEXI RAY

WILD THING

Copyright © 2023 Lexi Ray

Editor: Tracy Liebchen

❁ Created with Vellum

# PLAYLIST

*Reputation*—Post Malone
*What Do I Tell My Friends?*—Bree Runway
*While You're At It*—Jessie Murphy
*Ecstasy*—XXXTENTACION, Noah Cyrus
*Ghost(LA Garagetronic Mix)*—Luc
*Trouble*—Valerie Broussard
*I'll Make It Worth Your While*—Artificial Pleasure
*Pacify Her*—Melanie Martinez
*Too Far Gone*—The Plot In You
*Big Boss(Interlude)*—Victoria Monét
*Call Me Back*—DORA
*POOF*—DSL
*You Don't Wanna Play With Us*—TheUnder, Robyn The Bank
*Crazy*—Doechii
*Yellow*—Tyler Ward
*Louder*—Katéa

You can find the playlist on Spotify.

# PROLOGUE
## KAT

I WAS GETTING ICE CREAM AND ARGUING WITH A RANDOM GUY by the vending machine in the hospital when my mom passed away.

Sometimes, the most trivial things remind you of the saddest days in your life.

When I was eleven, Mom was diagnosed with cancer.

When I was eleven and eight months, she collapsed and went into the hospital, going in and out of ICU for the next several months.

By the time I was eleven years, eleven months and twenty days, I was spending every afternoon after school in the hospital, doing homework, and watching movies on my iPad in Mom's room.

It had become a routine. In the rare moments Mom came to, I tried to spend every second around her. Talking constantly because she barely could. Stroking her weak hand because she had a hard time moving. Bringing up the happy moments of the past as if I could bring my old mom back, make her look like she used to, with twenty more pounds, without sunken eyes or chapped lips.

By then, Dad had come back from overseas once again. That day, he'd gone to run errands, and I'd just woken up from a nap in the armchair next to Mom's bed.

It was an ordinary day, sunny outside but the hospital room was dim because they kept the blinds closed. I hated dimness. And hospitals.

A nurse came in. Nurses are constantly around the sick and the dying. I decided right then and there I'd never be one.

I was about to bury myself in my iPad when Mom stirred. Her eyes were unusually sparkly, gazing at me from the dark sockets, shades shifting on her sunken cheeks as she whispered, "Kit-Kat," so quietly I thought I'd imagined it.

"Mom?" I came up to her bed.

Her finger twitched—she couldn't lift her hand by then. Nor could she move, really.

I wrapped my hand around her finger, her skin unusually hot to the touch.

She smiled just a tiny bit. She couldn't lift a finger but she smiled—that was my mom, finding strength in the worst times.

She whispered something.

"What was that?" I leaned in closer, hating the smell of meds and hospital sheets. The smell that didn't belong to my mom. I just wanted her back.

"Take care of Dad," she whispered, closing her eyes.

I laughed. "Silly." Dad was a giant warrior. Only Mom could take care of him. That was Mom—Wonder Woman.

"Thirsty," she said. And though she was supposed to have only water, I wanted to cheer her up. She always liked ice cream. At that moment, all I wanted was to get her an ice cream. So I went out to the vending machine room at the end of the floor.

I was unwrapping the vanilla cone when some rude guy with a bald head and thick glasses said, "You should be in school, like other kids."

Did other kids have their moms in the hospital for three months?

I said something rude, my mouth already too snappy for my age. He reproached me. I bickered, wasting my time on him.

I remember the voice on the loudspeaker. "Nurse, room 312." My head snapped in that direction because I knew. I just knew.

I remember the nurses hurrying into the room, *Mom's* room, as I ran toward it.

I remember the sound of the heart monitor so unusually monotonous and annoying that I wanted it to go away so it didn't bother Mom.

"Mom?"

I remember the nurse hovering over her bed, another one running in and pushing me aside.

"Mom?"

I remember someone's voice, saying words that didn't make sense. "She's gone, sweetie."

She wasn't. She was right there. Covered by those awful

sheets. Smelling of those horrible meds. She was tired, too tired to open her eyes again. And that awful monotonous sound—God, she needed peace and sunlight.

"Mom?"

But she didn't respond.

Nor would she ever.

And I stood by her bed like a statue, ice cream melting down my hand, mixed with the tears that dripped from my face.

# 1

## KAT

"Archer? Archer, sweetheart?"

I tap his cheek with my palm, but there's no response.

Everything is wrong. *This* is wrong. He barely has a pulse. And the memory of that awful monotonous heart monitor from the past starts fading in and out in my mind.

My heart beats for the two of us, so fast I have to take deep breaths to figure out what I'm doing as I sit on my knees on the floor next to him.

I dial Marlow.

"Marlow!" I shout into the phone when he picks up. "Archer overdosed! I need a doctor at his house! Now!"

Then I dial Dr. Hodges's private number and shout into the phone.

"Archer, baby," I murmur, patting his cheek, his head bobbing.

It's an awful moment—me next to him, my red party dress in pretty contrast with his black clothes, like blood and ashes, the air suddenly sucked out of the room, the piano tunes of Billy Joel's song softly filtering through the room.

I hate feeling helpless. I always know what to do in emergency situations. But this is different because it's not just anyone. It's *him.*

"Archer." I cup his face and rub his cheeks with my thumbs, trying to wake him up.

His eyelids flutter, and my heart lurches in my chest with momentary relief.

"Archer, baby, look at me," I plead just as the front door slams, and Marlow darts into the living room, falls to his knees, and slides across the floor toward me and Archer.

"Fuck-fuck-fuck." He pushes my hands away and slaps Archer on the face too hard, again and again, as I watch in trance.

Suddenly, there are more people. Marlow pulls me away as I register Dr. Hodges getting down on his knees next to Archer and barking something about Narcan and an IV.

Maddy—she's right behind him, on the floor, on her knees, quickly pulling equipment and tubes and packages out of a big tote.

We are all on our knees for Archer, and I want to weep. I did it again—lashed out and ran my mouth minutes after Archer found out about his dad's death.

The quick conversations don't fully register in my head.

"What did he have?"

"Black heroine."

"Shit."

"Pass me Narcan."

"Hold him."

Archer's head moves slowly from side to side. His half-open eyes hold my gaze for a moment then shift elsewhere. He tries to push the doctor away, but Dr. Hodges won't have it.

Panic rises in my chest as I watch all this—Archer's strong body, sleeves rolled up, an IV needle going in—the sight that's supposed to be a relief but makes my hair stand on end.

And then he inhales sharply, his body shifting as he tries to get up.

*Archer…* I want to say his name, want to kneel before him, and wrap my arms around him.

His unfocused eyes shift between Dr. Hodges and Maddy, who keep talking to him, checking his eyes and his vitals. Then his gaze meets mine again, just for several seconds.

*I'm so sorry.*

I hope he can see it in my eyes, but he looks away, shaking his head slowly as if trying to shake off what just happened.

I can't…

I can't keep watching as the most powerful man I've ever known is confronted with what he just tried to do. Was that an accident? Intentional?

The horrible thought is lodged in my head, piercing me with so much guilt that I feel like throwing up.

I run outside, where nothing reminds me of the horrible words I spoke an hour ago. The words that possibly caused this. Was I really so mean that Archer attempted to—

I can't finish the thought, the sobs shaking my chest so

strongly that I finally give in, and tears start streaming down my face.

*You are such a piece of shit, Kat.*

I lean with my back to the wall next to the front door and slide down, closing my eyes and taking deep breaths. It doesn't work. They are jagged and sloppy. My chest shakes. Tears come like a freaking waterfall.

I inhale deeply until I know I can talk, get my phone out of my clutch, and dial Kai.

"Hey."

"You have to come to Archer's, Kai. Right now. Please."

I don't wait for his response. If he cares, he'll be here.

Only five minutes pass when I see a dark silhouette approaching. Kai. I knew he'd come.

"What happened?" he asks.

"He—"

And then it's back—that monstrous thought that this whole thing wasn't an accident.

"He—" A sob escapes me, my chest shakes, and I have to inhale to calm down.

"Kat?" Kai's voice is panicky. "What the fuck happened?"

"Kai…" I can't breathe.

Kai darts inside, his hurried footsteps disappearing as the door closes, then opens a minute later.

"You alright?" It's Maddy, always so calm.

"Is *he*?"

"Yeah. He's fine. He *will* be fine. We got here on time. You did good."

What a joke. I want to punch myself.

"I'm gonna go to him," I say, rising to my feet, barefoot —I just remembered I tossed my shoes into some bush.

Maddy blocks my way. "Don't, Kat. Let it go tonight. Kai is there. Archer will probably feel uncomfortable with someone else around. After, you know…"

"How are you letting him be by himself?" My voice breaks. "Everyone left him when—"

"Kat, calm down."

Right. I wipe my face with my shaking hands. "Do you think it was an accident?"

I need to know it was. That it wasn't my horrible words that could've killed him. I'll never forgive myself for what I said. *How* I said it. *When.*

The door opens. Dr. Hodges and Marlow come out.

I stare at the doctor with hope. "How is he?"

He nods. "He'll be fine."

Everyone is just fucking fine.

"And you are letting him stay home tonight?"

"He won't have it any other way. I have his vitals connected through his bracelet to the app on my phone. He'll be monitored."

"How?"

"Every bracelet does that."

Right. *I'm* not allowed to monitor him, but the freaking bracelet is.

"Give him space," he says softly, looking away. "He needs it. Tonight is a dark night."

## 2

## ARCHER

My heart is heavy and empty but pumping like I just raced for miles.

I need air or more drugs to bring me back to where I was supposed to be—nowhere. The hollowness that wraps around me is too much to bear, a thousand-pound weight on my chest.

I have no idea how much time has passed since Doc and everyone left. Marlow was here. Maddy. Kat.

I was on the floor, then on the couch.

My head spins as I finally rise from the couch and right away trip on the IV bag.

"Hey, man."

And there's Droga. Out of all people, he's here, rising from the couch too and holding his hands out for me like I'm a fucking princess who needs to be catered to.

His phone beeps. They're probably giving him instructions on how to babysit me.

Was that cardiac arrest? That happened before. Exactly the same fucking way. And someone brought me back.

I know what happened, but my brain works faster than the hormones adjust to the drugs and medication in my system. Right now, I feel nothing but suffocation.

"I need to be outside," I murmur, grab my cigarettes, and drag my feet out onto the deck.

The pool is still bright neon blue. The night air is heavy with moisture and heat. It's quiet, except for the soft trickling of the pool waterfall.

Quiet hell…

I lower myself onto the terrace steps.

Droga comes up quietly, takes a seat next to me, and lights a cigarette too.

I don't know why he's here. Pity? I don't need that. Obligation? They all want me well and alive because Zion's well-being depends on it.

An hour ago, I felt angry, hopeless, maybe. Now I feel pathetic like I failed at one more thing—keeping my face.

Silence burns between us with a tobacco smell and a metallic taste in my mouth. When my cigarette is burned down to the filter, I light another one, inhale deeply, scorching my lungs and summoning the courage to talk about the incident that left everyone scarred a year ago. Kat doesn't know the full story. But Droga should.

He's quiet, like he's waiting for something.

"There were two nights in the last year that were absolute hell," I start the confession that I've done so many times in my mind.

The person next to me is the only one in this world

who'd understand and hopefully forgive me for something that everyone considers my fault.

"We didn't get to her on time," I say quietly, not recognizing my voice, the memory of that night sending shivers down my spine.

Droga turns to look at me, but I don't meet his eyes. "Who?"

"Olivia."

When her name is brought up in occasional conversations among the guards, it's still said in a low tone and with the heavy followed silence that swells with the horror of that night.

"The night Olivia was taken, we had a party," I say, the words eerie in the night silence.

We've lost over a dozen people on Zion since the Change, but it's Olivia's story that's the darkest.

"A big party," I continue slowly. It's hard to put words together like my mouth doesn't belong to me. My brain is fuzzy. "Letting loose, you know, after being cooped up in this place for a year."

I have to pause and take a deep breath to summon the thoughts and courage.

"When the surveillance team got ahold of me that night, we sent the boats to the Eastside. Within minutes, I was at the surveillance center, and when I watched the cameras..." I close my eyes, wanting to forget, but it has an adverse effect, only making those horrible images more vivid. So I open my eyes and stare at the blue water in the pool. "You guys had already found Olivia, so I called the team off."

Droga shifts. My cigarette is burned down to the filter

again, and I crush it between my fingers, letting the searing pain distract me for a second.

"We rewound the footage to the beginning of the attack on your village. Saw one of your guys getting shot. Then Olivia being dragged into the jungle. And then…"

The images from the footage still haunt me in my worst lows and drunk nightmares.

I inhale deeply, feeling my chest tighten so hard that I can't breathe. "And then… Several Savages, who lost their moral compass a long time ago. One girl…" I don't want to talk about it but have to. Droga has to know. "They didn't even make it to the Ashlands, Droga. They did it"—I pause to search for words and can't find them—"right there, in the jungle…"

My chest shakes. I rub my face with both hands, but it doesn't erase the horror show in my mind. Never will.

Droga is quiet. A year ago, he and the other guys found Olivia's body. They knew what was done to her.

"I couldn't watch the footage, Droga," I say almost in a whisper. "I couldn't—"

"You don't have to talk about it," he says quietly.

"No. But I need to. I had a *party* that night, Droga. I left my fucking phone at the bar. And security had instructions not to interfere with the Eastside unless it was an emergency. It *was* a fucking emergency!" I snap. "But it took them forever to get the clearance. Because *I* had a *fucking* party! While *she*…"

I want to scream, but bile rises in my throat, and I hold my breath so I don't vomit.

My eyes burn. The lump in my throat is the size of a golf ball.

"And if—" I exhale quickly.

"It's not your fault, Crone."

I chuckle, disguising a sob that's hard to hold back. "But it is, yeah? They say I'm responsible for everything on Zion. They all blamed me. *You* blamed me, I'm sure. I blamed myself, who else?"

I shake my head, knowing I'm right.

"My guys—the ones who were on surveillance that night—watched the footage. They served in Afghanistan, Somalia, Syria. They've seen it all. And they couldn't meet each other's eyes that night. We're Gods here on Zion, you know. Shit like this is for war zones, not the pretty island. That's what the Change taught us—that before, we, the West, were lucky to be shielded from the worst humans are capable of. No human should see anything like what happened to Olivia. Moreover, experience it. And those with deranged minds are not human. They shouldn't be living in a society."

"No," Droga says almost in a whisper.

"I'm glad Olivia is dead."

Droga's head snaps in my direction. "Dude…"

"I am," I repeat. "Because if she survived that—*them*— that night… I don't know how one can live with the memories of that… How a *girl* can possibly mentally survive *that*."

He knows I'm right. PTSD can be more destructive than the actual traumatic experience.

I open my eyes as wide as I can, hoping they'll swallow back the tears that are about to spill.

*Fuck.*

"Scum like them should be dead," Droga says with an edge in his voice.

"They are." I finally turn to meet Droga's confused gaze. "Don't look at me like this, Droga. They *are* dead. That's why I have contractors—to do the dirty work. And after what they've seen in their lives, they don't mind cleaning this earth of scum. Even if it's self-served justice. I don't give a shit about anyone who wants to preach morals in this scenario. They can fuck off. Those Savages didn't deserve to breathe."

Droga nods, and for the first time, I feel relief, like I finally said something right.

He lights a cigarette and passes it to me, then lights one for himself.

It's on peaceful nights like these that the awful memories always cut the deepest. Mom and little Adam. Droga's accident. The night the world went dark. Olivia.

"What was the other night?" Droga asks quietly.

I manage a smile because that other night started something that made him happy. It's peculiar how horrible events can eventually lead to someone's best days. "The night the boat with the new arrivals crashed in a storm."

# 3

## ARCHER

Three new recruits and the boat crew died the night the boat got caught in the storm. For once, no one blamed it on me. I wasn't even the one who gave the clearance. The boat company was paid big bucks to bring the new people to Zion. They fucked the weatherman and got greedy.

"I'm surprised you cared so much about strangers," Droga says.

"Not the strangers, just her."

Droga's voice is etched with surprise. "Callie?"

I don't mind confessing again, because life is unpredictable. I could've died tonight. It's easier to breathe when you let the dark thoughts out.

"I got her for *you*, Droga."

"I know."

I suck in a sharp breath, remembering everything I put those two through. "She was meant to be a peace offering. And the night we got the word that the Coast Guard lost the signal from the boat, I stayed up all night, feeling the same horror as I did after your accident. If she died, I would've fucked things up for you for good. I would've never forgiven myself. Nor would you."

The silence between us is not heavy anymore. If anything, it's liberating.

"Wanna have a drink?" I offer, getting Droga's loud snort in response.

"No. I think you've had enough for tonight."

"Look who's playing mom."

"Booze is not a solution."

"I'm not looking for a solution. Just something to make life a little easier."

"People who care for you do that."

I laugh and right away feel my chest tighten. "You realize, I have no one left. Besides uncles, aunts, and some cousins, who don't give a flying fuck about me but are already hiring lawyers to dip their hands in Dad's money. And it's only been hours since he's been gone."

"I'm sorry, Crone."

I shrug.

"A lot of us don't have anyone," he says. "That's what you don't understand. You think people are angry at you? They are just angry at life. And there you are, who has it all. The Change didn't affect you in the slightest. If anything, it made you richer."

I never thought of it that way.

"I don't have anyone but Callie," he says.

"See? You have her."

"If you weren't such a dick, you and Katura could work things out."

"Bullshit."

"She saved you tonight."

"She was in the right place at the right time. You should've heard what she said half an hour before that. I fucked it up with her like I do with everyone else."

"Crone…" Droga ruffles his hair dramatically. "She's the one who called me and asked me to come here. She knows you. Cares. And while we were fussing around you in your living room, you know what she was doing?"

Kat saved my life—ironic. "Let me guess, giving instructions to Doc?"

Droga's silence is too long. When I turn to look at him, I recognize that gaze—judgment. "Maddy said Katura sat outside your front door, crying hysterically, her hands shaking."

Kat, crying… I could've never imagined that.

Droga flicks the tip of his cigarette. "I hope soon, you figure out who on this island really cares about you."

Does she? That's wishful thinking.

Droga and I shoot the shit for some time. They say tragedies unite people. I'd have to go through a few to reconnect with everyone I've pissed off in this life.

Soon, I have a hard time keeping my eyes open.

"I'm gonna sleep, Droga. Thanks for being here." I get up slowly, my body heavy like it's made out of iron as we walk to the living room. "I'll see you tomorrow. It's gonna be chaos with the board members and Dad's estate and the White House business."

"I'll see you when you wake up."

I scan the floor that's littered with empty med capsules and the lonely IV, but no syringe in the vicinity.

"You don't have to come and check on me." I rub my eyes. "I'm not that pathetic."

"Oh, I'm not leaving tonight."

My eyes shoot to Droga, who smirks, plopping theatrically on the couch.

I frown, confused. "Don't be ridiculous—"

"I'm not leaving, Crone. Not a chance. Gonna make sure you don't do anything stupid. Your couch is fine."

I want to interject, but there is this fuzzy feeling starting in my chest when I watch Droga kick his shoes off, a phone in his hands as he gets comfortable. "Sweetheart, bring me a blanket, will you?" he says without raising his eyes off the phone.

I stall for a moment, then realize he's trying to be funny. Droga. *Joking*. With *me*.

The feeling in my chest is like a roller coaster ride at the highest point.

Droga is reconciling with me—whoa!

I shake my head and try to swallow the fucking lump that's back in my throat. Because for the first time in years, he's sticking around.

I grab a blanket from the closet and toss it onto the couch.

"Just don't jerk off on my couch," I throw at him.

"Fuck off."

"Corlo, good night."

The living room goes dark, save for the dim glow from Droga's phone.

I am walking away when Droga's voice stops me.

"Hey, Crone?"

He doesn't take his eyes off the phone when he says, "If something happened to you tonight, I would've lost the only brother I ever had."

The words make me clench my jaw so hard that I feel my teeth grind.

"If you ever need to talk," he adds, "you know where to find me. But for that, bro, you need to be alive, yeah?"

*Bro…*

I don't answer.

The word rips me apart, and the open wound inside me finally gushes with all the emotions I've held pent up for years. They come like water through a broken dam, deafening me, making my mind spin and my heart pulsate, the lump in my throat expanding threefold, my eyes burning.

And I take it all to my bedroom where no one can hear or see the king of Zion finally on his knees.

# 4

## KAT

"What do you mean he left?"

The air in the break room at the Center seems too still as my eyes burrow into one of Archer's assistants.

"Mr. Crone left this morning, around seven," she explains, pouring herself keto coffee with an indifferent look like it's an ordinary day. Right, she doesn't know about Archer's episode the night before.

I got to work at around nine, wondering what it'd be like after the news of the Secretary of Defense being dead and all, absolutely sure that Archer would be around, on the phone, or in the conference room. I was hoping to see him, called Maddy this morning to see if Dr. Hodges had an update about him.

Instead, I get this news.

"He took the jet," the assistant says with a quick smile. "With seven others from the Eastside."

"Oh."

My heart breaks at the thought that he should be

watched by a doctor instead of flying around and dealing with his father's death. Someone should be with him. A friend. A relative. Does he even have anyone who cares?

The last thought is heavy.

On the way to my desk, I type a message to him.

**Me: How are you today?**

No response—I'm not surprised, don't expect any.

The Center goes on in its usual way, the nature soundtrack annoyingly peaceful though my mood is so grim that I stare at the screen of my work laptop for what seems like an eternity after it lights up, then finally dial Dad.

"I heard the news," he says instead of greeting me.

I stare down at the desk instead of him and nod in silence.

"I'm assuming Mr. Crone will leave for the mainland if he didn't yet?" Dad always calculates everything. Just like Archer. They're so alike, it's scary.

"He..." I look around, making sure no one is close, then put the headphones in. "He overdosed yesterday," I tell Dad quietly. "Only a handful of people know."

The next five minutes are a slow exchange of phrases that leave my mouth without much apprehension.

"So. O'Shea. Did you get my message?" Dad asks.

The message seems like it happened days ago.

"Right, O'Shea."

Everything around feels like mush—reality, employees at the computers, time. Like my brain is malfunctioning. O'Shea is the last person on my mind.

"So, he's connected to Tsariuk and was sent here by him. Possibly with Cunningham," I say, trying to shake off my thoughts about Archer. "What do we do? And what *can* we do without Archer being here?"

"Nick Marlow is in charge of security. So I'd like to get on a conference call with him and you. And someone who knows the security inside and out besides him, someone trusted. This last piece of info creates a bit of a problem. The longer we wait, the more likely O'Shea is to do something that can put Ayana in danger, being on the inside and all. So let's get this call scheduled."

I call Marlow, and an hour later, he comes in and motions me to follow him to Archer's office.

"His online connection is encrypted," he says, closing the door behind us. "He gave me the clearance."

So, Marlow talked to Archer, but Archer didn't find a second to text me back—understandable, though it pricks me with hurt.

"Is he alright?" I ask, not looking at Marlow so I don't give away my emotions.

"I guess," he says.

The door opens to reveal Raven, making me tense in momentary surprise. He's the guy from the beach, the same one we saw at the Carnage fight club weeks ago.

Raven is built smaller than Archer but looks so much more intimidating. Dressed in all black, long sleeves, jeans, and Vans, with his jet-black messy hair, he looks like a devil and emanates danger. The only thing missing is the cigarette that usually hangs from between his lips, smoke curling around him.

He's silent, but his presence fills the room, his prying gaze turning my stomach in slight unease.

"Kat, this is Raven," Marlow says without looking as he sets up the call on the big screen on the wall. "Raven, meet Katura."

"Nice to meet you," I say.

He shakes my hand with a nod but doesn't say a word. There's something odd about him, which I can't pinpoint yet. He's not a spring-breaker or rich. A stray—used to be, I assume—but of the worst kind, someone you don't want to get into a fight with in the wrong part of town but someone you'll probably be safer with in those same places than any trained soldier.

I know this kind. I used to work for them on the streets of Bangkok. High loyalty, gray morals, and little value for human life. This guy doesn't need tattoos head to toe to scream danger. He's been to hell and back, on the edge of a syringe and at the end of a sharp knife. It's in his calculated movements and the way his jaw shifts just a tiny bit like he's tasting fresh blood. In the way he doesn't have to look at you for you to know he hears everything, and when he does look—his gaze is razor sharp, making you look away.

He walks past me—slowly, as if he's circling prey—then pulls a chair from next to the desk and motions for me to sit down.

Well-mannered, huh? Maybe not a street guy after all, but definitely someone on the other side of the law.

Somehow, I feel like he talks even less than Archer. And somehow, I know that he's the type of person who gathers a lot of info and uses it against people. His eyes don't leave my face, not even for the moment he takes to pull two more chairs out. Like he's profiling me.

"Alright." Marlow navigates the arrow on the screen to a conference app and finds my father's name, then starts the call.

Considering, I came here undercover only several months ago, the conference call between the almighty of Zion and my dad is strange, to say the least.

"Mr. Ortiz, nice to see you again," Marlow says as soon as my dad's face appears on the screen.

Again?

"Hi, Nick."

Since when is Marlow Nick to my dad? Am I freaking missing something?

Marlow introduces Raven, and when Raven says, "Nice to meet you, Mr. Ortiz," I hear his voice for the first time— low, business-like, but soft. Whoa, I need to learn more about this guy.

"So, Katura already told you about O'Shea." My father spends some time giving more detailed intel on him, all the while looking calm and relaxed like he deals with Russian mob spies on a daily basis. The best part of this? Marlow and Raven's eyes are glued to the screen, and my chest bursts with pride for my pops.

He's the only one talking, in that monotonous voice of a lecturer. "We need to isolate O'Shea and Cunningham. You need to figure out who they are close to. If you give Katura their work schedules and GPS tracking prints for the last month, she'll share with me any info that might seem suspicious. There might be more guys in their crew. And that creates another problem. You need to restrict their movements."

"Restrict?" Marlow finally asks after a prolonged silence.

"Detention. Incarceration. Whatever amenities you have at Ayana. No form of communication with anyone while they are detained. But that's where you have a problem."

He pauses, and it's Raven who speaks now. "Who is reliable enough to handle and guard them."

"Correct." Dad nods. "You only need two-three guys who can do twenty-four-hour remote surveillance. But those guys have to be trusted. And by the looks of it, you can't trust a single security guy at Ayana right now. In theory."

"And in practice?" Marlow asks.

"In practice, you have to compromise. I assume Mr. Crone's private security team left for the mainland with him." He nods when Marlow confirms it. "You have no choice then. Someone has to do the job. I can look through the files again and make suggestions. Then there's the next question."

"Which is?" Marlow asks again, his foot tapping the floor—I can't tell if he's worried or excited.

"You need to get O'Shea and Cunningham to *talk*."

I know by the edge in my dad's voice what that means.

Marlow gets the idea. "Talk," he repeats like he's savoring the word.

Dad clears his throat, and I see Raven's eyes snap to Marlow and then back to the screen. He gets it.

"Not pep-talk, Nick. They are not office employees. And you know who might've sent them. You need to interrogate them."

I glance at Raven. His eyes narrow just slightly, his cheekbones sharpening as he sucks in his cheeks, which gives him an even more vicious look.

Slowly, he shifts his eyes to meet mine.

I stole a glance at the missing phalanges on his left hand before—he comes from experience. There's no doubt in my mind, that to Raven, doing this sort of *talking* is child's play.

# 5

## KAT

THEY BEAT O'SHEA FOR AN HOUR, THOUGH HE SEEMS TO BE immune to the pain—occupational habit.

"To loosen him up," Marlow says as we sit in the safety of the Center and watch it on the monitor. O'Shea's in a holding cell. No Cunningham in sight, but they got him, too.

There are three guys in the cell with O'Shea.

It's some guard who does the job, meticulously and catching O'Shea by surprise now and then.

"That's the trick," Marlow comments as if he's done it before. "It's a preparatory job."

"Aren't there more sophisticated ways these days?" I ask.

"Just watch."

Another guy in the cell is Chase Bishop, a legend, an expat, and a loner who lives in a bungalow up at the Divide. I've heard about him. He's lived in Port Mrei for years and moved to the middle of nowhere after the

Change. He's tall and muscled, with long wavy hair hanging down to his shoulders. I'd say a biker, but supposedly, former undercover, though seemingly in his early thirties and a bit too young for such an intense background.

Bishop leans against the wall with his arms crossed at his chest, looking bored.

Raven sits on his haunches, with his back against the wall, peacefully smoking.

It's the first time I see Ayana's holding cells, converted from former storage units, a gloomy sight compared to the slick interior of the Center.

I saw plenty of brutality on the streets of Bangkok. Let's just say that a thug making a guy bite the curb and smashing his foot on his head, breaking half of his teeth was something I can't unsee for the rest of my life.

"There's gotta be a different way," I say, annoyed.

"There is," Marlow says. I'm wondering why he's so calm. "This is just a usual routine Bishop wants to try."

Everyone in the holding cell is silent. I guess it'll be Cunningham's turn at some point.

"Psychological impact," Marlow explains. "That's what Archer says."

Archer's instructions?

"You start by giving him an idea of what's to come. And when he's getting the clue, you switch."

"To what?" I ask, cringing at the thought that Archer has some twisted tactics planned out, but Marlow only nods toward the screen.

Bishop stirs. "Do you know what the Pear of Anguish

is?" he asks, casually rubbing the floor with the tip of his boot. "We can go old-fashioned tonight."

Even I know the nasty torture device, shaped like a pear with metal petals hinged at the top and a crank on the other side. It's inserted into orifices. Turning the crank opens the petals that cut like blades into flesh. Bishop is definitely not a biker.

O'Shea doesn't answer. He knows.

"Your mouth, O'Shea," Bishop says indifferently, "looks like a good choice."

O'Shea spits blood on the ground and tries to shift, his body tied to a chair slumping. "You do that, I won't be able to tell you what you want to hear."

"True." Bishop only nods, hands in his pockets now. "There are other cavities. More sensitive."

"Cut the bullshit. I know I don't have a chance."

Bishop pulls out a phone from his pocket, checks it, then sticks it back in.

"Smart," he replies in a slightly different tone. "Here's the thing about Zion. We're all civilized people here."

O'Shea sucks his teeth. "Right."

"I don't usually take the easy path, but Mr. Crone is a nice guy."

Bishop turns and picks up something from a tray on a small table that I notice only now.

I lean closer to the screen. "What's that?"

Marlow leans closer to the screen, too. "Benzodiazepine, ether, psilocybin, I don't know, there's a concoction of them. Ask Archer. I'm not a chemist."

"How does it work?"

"It's illegal, I'll tell you that much. As to what it does, I'm sure we'll see soon."

Illegal, but obviously not on Zion. But the fact that Archer chose a more humane way makes me relax just a little.

O'Shea doesn't struggle when Bishop injects something into his arm, only looks at him with a bloodied smile.

"We are a small tight community here on Zion," Bishop explains, slowly walking back to the tray to place the empty syringe there, then picks up another and injects O'Shea again.

Raven is still smoking. Now that the beating stopped, the whole thing is like a chat between close friends. Minus the blood.

Bishop casually sticks his hands in his pockets. "We need to know who else Tsariuk sent. What you found out. Who you talk to on Zion." In a simple t-shirt, army pants, and boots, he reminds me of my dad. Granted, they have a similar past, which is a strange coincidence. "So let's start with Tsariuk."

O'Shea laughs. His laughter is relaxed, considering they beat him for an hour. Whatever was in the syringe is working fast.

"Now tell Mr. Crone how many people Tsariuk sent to Zion," Bishop says, calm like a therapist.

I don't get it. "Are they recording it for Archer?"

"Archer has the surveillance stream televised to him," Marlow responds. "Shh."

*Oh.*

He's on the other side of the screen, just like me and

Marlow, just like my dad. He has time for this but obviously not for me.

A barely audible sound escapes O'Shea.

"What was that?" Bishop asks.

O'Shea's head bobs, then he rolls it around as if cracking his neck, but the movement is extremely slow.

Marlow shifts next to me. "Must be working, whatever that shit is. Could be strong, too."

"Tsariuk," Bishop repeats louder. "How many people did Tsariuk send?"

"No can tell." O'Shea's speech is slow as if he has a hard time moving his tongue. "Haven't talked to Tsariuk in years."

"He sent you. I saw your file, O'Shea."

"He didn't. He—" O'Shea breaks out into a low continuous chuckle, but Bishop doesn't interrupt him. "I came by myself. With Cunningham."

"Okay." Bishop's tone changes to that of a teacher talking to a slow child. "Let's try again."

"There's nothing else to say. Tsariuk killed my family."

Okay.

My mind goes to the info in his file as he recaps it in a slow bitter voice.

"I had an affair with his sister while I worked in Petersburg. Yeah, shoot me. It happened. I'm not a good man, okay? I should've known I was signing my death warrant. Tsar tracked my wife and newborn, set my house in England on fire, with my wife and child in it."

The words are eerie, considering there's a faint smile on O'Shea's face.

"I ran. They would've killed me too. I could never come back to Russia, never saw my son or his mother. But as soon as the rumor spread around that Tsariuk's daughter went missing after the Change, the whole fucking world started paying attention."

The cell is quiet. I hold my breath.

O'Shea looks way too relaxed. Slurring, he almost sounds high, but his words are coherent, and there's a permanent smile on his face. Whatever concoction Archer got ready for him must have multiple effects.

"I know I'm fucked." O'Shea looks around aimlessly, then tilts his head back and closes his eyes.

After a prolonged silence, Bishop asks, "And your buddy, Cunningham?"

"He's in for the ride. We wanted to do an extraction and sell Milena—if we were to find her—to the highest bidder. I'd kill Tsar if I had a chance. Her? We are not women-killers, but we'd make money, and whoever bought her, she'd deal with them, and they'd deal with her father."

O'Shea sniffles and smiles broadly, blood on his teeth, drooling onto his shirt.

"Tsar is desperate," he continues in a slow raspy voice. "She's his only child. He's getting old. His wife has cancer and is dying. Why his daughter is in hiding—well, I can imagine. Aleksei Tsariuk is not a fucking saint. Not even to his wife or daughter. But things change. She might be dead —he's not stupid. Hundreds and thousands went missing during the bombings. He's been searching the mainland— shelters, hospitals, internment camps, prisons, survivalist compounds. You name it—Tsar has already looked into it.

And the only thing that can stop him is her dead body and DNA proof. But this island, it's of special interest."

The cell is too quiet and motionless except for the smoke from Raven's cigarette curling into the air.

"Here's the thing." O'Shea licks his lips for the longest time. He's thirsty—must be the effect of the drug. "You think Tsariuk sent people here? I bet he did, through any hole possible, Zion has many. But... So did the Cosa Nostra, who had a falling out with him. So did the Arabs, because they want leverage. So did the Chicago Outfit, because they want to kiss his ass. Yeah. You guys became the most targeted island in the world. Finding Milena Tsariuk is like the almighty's most exciting Easter egg hunt. Zion security?"

He laughs, loud and long, then goes into a long coughing fit. Bishop stands with his arms crossed. Raven lights another cigarette.

"Security is fucked, 'cause there are probably more moles there than you think. Your surveillance team—same-same. Staff and service people—that's your weak spot, and there's no chance in the world you'll catch anyone. Because guess what? The old lady who cleans your house—she could be a spy. The gardener—could be a snitch. The kid cleaning the dishes at Tapas notices every person who goes in and out and marks down their names—probably works for the locals."

My insides grow cold.

"If Milena is here, she doesn't have a security entourage. She could be snatched away, and Tsariuk will never find out. That's the trick. She could be a weapon against him.

Even the—" O'Shea coughs loudly. "What's that thug's name? The mayor? Butcher, right. He announced a bounty on Milena's head about half a year or so ago. Guess what? To any average fucker in town that's on your payroll, it's like winning a lottery."

O'Shea isn't giving any concrete info, nevertheless, everything he says is like opening a can of worms.

"There's only one thing that can keep your island from everyone in the world sticking their noses in. If you find that fucking ghost girl yourself. Or someone does. Or her body. Show Tsar the body of his daughter—case closed. Until then, Zion is an open target."

# 6

## KAT

"IT'S IMPOSSIBLE TO CHANGE THE ENTIRE SECURITY AND surveillance team in one go. It's hundreds of people," Dad says when I get on a video call with him.

For the first time, he looks worried as he rubs his forehead.

I don't say much when we talk about Tsariuk business. Not when I'm at my desk, and though I use headphones, technically anyone within earshot can hear what I say. Suddenly, O'Shea's words acquire a new meaning. Being in the Center is like being in a den of vipers.

So I limit my responses to occasional nods.

"The only way to make sure Milena Tsariuk is not on Zion is to go through every female resident's file and confirm her identity. For that, Archer is the only one who can give clearance. I'll talk to him."

Everyone talks to Archer, but I'm a no-no. Our messages don't go beyond me asking how he's doing and him responding, "Fine." Nor does he say when he's coming back.

"I have info on Raylin Reyes, Ty's lost sister," Dad says, changing the topic. "She was at the Bryne's Hospital right after the bombings. For half a year."

My heart pounds so strongly that I forget all about Tsariuk and O'Shea. "She didn't die?"

"Well, not during the bombings. I found medical records. She was badly injured, incapacitated. She was transferred to a physical rehab facility, which was shut down due to the increased radiation levels and relocated, and that's when she went missing."

"What do you mean missing?"

"Kit-Kat, look it up in the dictionary."

Jesus, whatever. "So, now?"

"So, now we need to dig more. But not a word to her brother. There's no hope until…"

O'Shea's words come in handy—a death certificate or a body and DNA proof. The Change screwed many people. The worst part is not knowing what really happened, how many went missing and are still alive but for various reasons are in hiding. Off-the-grid is the new black.

We change the topic to Ayana and me. Not a word about Archer, though he's the only person I'm truly concerned about. And when the talk is over, I can't help but think about the papers I stumbled upon the other day.

They were in the folder with the documentation of the companies that used to contract the guards before the Center was officially set up and the security contracts were under the Gen-Alpha umbrella. The files were the transfers between the different companies and bills to independent contractors.

One paper caught my attention—a notice of the leftover budget transferred from a private foundation to the one adjoined to Gen-Alpha.

Odd.

I searched for it online, didn't find anything, then put it in a database search on the Center computer.

One name, just one name came up, and it told a story that no one knew—perhaps still doesn't.

Kai Droga and the fund created for him by the independent non-profit foundation, attached to Gen-Alpha that back then was just a small company. The foundation covered the cost of reconstructive surgeries that weren't covered by Kai's insurance.

Not a chance Kai knows about this and probably shouldn't. This was a pay off—silent, secret. When the right time comes, I'll ask Archer. He has too many traumas he tries to cover up.

Whew.

I'm about to leave the Center when I see Margot strolling out of her office and in my direction. I can't imagine what she can possibly want from me, but her posture is way too arrogant.

We haven't talked about Cece's birthday. In fact, the incident with the picture of me naked in Archer's pool took a backstage after the news about his dad's death.

So when the Pink Medusa stops at my desk and folds her arms across her chest, I cringe at the smell of her perfume and the sight of her bright-orange jumpsuit.

"Going as a pumpkin today?" I don't bother meeting her eyes as I clear the files into the desk drawer.

"About that picture that was passed around," she says with poison in every word.

"About you and I—stop talking to me, okay?" I shut down my computer and rise from my chair.

"I was the one who sent it to everyone."

My head snaps in her direction.

She's admitting it? Is she asking to die right now? I had a feeling she was involved, and her confession is way too bold.

"And I apologize," she adds quickly.

I look around, frowning. Did I just hallucinate? Is there a hidden camera? Another prank?

"What?" I say with a frown like I misheard her.

"That wasn't cool. I'm sorry."

No shit.

I'm about to wrap her pink hair around my fist and bring her to her knees—that would be a more appropriate apology, considering how mad it made me and the things I told Archer, ruining whatever we had going on—but she turns around and hurries away.

What the hell was *that*?

Not that I like having Margot occupy too much real estate in my head, but she's still on my mind as I walk out into the warm humid afternoon and go home to change.

There's a beach get-together. Outcasts and—surprise-surprise—Marlow and Axavier. The last days were a roller-coaster, and this party is the only thing that might help my mind escape from the never-ending thoughts about Archer.

# 7

## KAT

Did I interrupt something?

The door of Kai and Callie's bungalow finally opens after the third knock. Kai's hair is messy and his face is flushed but he has an unmistakable smile when he lets me in.

Yup.

"Busy?" I ask with a snort as I walk in.

Callie fixes her messy pigtails as she goes about the room, picking up random things and shoving them into a beach bag.

"Hey, Kat. How is it going?" Her voice is lazy but out of breath, and when Kai walks past her and pinches her butt, she blushes and swats his hand away with a quiet, "Stop it."

I wrinkle my nose. "Oh, gee, don't tell me I caught you guys in the middle of it."

"Actually, at the end of it. All yours now." Callie chuckles, still not meeting my eyes.

This girl… First, she gets on an island where both her ex and her ex's ex-best friend that she had a thing for play war. If that's not complicated enough, she starts another war between them, then gets a chance to leave but comes back and is now on a permanent honeymoon. To be fair, if someone deserves a cheesy as hell happily ever after that's her and Kai, and I'm a bit envious of their bliss.

"So, a lot of between-the-sheets-action these days, huh?" I ask, strolling around the room as she gets ready.

"Shh." Callie presses her forefinger to her lips.

"Why?" I snap, then hear a voice in one of the bedrooms, a kid's voice. "Oh…"

I cover my mouth with my hand. I forgot they have a kid now, a foster kid, or whatever this arrangement means.

Just then, he comes out of the room, chatting with Kai. He looks like a surfer kid, eight or twelve, it's hard to tell. He's gained some weight but is still skinny.

"Little, this is Katura," Callie introduces us, and the kid shakes hands with me.

"Sonny Little," he says proudly with a half-smile.

It's the second time I've seen him, and now he's dressed in shorts and a t-shirt that are actually a child's size, barefoot, his hair still a mess, down to his shoulder.

He's a Chatty Cathy, for sure, as he slides his feet into flip-flops, chirping non-stop about *The Wizard of Oz*.

"He's obsessed with movies," Kai explains as we all leave the bungalow and head for the beach.

There's already a small party assembled there. Beach umbrellas, coolers, beer. Rap music blasts from a portable speaker. A small but rowdy crowd, Outcasts, like the old days—Owen, Ya-Ya, Guff, and Kristen among others from the Eastside. Surfboards lie in a line on the sand. It's overcast, but the waves are perfect for surfing, the mood is cheerful, and I'm right away handed a beer—Belgian, not the Port Mrei swill we used to drink on the Eastside.

Ty, our Eastside Tarzan, is here. His dirty-blond hair is past his shoulders, and his smile is bigger than ever.

"Look at you, all lovey-dovey," I say to him.

As a confirmation, he wraps his arms around Dani from behind and kisses her on the cheek, then nuzzles her neck.

"Oh, young love," Marlow coos as he stands by the beach chair where I sit and fixes a joint.

I snort. "Like you're older or something."

Marlow lights a joint, takes a hit, and passes it to Ty. "My grandma used to say"—he inhales and holds his breath—"'you should have one big love in your life. Just one. Forever.'"

"Oh, yeah?" Ty squints at him as he takes a hit and passes the joint to me.

"Yeah," Marlow says on an exhale, a cloud of smoke forming around him like a halo. "So I go, 'Grandma, who was your one big love? Grandpa?' She goes, 'Bikers, sweetheart. My one big love was bikers.'"

We all break out in laughter.

"Bullshit," Ty says and lets go of Dani. Before Marlow has time to react, Ty lunges at him and has him in a headlock. "I'll show you love, sweetheart."

In one fast motion, he licks Marlow across his cheek.

Marlow fights back. "Fool!" He wrinkles his nose while the rest of us laugh. "Ew, that tongue, it's like cow-size."

Ty is back wrapped around Dani. "Someone likes it."

"Yuck."

"Someone's yuck is someone else's yum. Right, angel?" He kisses the top of Dani's head and winks at me.

Marlow kicks the sand in his direction. "Yeah, teach the kid your nasty ways."

But Sonny Little has a permanent grin on his face as he sits right on the sand with an open bag of potato chips and watches everyone with amusement. To say it's weird to see a kid among us is an understatement, but it sort of gives the whole gathering a family vibe.

My phone beeps.

"*Chyo nos povesila*?" Marlow asks me why I'm down. "Sent you something."

It's a picture. I pull the screen closer to me so no one sees it, and my heart starts beating wildly.

It's the only picture of us—Archer and I at Cece's party, on the dance floor, dancing *bachata*. My back is to him, his hands are on my waist. I smile at nothing in particular while his eyes are on me like he's just seen the most beautiful woman in his life.

"Thanks," I say quietly to Marlow and put the phone away, though I want to stare at the picture for hours, studying every little detail.

My friend, Jonshu, used to say that attraction is a chemical reaction spiked by testosterone. So if you are a girl, as long as you have enough alphas around you, it helps to curb the need for it.

I can say with certainty that it's rubbish psychology, because Kai, Marlow, Ty, Owen, Bo, and all the others combined can't erase the feeling of something missing without Archer around.

I'm surprised to see Maddy here. Every time I run into her, I ask the same question: "Let's hang out sometime. Maybe, go to a restaurant?"

"Sure," she says indifferently every time, and somehow it ends up being a no. Maddy is always alone, and it feels like she prefers it that way. The only time she opens up is with the Outcasts. And Bo.

Bo is here too, which is an even bigger surprise. He's fully recovered, now on payroll with Archer, taking on the giant task of managing Ayana.

Ty, Kai, and Owen pick up their surfboards, ready to conquer the giant waves brought by winds and the upcoming hurricane season.

I remember Archer mentioning surfing and ask, "Is it true that Archer used to surf?"

Ty, Kai, and Owen immediately turn their heads to me.

Archer told me this once, to which I bulged my eyes at him.

"Why are you surprised?" he laughed then.

"Because it's like, salty, and wet, and God forbid you get dirty."

The guys stand with beers in their hands as the rest of us sit on the sand or chairs in a semi-circle.

"He used to," Marlow answers. "Used to be great."

Kai narrows his eyes on the ocean. "What is he not great at?"

Owen snorts. "Keeping his shit together."

Some Outcasts are still bitter about the last two years. I

shouldn't have brought it up. The guys leave their beers and walk off toward the water. The rest of us chill and watch the surfers, me and Maddy chatting about nothing.

This feels like being on the Eastside again until I turn my head and scan the majestic Ayana resort, splayed above us on the lusciously green hill.

The peak of Zion is weighed by giant fog. It rained earlier today. My butt is wet from sitting on the damp sand. Maddy passes me another beer, and I chug it just to kill my bad mood.

Bad idea, I know. The more I drink, the more I think about Archer. Maddy and I share another joint, which makes it worse. The warm wind against my skin reminds me of Archer's touch.

And then I do what I do best—being drunkenly annoying as I pick up my phone and text him.

**Me: Are you doing alright?**

There are three messages just like this already above, answered, "Fine." More of, "Wanna talk?" answered with, "Have a lot of things going on right now."

I regret this message right away. Until the sound of an incoming message makes my heart jump out of my chest.

**Archer: I'm fine, thanks.**

It dawns on me that it's an auto-response, or one of those pre-made messages.

I dial his number, ready to jump up and walk away for a talk if he picks up. He doesn't.

Callie laughs cheerfully as she shouts something to Kai in the water. Dani cheers. Marlow whistles. Everyone seems so happy. Do they know how precious this is?

I'm not depressed. I'm not. I keep repeating this to myself, but I don't even feel like going for a swim, taking my boots off, or even being here. I down the beer, trying to fill the emptiness inside me that's become almost permanent lately.

I've been wrong about Archer. Everyone talks about how he doesn't care about others. Truth is, Archer cares a whole lot, just never shows it. About Kai and Callie, the Outcasts, Ayana, even the medication they develop, and the people who need it. He's like a Jedi, in charge of this small world called Zion. And it's not just about the lab, no matter what they say. Otherwise, he'd move to Australia and work from there.

The night of his father's death made me realize that he feels alone. I remember his face when he came to it after the overdose, gloomy, hopeless, as if surprised that he was still alive. Like it was a mistake. Like his actions were premeditated.

The thought rips my heart. My hand instinctively goes to my neck, and my fingers brush along Archer's gold chain. I still wear it, the subtle reminder of what we had.

The lump in my throat is growing at the thought. Just then Maddy turns to me and asks, "Are you doing alright?"

This. Fucking. Question!

Tears well up in my eyes. I'm so *not* alright. So lost. So missing him that any other response would make me break down crying, so I blurt out the only easy thing that people who are not alright do:

"I'm fine, thanks."

# 8

## KAT

A MONTH WITHOUT ARCHER ON ZION CREATES A VOID INSIDE me until I feel like I'm a zombie, carrying on from one day to another on autopilot.

We were expecting the heads up about Archer's return, but nothing about Archer is casual. He left after the terrorist bombing and comes back with another bomb.

It's early afternoon, and Marlow and I sit on the terrace gazebo by the pool at his villa. It's raining, the sky gloomy and heavy with gray clouds, and the air is sticky with warmth and humidity.

It rains almost every day now. Nature seems to be crying for the good old happy times.

I finally made it to Marlow's home three weeks ago. A one-hour tour gave me an idea of what millions can buy. His villa is a little smaller than Archer's but nevertheless equipped with a multi-level pool and hot tub, a gym room, a sauna, and a giant bathroom with a tub in the middle like a lonely boat in the ocean.

"Don't tell me you take baths, Marlow," I said, eyeing the damn thing and wondering what one can possibly do in a bathroom big enough to have a party with a hundred people.

"I do." Marlow frowned like I'd offended him.

I don't want to picture Marlow in a tub. Rose petals and candles? Marlow is a mystery. Shooting guns and playing the guitar. Handling Ayana security and composing love songs. All muscles, gym workouts, and half-unbuttoned metrosexual clothes, colognes and jewelry. I know there's a part of Marlow that could knock my socks off from surprise, but it's probably reserved for someone special. I only hope he meets her soon.

There's also a recording studio with guitars lining up the walls and a drum set. There's a game room.

"Axavier likes testing out his new projects here," he explains. Axavier designs video games with immersive experience measured and altered by the sensor pads attached to the players.

"Cool," I repeated over a dozen times during the tour.

But just like anything else—seen enough times, luxury doesn't shock you much anymore.

Right now, sitting in Marlow's villa, I feel like I've been hanging out with rich people all my life.

"It's grim today." I stare at the pool rippling under the raindrops as Marlow opens the beers for us.

"Hungry?" he asks.

"Nah." I study him for a minute as I take sips of the cold beer. "I like hanging out in your kingdom. Just wondering where your princess is."

He snorts and starts humming some Russian song.

He's wearing board shorts and flip-flops. His elaborate tiger tattoo wraps around his arm below the short sleeves of a Da-Vinci-painting-patterned shirt, unbuttoned halfway down, giving me a peek at his nipples.

"You have your nips pierced?" I gape.

He looks down as if making sure they are still there, a smile tugging on his lips when he takes a swig of beer and leans back in his chair as he winks at me. "Wanna know what else I have pierced?"

*No.*

We hang out more than usual lately. Days off are spent at Marlow's or Kai's or Ty's as we all bond and wait for something bad to happen again. This island has a curse. Now and then, the universe sends a disaster to disrupt paradise.

Raven and Marlow took Kai to the jungle to shoot guns but never took me, though I've asked.

Axavier ditches us more often lately. Marlow thinks he has a new fling. I'm not even a bit curious. All I want to do is talk about Archer, considering Marlow talks to him every other day, but Archer hasn't returned a single one of my phone calls. It's been almost a month since Archer left for the mainland, and I don't feel like being on Zion anymore. He seems to be integral to everything that this island is.

The beer bottles are covered with condensation. The drizzle turns into a rain shower.

Marlow's phone rings, and he picks up with his usual, "Hey, man," then goes quiet for a moment.

Is it Archer?

I stare at him like I can extract any info by reading his mind. He takes a swig from the bottle. "Got it." He hangs up.

"Archer is back. He wants me to meet him at the airport."

I try not to show that my heartbeat spikes like a rocket into space.

"Will he come to your place?" I don't hide my anticipation.

"Not sure."

"Will you?"

"If not, I'll text you."

"Marlow, I wanna know everything! Hurry up!"

While he's gone, I'm on pins and needles, my mood changing from euphoria to anxiety as I walk to Marlow's giant kitchen and grab another beer from the fridge, then smoke half a joint to calm down, all the while checking my phone every minute to make sure I didn't miss a message.

There are no messages, but I hear the front door open and dart inside to see Ty and Dani.

"Hey, you." Their smiles are confused. "Is there a party or something?"

Equally as confused, I hug Dani, then him. "Is there?"

"Marlow texted, told me to be here ASAP."

"Huh."

After another half an hour, Marlow walks in and stops at the entrance.

Our heads turn in his direction as we sit up on the couch.

"What's up, fool?" Ty asks, and after Marlow doesn't respond or move from the door, I sense something's up.

I've spent more time with Marlow than anyone else on this island and have seen his sad moods, which are rare and short.

What I see on his face is panic.

"Marlow?"

He licks his lips, his hands smoothing his hair, again and again. His eyes aimlessly roam around, but he doesn't move away from the door.

Did someone die?

"Is it Archer?" I murmur, exchanging looks with Ty and Dani, and the three of us rise from the couch.

"Dude!" Ty says, all of us suddenly anxious because Marlow looks scared or lost or about to have a meltdown, and I don't understand it. His silence can be a sign of horrible news, and I've had enough for a decade.

"Marlow!" I shout.

Then I see *her*…

What I register first is blond hair cut to a bob with straight bangs as the girl slowly steps through the front door behind Marlow and into the hall. Big eyes, filled with the same panic as Marlow's, full lips, slender figure, long-sleeved shirt with street logos, jean shorts, black leggings, and Converses.

Who the hell is she?

The villa is silent as I stare at Marlow and the girl at the entrance.

"Oh, God." That's Dani's whisper, followed by a choking sound and a whimper that comes from Ty.

I turn my head to look at him, and my hair stands on end.

I spent several weeks on the Eastside, and one thing I know is that I never saw Ty without a smile. He's famous for his smile. Notorious for his jokes and fooling around that can make even the dead laugh.

Except now, his eyes are wide open like he saw a ghost and full of tears. His parted lips are trembling, and his chest is rising and falling rapidly like he's having a panic attack.

Dani touches his arm, and a sob escapes him, tears spilling down his cheeks.

"Ty?" I whisper.

"Ray-Ray," he echoes, the name sending shivers down my spine, then starts walking—a broken stumble like a zombie.

The girl who just walked in starts smiling. I want to say it's a happy, hopeful smile, despite the tears that now stream down her pretty face.

She's the most beautiful girl I've ever met. Ty's the most shaken I've ever seen him. This moment is heart-wrenching as I hear Ty break down into loud sobs when he reaches her and sweeps her into his arms.

Love. Hope. Family. The Change ruined so many beautiful words but also filled them with a much deeper meaning. Nothing compares to the overwhelming feeling of witnessing people who never hoped to see each other reunite.

There are sobs first, then crying, then laughter as Ty holds his sister in his arms, her feet dangling in the air a foot above the floor.

Marlow finally walks up to us, still avoiding eye contact. His red eyes are an indication that for some reason, he's too invested. My eyes shift between him and Ty, who sets his sister down and strokes her hair, smiling, crying, whispering something, kissing the top of her head, and sobbing again.

I should look away, but I can't. My heart explodes from being happy for them, proud of my dad for finding Raylin Reyes, and grateful to Archer for making this happen.

"Let's go to the terrace," Marlow says and walks out, Dani and I following, leaving Ty and his sister in their happy bubble.

Dani sniffles, a smile flickering on her lips.

Marlow's hands shake just a little as he lights a cigarette.

And I—all I can think about now is Archer. He's here. And seeing Ty getting his loved one back, my chest tightens at the thought that I might have lost mine.

I do what I've done so many times in the last month. I break the silence and ask the usual question:

"How is Archer?"

# 9

## ARCHER

After never-ending meetings, I want to be alone. My house is just fine. Four gray walls. Dimmed lights. No music. It's good to be back.

Ty barged into my office earlier and pulled me into a bear hug, tears in his eyes, hands grabbing my head and pressing his forehead to mine.

"I owe you man, big one, the biggest fucking favor you ever need, my life, anything," he blabbered like a madman, hugging me again.

"It was Mr. Ortiz, not me," I said when he finally let me go.

Now I stand by the window of Cliff Villa, a drink in my hand. Just like before I left. Nothing much changed. Definitely not my mood.

It's pouring outside, but the sound of the rain is muffled and barely reaches inside. My cave is my fortress.

Except when I turn and catch sight of the painting on

the wall, the red splash amidst the shades of gray reminds me of…

Her, yeah.

I've been through hell in the past several weeks. Kat's harsh words that fateful night are always in my head, chased by the images of her beautiful face in front of me when I came to it after the plunge, on her knees, red lipstick, red dress, my heart bleeding red as she brings me out of the darkness.

No matter how I try to shake her off, she tiptoes back and, in drunken times, barges into my head. I want her to go away but crave her at the same time. She has some strange power over me that weeks of not seeing her didn't erase, only made worse.

After the mainland, Ayana seems strange. It's home, but so small and suffocating, with so many dramas and traumas but also happy moments. It's all in here.

I try to read the latest bio-genetics research article Amir sent me, but words get lost in my thoughts.

I wanna go to the Southern Cabanas where the on-site scientists reside. When I'm among the regular folks, I feel like I'm in a normal world. With normal people. *Older* people. There is something unsettling about not seeing many elder people around except in the lab. Or children. Zion is an island of youth but with no future. We need change, that's for sure, and that idea got lodged in my mind during the weeks on the mainland. I just don't know what to change.

I dial Bishop. It's an enigma, really, but he gets along well with me and actually likes me. He's a recluse, but

O'Shea's business brings him to Ayana more often now, and he's one of the few people I can trust.

"Bishop," I say with a smile when he picks up. A decade older than me, he is the one person I don't shy away from when it comes to security advice.

"Do you entice security breaches at Ayana out of boredom, Archer?"

The humor in his voice makes me smile. His is one of the very few voices I actually don't mind hearing right now.

"I like living on the edge," I joke, noting in my mind how ugly the truth is, considering what happened.

Bishop laughs into the phone. He has an intense past, a sharp brain, and a fuck-all attitude, but is one of the easiest people to shoot the shit with. Maybe that's because he's not in my circle and doesn't feel pressured.

"Well, welcome back," he says after we chat for a minute. "Right back to Ayana mess. That security breach two months ago, now the spies. Jesus. I don't know if you want to hear it, but most of the issues with your security have to do with Butcher."

"Why do I hear that name too often lately?"

"Trust me on this one. You heard O'Shea, Butcher is involved. He's not as dumb as we think, despite being a thug. He lets the Savages do all the dirty work. He probably pays off your guys at the port."

"No fucking way."

"Archer, corruption is an integral part of any structure. Otherwise, we could've built a Utopia a thousand years ago. There are too many dealings going on in Port Mrei, too many fuckheads, ready for anything and getting restless. You need more patrol in town. Raven handles the peace talks and has leverage. He does what he has to, but he's not enough. Raven is a one-man-army who has too many important responsibilities, and we don't have many guys as smart as him who are not afraid to deal with the thugs and get their hands dirty."

Bishop is as good as Raven. So when he talks like this, I listen.

"Hey," I say, really thinking of taking a trip to the Divide and chilling with him. "We need to discuss Butcher and all that. Let's get together. What do you say?"

"I can swing by."

"How about *I* swing by instead? Maybe take Raven with me. Hang out for an evening."

"To what do I owe the pleasure? Tired of your fortress, jets, and an army of minions? You want to do a house swap?"

He actually makes me laugh this time. "Yeah."

"As long as your crib comes with that pink fire on legs —sure."

I grin. He saw Margot once. It didn't go well. So, naturally, he probably has wet dreams about her.

"Seriously though. We need a meeting. I want you to meet Alex Ortiz. He's former undercover too and the guy I trust with all the security advising right now. Let's get the boys together, figure out this O'Shea business, and have a drink."

"Any chance that pink doll gonna be there?"

He is adamant.

"No."

He laughs through his nose.

I snort. "Sounds like you've been a no-woman kinda man for a while now, huh?"

"Discipline above all."

"Has nothing to do with discipline. You should come here more often. You are an impressive man, and many girls are bored out of their minds."

"Asceticism helps to clear the mind."

"Don't go Scarecrow on me, Bishop. I like your mind. So let's shoot for tomorrow afternoon so we can figure some stuff out."

If we ever do. Fuck if I know.

I'd gotten the updates about the British spies while I was on the mainland, but there's much more to be done. The entire security team is in question. Only a handful can be trusted. Who knew that we'd be so fucked? And all because of some Russian princess who might be long dead by now. It's always a girl.

Speaking of the devil, Kat is on my mind again. She's my heart defect. Life got crazy on the mainland. Funerals, White House meetings, FBI giving a briefing about classified info like I have anything to do with it, family lawyers, Gen-Alpha lawyers and advisors, estate managers, accountants. You name it—I had it. Who knew that one death can make thousands scramble? My dad can. Granted, he is—was—one of the most important figures in the government. He still holds that power even after he's gone.

And yet, amongst all that turmoil and grief that somehow

turned into apathy and indifference, Kat was on my mind constantly. Even during my dad's funeral, when I didn't want to see a single face but wished I could talk to her.

And then I flew in Mr. Ortiz and Raylin Reyes, who I'd never met before, though I've been friends with Ty since Deene.

Mr. Ortiz seemed more approachable in person, jeans and a hoody and a baseball hat, but broader and taller than me—an impressive man. I felt like a conspirator chatting with him, knowing that Kat doesn't know about this meeting.

Her texts were the sweetest unsolicited drug but also a reminder of how things ended with us.

*Are you alright?*

Fuck…

*How are you doing, Archer?*

And then the memories of her assaulted my brain.

How am I fucking doing, Kat? Why don't you tell me again how shitty of a person I am?

And here they are again, the harsh words spinning in my mind like a pack of flies.

I try to calm down. Emotions are a formula. Everything is. But Kat doesn't follow any explanations or rules. She's some kind of enigma that was dropped into my life out of nowhere. And I'm done trying to fit our relationship into a formula. That's not how my brain works. Or heart. Or whatever it is.

I want to be angry, but as I take the last sip of my drink before going to bed—I limit my drinks even more these days—I wish she was here, stayed quiet, let me fuck her, then cuddled with me like she did that one time.

"Corlo, lights off."

My living room sinks into darkness. The only lights coming through the window are the blue neon of the pool.

Neon blue...

I open my phone and find that fateful picture of naked Kat in my pool.

I should feel bad for taking it, but I don't. I did confront Margot when I called her from the mainland, and she eventually admitted her fault and how she swiped that picture off my open phone the night of Cece's party when she stopped at my villa.

I told Margot that she's going to the mainland. She freaked out. I told her she was acting like a high-school cunt. She poured a whole bunch of dirt and feelings on me. She wanted to be heard, and I listened, though I knew everything she thought about Kat and me and didn't care.

I hate making women cry. And Margot did. Groveling is not her forte, but she screamed and then broke down in tears.

"What do you want me to do, Archer? I can't change what happened."

"Apologize to her."

"No fucking way!"

"You are a grownup. You ruined Cece's birthday."

"No, I didn't."

"Bullying is for high schools, Margot. We are a tight community here at Ayana, and no matter how much I value you, I won't let you fuck with people."

She said she apologized.

I stare at the picture of Kat in the pool and can't get enough. I can't part with it. But I will, along with the rest of my Kat-porn.

My phone beeps.

**Kat: Can we talk?**

I don't need a pity fuck. Everyone is concerned, and so is Kat. But even before she said those harsh words to me the night of the incident, before the picture was passed around, she walked away from me on the dance floor, right in front of everyone.

**Me: I'll see you in the office tomorrow.**

Bitterly, I press send and pull up the videos from my cam archive.

I've rewatched them drunk so many times while away that they started to feel like someone else's life. They are a thing of the past.

Me going down on Kat on my coffee table.

I glance up at the table as if to make sure it's the same one, then on impulse, press the delete button on my phone.

Gone. Like it never happened.

The one with us naked on the couch, fucking, then talking for what seemed like hours.

Delete.

The one where she insisted on cognac-tasting, though there isn't much you can see on cam besides my tall figure and Kat's hands on my ass. Then me fucking her from behind.

I rewatch it again, my dick hard as a rock by the time I finish.

Delete.

The pool one.

I want to rewatch all of them again, already hard and wanting to get off. But it feels wrong, almost illegal, especially after the effect of that pool picture sent out to the entire party.

Delete. Delete. Delete.

It fucking hurts—erasing parts of her, one memory at a time.

There was another video—the night my dad died. I watched it once, on the mainland, the way things went down, how Kat ran into the villa. I deleted it right away, couldn't have the evidence of the night I failed myself and Zion.

I turn off the villa cameras. There aren't any videos of Kat left, only pictures. The ones from the Eastside and the pool one. My thumb hovers over the neon-blue screen and the delete button, but I don't have it in me to get rid of this one. I need something of her. Just a morsel.

There's one more.

Two weeks ago, Marlow sent a picture from Cece's party.

**Marlow: I thought you might want this to cheer up.**

I pull it up again, though I've stared at it so many times that I have it engraved in my mind.

It's a shot of Kat facing the camera, in her high heels, red dress, and loose hair, head turned sideways as she smiles to herself. I'm behind her, my hands on her waist as I gaze at her like the guy who just met the girl of his dreams. We are dancing *bachata*, two of us caught in the darkish shadows of the night and the soft glow of the lanterns and party lights. It's the only picture of us, but I've never seen anything more beautiful and intimate.

I'm keeping this one. Even if there's no more chance of us being together, I'll keep this as a reminder that once upon a time, we were happy.

## 10

### KAT

I stare at Dad on the computer screen, not believing my ears when he tells me a story of how he extracted Raylin from some compound where she was kept against her will.

"Why didn't you tell me that before?" I ask, almost hurt that he kept this secret, as well as the meeting with Archer. Archer met my dad—the news is shocking yet heart-warming like we have one more connection despite being so badly broken.

It's not even nine in the morning, but I'm already at the Center, and my heart thuds in my chest when I see Archer come in.

"We'll talk later," I cut off Dad and say, "Hey," to Archer, who only nods and disappears into his office. The brief seconds of seeing him after so long, in his usual black t-shirt and jeans, make me nervous like I just saw my idol.

After summoning my courage for ten minutes, I knock on his door.

"Hi. Can we talk?" I take slow steps toward his desk, studying him.

"Sure." He gives me a work smile that doesn't reach his eyes as he clicks on something on his computer like I'm one of his assistants who interrupted his morning.

"Can we talk about what happened?" I ask, my heart racing.

He flicks his eyes at me only for a second. His professional mask is too familiar. "Thank you for what you did." His expression is icy-cold.

There's a loud knock at the door, followed by Margot walking in without waiting for a reply.

"Oh, busy?" she asks with pretend-concern but keeps sashaying toward the desk, giving me a condescending look like I got lost.

I roll my head. It's the first time I get to talk to Archer, and she's interrupting.

"Will you just fucking disappear for a minute?" I snap.

She stops and stares like I have a third eye, then glances at Archer as if waiting for his response and back at me.

I take a warning step toward her. "Or I'll drag you out by your pink hair. It won't be pretty."

She backs out, closing the door with a mortal stare, and when I turn around, I think I see a flicker of a smile on Archer's lips that disappears too quickly, his gaze back on his computer.

"That's not what I wanted to talk about," I continue, irritated. "I meant what I said that night, *why* I said it."

"Kat, you don't have to explain your opinion to me."

"It wasn't an opinion—"

"Kat," he cuts me off in a businesslike manner. "If you came to apologize, please don't. And I don't need an explanation of why you think the way you do. It's alright. Water under the bridge."

His phone rings. Goddammit!

"Is there something else you wanted to talk about?" he asks, his face devoid of emotions as he picks up his phone, a clear sign that he doesn't want to talk. "I really have to take this."

I have his gold chain in my pocket, and I grip it as hard as I can, counting seconds in the hope he'll say something else. I wanted to return it. But now, I'd be doing it angry, so instead, I nod and walk out.

A week goes by without Archer talking to me. The traffic in and out of his office is like that of a President. Assistants, lab personnel, surveillance. We act like strangers, the sight of him piercing me with regret for the harsh words I said every time I steal a glance of him.

One day, Ayana is rattled by the sound of helicopters, then a jet, and another one. An hour later, an echelon of golf carts pull up to the Center, and before the "guests" walk in, a dozen or so security guys sweep in, clearing the path to a conference room.

"What's happening?" I ask one of the office guys after security asked me to move away from my desk.

"The board members' meeting."

A group of fifteen or so people walk into the Center, most of them much older, dress shirts and sunglasses, smiles and chatter. They could be Wall Street guys. Or Palm Beach golfers. Except they are not.

Archer is among them, so young he almost looks out of place, in a white dress shirt, sleeves rolled up. He looks so sexy that it takes my breath away.

"A couple of them are the richest men in the world," the guy next to me murmurs as if it's a secret.

I know that.

"Wonder if any of them are responsible for the Change?" he asks with a snort.

I'm not into conspiracy theories, nor do I like politics. So I leave the Center.

The almighty with an army of guards crowd Ayana for the next several days—restaurants, bars, yachts, and villa parties. When they leave, Archer reappears at work, but it's silent treatment again.

I sit at Marlow's one evening—for the first time in more than a week, because Marlow is in the wrong place mentally, either spending evenings at Ty's, because, right, Raylin is there, and he still didn't tell me what his history with her is—or he's sulking by himself and doesn't pick up the phone.

Right now, I'm on his couch in his lounge room, listening to him play the guitar, plucking at the strings some melancholic notes. We're barely talking, both of us lost in our thoughts, ignoring his phone ringing.

Only when the front door opens—Axavier is supposed to come—do we both stir.

But it's Archer.

I'm so taken aback to see him outside the office that I freeze. We stare at each other, and I feel like his worst enemy, considering he avoids me like the plague.

"Wanna chill with us?" Marlow asks without getting up while I stiffen and keep staring at Archer.

"Just dropped by to chat about O'Shea, but..."

But I'm here. I get it.

"Don't want to interrupt your evening." Archer attempts to smile. "I'll catch you later."

Marlow and I exchange confused looks when the door closes, and we are left alone.

"I told you. He hates me," I say, not hiding the hurt in my voice.

Ain't that the truth, because two days later, after work, I'm at Ty and Dani's place, trying to make small talk with Raylin, who is cool and mesmerizing but too reserved. I'm not into girls, but I can't stop looking at her. Her beauty, those doll eyes and puffy lips, is truly hypnotic. She would be a ten if she didn't have that lost look on her face, like she's not quite there. By God, can anyone be more introverted!

That's when Archer shows up, halting as soon as he sees me.

Ty—freaking Ty, the golden boy with millions in his trust, who had to live on the Eastside like a hippie because of Archer—now greets him like they are best friends.

Everyone does.

For the first time tonight, Raylin smiles broadly and rises from the pool chair to give Archer a hug.

But when I catch Archer's glance at me, I feel it—I'm not wanted here.

I know what's gonna happen next—he'll say he stopped

by for a second, will turn around, and leave, not wanting to breathe the same air as me.

But he deserves this—friends, some chill time with them. So I rise quickly and throw, "I have some things to do," to no one in particular, and leave.

No one stops me. No one cares, really. We come and go. Ayana is easy. Friends are easy. I've never had many, but I don't want to steal them from Archer or be in a competition where it's either him or me.

So I walk through the twilight with my eyes burning from tears.

What did I do to him?

I said awful things. I left him in the middle of the worst night of his life. We can talk it over. But we don't.

He barely acknowledges me in the Center when he comes and goes, and I usually leave in the afternoon to work from home.

Hurt builds up for days and days until I realize that if I don't talk to someone, I'll lose my mind.

There's one person who might understand, who won't share, who always keeps things to herself.

"I'm going crazy, Maddy."

I sit on the examination table in one of the rooms in the medical ward, head hanging low, feet dangling as I study my boots.

Maddy leans on the wall, arms crossed at her chest, a soft smile on her lips. "I have a feeling you always were."

"No. I feel like I'm bipolar. One day I'm happy, grateful to be here, then miserable the next one, feeling that I don't belong. One moment, I feel like I can take on the entire world, and the next, I feel like any girl here is better than me."

"Any girl?" There's humor in her eyes when they meet mine. "What does it have to do with girls? Or is it about a guy?"

It's like she can see through people. Maybe it's the goodness of her character that allows her to dissect others' emotions and rationalize them.

"You're a strong woman, Kat. You can take on the world. Of all the girls I know here, you are the one who can. But here's the thing."

She pauses and waits until I meet her eyes again. Hers are kind and understanding. I can see why Kai once said she has a heart of gold. I know—or rather feel that being around her—why everyone is drawn to her.

She's only several years older than me but wise, soft-spoken, and kind. A minute of us talking like this, and I want to tell her my deepest thoughts. She's like a saint. A mother. A sister. A best friend. A pretty girl with a golden personality. It's rare in today's world. Why she doesn't have a man who carries her in his arms and showers her with presents and love, is a mystery.

"When you start doubting yourself," she goes on, "and look for approval, and I mean the approval of one specific person, a guy at that—your heart is too deep in it already. It's not about you or what you are worth or capable of. It's about that person who makes you too self-aware. What solves any issue you have is talking it out with that person."

I snort. "Have you met that person?" Archer and I never

really talked heart-to-heart. We spent too much time playing until I got caught up in my own games.

All-knowing Maddy smiles softly. "I have. And he has the same problem as you."

"Which is?"

"You two come from different sides of the track but are very much alike. He can take the entire world. And he has. But he might be scared of his feelings, Kat. Just like you are."

"How would you know that?"

"Because things like this are much more obvious to the bystanders."

Her smile calms me and makes me wanna talk more. I bite my lip, trying to suppress the emotions that rise like high tide.

"Maddy," I say quietly, not looking at her, as I am about to say the scariest thing that ever left my mouth. I can't explain the feelings simmering inside me, except now they are boiling, and I don't know how to keep them from spilling over for everyone to see. I finally raise my eyes to her again. "Have you ever been in love?"

# 11

## ARCHER

FOR ONCE, IT'S SUNNY OUTSIDE. WHO KNOWS WHEN I'LL GET another chance to ride a motorcycle. I need to get out and clear my head, and I need a partner in crime.

I call Droga.

He's been with me through the best and the worst of it. We talked several times while I was on the mainland. But I still feel anxious as my thumb hovers over the "call" button on my phone screen right under his name.

"Wanna go for a ride and share a bottle?" I ask him right away when he picks up.

It's an invitation. Those were the code words for when we wanted to fuck off from the usual Deene crowd to some strange locations no one knew us, drink, and talk about life.

"I'm in," he says so easily like it's a usual weekend at Deene.

It's afternoon when Droga rings the bell, the only person besides Doc to do so. Surfer's tank, shorts, sneakers, and tattoos that cover his skin, painting it black and all colors of the universe. It'll take me a while to get used to the sight.

I don't invite him in. Instead, I lead him around the villa and open the garage doors.

"Fuck…" Droga's eyes dart around the wide space and three sports bikes that stand there.

"Wanna remember the good old times?" I offer.

I haven't raced with anyone on this island. These bikes haven't been ridden by anyone but me.

"Where? On the small Ayana roads?" He walks over to one bike and inspects it, hiding his amazement, then walks over to the next one.

"Nah. The dirt road along the south coast. C'mon, Droga. It'll be fun."

My heart starts beating faster as I watch him walk over to the third bike, the Ducati Panigale V4 R, his favorite. I always wanted that bike back at Deene. It was Droga's dream, but he couldn't afford it, so I never got it not to rub it into his face. I did get it after the Change though, hoping that there would come a day like this.

"Fucker," Droga murmurs, sending me a fake glare, then grins, swinging his leg over the seat and clutching the handlebars, measuring up to it.

"You take the Ducati. I'll take my Streetfighter," I say, passing him the helmet. "Go slow the first half a mile past Ayana's southern gate. After that, when you pass the parking lot, you can take it up to a hundred. I did more than that a couple of times, but I was stupid. Just follow me."

We drive carefully through Ayana, heads turning to look

at us, the two sports bike engines making a racket, and I feel a lot of things at once. Riding side by side with Droga is like riding into the past, the memories of how many things I fucked up, the ones I got back, ups and down, the fucking roller coaster that life is, losing loved ones, gaining new friends, death, life, and everything in between.

When we leave the southern gate, we pick up speed.

I know we won't do this often. I know every meeting with Droga will be like Christmas in July, a waterfall of emotions, a flood of memories, until, hopefully, it becomes the new normal again.

An hour later, we sit on the beach and drink whiskey straight out of the bottle. It feels like back in Mexico on our cross-country trip years ago. A time when life seemed easy and we thought we could be reckless and start all over again any day.

"Callie is not worried I'm gonna take you out and do something awful to you?" I joke.

Droga snorts loudly. "Dude, when you're sober, you don't have a chance. I hate to break your heart, but I'd take you down any time."

"Maybe." I nod, grinning.

We are getting drunk, discussing Ty and everyone else.

"Marlow and Raylin, fuuuuck," Droga says with a chuckle. "Marlow is so head over heels. And she's messed up. And they have a history from before the Change, not exactly a pretty one, and she went through some dark stuff after the Change that even Ty doesn't talk about. So now her and Marlow are playing these love-hate games."

"Yeah, I figured."

"You are like Ty's favorite person now. He is so happy she's here. Can't shut up about how you are his new hero. Well, and Kat. Ty sent a big check to her father."

Then there's silence, things we don't talk about. It's up to me to bring them up. I've held back too much shit before, too many things I didn't tell people who are now gone.

"I tried to stay away from you after that fire because I thought that you were just like my dad," I finally say, feeling uneasy, but the booze is doing its job and letting me loose.

Droga turns his head to me.

"After losing my mother and brother," I continue, not looking at him because I can't face him but I need to let it out, "I felt alone. You know my dad. He got all weird when my mom died. He didn't care much about anything but work and power games and women. Definitely not about me. I despised him for that. And when you came around, I swear, I realized one day that I cared about my best friend more than about my own father."

I think Droga always knew that. That I valued him above all the rich kids I used to keep around—a fucking football team of them and an entire stadium.

"I was so fucking mad after that night you spent with Callie. Like you betrayed me. Like you were turning on me just the way my dad had. So I said, fuck it. I was in a bad mental place. And I overdosed that year, yeah..."

Droga doesn't say anything, but I feel him shift—I know when he's uneasy.

"You know what Dad did?" I can't help but smirk. Maybe that's why I didn't grieve him so much—he was an embodiment of a parent who didn't care. "He sent his assistant to the hospital because he was too busy. And flowers." I laugh, but it's a sad laughter. "That was my fucking father, you know? He said afterward that I'm weak for getting so wound up about the people who don't value me in their life. So I stayed away from you. Pretty pathetic, huh?"

Droga takes a slow gulp from the bottle and loudly smacks his lips. "You know what always bothered me about you, Crone?"

Here we go. "A gazillion things?"

"Just one, actually—it defined everything about you, though—that you find genuine feelings pathetic."

I stare at the horizon and the ocean, the loud sound of the crashing waves drowning my unease.

"I understood it about you when I met Callie," he says. "Yeah, I know you gonna smirk right now."

I catch myself smirking. "I'm not smirking."

"I thought I was pathetic when I fell in love with her back at Deene. But that's because you constantly taunted me about it. Like I was a loser because I fell for a girl. And you going behind my back and roping her in didn't help."

"Droga—"

"I know, testosterone and all that. We had too many girls around, never cared about them. But after the Change, when Callie came to Zion, I realized that pathetic"—he pauses, letting it sink in—"is having feelings for someone or caring for others and acting like it's something to be ashamed of. You were like a brother to me at Deene."

The words make my eyes burn.

"And only once did I see you show genuine feelings—the night in Mexico when you got drunk."

"Whatever. I was wasted."

"Stop. Fucking. Brushing it away like it's nothing!" He raises his voice at me. "Can't you see? You tried to pretend that the night when you let go and finally talked about your mother and Adam didn't happen. *That* was the night that showed you trusted me. And I trusted *you*. It meant more than any other night. More than the other stupid shit we did for fun. But you never brought it up again."

True, though I still have the pictures from that trip in my drawer.

He kicks the sand with the heel of his foot—irritated, I can tell.

"And what made me mad after the Block Party was not the shit that you put Callie through. Not even the fucking accident, though I gotta admit, nothing topped that until the Change."

I swallow hard and turn to look at him.

He turns to meet my gaze. "What got to me is that you chose not to deal with it or talk about it. You came to the hospital *once* after the fire—*once*, Crone—and I was so mad that I sent you away." His voice is rising, his words are sharper, and so is his stare. But I don't break the gaze, because he needs to let out, and I need to take it like I should've years ago. "Yeah. That was the wrong time to come to me. But after that, Crone, after *all that time*, you gave up and acted like you didn't give a shit. As if admitting you were wrong would've somehow made you less than what you were. Like you didn't want my shitty trauma in your life."

My heart explodes in shame and guilt at the words. "Not fucking true," I say quietly and tear my gaze away from him.

"Well, your arrogant smug face didn't show it. Not when you partied hard every weekend with everyone, posting on social media how great life was when mine was ruined."

"Sorry." I nod and nod, looking down at the sand like I can bring those years back.

"You apologized. I don't need to hear it again. And now you tell me you went through a lot of shit, too."

"You don't know how heavy guilt can be when it overlaps the past mistakes."

"I know. That's not why I'm telling you this, Crone. What brings people close is letting them know how you feel. Not shoving your feelings down the drain, hoping it won't get clogged."

"Yeah, fine, I have a problem."

Droga snorts. "You have many. But confronting your feelings… Yeah… You might need a shrink or Katura to sort it out."

A chuckle escapes me.

"So. My point." Droga exhales loudly, then drinks from the bottle and licks his lips, taking a moment to wind down. "You and Katura—now that we are on the topic of feelings —spill."

## 12

### ARCHER

DROGA IS A BETTER MAN THAN ME. I'VE PUT HIM THROUGH hell, and he's the one making an effort to bond.

I still feel like there's an invisible wall between us, but it's getting thinner. I'll fucking humble myself to make it vanish. I never thought I'd be like this. But Dad's death did a number on me. The overdose—another one. Kat saving me...

Well, let's just say you learn to reevaluate things. I was always the top one at everything but confronting my own feelings. Maybe, I should top that too.

I light a cigarette and let out a smoky sigh. "Kat is wild," I finally say.

"Here we go."

"What?"

"What?" Droga mimics. "Using nicknames and mockery to hide feelings. That's your problem."

"What are you talking about?"

"She gets to you, huh?"

"Yeah."

"Yeah. Like no one else, huh?"

"Yeah."

"Yeah," he mimics again. "What's bothering you, Crone? I know you like her. *Really* like her. And that's an understatement. You thought I was starry-eyed when I met Callie at Deene? Have you seen yourself around Katura? At Cece's? You were glowing like a fucking Christmas tree."

I turn to stare at him in confusion.

Droga leans back on his elbows on the sand and crosses his legs at his ankles.

"Yeah," he drawls, "fuck off with your inner guard. There are flames in your eyes when I bring her up. And I bet your dick is hard when you think about her. But unlike other girls, you let her sleep in your bed, and stay till morning, and make a mess in your villa."

Instantly, the memory of her panties stuck between the couch pillows makes me smile.

"—and break the rules," Droga continues, "and you probably already told her things about yourself you never told any other girl. When she's around, your body reacts with every fucking cell like you are connected by live wires. And when she's not, there is an empty space that nothing else can fill. Am I right?" He doesn't hide a smile. "Or am I right?"

His smile is too wicked, and when he elbows me, I can't help but grin, turning away. It's not fucking funny, considering I'm miserable just being in the same building with her and not talking, yet the fact that she exists—that one simple fact—is enough to make me feel like I got blessed.

"You are a scientist, Crone. You'll tell me it's hormones, and it will pass, but you can fuck off. I've never seen you like this with anyone."

Kat makes me feel things I've never had room for in my life before. Feelings, period. They were never part of the equation.

I exhale, summoning all my courage to spill the shit to the only person I ever confided in before.

"Listen," I start, feeling the buzz of whiskey in my head. Booze makes it easier. I might regret this moment of honesty tomorrow, but fuck it. "You and I... That shit started because of the girl, yeah? To be precise, because I didn't understand why someone would go apeshit like you did about Callie back at Deene. I mean, I had Anna Reich—that was after your time. She was smart, pretty, charming. All the checkmarks, yeah? I was content for some time, pissed when her father took her back to the mainland after the Change. But by then, I was tired of her. Shit wasn't working out. I didn't understand why. Sex and all, if she could deliver, I didn't understand why it didn't work, why I was so damn bored."

I dig my heels in the sand and take another gulp from the bottle, hissing as whiskey burns my throat and chest, then pass the bottle to Droga.

"With Kat, though, right from the start, I was fascinated. Fas-ci-na-tion." I chuckle through my nose. "That word faded out of my life a long time ago. She surprises me. She makes me mad. She constantly makes me feel so many different things. I don't stop *feeling*. She is different. You're right, she fills some invisible holes in my life that I didn't even know existed. I want to spoil her, protect her, like she's some rarity I've never encountered before. Just being with her is fucking overwhelming. And… Fuck… I want her to care as much, you know? It's… scary, really."

"My man." I turn to see the fucker grin. "You are falling in love. In fact, you are already there and just trying too hard to deny it."

I shake my head, trying—yeah, fuck—to deny it, if only to save my pride. "That's the problem, Droga. Because she said some awful things to me, so I don't know if I was just another mountain for her to conquer. And because we both think we are tough shit. We don't let each other have the upper hand."

"You can't. You kidding me?"

Droga gives me a gaping look like I have a third eye. I snatch the bottle out of his hand and take another gulp. He snatches it back, takes one more swig like it's a duel, his eyes slightly narrowed and shiny, whiskey-buzzed—welcome back, Droga—then pokes my shoulder with his finger a little too roughly.

"If there's one thing you can't do with a woman, it's have the upper hand. You can't even make her feel like you do. You are a man, bro."

*Bro…*

The word tugs at me with its unexpectedness, and I still at the fact that we are drifting to the way we used to be with each other four years ago.

"Callie and I played that game for a while," he says. "Until I realized that if I lost her, life would be pathetic and meaningless. I might actually say thanks to you for the mud you dragged us through. Because in those few days on the Westside, she changed. *I* changed. When we thought we might not have another chance with each other, it broke down the walls between us. So fast, I was in awe. We both were. The awkwardness was gone. And it was fucking beautiful. I was a fool playing it tough. Men shouldn't. Ever. Not with women they love." Droga's voice is loud and passionate—he's drunk, but I only watch him with a smile, not interrupting. "You can't drop your armor as easily, Crone, I know you. But trust me, there'll be a breaking point, and you'll have to let her know how much she means to you. You'd better not fuck it up."

"What if she doesn't feel the same?" I say the words too quietly, digging into the sand with my heel like I want to hide my head in it.

"Wow, Crone. You are farther along than I thought. And a coward." He chuckles.

"Fuck off."

"Co-ward!" Droga sings drunkenly, stabbing me with his forefinger. "You seduce with kindness, not pressure."

I shrug. "Pressure makes diamonds."

"Yeah, and breaks fine china."

"Kat is the last thing from fine china."

"Well, pressure also started a nuclear war."

"Alright. I get it, I get it."

"You're always the first in everything, Crone. So make the first step. Take a break from being a dick."

I chuckle, but Droga doesn't smile. He's always had that rational side to him. A fucking philosopher. A noble one.

Maybe that's what drew me to him in the first place—the awesomeness that's opposite to my shittiness.

We stay quiet for a moment, watching the ocean and taking turns from the almost empty bottle, smoking. I fucking missed him, this, our conversations.

"You are the most brilliant man I know," Droga says. He's one of the few people I actually accept the compliment from with pride. "But you still have plenty of things to learn. Like women."

"Yeah, okay."

"Okay," he echoes. "You know how to use them, but you never tried to understand them."

"Alright, Droga! I get it! Drop the fucking topic."

He doesn't. "There's a sure way to put yourself out there before her."

Alright, I'm a little curious. "Which is?"

His grin is crooked. I know that shitty grin. "You can always fuck Kat while you're spilling your feelings. She won't be able to run."

I pick up a handful of sand and throw it at the bastard before we both burst out in drunk laughter.

## 13

## ARCHER

It's already close to midnight when Droga and I drive through the southern gate to Ayana.

I'm drunk, yep, because I tease Droga in the worst way as we slowly ride up the main Ayana road. "Hey, do I need a bulletproof vest?"

"What?" He wrinkles his nose—he does that when he's drunk.

"In case Callie is hiding somewhere around with a gun, ready to shoot me."

"Oh, fuck off," Droga snaps.

"She's probably scouting the area with night vision goggles, looking for you, setting buildings on fire."

Droga lets a quick burst of laughter escape and shakes his head. "I'm gonna punch you."

I grin and slow down as we pass a group of scooters.

I see Raven on an ATV, approaching. I wave him down, taking in his bruised face, his gaze grimmer than usual in the light of the street lamps.

"Carnage?" I inquire as Droga pulls to a stop behind me.

Raven cracks his neck. "Got a couple of punches. Going to Doc's, too lazy to do it myself."

"You won?"

Raven doesn't answer, and the fact I even asked means I'm quite drunk. Raven never loses, and Carnage cage fighting is his monthly thing. He's not as tall or muscled as me, but his feistiness and precision in his moves makes him one of the most dangerous opponents. They keep upping the weight limit for his rivals at his own request, but there are very few who want to take their chances.

"I'll catch you at Doc's," I say. "Need to talk."

I've been meaning to talk to him for a while. It's midnight, and I'm drunk but don't want to go home yet. What I want is to storm into Kat's, throw her on the bed and fuck her senseless. But I've been drunk too many times in my life and know that I should stay away from any emotional stuff if I don't want to hurt people's feelings.

"Droga, take the bike to your place," I say when Raven takes off.

"Nah, I'm fine."

"Seriously. Take Callie out for a ride. No one will appreciate this beast more than you. I gotta have a chat with Raven."

I take off before Droga objects again.

When I come to the medical ward, Raven sits on the examination table in one of the rooms as he waits for a nurse. In the bright light of the small patient room, dressed all in black, he looks like a dark angel, and the bruise on his face gives his already sharp features an even deeper edge.

I fall into a chair and slump, exhaling loudly and rubbing my face, tired but unusually relaxed. I lazily study Raven, who sits with his face raised toward the ceiling, eyes closed, like he's meditating.

Even after years of knowing him and working closely with him now, the guy is a fucking mystery to me. On the mainland, he used to be my connection to anything off-limits. Money can buy anything, but without a person who knows how to get it and who will keep his mouth shut, you are nothing. Raven wasn't just a regular dealer, he was the dark web guy, mysterious, with plenty of rumors to make me cautious around him yet trust his connections.

He heard my conversation about the Spring Break on Zion before the Change.

"Take me with you," he said, and I almost choked in surprise. The nerve. "I can be your mule. Anything you want—I bring it with me. I get caught—it's my responsibility and jail time." Not that private jets get searched. But he had balls.

So I took him with me. And blow. Shrooms. LSD. Ayahuasca. Guns. Illegal fireworks.

And there's the lesson that life teaches you.

When shit went down, there was no better person to know than Raven, who found guys through his old connections on the dark web who knew guys all over the world and could get shit done amidst world lockdown.

Money was the best weapon. With the unlimited access that I gave Raven, he managed to acquire the chemical compounds for testing, keeping Gen-Alpha in the clear, and the biological material without waiting for months of approval. He made the first shipment of weapons happen like it was nothing.

Shit, the dude never went to college but knew the military codex as well as the laws of bringing heavy arms to a US territory. How?

In two years, Raven became *the* Zion connection. Arms, security specialists from war zones, black market, white market, government contracts, test animals used before FDA approval because paperwork took too long and we needed to run test-and-error.

He had a meeting with my dad, for which I got Raven dressed in one of my Armani suits, and holy fuck, he looked like a Yakuza top-echelon boss, his pitch-black hair slicked back, his speech flawless. He didn't swear, still doesn't, like it's a taboo. My dad, the Secretary of fucking Defense shook hands with him, and only the two missing phalanges on Raven's left hand gave away a story that didn't fit with the picture of a sharply-dressed no-nonsense guy. And the scars that etch his body—I've seen those, but he hides them well enough underneath long sleeves. My dad had connections and all the power, but amidst the shaky political situation at that time, Raven was the middle guy who was willing to take responsibility and fault for military contracts.

What I know is that Raven deserves every bit of his reputation. I would trust him with my life and definitely would never do anything to get on his bad side, knowing where he comes from and all.

"Feel like having a drink at my place?" I ask.

Raven lowers his head to look at me with a glint of

amusement in his eyes. "You look relaxed, Archer. Despite what happened to your father, you seem to have it together like you used to."

There's a soft knock at the door, and Maddy walks in, right away giving me a surprised look. "Archer! How's everything?"

Her movements are soft but precise like she knows the room by heart and can do things with her eyes closed. It's soothing, and so is her voice when she asks me a couple of questions, then turns to Raven.

"Mathew Levi," she says the name that I forgot as she studies him up and down. It's odd to hear Raven's real name which sounds extremely Biblical.

"It's Raven," he cuts her off in his low voice, staring her down in his deliberate intimidating manner.

"Well, you are a patient, so it's Mathew Levi."

"It's Raven."

There's a pause between them, Maddy facing him as she slowly puts his file on the desk, then takes slow steps toward him.

"What are we dealing with?" she asks.

"You are dealing with my face," he says slowly.

"Alright." She attempts a smile. "I need you to move closer to the edge of the seat."

And when Raven does, his jaw tightens a little. He's injured—I've been to cage fights enough times to know.

Maddy notices, too. "What's with your ribs? Are you hurt?"

"I'm fine."

"I need you to take off your shirt."

"I said I'm fine," he says just as quietly yet with danger etching his tone, his eyes never leaving hers.

She doesn't flinch a bit. "You're my patient, and I'm asking you to take off your shirt so I can *make sure* you're fine."

"You're going to do what I came here for. My face, that is."

I think I might've sobered up at this conversation.

Maddy's expression doesn't change, not even a fraction. And that's an achievement, considering most people can't look Raven straight in the eyes without giving away unease.

"Man, let her do her job, huh?" I smile, trying to ease the tension. I don't like his sharpness with Maddy. "Maddy, he's just stubborn."

Raven only cocks his brow in response.

Maddy turns to me with a soft smile. "Give me a minute," she says and walks out.

I shake my head at Raven. "What's your deal? Maddy is like the nicest person on this resort. The girl can save an army if needed."

"And she has a job. And can follow orders."

"Oh..." A drunk laugh escapes me. "I see what you're doing, man. Is this some kind of tough guy mating ritual? If you think you can win with her—nah, dude, not a chance. She's tough, through and through. And honest. So give her a break, will you?"

The door opens again, but before I see who it is, Raven's eyes flash in that quick unmistakable anger.

"Gentlemen! Late night?" It's one of the other nurses, a

girl in her mid-twenties, who was selected to come to Zion a year ago. She starts chirping away, her ponytail awfully jumpy, just like her high-pitched voice and permanent smile.

"Where's the other girl?" Raven asks, his voice suddenly steel-cold.

"Maddy? She's busy, asked me to take care of you."

"I want *her*."

"I can help you—"

"I said"—Raven cuts in—"I want *her*. Bring her back."

The girl helplessly looks at me, but I only shrug, enjoying the show, and she walks out with disappointed hurriedness.

"*I. Want. Her*," I slowly echo Raven's words and study him in slight disbelief. "What are we dealing with here? Maddy is too nice to mess with."

But I know it's pointless to argue with Raven.

The door opens again, and Maddy smiles at me, her smile waning as soon as she turns to Raven and takes several slow steps toward him, her chin slightly raised in defiance.

No one has ever looked so calmly into Raven's eyes, not even me. And I can't look away and cheer for Team Maddy when slowly, as if putting up a show, Raven reaches behind him, pulls his shirt over his head, then tosses it onto the chair, the entire time keeping his eyes locked with Maddy's.

There's a bloodied bruise on his ribs—Maddy was right about needing to look into it. Many bruises and cuts etch his muscled torso. The fragments of the giant raven tattoo on his back wrap from behind and claw at his biceps.

I feel bad for leaving Maddy with Raven one on one, even though Maddy is not a bit shaken by his almost murderous stare. But this is not my business.

I get up slowly, swaying from booze. "Listen, stop by my villa after this," I tell Raven. "Let's have a drink and chat. We have things to discuss, and I'll be up for a while."

"Sure," Raven says without taking his eyes off Maddy, like he's trying to stare her down.

"Maddy, you can handle him?" I ask from the door.

"Absolutely," she responds, not turning.

"Sure? Raven is a handful."

She doesn't look at me, only him when she says, "We'll be just fine," like she's talking to a sedated tiger that's not dangerous anymore.

Raven took the world by storm. Maddy takes others with kindness. Raven just doesn't know that kindness is a bigger weapon than the Swiss Army knife he carries on him at all times and, rumor has it, is an expert with in cutting through a bone. But if there's anyone who can stand their ground, it's Maddy.

And as I close the door, that's the last thing I see and hear—Maddy taking a slow step toward Raven, saying in a voice that could dull a Swiss Army knife, "Let's take a look at you, shall we?"

## 14

### KAT

IT'S BEEN MOSTLY SUNNY THE WHOLE DAY, BUT NOW, AT midnight, it's starting to rain. I don't mind, except the moisture makes my hair frizzy and no amount of coconut oil can tame that dark halo around my head.

I stare at the phone like I can talk myself out of texting Archer. It's too late, but I can't sleep, and Archer has insomnia.

*Here you are, Katura, good job, fixated on a guy.*

Self-taunting doesn't work, because in a moment, I dial his number.

Of course, he doesn't answer. But that's the one thing I'm looking for tonight—the answer to what's happening with us. I won't pry it open from him, but there're ways to know. And before I leave my bungalow, I put his gold chain in my pocket.

I love everything about the tropics but the frequent rains that eventually make the resort look like a playdough kingdom that stood erect for some time and is losing its shape.

It's dark. My skin is coated by moisture. The rain drums against the leaves, rustles against the tiki huts, and rattles against the tin roofs.

I could've rung the bell of Cliff Villa, could've knocked. But if Archer senses it's me, he'll ignore me as always.

I used to feel adventurous sneaking into his villa. Now I feel like a trespasser.

So what do I do now? Sneak in again. Because if he's with someone, if he has company, I'll feel embarrassed standing at his door, explaining that I want a minute of his time.

I go down the path along the lower level of Cliff Villa and crawl over the stone fence among the bushes—I feel awful doing it, but I did it the night of the escort party, and I'm great at making the same mistakes.

I walk along the waterfall wall and up the shadowy stairs toward the pool. It glows blue, like it always does, rain or shine. My face is wet, and so are my hair and clothes. I creep up as I near the pool level and hear a splash.

Someone's in the pool, in the rain. I walk up the steps that lead to the terrace and take a look.

It's Archer. Swimming butterfly-style along the pool length.

My heart starts racing at the sight of him and what we used to do in this very pool.

He reaches the end, sets his elbows on the paving edge, and glides his hands along his hair, squeezing out the water, then hangs his head between his arms and bobs above the water for some time.

There are no thoughts in my head, only feelings and senses. The sound of the rain against the stone deck. The sound of my footsteps as I walk along the side of the pool. The sound of blood pounding between my ears.

When did approaching him become so scary?

Another splash, and Archer pushes off the side and swims on his back, rain dripping down his face, his muscled arms making powerful strokes in the water.

Feelings simmer in me with more force than ever. The regret about the things I told him. The hope that he will forgive me one day. The day that will be brighter and happier than any of the previous ones when he wasn't around.

My heart is ready to explode when he suddenly notices me, turns around in the water, and stops.

"Hey, Arch," I say, the sound of my voice so overly cheerful, I hate myself for pretending.

He swims toward me and gets out of the pool. Water drips down his toned muscles as he stands in front of me in all his glory. There was a time when all I could think about was his body next to me. There was a time where I could tease him and claim him any time I wanted. All that's left now is his indifferent gaze, almost confused as if I stumbled into his villa by accident.

"Did you want something?" He picks up a towel from a chaise lounge and ruffles his hair with it, though the rain will get it wet in seconds.

Do I need something?

*To talk. To spend time with you. You.*

I lick the rainwater off my lips, blinking fast as it gets in my eyes. "Are you busy?" This must be the stupidest question right now.

"I'm expecting someone."

His movements are a little too edgy, his eyes sparkly, his blinking too slow. He's been drinking. I know Archer by now. This might not be the best time to have a conversation after all.

I dig into my pocket. "I came to return this." I stretch my palm toward him, his gold chain coiled in the center of it.

He keeps drying himself with a towel, staring at the chain in my hand.

*Don't take it. Don't take it. Please, don't take it.*

I might be silly, but that's the only way to tell if he still wants to share something. Even if it's just a stupid chain.

*Don't take it.*

Slowly, he raises his eyes to meet mine, then reaches for the chain, his fingers, unusually cold, brushing my palm.

"Thanks," he says.

My heart falls. So he's accepted it...

The sound of the phone ringing comes through the open terrace doors. We both turn to look at the lit-up windows— a dark shadow walking through the living room, Raven.

"I should go," I murmur, hoping Archer stops me.

He doesn't answer. We're still both staring at the living room like that shadow came to give us the final judgement. The air is thick with unspoken words, the emotional storm inside me making it hard to breathe. My legs feel like they're made out of stone when I turn toward the terrace doors and take slow steps away from Archer.

That's right. I came into his life like a spy, sneaking in. And I go out through the main door, not a word from him as I leave Cliff Villa.

# 15

## ARCHER

"I can do some research," Raven says. "I'll talk to Shepherd. He has guys who wouldn't mind making some money. They can snoop around and find out if there's any word on the street about a deal with Tsariuk."

"Shepherd?"

"Butcher's cousin. They are at war right now."

"Like us and the Eastside were?"

"Their stand-off is not public and extremely vicious. Bodies show up here and there. There are riots. Port Mrei is divided into two factions. And Butcher is a psychopath, a criminal, and an animal."

I frown. "This is all happening in Port Mrei?"

"Archer, I've been telling you this for months," Raven says indifferently. "You were in a daze."

"Are you lecturing me?"

"No. Just reminding you. Port Mrei is doing bad. The Ashlands even more so. There's a rumor that Butcher is outsourcing people there for all his dirty dealings."

"What dirty dealings?"

"Weapons. Collateral. Sabotaging Shepherd. Messing with Ayana's security."

"I'm not worried about the Ashlands."

"Too bad. That's where Butcher gets fearless high trash."

"Didn't we make a deal with Butcher?"

Raven stares at me like I'm a child who asks silly questions.

He grew up in foster care, graduated to the streets, and went into the dark web business. Unlike street dogs, he is extremely smart. He analyzes everything he sees. He reads people better than a fucking lie-detector.

"Our deal with Butcher is like that of America and North Korea but without a moral code," he explains calmly.

I sigh in irritation. "So sit down with Marlow and discuss it. Fuck. We put millions into security. Why, suddenly, in the last month do I not feel safe anymore? Suddenly, I find out Butcher gets weapons while we are supposed to control every damn thing that comes to this island."

Raven lights a cigarette. "If we start tightening the bolts right now, we'll get a rebellion from Butcher, and then it's war. So the first thing is to tighten Ayana security so we are prepared. We can't exactly do that unless we change it completely, but you don't need Mr. Ortiz to tell you that it's impossible with Tsariuk's interest in Zion."

Right. Today was one of the better days. Drinking with Droga. Talking about anything but business. But just like the weather, the day goes to shit.

"Someone should really go through spring-breakers'

files once again, with a fine comb," Raven says, puffing smoke and flicking ash into an ashtray that sits next to him on the couch instead of the coffee table, because the table is untouchable, and Raven is respectful of others' requests.

And the table reminds me of *her*.

*Everything* reminds me of her. I went into the pool for the first time since her and I were there. And what do you know, she's like an apparition standing on the edge of it when I come out from underwater.

"If we want to find Milena Tsariuk," Raven interrupts my thought, "we need to track every relative of every female spring-breaker, contact them and find out why the particular spring-breaker didn't return to the mainland. Everyone has reasons."

"That's a lot of work, and I can't just trust anyone with the private files. You understand some of them are the wealthiest people in the Western Hemisphere."

"Then?" Raven looks at me with that same indifferent expression.

"The last time, I did the work myself. It took me a lot of fucking time, and I didn't find Tsariuk's daughter."

"Get Marlow to do it. We need to find time for this."

Raven takes a drag off his cigarette and looks out the window like he can see through the darkness that forms a wall behind the pool.

I make Raven and me another set of drinks and sit on the couch, enjoying the silence.

That's the thing about Raven. I feel calm around him. I know he doesn't sit well with most people. But I know him. Under that cut-throat energy is a man of reason and loyalty.

"I wanna do a line of coke," I say out of context, feeling restless. Wanting *her*. Wanting to party and drink and fuck and remember what made me feel alive.

I can't. I know I won't stop for the night, and that's the problem.

"You in?" I know perfectly well that Raven drinks but doesn't touch anything else. Because of what happened to him in the past. Because of his lifestyle. He sells anything illegal and dangerous and deadly but doesn't indulge. It's another thing I respect about him.

Slowly, he turns his head to me, his eyes probing.

"You do this for the wrong reason, Archer." His voice is always fucking calm.

"Oh yeah? Enlighten me."

For the first time this evening, there's a trace of a smile on his lips when he says, "If I tell you what I think, you won't bear a grudge?"

Whoa. If Raven has to ask me—*Raven*, who I saw break bones in Carnage during cage fights—I wanna hear what he has to say.

"Shoot."

"You are like a young dog, Archer. A crazy young dog that's trained but still has so much energy that it's over-whelming, making it occasionally snap and rush to its death. You have no sense of reason or preservation when you slip. You are a sophisticated grenade without a safety switch. And the worst part is that you are affected by a girl."

"Spare me, Raven." I roll my eyes in annoyance. What's with everyone bringing up Kat today?

"You asked, I answered. It's not a tragedy that made you shoot up a month ago. You went through plenty. It's a girl, isn't it?"

I tense and don't look at him, only take a slow sip of my drink. "How do you know?"

I don't have to ask. Raven is an all-seeing-fucking-eye.

"I have emergency sensors hooked up to my phone. Several people from the upper echelon."

"Why?" Stupid question. Same reason why Raven knows everything about any given person at this resort.

"Safety. My safety, too. My well-being depends on yours and several others." Sometimes, Raven scares me. "You were sinking for some time, Archer. This"—he taps his temple—"is messing with you when you do too much booze and drugs. You've been on a bend for months then started doing better when you were sneaking around with that girl, Katura. Then she turned on you, or whatever the story is."

I snort. Raven is perceptive and insightful.

"You have to know where you two stand," he carries on. I've never heard him talk so much on the topic of a relationship. "If you are not on the same page, let her go, get over it, get her off this island so she doesn't bother your ego, and get yourself straight. If you are on the same page, get over your ego and make things right with her so you can function like you used to."

"And you?" I ask him with a smile. I feel that even drunk he's as sharp as a nail. And I've never seen him drunk.

"What about me?"

"What do you drink for?"

"I just enjoy it."

"Nuh-huh. Bullshit. I've come to know you, Raven. You are sedating your shitty past. And I'm avoiding the pointless future. That's the difference."

"You are making the future happen for a lot of people."

"Well, I'm glad someone is optimistic about life."

"You think dealing with rich snobby assholes is a burden?" There's a little smirk on his lips. Every emotion is just a tiny indication on his face, like he drained himself of all of it a long time ago. "Try dealing with guys who shake hands with you but can put a bullet in your head if they don't like your shirt."

"Raven, you are one of the most important guys on Zion."

He nods. "But if Butcher decides to put a bullet in my head one day and I'm not prepared, I'll be gone in a matter of seconds. And it'll probably be a bullet Ayana paid for."

A sad smile curves his lips. There's too much I don't know about his deals in Port Mrei. Maybe I should. For now, I'm glad I have people like Raven and Marlow in my life who cover other bases.

Droga, too—he's finally creeping back into my life.

And Kat. I wish I still had her. But we played our games, and now she's done with them, feels bad for saying awful things, and wants to receive an amnesty so she can stay on the island because by now, she has friends and enjoys it.

"Did Maddy patch you up?" I ask, just to change the topic and out of genuine curiosity.

Raven plays deaf.

"Are you avoiding the conversation?" It's my turn to smile.

He shakes his head, finally meeting my gaze, his expression too cold like I just brought up his enemy. "She did fine."

"No more conflicts?"

"She's good at what she does. Especially when she follows orders."

He flicks the ash of his cigarette into the ashtray too sharply. Uh-oh. Last time I checked, she got her way in the office.

"She's leaving for the mainland or staying?" Raven asks without looking at me.

I narrow my eyes at him. "Staying. Why?"

Raven only shrugs. "No reason."

There's always a reason with Raven. "You like her or something?" I ask, teasing him.

He stares at me for some time without a single emotion, then finally says, "Just wondered is all."

Raven never *just wonders*. But he is usually not a talker either.

"Women—they make things complicated, huh?" I smile, thinking about Kat and trying to distract myself from picking up the phone and calling her—the urge I've been fighting every night for the last month.

Raven only smirks. "A necessary evil. And that's too much credit."

I laugh, but as soon as Raven leaves, I sink into the never-ending thoughts about Kat.

No, not evil, not complication—pain. That's something I never knew women could bring, because I almost feel physical pain in my heart from missing Kat so fucking much.

# 16

## KAT

THE DAY AFTER THE FAILED POOL CONVERSATION, ARCHER ignores me at the Center as usual. He offers a curt "Good morning," and nothing else, then leaves the Center in the afternoon without a word, and there's no sight of him for the rest of the day.

When my phone beeps in the evening, I assume it's Marlow or Maddy. Callie, maybe.

But It's Archer, and just seeing his name flash on my phone screen triples my heartbeat.

**Archer: I have something for you.**

Cliff Villa is quiet when I come. No music.

"Archer?" I call out, slowly walking to the center of the living room.

"Here you are." The voice comes from the entrance to his bedroom, and Archer walks out in just a simple t-shirt and sweatpants. The informal sight of him is so unexpected that I wonder if he finally wants to talk properly.

There are papers in his hand. No smile. He's not even looking at me—just a glance, as if the sight of me bores him.

Something's off about him calling me over. "What's up?"

We used to do a lot of fun things in this villa. My best moments on this island happened here. Also the worst ones. Now it's just this—boring courtesy.

"There." He passes the papers to me as he approaches.

Studying his face doesn't help to figure out what mood he's in. Lately, his face is an indifferent mask. I get it. Trauma, losing family, work. The time we spent together seems to have been wiped away for good, making us this —colleagues.

I hate the word.

I stare at the papers in confusion. My face is on one of them, my dad's on the other—these are copies of our passports.

Why?

And then the word slaps me across my face—Australia.

"What's this?" I murmur, unease washing over me at the word that used to signify so much in the past.

"Your dream," Archer says, staring at the papers in my hands.

I swallow hard, the word "visa" not bringing the delight that it should. "Australian visas?'

"Yes. You came here for that, didn't you? We agreed that if you found useful info, I'd help. You did way more than that. So there. Plus the money as promised. I talked to Mr. Ortiz already."

"But…" Wait-wait-wait. "What's this supposed to mean?" I stare at him, willing him to look up from the papers in my hands. He's so close. The scent of his aftershave reminds me of what it felt like to have his skin against mine.

Archer finally raises his gaze, his eyes cold. "Your work is done, Kat. Thank you. Your father will continue to provide us with background checks. But you don't have to be here. I arranged for you to take a boat to the mainland tomorrow morning."

A breath catches in my throat.

*Tomorrow?*

"I can't leave!" I spit out.

"Kat, you really don't need to be here anymore. Raven and Marlow can handle things—"

"Are you trying to get rid of me?" I snap.

We're only several feet from each other, and they are painful. We used to look forward to crossing them. Now they feel like a mile.

My eyes burn. I hold my breath to suppress the emotions that start a storm inside me.

"Kat." Archer's voice is low and even, lifeless almost, just like his gaze. "You wanted this. You wanted to get the job done and leave. I'm giving you what you wanted. Australia is a fresh start."

"I don't want to leave."

"Why?"

"I… I… I can do more. Do more research. Help." I sound pathetic, I know. He's trying to get rid of me, and it's just too sudden and too… painful.

"You don't have to," he continues. "Australia will give

you more opportunities. New life. New job. College. Anything you want, Kat."

"But I want to stay!" I shout, forgetting myself.

"For what?"

His gaze is changing. It's growing more intense.

"Because I like it here," I say. "And I can help."

"You don't need to help anymore."

"I-I..." I don't know how to tell him that maybe he and I still have a chance. That I *want* a chance, whatever that means.

"Your work is done, Kat. You said so yourself."

Karma is a bitch. The words that I spat at him that fateful night when his father died come back. That's exactly what I said, and now he's giving me what I asked for.

But I didn't mean it. I was angry. We should've talked about that night, about what happened. But, right, we barely talked before. Even less so now.

"I'm staying," I argue.

Archer shakes his head. "You're leaving tomorrow. It's for the best. You just don't understand it yet. You got used to this place, but trust me, Australia has many more opportunities for someone like you."

"Someone like me? What's that supposed to mean?"

"You are resourceful."

"Resourceful?" I mimic him, getting angry and desperate. "As an employer, you should've at least given me prior notice."

"You were never officially on the payroll, Kat. Let's not dramatize this. You are leaving."

"I'm not."

"You *are*."

Tears start welling up in my eyes. I have to leave before I break down. Anger is not my friend. I don't know how to control it.

And here it is—in my fingers that start ripping the papers into pieces. I throw them in Archer's face like confetti, making him flinch.

"These are just copies," Archer says, motionless, not even his signature smirk tugging at his lips. "I have your passport, Kat. I'll get it to you for your trip tomorrow."

"Fuck you," I snap, taking a step back toward the door. "Fine! I'll leave!" I shout. "I won't bother you. Won't stay in your way. Won't irritate you with my reckless behavior. Won't embarrass you in front of your people. I remind you of the worst moments in the last months, don't I? Is that what it is?"

I storm out of the villa into the warm tropical evening and gasp in relief, because being next to Archer is too intense. Like I drank some freaking potion that makes my body all liquid in his presence, makes my brain all mushy when he's next to me.

Maybe if I leave Zion it'll get easier to breathe. But the thought of never seeing Archer again is devastating.

I stomp to the Center and open my work computer. I can't talk to Dad from anywhere else. Only here. Everyone's eyes are on me like I'm a spy.

Oh, wait, I was.

I try to collect myself as I wait for the laptop to boot, then dial Dad. But when his face appears on the screen, my chest shakes with a sob. So do my hands that I clasp together and dig my nails into the skin to distract myself.

"Dad…"

"Hey, Kit-Kat." His voice makes tears well up in my eyes. "What's wrong?"

I shake my head and lean with my forehead on my fingertips, hiding my face from him, from the several employees at their desks, from the world. I want to crawl into a hole and disappear.

"Sweetie, what's happening?"

I swallow hard and take a deep breath, finally summoning the courage to look at the screen.

"I'm coming home tomorrow."

What I don't expect from him is a smile. "You are, huh?"

"Archer has Australian visas for us." What used to be a dream suddenly feels like a punishment.

"I know."

"And…" *You are okay with that?* I want to scream. But then—goddammit—that was our plan!

And now it's a mess, a disaster, a subtle pain in my chest.

Dad's gaze is unblinking. "Why are you upset, Kit-Kat?"

"Because I don't want to leave!" I say too loudly and notice heads turn in my direction. "I… Dad, I…"

I'm about to burst into tears. So, I say, "Archer will send you an update, I'm sure. Talk to you later, Dad."

And without waiting for a response, I hang up. The screen lights up right away with a call back from Dad, but I slam the laptop shut and leave the Center.

One drink.

Two.

Three.

I don't want to get drunk but rather fall into a deep sleep and wake up on the mainland, forgetting that this trip ever happened.

I take the bottle and set it next to me as I sit on my balcony and stare at the dark jungle.

Marlow doesn't pick up the five times I call him. I text him the news. Now he knows I'm leaving. But he's busy with the new girl. Right. Who gives a shit about Kat, anyway? So much for friendship. If I go around saying bye to Maddy and Kai and Callie and Ty, it'll feel devastating.

I wipe away the tears and take a swig from the bottle, some sweet liquor Marlow brought once for dinner. It's half-empty by now and too sweet. Something nasty and bitter would've been more appropriate.

Wiping away tears doesn't help. They just keep coming.

My phone dings with a text.

**Archer: The boat leaves tomorrow at 6 a.m. Slate will pick you up and take you to Port Mrei.**

A sob escapes me.

How can he say it so easily?

**Me: Fuck you.**

I reinforce my answer with another swig from the bottle.

**Archer: That's not a very friendly farewell.**

**Me: I hate you!**

Another swig.

No filter.

Here we go.

**Me: You won't ever meet anyone else who will see you**

the way I do. But you don't need that person, right? Riiii-ight, Mr. Chancellor. GET A BIMBO! Ssssso much easier.

Me: Maybe the one with pink hair. Someone who'll obey your every word.

Me: Maybe I'll get an invite to your wedding one day. Barbie and Ken.

Only when I'm done venting do I curse under my breath.

*So classy, Kat.*

And drunk. My head spins as scream, "Fuuuuck!" and throw the phone against the wall, then light a joint with trembling hands and sit, my eyes closed, waiting for a reply.

But it doesn't come.

Because I break everything in my life, not just phones.

# 17

---

## ARCHER

Whoever said, "Out of sight, out of mind," obviously hasn't met Kat. She's a spike of serotonin with a dangerous crash afterward.

I deleted the videos from the villa cam and now regret it. So I pull up the picture of us from Cece's party, and my treacherous heart gives out a sad howl at the thought of not seeing her again.

A text pops up on my screen.

**Kat: You won't ever meet anyone else who will see you the way I do. But you don't need that person, right? Riiii-ight, Mr. Chancellor. GET A BIMBO! Ssssso much easier.**

Then another right away.

**Kat: Maybe the one with pink hair. Someone who'll obey your every word.**

**Kat: Maybe I'll get an invite to your wedding one day. Barbie and Ken.**

Whoa.

She's angry. Drunk or high. That's way more than she'd

usually let out, and the texts prick me right down to my soul just like the words she spoke that fateful night.

I used to tell people what I wanted them to say about me. I used to *make* them. When they didn't go along, I'd get angry.

That's what happened the day after the Block Party and the rumors about Callie and Droga—I snapped. I lost my best friend, and it taught me that anger can be curbed and that it didn't matter what others thought about me, only the ones I cared about. But my best friend didn't care anymore. That was the problem. There wasn't a single person, I realized, who cared about me. So I stopped caring about others too.

The four years between me being twenty and arrogant and being twenty-four and mentally fucked were the painful years of proving me wrong. The Change showed me how others folded seeing their loved ones dying. I had no one.

Sending Kat away is the last attempt to force her out of my system. I'm failing miserably, and she still doesn't say what I want to hear—that she wants to be here for me. Not Marlow. Not the job. Not the tropical paradise. Not the fucking suspense.

Me.

I'm a selfish prick. Yeah, the wild thing was right, what are you gonna do?

My reinforcement comes in the form of two drinks shot back to back. Then, for the first time in a month, I open the tracking app.

Kat's home. And that's where I'm heading, on foot,

hands in my pockets, skirting the dark buildings like a fucking vampire, because I don't want to see anyone else or talk to anyone. I dread every step closer as my heart flutters with some stupid-ass hope. It always does. Kat is an invisible trigger that has a control over it.

There's no logic in me sending her away. But I want her to talk, and not in that careful, "How are you, Archer? Are you feeling okay, Archer? How is it going, Archer?" Like I'm a fucking child.

Right now, I'm stepping into a fire. It'll scorch me. It might ruin me because I'm ready to step over my pride and put my feelings out on a platter in front of her. But she might not feel the same. Yet, the fire—*her*—is hypnotic, and I can't stop.

I don't knock when I walk up to her bungalow, but open the door and step inside quietly.

It's dark outside, and the only lights in her place are the dim lamp by the bed and the solar light on the terrace. There's a small dark shadow on the otherwise light floor—a broken phone.

It's quiet. I haven't been here in two months, and the scent assaults me with all that used to be so familiar—her smooth skin, her wild hair, her beautiful smile.

Her…

There's a soft sound coming from the open doors to the terrace—Kat's in the wicker chair, her head tilted back, eyes closed, her arm hanging off one side, a bottle of booze between her fingers.

"Are you done with nasty texts?" I ask, stepping out onto the terrace right behind her.

She jolts to her feet with shock in her eyes, staring at me —it's the first time I've caught her off-guard like that.

I lean with my shoulder onto the door frame, hands in my pockets as I study her head to toe.

She's wearing booty shorts and a tank. Her eyes are puffy and sparkly with tears, her face wet. The scent of coconut oil with a tang of cannabis is stronger here.

"Is there more to come?" I smirk, though my entire body is on edge at being so close to her, always is. "You could write a novel, *Hating Archer Crone*."

"Maybe I will," she says almost in a whisper, setting the bottle on the wicker table. It's almost empty. I wonder how much she drank.

"I don't see you packing," I say, trying to put as much indifference into the words as I can.

"I came here with nothing. I have nothing to pack. Save this for the next assistant."

That's the thing about Kat—she never asks for anything, doesn't cling to material things. It's unusual and surprising, considering she's been surrounded by luxury during the last several months.

We stare at each other in silence, then her lips curl in a smirk. "What do you want, Archer? One last fuck? For old times' sake?"

I fake a smile. "I'll miss that."

Then I take a step closer. If she's actually leaving, yes, I want to trap her here and fuck the living hell out of her, take every last drop I can.

There's slight surprise in her eyes, or hope—I can't tell. Her haughtiness flickers on and off—yeah, she's tipsy. So am I. Her closeness shoots down all the stop signs in my head. I'll fuck her my way too, rough and quick. As a payback for showing up on my island, starting a storm in my life, and messing me up worse than I've ever been.

"On all fours, wild thing. Now," I order in a low voice, my heart beating in anticipation of seeing what she'll do.

"Fuck you," she whispers.

There she is again, that pendulum. *Fuck me, Archer. Fuck off, Archer. Answer the phone, Archer. Leave me alone, Archer.*

"Excuse me?"

She takes a step toward me, hate and spite in her eyes just like that dark night, and my insides turn cold—no, she's not in the mood to play. That's it, I fucked up for good.

"If you want to fuck, then don't give me a half-ass pity fuck, Archer. I'm not a toy. Fuck me the way you drink. The way you used to get mad at me. Fuck me like you shot smack, desperate to forget the pain." The words stab me in the heart, but she's right. She does know me. "Fuck me the way you feel, all of it, good, bad, hot, ugly, and everything in between. Because that's you." She's slurring, angry, spitting the words out at me as she takes tiny steps closer, stabbing the air with her forefinger. "Under that calculated mask you put on every day lately is the guy who laughed at my silly jokes and shared his past and ordered a chef from the mainland only to pretend that it was nothing and that you do this for everyone. If it's over, I don't need your half-ass seconds."

"So, for once, you don't want to fuck?" I try to say it as

bitterly as I can, though my entire body feels like it's twisted in pain. This is rejection.

"I don't want a pity fuck from you. Or another hate fuck. I've had those."

"So what do you want?"

Her eyes are so beautiful, with pools of tears and so scared. I can tell. She's afraid she'll let her guard down and say something that'll shatter her image of the unapologetic tough girl that she is.

She's more than that. And I want it all. But I'm the last person she'll open up to. And that's what makes *us* impossible.

The silence between us is becoming too tense. It's our enemy. Everything that should be said always drowns in silence.

I wait for her to say what I want to hear. She waits for me to say something else. I could tell her that she's my madness. That I'm obsessed beyond any logic. That trying to drive her out of this place seems like the only cure but also feels devastating.

But Kat is silent too. Maybe she has nothing to say—I quote—*to a selfish prick who doesn't deserve people loving him.*

The words are still hurtful, echoing in my mind and in her gaze.

"Right," I say quietly, nodding, and turn around.

The walk toward the door is heartbreaking.

Just like her walking away from me the night of Cece's party.

Not a sound comes from her as I open the door and walk out of her bungalow.

## 18

## KAT

GONE.

He's gone.

I'm such a coward.

Desperation sends my pulse through the roof when I finally pull myself out of my stupor and rush toward the door, outside, and up the path toward the road.

"Archer!"

I stop, staring into the darkness for any sign of him, my heart pounding in my ears.

I'm so messed up and so, so scared that I lost my last chance with him.

"Archer," I whisper, willing him to come back.

Tears start streaking from my eyes, and I run my hands over my hair, trying to hold back the emotions.

It's hard to breathe. Sobs suffocate me. Tears won't stop as I stand here on the loneliest night of my life, the scariest too, topped only by the night of Archer's incident.

A lone parrot screeches in the trees. There's a muffled

beeping sound coming from behind me. I breathe in and out slowly, trying to calm my heart which seems to pulsate through my entire body.

I turn around slowly and walk toward the lit-up porch, staring at my bare feet, wiping my face, and see—

His feet…

My eyes slowly rise, following the body, *his* body, and I stare in shock at Archer, who leans against the side of my bungalow, arms crossed at his chest as he gazes back at me. He pushes off the wall and steps toward the door, holding it open for me, his eyes never leaving mine.

What's happening?

I step toward him, my heart pumping even faster. I think I might be having a heart attack.

There's that strange sound again coming from his pocket. I'm so confused about everything that I don't even fight when Archer grabs me by my arm, pulls me inside, and, kicking the door closed, whips me around and presses me against the door.

"Why are you crying?"

His voice is harsh, but his gaze is too intense, letting me know he's not angry but upset. My future depends on the answer.

"Is it Zion? Friends? Marlow? Fucking talk, Kat. We've been here before. Me, pinning you to the wall, prying words out of you. You choking and handcuffing me because you are used to fighting back."

How does he not get it? "You are such an idiot."

A glint of bitterness etches his eyes. "So explain it to me, to the idiot that I am. I can't chase you, Kat. I can *force* you to do and say what I want, but I won't. Out of all people, I won't do it with you."

"Why?"

"Because you are important to me. And if you don't feel the same, then I have to let you go."

"Don't." I'm begging. This is the lowest I've been with a man. I should be ashamed.

"Say it," he urges.

"Say what?"

"Tell me why you want to stay."

I feel like I'm kneeling but I haven't moved an inch.

"I have a picture of us on my phone," I say, my chest tightening at the words. "Us dancing at Cece's party. It's my screensaver. It's us."

I hang my head, tilting forward and pressing my forehead to his shoulder. It's easier to talk if I don't look at him, though his scent drives me insane. "I know I acted like a brat that evening," I say in a shaky voice, swallowing tears. "I know that later, I said some awful things. I let you down in your worst moment, and you might be hating me for that. And maybe that's the reason you keep your distance lately."

This will only work one way—if I show all my cards.

"I want you," I say quietly, summoning all my courage. "More of you. What we had. It's frustrating. And worst of all—" I swallow hard. "It hurts, Archer. Because we don't talk anymore. Don't laugh together. We don't have *anything* anymore."

My head is dizzy, and my heart is ripping apart. From

booze. From the emotions I can't hold back anymore, letting him see me this way, the mess that I am.

His fingers brush off my tears, and just his touch is enough to make my knees buckle.

"I'm drunk. I'm sorry." If I weren't, I would've never told him even a fraction of this. "If you don't care—"

"Don't finish the fucking sentence, Kat."

My feelings are way over the top, spilling onto my face in embarrassing tears.

"I want so much more of you, Archer." I stare at his shirt, at his arms moving as his hands gently cup my face, then down at his feet—anything but his face, as if meeting his eyes will kill me. "But if I can't have that, it's alright. I'll be fine. But let me stay for a little longer."

How do I tell the man who avoids me that he haunts me every hour of every day? That every time he walks out of the room we are in, I pray to see him again in the next minute. That the world feels empty when he's not around. That I constantly imagine what it'd be like if there *was* an us. That I lie sleepless in my bed at night, for hours staring at the ceiling, remembering every second we spent together. How scary it is to realize that I crossed some red forbidden line where there's no return. No return from the person who consumes me completely.

"I won't bother you," I whisper. "Won't annoy you. Won't get on your radar, I promise. But I need more time with you. If only at a distance. So I can part with Zion my own way."

The air burns between us. There's silence and waiting,

me waiting for his response that doesn't come, and I finally summon the courage to lift my face and meet his eyes.

His gaze is so intense that I want to disappear from shame.

"I can't, Kat," he says.

The words are like a death sentence.

"I can't do that," he repeats.

They're deafening. I want to scream. My tears will soak the floor soon, but that's not as devastating as the fact that he won't give me another chance.

"I can't let you stay here at a distance." My words out of his mouth sound bitter. "It doesn't work. *Won't* work."

*Right.*

Another sob betrays me. I push at his chest with my weak hands, wanting to walk away, but his strong rigid body won't budge, and I look down, burning from shame. *Stop touching me, then.*

He's my weakness. I should've left a long time ago.

"If you stay," he says even quieter, his face inching closer to mine, his hands still holding my head, tilting it up again so I look at him, "we can't play games anymore. We can't pretend like we're here for a fun ride. I'm done with those."

His nose brushes my cheek, his warm breath making me lose my mind.

"If you stay, Kat," he says so softly that if this sentence ends in the most devastating way, I'll *have* to leave. "Then it's you and I. Together. Officially."

My eyes widen in surprise. His eyes are so close and so intense and full of every possible emotion besides his usual arrogance that my head spins. One inch and I could kiss him. One inch and we *could* be together.

"If you stay," he whispers, his fingers lacing into my hair, "you are mine."

"Yes," I breathe out so quickly that it scares me, and before I can think or say anything else, Archer's lips mold with mine in a kiss.

That inch… It can create an abyss between two people. But as soon as it vanishes between us, my world spins on its axis.

His fingers sink into my hair and grip so tightly that there's no way to escape the deep plunge of his tongue that makes me moan into his mouth. The kiss is so deep that I feel like I lack air to breathe. But I don't need air. Just him.

I fist his shirt, pulling him even closer, wanting to jump into his arms.

He pulls me off the door and into him, taking steps back toward the bed, his lips taking mine in a ravishing kiss. His hands start pulling my tank up and over my head because our words can't keep up with our bodies that missed each other for far too long.

"We are together, in public," Archer murmurs between the kisses as I slide my hands under his shirt, seeking out his bare skin.

"Yes," I murmur, catching his lips again in a kiss, my head spinning at the realization of what he's offering.

"That's the only way it can work, Kat."

"Us. Yes. Yes." I'll say yes to anything at this very moment.

My heart is about to explode. And there's that beeping

in Archer's pocket. I hope it's not bad news or another Armageddon, though I won't let him check it, not until we seal the deal.

And I kiss him even harder so he doesn't get a chance to back away.

I pull his shirt up.

"I don't care about the workplace," he murmurs, letting me yank it over his head and toss it onto the floor. "It's my island, and we'll do whatever we want." He does the same to my bra.

"Yes," I answer, my hands on his sweatpants.

"No objections."

I push his sweats and boxers down. "No," I murmur, letting him do the same to my shorts as we both stumble, making little steps toward the bed and kicking the shorts and pants away.

"No hiding," Archer murmurs, his hands impatiently roaming my body.

"No hiding," I agree, my mouth greedily kissing his neck, tasting his skin.

We bump into the bed and fall into it.

"You have a problem—you come talk to me, Kat. Not Marlow or anyone else." He wraps his arm around my waist and pulls me flush against him.

My brain is fuzzy from his words and his touches and this sudden hope that's bursting out of me.

"You are mad—you let me know. Upset—tell me." He kisses me hard again.

"Yes," I blurt somewhere in between.

We are a hot mess as we rub against each other, finally naked, finally loose, pulling and tugging.

"You are happy—you tell me. I want to know it all, Kat." He kicks my legs apart and adjusts himself between my them.

"Ssssso happy right now." Wet face. Wet pussy. Look at me.

"Yeah?" He sheathes into me, and I moan a desperate, "Yeah."

He starts thrusting, and I'm a happy mess.

"Yes," I murmur, falling apart under him with a muffled moan.

# 19

## KAT

I'M A TAKER, REMEMBER? BUT AT THIS MOMENT, I LET ARCHER take what he wants. I'm always there for a ride, but this time, I want to give, ease his moments of sadness, and be with him when he really needs it.

Archer's hands slide in my hair as he kisses me like he's staking his claim inside me. He *is* inside me, and I want to take control, ride him, take what's mine. He *is* mine, but I want to let go.

We are a tangle of limbs and a furnace of feelings. He is fucking me like he hates me, like he wants to hurt me, though I know better. My thighs fall open to let him in deeper, and I still can't get enough. We kiss like there's a fight over whose tongue belongs in whose mouth. Archer pounds into me, and it feels deliciously good.

It's a physical-release fuck.

An emotions-drain fuck.

A we-haven't-talked-forever-and-need-to-blow-off-steam fuck.

A remember-how-this-feels fuck.

An I'm-yours-and-you're-mine-so-stop-the-bullshit fuck.

He doesn't say a word, just groans, that animalistic sound mixing with my whimpers and gasps because it feels so good to have him and I don't want to hold back. We are a mess of sloppy kisses, greedy hands gripping each other, teeth grazing, thighs slapping together until we are both spent, panting as we fall onto our backs.

We lie splayed on the bed, next to each other, staring at the ceiling for some time. My heart has never felt so happy.

I want to say so many things. Afraid of so many of them. And I don't want to ruin the moment. Ruining things is my bad habit.

I shift my hand just a little bit toward Archer and feel his, his thumb brushing against mine, intentionally, back and forth.

One touch. It can mean so much. Our fingers aimlessly brush together, and it might be the most intimate moment yet.

I turn my head to study him. This beautiful guy, so strong, so powerful, and so full of feelings.

He turns his head to meet my gaze.

"Just remember I warned you, wild thing," he says, a smile on his lips too playful to be a warning. It's one of Archer's bedroom warnings. These are my favorite. "You just said yes to a selfish prick."

I chuckle. This shouldn't be funny. I called him that in his darkest moments, but I'll fix that. "But you are *my* selfish prick now, right?"

I bite my lower lip, trying not to grin, my heart flapping invisible wings.

Archer shifts onto his side, propping himself on his elbow, pulling me toward him with his arm snaking around my waist.

"This is it," he says, his eyes roaming my face.

He smiles. I smile, my skin crinkling from dry tears. We're ridiculous.

I lift my hand to brush the back of my fingers against his cheek, the way he does to me.

"Boyfriend…" I murmur dreamily and then repeat it in my head like I want to get a taste of it. I thought he was kicking me off the island, and now this—*us*. There *is* an us.

"You are so screwed, kitten. You have no idea."

The best news ever.

"Good thing I like being screwed by you," I say cheekily before our smiles meet in a kiss.

Aaaaaand, we are back!

I break the kiss to whisper in his ear, "Are you gonna fire me if I tell you that I don't really care about the job?" I nibble on his ear, inhaling his scent. "Just you, Arch. All I care about now is you."

I kiss his neck, but he gently tugs at my hair, pulling me away.

"Kat, look at me."

"Nuh-huh," I murmur, trying to bury my face in his neck, embarrassed at what I just said. That sweet liquor is some wicked truth serum. I feel like I just spilled classified material.

Archer's movement is quick and overpowering when he

flips me onto my back and pins my hands above my head. There's nowhere to look but him. My heart pumps heavily as Archer's lips stretch in a smile that's not cocky for once but happy, his lips parting to say something, but he doesn't. He knows better than to taunt me in moments like this.

Instead, he sags against me, his hard chest against my breasts, his strong thighs between mine, and kisses me.

We kiss for the longest time. It's our first time opening up, even if only in this way. I free my hands and run them along his muscular body, letting myself touch him for myself, absently, feeling him under my fingertips rather than deliberately calculating the touch to turn him on.

I've watched Archer for months, learning his every move and gesture. Right now, I learn him through the way his body responds to mine. The way he deepens the kiss when my hand glides over his cock that's hard again. My guy is hard everywhere.

*My* Archer.

I slide one hand up his torso and into his hair, tugging at it. I can't get enough of his smooth skin and hard muscles. I've taken it for granted before. Now, every minute feels like I might lose him again—it's emotional PTSD.

His tongue swirls around mine in deep strokes. This guy is a perfect kisser. When he takes his time, he can probably make me come just by doing these soft velvety licks into my mouth.

Every time he pulls just slightly away, my heart jolts at the thought that he'll leave. And when we finally break apart, I don't take my hands off him.

"I like kissing you," I say.

He brushes his thumb against my lips. "I told you I love your lips."

I love his confessions, but they make me too vulnerable. "Your phone was going off the hook. Better check it," I say to change the topic.

His chest shakes in a silent chuckle. "Emergency alert."

My smile is gone. "For what?" Like we don't have enough emergencies on Zion.

"For your heart rate."

What? It must be some kind of joke because Archer is grinning, that familiar devilish sparkle in his eyes.

"I have a vitals alert activated on an app and connected to your Ayana bracelet that tracks your health."

"You're kidding me, right?" This guy is a first-class stalker.

"It's true. Just want to make sure you're alright." Now he brushes his thumb on my cheek. "It alerts me when you're in extreme distress or your vitals fail."

I don't need to ask why it was beeping like mad in the last twenty minutes. I'm surprised my heart didn't jump out of my chest and plant itself at Archer's feet.

He nods toward the floor. "Looks like your phone is broken."

"Yeah." I wrinkle my nose. "It broke."

"It *broke*?" He snorts. "Or *you* broke it?"

"I got a little upset, and it slipped out of my hand."

"A *little* upset?"

"Yeah." I peek at him from under my eyebrows.

"I see. It probably couldn't handle the rude texts you were sending me and leaped to its death."

"Maybe it felt heartbroken."

"Oh, big words, Miss Ortiz."

He's teasing me, and the difference between the Kat a month ago and Kat right now is that this Kat doesn't even care. I want more of this, him teasing, taunting, even making fun of me—that's us.

I don't want him to leave. I'm about to say just that but then stall, drowning in the feeling of his skin under my fingertips and the way he rakes his fingers through my hair as we lie wrapped in each other.

"Kat?" I flick my gaze up to meet his. "Spit it out."

Of course, he can read my freaking thoughts. I bite my cheek, slightly nervous. "Will you stay here tonight?"

Archer likes pristine cleanness. My place is anything but. Jesus, we didn't even bother undoing the bed. There's a trail of our clothes on the floor from the door to the bed, and some of my shirts are splayed on it. I could clean up real quick, if only he stayed.

A smile grows on Archer's lips—that familiar amusement like I said something crazy. And then he starts chuckling.

*Shit.*

I'm pushing it. Of course. He offered this dating thing, and I'm jumping head in.

*Tsk.*

I cast my gaze down, aimlessly drawing some abstract shapes on his bare chest with my fingers.

His hand reaches to push my hair behind my ear, and I freaking blush like a little girl.

"Kat, Kat, Kat…"

Here it comes. As always, I got carried away.

His fingers slide under my chin and tip it up so I look at him.

God, I love his smile. Maybe I should say more stupid things just to cheer him up.

He leans down to brush his lips against mine in the softest kiss yet. My body turns into a pool of want beneath his, but I'm afraid to move and let him go earlier than he decides to.

"Wild thing, even if you choked me out, dragged my body out of here, and barricaded the windows and doors, I'd still find a way to get back in here."

He's grinning. So is my heart, which is doing a winning drumroll.

"I'm not planning on leaving," he says. "I was hoping for breakfast. And I'd like to have two of them. We still haven't made it to that part."

I remember every time we were together.

"And"—his gaze slides down my body—"I didn't have my dinner yet." Horny bastard! I squeal inwardly in delight. "So there. I'm staying tonight. Thanks for asking and not making me invite myself."

He kiss me again, and my heart is pretty much like that emoji with blissfully tight-shut eyes and a tongue sticking out.

## 20

### ARCHER

Will I ever tell her that I bluffed and wouldn't have had the guts to send her off this island?

Will I ever tell her that I've never wanted anything more than her?

I might in the future. I've never looked forward to the future so much.

And I've never been so much in the present as I am now, slowly thrusting into Kat, kissing her non-stop, gliding my hand along her warm thigh, her legs wrapped around me, her moans seeping into my mouth.

She's letting me in deeper, and I'm not talking about my cock inside her, throbbing again, even though we just fucked. Her words spin in my head, every kiss laced with them, every thrust, every brush of her hand against my skin, her fingers twisting into my hair. The scent of her.

*I want so much more of you.*

I want *all* of her.

We fuck slower this time. I need to fuck her a dozen more times just to catch up on how much I missed her.

"I'll fuck you to death, my beautiful spy," I murmur, drawing out every thrust like there's some existential meaning in it.

"That was the promise yet to be delivered," she blurts out.

I thrust harder into her—I've yet to fuck this clever mouth of hers properly.

But before I pick up the rhythm, she pushes into me, flips me onto the bed, and pins my hands above my head.

"There," she exhales, sinking onto my cock.

I'm startled. She holds my hands pinned with unusual strength. Not that I can't overpower her, but this feels good. My woman taking charge is arousing as hell. There's unexplainable pleasure in relinquishing control, let alone the sight of my kitten riding on top of me, her torso arching in waves, her perky breasts right above me, her hair falling down onto my face. She is a warrior in bed, and I fucking love it.

I lace my fingers with hers. She leans over and kisses me greedily. Even our tongues are at war.

No, not a fucking chance I would've let her go. She is my biggest addiction yet. With the biggest hangover I've had in the last month.

I thought she was a drug I needed to try and then toss away when the initial curiosity wore off.

I couldn't be more wrong.

She's the cure for the darkness that anchored inside me

for the longest time and the loneliness that had taken root deep within it.

I let her ride me for a little longer, feel her hold loosen, then tear my hands out of hers, flip her onto her back, and start driving into her until she cries out and the mere sound of her orgasm makes me come right after.

We lie on top of the sheets for some time. She's being unusually quiet. I want to lie like this forever, but also to fuck her again, kiss her, talk, laugh—all at once, like there's no time to do everything I've wanted to do with her. The last weeks without her were torture.

Her beautiful body is splayed on the bed. There's that lazy cum-buzzed look on her face. Her voice is soft, though intending to be more confident, when she finally asks, "Are you hungry?"

I turn my head to meet her playful smile. She always changes the topic when she feels vulnerable.

"Yeah, I could eat something."

Needing a cigarette, since I just went through a turmoil of emotions, I put on my boxers, pad toward the terrace, and lean on the doorframe as I smoke, exhaling into the warm night air. I hear the fridge opening and closing, and when I turn, I catch Kat's gaze on me, her eyes dropping to her hands right away, a little smile on her lips.

She's put on a long baby-blue surfer tank that goes just below her ass but leaves the sides of her torso open and makes her long tanned legs look even more gorgeous. Her hair hangs over one shoulder, her face slightly puffy from crying, lips swollen from my kisses, cheeks flushed from me working her up twice in a row—my doing, thank you very much. And I can't hold back a smile as she fusses with the bowls and a pot, grabs something out of the fridge, closing it with her foot, then licks the spoon she just used to stir the pot.

Kat. With a pot. In her kitchen. Warming up food for me.

There are dozens of little things about this scenario that would've seemed ridiculous and impossible a month ago.

And yet…

"It's nothing fancy," she explains almost apologetically as we sit down side by side at the kitchen island and dip our spoons into the bowls of soup. "It's *Caldo de Res*, a Mexican soup. My dad's friend used to make it all the time."

"It's good," I say, taking spoon after spoon of the beef-and-vegetable soup, the taste of it lost on me as I still can't believe what's happening. Now that I think of it, I'm pretty sure no girl I ever dated cooked for me. Most grew up with maids.

There's a knock at the door.

"Expecting anyone?" I ask, jealousy scratching at my heart at the sound. This resort used to be full of my friends. Now, Kat has more friends than I do.

She gives me a reproachful look. "I was supposed to be getting ready to leave tomorrow, right?"

*Right.*

The knocking turns into banging.

"Kat! Open up!" Marlow yells angrily as he jerks on the door handle.

Slowly, I rise from the table and pad to the front door,

not a bit flustered at the fact that I open it only in my boxers.

Marlow's scowl is the first thing I see, which changes into gaping as his eyes scan me up and down.

"I guess it's all sorted," he murmurs, his expression softening.

I lean with my forearm on the doorframe. "What is?" I want to hear it from him.

He rolls his eyes, cocking his head. "Dude, she's not leaving, is she." There's no question in his voice but an angry reproach.

"Not alive, no."

He snorts and is already walking off. "Have a good night," he says without turning, and when I close the door, Kat is aimlessly stirring the soup in her bowl, trying really hard not to grin.

I want to do all sorts of things to her, but we are both exhausted. Cortisol and adrenalin get released into the system, triggering excessive production of serotonin, all of which eventually start running low.

We are drained, but I know that I'm falling asleep in her bed, and tomorrow she won't run away. For now, we are good.

We put out the lights and get in Kat's bed.

It feels surreal, like I've finally gotten close enough to her, feeling her next to me under the sheet though she doesn't come close.

"Come here," I whisper.

"You are not a cuddler, remember?" she whispers back.

Unbelievable. "I said, come here."

She shimmies over, but not close enough.

"Katura," I warn her. She's playing, little spy.

"Using big words, Mr. Chancellor?" Kat is back, the sassy thing that she is.

I slide my arm around her waist and pull her flush against me. "If you don't shut your pretty mouth, I'll fuck it. I still have a lot pent up inside me, and I haven't gotten laid in weeks, and you can't keep up."

She adjusts against my side, producing something like, "Uh-huh," under her breath.

"And then I'll fuck your sweet ass to prove my point. So be very quiet, yeah?"

I know she's smiling as her arm eagerly slides around my waist.

And that's how we fall asleep. Me thinking about doing just that to her sometime soon. Her considering it in the future.

## 21

### KAT

IT'S BRIGHT OUTSIDE. FOR A CHANGE, I WAKE UP HAPPY, because there are familiar arms wrapped around me.

I'm afraid to stir. Archer might get up and leave right away. I just want one more minute, like it's a dream, and I don't want to open my eyes in case I got drunk last night and imagined all of what happened.

Archer finally stirs, his fingers brushing against my shoulder. I brush mine across his hand slowly, like I'm half-asleep. His slide lower, his body stirs just an inch, a tense inch that's an obvious sign he's turned on. We play this game for a minute until our movements turn into nuzzling each other. Our hands slide lower to the more intimate areas, I shift with my back toward him, pushing my butt against him, and he slides his erection inside me, filling me up, and we both grunt.

We fuck slowly. Don't say a word. Lie quiet for a minute afterward. It's not enough. Not by a mile. Won't be for a while. I feel like I need to get under his skin to be closer to him.

"Just remember what I said yesterday," he says too seriously for my liking after he takes a shower—*Archer* takes a shower at *my* place, I'm taking a mental picture of this—and walks up to me dressed in his shirt and sweat pants.

"Remind me," I tease. "Which part?"

He cocks a brow at me, and I laugh.

"When something bothers you, worries you, makes you angry—you talk to me. We'll have to talk about a lot of things. And we're not good at it."

"We're okay."

"You are already avoiding this conversation."

"Pff. No, I'm not."

"Your eyes say otherwise, kitten."

I love that he calls me kitten again. But his voice is not playful. Rather, intense.

"What do my eyes say?" I tease.

"That if you dropped your guard, you and I could make things work."

"We can make it work if you drop your pants right now." God, I'm stupidly horny around him. Even the thought of him walking out the door makes me miss him already. And yes, his gaze makes me feel way too vulnerable.

"There you go. That's not what I was talking about."

"If you dropped your know-it-all attitude, Archer, I wouldn't have to have a guard." I lick my lips, trying to come up with words that won't make me sound weak. "It's not about having a good time anymore, is it?" I ask quietly, careful about what I say because we messed around until we realized that we started messing with each other's feelings.

"It's not. Hasn't been in a while." He's making me uneasy like he can read my thoughts. "It's called a relationship."

Something changed in him after that evening when his world crashed. He is calmer, quieter, less cheerful—understandable. He looks at me differently. It's too open like he sees something he hasn't seen before, and it takes him by surprise. He joked before that he has it all figured out. I thought so too. Until the night I almost lost him.

*Lost him*—just the thought of it sends my mind into panic mode.

So does the word *relationship,* which has never been part of an equation in my life. This is getting too deep. We're taking the next step, without any tricks, which is a freaking achievement on our part.

What's happening is amazing, because before Archer steps out, he walks over to me and pulls me into him.

"I can't read you very well anymore. So we have to talk about things."

*Things* are feelings, I get it. "I thought I was an open book."

I can't hold back a smile when I look from under my eyebrows at Archer as he tongues his cheek.

"Yeah," he drawls. "There are a lot of pages."

"I thought you can speed read."

His arms around me tighten. "There's your mouth again."

"I thought it was your favorite part of me."

"Don't test my patience. I'll see you at work, yeah?"

He kisses me, long and deep, stirring me up like we didn't just go at it twice.

I pull away and pick a thread off his shirt. "You won't leave if you keep kissing me like this."

He only laughs through his nose, then takes my jaw between his thumb and middle finger. "I have a feeling the office is gonna be one of my favorite places again," he murmurs before his lips touch mine in a soft kiss again. He kisses me like he's trying to figure out if I taste different as a girlfriend than the casual lay I used to be.

Then his hand slides into his pocket, and he reaches behind my neck.

His gold chain—he puts it back on me, like he's branding me.

"Until I get you something worthy of you," he says in a voice that sends me to the damn moon.

And then he's gone.

## 22

### KAT

*No holding back.*

Archer's words were full of promise, and as I take a dip in the ocean before going to the office, I already anticipate the workday.

I'm at the Center before him, and when he walks in, I expect him to carry on with his day.

"My office." He nods toward the door, and I melt in his arms when I get a kiss as soon as I walk in.

"We need rules," Archer says when my hands go slightly lower on his body than is appropriate, considering anyone can see through his office window.

"Rules?" I murmur.

"We meet every other night," he says.

I'm startled. "Ohhh-kay? Why?"

"We need to take things slow. Because otherwise, we'll fly off the handle and do something stupid."

I can read his body very well. Right now, his rules don't

make sense. Not when his fingers brush against my back in a very obvious way—he wants me again.

My fingers go to the buttons of his jeans, and Archer cocks his brow.

I pause. "I thought you said no holding back."

His beautiful lips curl in a tiny smile. "I want to take you on a date before we do anything else."

"I see," I murmur, not taking my eyes off his, and unzip him anyway, reach inside his jeans, and give his cock a few soft strokes through his boxers.

He's semi-hard and grunts, his hand snaking into my hair and pulling at it gently. "Kitten," he warns.

I know he can't resist it, but there are rules, so, I'll abide. For now.

I give him one last stroke, teasing him just for the hell of it. Archer sucks in his cheeks in tension—he does it sometimes, so cute. Slowly I zip him back up, which is a struggle as his cock swells and refuses to fit back in.

There's disappointment in his eyes. He's horny. Holding back is a bitch, but he's the one who insists.

"I'll follow your rules," I purr.

He smiles at my words as he sets his hand on my hipbone, pulling me closer, licking into my mouth just once. "You are a tease, kitten."

That I am. And wet. "You are being unfair."

"Oh, I'm very fair. There." He pulls away abruptly and retrieves a new cell phone from his desk. "This one has a camera, so you can take pictures. And it's cleared, so you can do video chats with your dad."

And that's what I do next. I snap a selfie with Archer,

who doesn't even look at the camera, just at me, as I'm being goofy.

I'm already calculating in my mind all the dirty selfies I'm gonna take and send to Archer to make him lose his mind. I don't like rules.

The entire day, we tiptoe around each other like there's something fragile between us that we're afraid to break. We said some sensitive things the night we broke the ice, but we don't talk about feelings again.

I catch Archer's glances at me through his office window. Then more of them every time he goes in and out of his office. Before the work day is over, Archer sends me a message.

**Archer: Any plans for tonight?**

I'm being ballsy, not knowing why he asks.

**Me: You.**

I glance at his office and see a smile on his face as he types on his phone.

**Archer: Good. Dinner at my place tonight? Seven?**

There are question marks in his texts like he's not sure I'll agree. You kidding me?

**Me: Can't wait.**

I try really hard not to grin like a happy fool.

**Me: Are you gonna deliver on your promises?**

**Archer: Which are?**

**Me: No holding back.**

**Archer: Are you good with multitasking?**

**Me: ?**

**Archer: Eating, talking, and fucking at the same time.**

I burst out laughing and cover my mouth with my

hand, then shake my head and get up, holding Archer's gaze through the window.

"See you," I mouth, and his mischievous cocky stare burns me all the way to my core as I leave the Center.

I've never gotten ready for dinner so meticulously. My heart beats like a moth against a bright lamp at night.

A dark-green slightly loose string dress.

Boots—they'll come off right away, maybe after my panties.

Makeup—I've never put on makeup as many times in my life as I have here on Zion. But that's another thing about women's psychology. We doll up even when the guy is already into us, like peacocks spreading our colorful feathers. Wait, it's male peacocks that do that. I laugh at the thought as I walk to Cliff Villa, my heart racing in anticipation as I approach.

We used to play a cat-and-mouse game. Now we are in a relationship that's almost as fragile as a house of cards, and I so desperately want it to work out.

Yeah, guys hustle before a date too—I hold back a grin as I swipe my gaze along Archer's body when I walk in.

He's dressed in jeans and a black button-up, casually untucked, sleeves rolled up, unbuttoned at the neck. But I can tell his tasseled hair is too perfect—he's spent time on it, the sight as sexy as a waft of his cologne when he kisses me on the cheek.

"Aaaye, look at you, miss!"

Alma's voice makes me turn around. The maid's hands are clasped at her chest in prayer as she studies me with genuine admiration.

"Have a good evening, Mr. Crone." She bows slightly, beaming as Archer graces her with his smile, and leaves.

"She's made dinner for us."

"Do you ever cook?" I ask Archer as he walks me out onto the terrace by the pool, a small table with candles, flowers, and silverware set up in the center.

I have butterflies in my stomach—it's an actual date.

"No," Archer replies. I can't picture him cooking anyway.

I set my phone on the table and take several steps toward the pool.

It's getting dark, but the terrace is set in a warm glow of the lanterns and the blue pool lights.

This pool has seen many of my and Archer's moments. Now it's witnessing a date.

My phone beeps, then again, and again in a fast warning succession.

I have no interest in answering, not when I'm with Archer. The world can wait.

It beeps again, and I turn to see Archer glance at it with curiosity.

"Are you hungry?" he asks, hands in his pockets as he openly studies me.

"For food?" I ask, innocently raising my brows.

He chuckles.

The phone beeps again, pulling Archer's gaze from me.

"Someone wants you tonight," he says, picking it up. "It might be another Ayana drama." He frowns at the lit-up screen, then swipes it open as he takes several steps toward me.

"Trust me, I'm in no mood for anyone but you," I answer cockily when Archer suddenly stops, his smile disappearing.

"What is this?"

I have no idea what he's talking about, except his expression is suddenly way too serious for my liking.

Slowly, he raises his gaze at me. "What the fuck is this, Kat?"

Nothing can ruin tonight, except some stupid joke, or another prank picture.

I take the phone from his hand.

For a minute, I'm confused, because the dozens of texts from Marlow don't make sense.

**Marlow: U r in my head.**

**Marlow: Under my skin.**

**Marlow: I see u look at me but u don talk I just…**

**Marlow: Will you ever forgive me for that night???**

I'm confused. What the hell is Marlow up to? One way to screw me up is to send ambiguous texts that my boyfriend just so happens to read.

Then another message comes in.

**Marlow: Fine, go to Axavier or whoever.**

My breath catches in my throat, horror surging through me.

**Marlow: I wanna be with u tonight. Dont ignore me. U cant. Come to my place.**

Jesus, Marlow.

**Marlow: One night. All I ask. I know u miss me.**

What.

The.

Hell.

I raise my eyes at Archer, and he's staring at me like he saw a ghost, his face white.

"Axavier? Really?" His voice is low but so cold that I can feel it in my bones.

"Arch. That's not—"

"Marlow, too? Are you serious?"

"No! It's… Arch, it's a joke or something…"

He snatches my phone out of my hand, turns on his heel, and walks inside, leaving me startled.

"Archer!"

But when I run through the living room and outside, he's already fired up the Streetfighter and zooms away from the villa as I start marching toward Marlow's.

*Marlow, you stupid ass.*

I hope there's no murder tonight.

## 23

---

## ARCHER

I'm angry and in shock. I want to punch walls and faces, mostly Axavier's and Marlow's. Marlow knows Kat is with me and still talks like this, even after I warned him once.

I pull up to Axavier's villa. The lights at his place are off but his bike is parked up front. His door is locked, but I ring the bell continuously until I hear, "Alright! Alright! Jesus!" and Axavier's face appears in the door cracked open only ten inches or so.

"What the hell?" He's dressed only in boxers. Seems like a too-early night for him.

"Let me in. I need a little explanation," I say, trying to walk in, but he almost shuts the door in my face.

"Not a good time, Archer. What's up? Could've called."

Oh, hell no, I'm not taking this.

I slam into the door, sending Axavier stumbling backward, and walk in, kicking the door shut.

"What the fuck, dude?" Panic flashes in his eyes.

He looks scared. That means something's up, and I wanna know what it has to do with my girl.

"Explain," I hiss, pulling out the phone and showing him Marlow's message.

He frowns and rubs his hair with both hands. "No idea. What's this about?"

But his cowardly expression is a giveaway.

"I said, explain. Now." I step into him, and he backs away but toward the door as if trying to lure me outside.

"No idea, Archer! Dude!"

I stab him in the chest with the phone, anger rising in me. "What the fuck do you have to do with Kat?"

A cellphone rings in his bedroom, and then there's a muffled voice. In his bedroom…

I freeze in surprise. "Company? Who are you fucking now? Everyone's girlfriends?"

Axavier grabs me by the shirt when I take a step in that direction. "Dude, none of your business!"

I tear myself away, stalk toward the bedroom door, and throw it open.

"Hi!"

The sight is so unexpected that I pause for a second, staring at the king-size bed in silence only interrupted by Axavier's quiet, "Fuck," behind me.

I was expecting anyone but not this, a slender naked body with the sheet covering the crotch, flat chest, and blue hair—Milan, Cece's stylist.

"It's not what you think, man," Axavier murmurs behind me, but I'm too shocked to answer, and… fuck, relieved.

Milan smiles and shifts his gaze to Axavier. "Oh yeah? I needed a place to crash," he says, returning his gaze and a sarcastic smile to me.

"Yeah, he just needed to crash," Axavier echoes.

Milan's gaze hardens as he cocks his head. "And I figured that Xave's sweet ass is just the right place."

A mix of a heavy exhale and "Fffuck" comes from behind me, and I have to hold back my laughter.

Axavier's embarrassment is precious as I turn and walk past him, the sound of his bare feet against the floor following me.

"Archer, man, I can explain."

I turn slowly. He doesn't get it—I have my answers.

"Kat?" I ask, just to make sure.

"Dude, I never touched her. I wouldn't. She wouldn't. I mean, like fuck, are you still sleeping on this? She's all about you."

I nod and turn to leave, but Axavier grabs me right before I reach for the door.

"Dude, about that…" He nods toward the bedroom.

"How long?" I ask him, and that's for my personal math exercise.

He looks away, hands on his hips. "A month."

"Hhm."

"Maybe two."

"I see."

"Or three. I don't know. It's complicated."

"Isn't it always."

"Just don't—"

"Axavier, chill. It's no one's business but yours."

I have my answer, but as soon as I get on the bike and think of Marlow, anger starts simmering in my blood. I pull up at his villa when Kat's phone in my pocket beeps again, this time with a voice message from Marlow.

I kill the engine and press 'play.'

Marlow's soft voice turns my stomach inside out.

**"Baby... I really miss you..."**

I'll fucking kill him.

## 24

## KAT

Wrong words said at the wrong time can ruin a life.

Marlow didn't mean what he said. But I'm not even mad at him, just shocked, the thought of it making my breath catch in my throat as I stop in the middle of a darkish avenue and rub my face, trying to wrap my head around what just happened.

Archer has my phone. He'll break it. Worse, he'll break it against Marlow's head.

*One night. That's all I ask.*

What the fuck, Marlow?!

I don't know how long I stand in the shadows, trying to come to terms with the messages from Marlow.

Deep breaths don't help with the panic that's rising in my chest, so I start walking again, increasing my pace until I'm almost running.

My heart jolts when I see Archer's bike next to Marlow's front door.

*Shit.*

I almost rip the door off its hinges and dart inside.

The smell of booze and pot assaults my nostrils. It's dim, only an arc lamp on, but I register a giant mess in the living room and—

They are fighting!

It's the first thought that comes to my mind when I see Archer and a shirtless Marlow struggling halfway down on the floor.

Then I hear bleating. There's no other way to describe the sound that comes from Marlow, who can't talk, let alone stand on his own.

"Get the fuck up," Archer barks, grunting as he tries to haul him up.

"Arrrrtsch…" Marlow growls like a freaking pirate, then laughs drunkenly as Archer finally pulls him up and wraps Marlow's arm around his neck.

"Come on. Bedroom."

I watch in shock. Marlow is lit. The guy can hold his liquor, but his drunk state is less than macho. And holy shit is he incapacitated.

"Do you need help?" I ask, approaching carefully, trying to gauge Archer's mood.

"I'm fine," he blurts without looking at me as they both stumble toward the bedroom.

I follow. Any other time, I would've laughed, but this time, it's serious. What Marlow said. What Archer thought.

Archer drops Marlow onto the bed and pulls off his sneakers.

"Love yooooou, maaaaan…" Marlow drawls drunkenly, then laughs, hiccups, and goes quiet.

Archer turns around slowly to meet my gaze.

"Archer, let's talk," I say quietly, searching his face to figure out how he feels.

"Come." He motions toward the living room, walks past me, and I follow with a heavy heart like I'm going to the principal's office.

He sits me down on the couch and pulls my phone out of his pocket.

*Shit. Again.*

He stabs the screen, and Marlow's voice message starts playing, his voice low, drunk, and slurring.

**"Baby… I really miss you…"**

"Archer, that's not—"

"Shhhh." Archer presses his forefinger to his lips, silencing me.

There are inarticulate sounds in the message, something being dropped, a muffled, "Shit." I figured, now that I glance around and see bottles of beer and booze, ashtrays, a broken bowl, the smell of tobacco and cannabis too strong, that Marlow let really really loose.

**"I… I… I wanna see you… Right now… Talk. Les' talk, baby…"**

What's with baby? *Jesus, Marlow.* His drunk voice is full of gasps and grunts.

**"I can't deal with this. You an' I, we go waaaay back. An'… An' I never forgot tha' night."**

My heart twists. What night?

**"Les' talk. I miss you. I've missed you all this time, Ray-Ray."**

My heart slams in my chest at the name, and my eyes snap up at Archer, a smile twitching on his lips.

"Jesus…"

Archer ends the message, tosses the phone aside, and just stares at me.

The relief inside me is so great that I laugh nervously. But a bigger realization assaults me like a hard blow— Archer thought I had something going on behind his back.

The thought cuts off my laughter, and I try really hard not to show it, but bitterness creeps in like a snake, making my eyes burn.

Archer looks at me and notices. "Kat," he says softly.

But I'm already on my feet, shaking my head. "You really thought I'm that kind of person, Archer?"

My voice is cracked. I'm many things, but a cheater is not one of them. Nor have I ever considered any man besides Archer since I came to Zion.

"You…" I want to laugh in that evil shocking way that people who are fucked up do but can't. "You actually thought I could—"

"Kat, listen to me." He reaches for me and tries to stop me. I try to pull away, but he only pulls me tighter toward him.

"I can't believe you thought it even for a moment, Arch," I snap, pushing my hands against his chest, though he doesn't budge.

"Kat, Kat, chill." He wraps his arms around me tightly, holding me in place, his face lowered to mine. And that's one thing I can never resist—his touch. "I didn't believe it. Didn't want to. But I could've become a murderer tonight."

His hand goes up to stroke my hair. The bastard knows how to calm me. My heart can barely handle this and all the ups and downs we go through. He'll make me one of the twenty percent of women who die of heart failure. Or a broken heart. Either or, my heart is his.

He kisses the corner of my mouth. "I swear, I could kill anyone who even thinks this way about you. I didn't think straight. Just…"

*Bastard.*

His hands do the magic, touching me everywhere. They finally come up to my face and hold it in place, tilting it up so I can look at him. "I'm sorry, okay? I over-reacted."

"You think?" I snap, my chest heaving from frustration, but my body is already inching toward his, always does, the freaking traitor.

"Tell me something." His thumbs start stroking my cheeks, his body pressing into mine, distracting me from the anger that was simmering in my blood just seconds ago. "Tell me. If you saw messages like this on my phone, would you not be upset?"

He kisses the corner of my mouth again, our warm breaths colliding, my hands already stroking his torso though I try to keep it together.

"Absolutely," I breathe out. "I would've set the person who sent them on fire."

"There you go."

The first kiss is soft and quick, calming me as my brain tries to push away anger.

"You make me crazy," he whispers, and the next kiss is

longer, his tongue plunging so deep in my mouth that my head starts spinning.

I can't hold back with this guy. My brain short-circuits when our lips touch. And they are like magnets. His hot mouth latches onto mine, his tongue licking into it, and I'm a goner.

His kiss is possessive, his tongue swirling deeper into my mouth like it belongs there. It does.

*Welcome home, babe.*

He's pulling me toward him, backing up, going some-where—I don't know where, I don't care—couch, floor, against the wall. As long as his lips are on mine. As long as his kisses grow impatient, his mouth swallowing mine.

Our hands roam each other's bodies. We stumble, but nothing matters in this moment when we're at our best, with each other.

Archer's hands slide under my dress and squeeze my butt, hauling me up, pulling me against the hard bulge in his jeans.

"Your house?" I murmur in the second I manage to tear my mouth off Archer's.

"In a minute." His greedy mouth comes back to mine.

It's a minute that will last for as long as we need to fuck this away—we're so predictable.

"Cameras?" I ask.

"No," he murmurs, coming up for air, then kisses me again.

His fingers slide under my panties and between my legs, pressing in just the right places, making my body simmer with heat.

I whimper. This guy coaxes the most embarrassing sounds out of me, but I can't help it.

Archer must know this place by heart, because we are still kissing when he suddenly spins me around and lowers me down, my butt landing on a small hard surface that feels like a coffee table. His hand between my legs vanishes and appears at my chest, yanking my dress down to my waist together with my bra.

He takes my breast in his mouth, making me moan, then the other one, his kisses turning into open-mouth bites so delicious, I seep with want.

He leans into me, lowering me onto my back, and I scramble for any surface to prop myself on when my hands find the couch right behind the table. Archer yanks the hem of my dress up, pulls my panties to the side, and his tongue does a long swipe along my slit.

"Archer," I whimper.

Another swipe. Then another. His hands hook under my thighs. He's not playing a sensual game, not teasing. It's raw licking like he's trying to swallow every drop of want I have to offer. I moan, needing more, so much more of him.

"Not enough," I blurt out. "I need you, Arch. Right now."

We need to fuck this obsession out of our systems quickly so we can use our brains and do things at a normal pace. We're impatient and unapologetic about our sexual needs. It's too obvious when Archer straightens up and hurriedly undoes his jeans, then pushes them down his hips and drives his hard cock into me in one thrust.

I cry out.

The cry is chased by another when Archer starts pounding into me.

*Properly fucked…*

I never understood the words until I got to know what passion can do—unravel me, scorch me, strip away my shame and dignity.

I'm balancing on the small coffee table, my hands behind my back, holding on to the couch arm for dear life as Archer holds my hips and fucks away like a psycho. He lowers himself onto me and takes my mouth in a violent kiss. I can taste myself on him. It's raw and sexy. He grunts into my mouth, the sound that drives me wild because I'm the cause of it. My calculated Archer loses his cool in moments like this, and I love seeing him unhinged.

I can handle anything this guy gives me. But the coffee table can't. It wobbles, swinging on its legs harder and harder with Archer's every thrust. I'm so gone, it feels so good, like I'm on a rocking horse, that I only catch myself when my body feels like it's free-falling, and the table gives a loud cracking sound and starts descending under me. My legs wrap around Archer's torso. His cock slips out of me. In a split second, I squeal, but Archer's arms around my back catch me.

"Fuck," he grunts and trips on the table that collapses onto the floor with a loud crashing sound.

I'm wrapped around him like a monkey, but he doesn't halt. In a moment, he lowers me onto the floor next to the couch and the broken table. In one swift thrust, he's back inside me, reigniting the lost spark. He places his hands on the floor on each side of me and starts pumping.

This is next level madness. We are animals. My thighs fall open to take more of him as he pounds away. I'm a sweaty mess, my hands somewhere on his body, but I don't register much as the heat in my core turns into a fireball and sweeps across my body, making me cry out in an orgasm. My blood is on fire, the center of the blaze my pussy that Archer keeps ravaging with his cock until he grunts like a beast and falls on top of me, panting.

There's a minute of heavy breathing, then Archer falls off me and onto his back.

"Holy shit," he murmurs.

I grin, lying like a starfish on the floor, the dress bunched up around my waist, panties skewed to the side, exposing my bare pussy, boots on my feet—yep, I'm classy, not, and I love it. I've never felt so sexy, so undone, so shameless, and yet so wanted as I do with Archer.

He wipes his face with both hands, exhaling through his puffed lips, and I grin. My sexy guy. Undone just like me. On the floor, his jeans still around his thighs. His beautiful cock out—his trademark pose when he's with me.

"Dinner must be cold," I say, smiling, as I fix my wet panties and rise to my knees.

Archer chuckles and squirms on his back on the floor, pulling up his jeans. "I'm down for whatever cold dinner, kitten. As long as you stay the night."

Our smiling gazes meet. Fuck, how I adore this post-sex smile of his—cocky yet warm, giving a glimpse of his gentle side before he turns back into the calculated reserved Archer Crone.

I'm about to bite back with a clever comeback when

there's the soft sound of the front door opening, and we both freeze like opossums.

Soft footsteps follow, and I glance from behind the couch to see Raylin, Ty's sister, walk slowly through the living room toward the bedroom.

She doesn't notice us on the other side of the room.

"Raylin," I mouth to Archer, who cocks a brow, and we both hear her soft voice from Marlow's bedroom. "Nick?"

No one calls him by his first name. Except her, apparently. That's the story I have yet to pry open from Marlow, about *that one night*, and *another chance*, and all that nonsense that almost got me in trouble.

But right now, I want a cold dinner with my hot guy.

We try to be as quiet as we can as we get up off the floor, and Archer helps me fix my dress, his large warm hand unusually gentle and protective on the smalls of my back as we creep out of Marlow's villa, the only sign that we were there—the broken coffee table.

## 25

---

## ARCHER

M‍Y FAVORITE THING ABOUT MY NEW ROUTINE IS WAKING UP TO an octopus wrapped over my body—Kat. I still don't admit to her how much I fucking love it. I don't want to get up, not when she's in my bed. I haven't slept so good in my entire life and grunt half-asleep in disappointment when she gives me a kiss and slips out.

I've set the rules of meeting every other day. We need structure, but it's complicated because I seem to crave her every minute of every day. Addiction, see?

Our plans don't work as intended, though we've been doing this for a couple of weeks now.

Most dinners are at my villa, and before we even have food, we claw at each other as we tear our clothes off, then continue in the same manner after the dinner. We are like animals in rut. A movie night turned into an edging game of heavy petting and stroking each other through our clothes during half of it, both of us completely missing the plot until Kat was soaked down to her knees and asked for mercy.

This is different from what we had before, before *that* night. That's what I call it in my mind, the night when things got too dark.

Kat brought it up once, but I avoided the conversation. There are a whole lot of other topics we avoid. Like the words that came out the evening we made up. The feelings that gushed out of her that night. Our conversations miss the right words, and every day is a struggle to hold them back. So we fuck like two maniacs—that's our love language.

This morning, Kat is off to her daily swim in the ocean. The girl is religious about exercise. Doesn't even drive to work—walks.

As soon as I walk into the Center, I kiss her good morning. No matter how early I come to work, she's already there, working those files like her life depends on it. And I'm working the bump in my jeans as I sit at my desk, watch her through the office window, and can't shake off the filthy thoughts.

If there's something to distract me, it's the fucking Tsariuk business that's on everyone's mind. And Mr. Ortiz is on my screen as soon as I dial him.

"Archer." He nods in greeting.

I asked him to call me by my name when we met up on the mainland. He reminds me of my father—no-nonsense, all business, the emotionless mask on his face. Except, unlike my dad, Mr. Ortiz cares about his child.

We chat for a minute about weather and politics and the latest news from the EU and Australia, then discuss Tsariuk business and make an arrangement to get Bishop, Raven, and Marlow on a conference call with him later that day. Something needs to be done about O'Shea and Cunningham. We can't just hold them forever, but we can't let them stay on Zion either. Can we let them go? That's the question.

And then our conversation switches to Kat. I try to lure little pieces of information about her out of him, wanting to learn more. But every time I drift off topic and get personal, Mr. Ortiz shuts down like I'm touching a sensitive subject.

The news that she and I are an item didn't seem to surprise him. Shit, the man has the best poker face I've ever seen. What bothered me when I told him that was that there was no visible sign of approval, like it's an experiment that might not work out successfully.

"Kat is good at researching and figuring things out. I gave her access to the spring-breakers' files," I say. "She handles the files like the CIA. I'm guessing it's your training. I admire her."

Mr. Ortiz is quiet for some time, staring at me unblinkingly, and for a moment, I think the connection is lost, because the screen seems to be stuck.

"Mr. Ortiz?" I ask, narrowing my eyes at the screen.

"I'm here, Archer."

He's not stuck. Then why is he so alert?

"Do you know why she got drug charges in Thailand but never went to jail though it's a severe offense there?"

The off-topic question catches me by surprise.

"That charge was mere bureaucracy," he explains. "It was pardoned. The truth is, she was undercover."

I want to laugh but hold back. "She was fifteen. Or sixteen?"

Mr. Ortiz nods, his expression unchanged. "She ran deliveries for local drug dealers. You probably know that. *I*, of all people, should've known that but was too absorbed in my work. I blame myself for letting her get into the street life that she shouldn't have been part of."

He goes silent for a moment, then continues.

"She was used as bait in one of the counter-trafficking operations."

I swallow hard, then frown. "And you agreed?"

He shakes his head. "They did so without asking me. Without letting me know. They asked *her*. *She* agreed. Because Kat, well, she thinks she is a tough cookie."

"It's illegal." I almost don't believe what he says. "She was a minor."

"It's Thailand. The operation wasn't approved by the higher-ups. And my own boss decided that seven other lives, or dozens, were worth it. They were, in theory. But not when you put a minor at risk. Not when it's *my daughter*. But then, again, gray areas."

Another moment of silence follows, and I almost don't want to hear what else he has to say.

"She wasn't hurt. Well—" He looks away, around, like he is following a fly, and it's awkward because I realize that this tough guy has a hard time talking about it. "She did the job, let's put it that way. She almost got hurt in the worst way you could think of."

I think of Olivia, and my stomach turns.

"Came about a minute close to something that could've traumatized her for life. If she ever feels like it, she'll tell you."

He looks at his hands, then back up at me.

"We left Thailand the next week, moved to Pennsylvania, to the middle of nowhere to stay away from all that, my work, to be exact. I realized that I almost lost the only person I loved because of my dedication to work. It's never worth it. And then she got in trouble again, because she's feisty and doesn't take crap from anyone."

I feel slightly hurt that she never brought up this wild story.

"The reason I tell you this, Archer, is because Kat is brave, but she's also reckless. She acts on the spur of the moment, and she refuses to accept defeat. Whether it's a particular scenario or…"

Or? There's gotta be a moral to this story.

"Or a person," he says, his gaze locked with mine.

Ohhh-kay.

"She is tough, Archer. She thinks she can do it all on her own. But listen carefully. If you hurt her. If you make her cry again…"

I stop my brow from arching.

*Again.*

He looks down. She must've told him about our little dramas.

"I only do this—Zion—because of her, you understand," he goes on, not looking up.

And then it hits me. My girlfriend's father is being over-protective and is… worried. Wow. It's endearing in a fucked-up way. And unlike other girlfriends' fathers in the past, he doesn't give a damn about my fortune.

"I am asking you a favor. Like a father with a daughter. Don't mess with Kat." His voice is calm, and maybe that's why I don't feel threatened. Not by him.

"I—"

"You know what I mean. You see a bad-ass pretty girl with a killer portfolio, and you think you can endlessly play games with her. I'm sure she plays along."

He looks around again like he's collecting his thoughts. This is awkward. I am having a conversation with the father of a girl who fucks me and fucks with my feelings and is the only one who manages to wrap me around her finger. Yet, he's worried about *her*. Did she say something I need to know?

"She's never really had a boyfriend," he finally spits out and turns his gaze to me, his expression serious. "Don't tell her I said that. I know she has experience." He slowly wipes his face with his hand. "This is awkward," he murmurs. "I'm sorry. She's never let anyone close. She's young. She'll learn. She might think this is serious, but she doesn't know better."

Ouch.

What shocks me the most is that Mr. Ortiz is slowly losing his emotionless mask.

"In time," he carries on, "she'll meet someone who'll value and love her for who she is. Someone much stronger than her who won't show it, won't try to top her. Someone she'll be able to rely on and trust instead of trying to impress. She has issues with trust, after Thailand and all that jazz. And she sure likes to impress."

Clearly, Mr. Ortiz is not my fan. "And you don't think she's met that person yet…" I smirk but hold his gaze.

Mr. Ortiz sucks his teeth. "You are cocky, Archer. You wear it like a badge of honor. With your achievements, it's no surprise. But you have a ways to go with women."

I try not to show my bitterness. I've had plenty of women in my life, yet he's not the first one to tell me I don't know shit.

"The problem is that I've heard how she talks about you, Archer."

"*Is* there a problem?"

"You are both young. I think I have an idea of what you are like with girls. You try to show Kat her place and dominate her. And she won't budge. That will only spur her competitiveness but will draw her away. So…"

So…

His words dig into me like a fishing hook. The fact that he brings up Kat's feelings means she's talked quite a bit about us.

"Step away, Archer. That's what I'm asking you. If you two are just playing games, leave it."

Not a fucking chance. Just the fact that he doesn't know me well and asks me to leave the girl I've gone far and beyond to finally have makes me angry.

But I don't show it. I might not be good at being humble, as per Mr. Fucking Ortiz, but I do know respect.

"You tried to send her away," he continues, "then changed your mind. Something is going on between you two, besides the good old dating thing. But if you can't be the person she can trust and rely on, let her go. You have a lot of money and power. It fascinates her. Money *is* power but not strength. IQ is knowledge but not wisdom."

"I never used money to attract someone. Certainly not Kat. And she wouldn't go for it. You know it."

"No. But she's already too deep in it. And if you don't feel the same, let it go. Because in no time, you'll hurt her."

He's silent for a while, studying me.

*Have at it, Mr. Ortiz.*

It's Daddy protectiveness, I get it. But he is the one who just opened up about his daughter, and I am grateful. And I finally find it in myself to talk.

"I think you should let us take it where it goes," I say. "We learn from our mistakes, not others, despite what wise men say. Sometimes, mistakes lead to the best things. I learned that through hard work and watching others. I care about your daughter. Care—" I stall, because I haven't told anyone but Droga how I feel about her. "*Care* is an understatement. *Important* is an understatement. I think you underestimate what's happening between us and underestimate *me*. Which is not surprising, considering my reputation."

A knock at the door interrupts us, and I want to send the person away because I need more time with Mr. Ortiz, but Kat's smiling face appears in the doorway.

I notice her ripped jeans, something I've never seen her wear before. "There's my girlfriend." I don't mean to rub it in Mr. Ortiz's face, but this time, I say it with even more pride.

Kat grins. "Am I interrupting?"

"Not at all. Talking to your dad."

"Dad?" She walks around and waves at the screen. "Hi."

"Hi, Kit-Kat."

I almost choke in amusement.

*Kit-Kat.*

"What were you two talking about?" Kat asks, wiggling her eyebrows.

"Work," Mr. Ortiz says at the same time I say, "You."

He doesn't flinch. Kat narrows her eyes at me in suspicion. I flash her the most charming smile. She doesn't know that I've talked to him more in the last few months than I talked to my own dad in the last year.

When I hang up, she walks around the desk like she's avoiding me. I've learned this means she's being playful.

"So, Kit-Kat, huh?" I drawl, leaning back in my chair and studying her with a smile.

She shoots me a warning glare. "Don't…"

I lick my lips. "Come here," I say, adding in a murmur, "Kit-Kat."

"I warned you, Archer."

I grin even harder, wanting to kiss that scowl away. "I'll stop if you come here and give me a kiss."

She lifts her chin in that haughty way of hers.

I'm planning on a little more than just kissing. There's one sure way to put my wild thing in a better mood.

# 26

## KAT

Archer offered me one of his bikes, but I prefer to walk everywhere.

The garage behind Cliff Villa has several motorcycles. We went for a ride on one of them. Not that I can tell the difference between a half-a-million dollar motorcycle and one that has a custom engine and was designed for street racing and therefore more powerful. No. Kai can. They take occasional rides and chat here and there. Archer seems happier.

I stroll into his office every day like it's my second home. In fact, I spend more time in his office than at my desk. Talking about work. Discussing O'Shea and Cunningham. Discussing the spring-breakers, whose files Archer finally gave me—a big step on his part.

Playing… Those office blinds are tired of sliding up and down, because we finally gave in to the "no holding back" in the office, and I got into the habit of wearing skirts and dresses. Easy access, remember?

Today, I walk in on Archer talking to my dad. Judging by the slip-ups here and there, he does that a lot.

"So Kit-Kat, huh?" Archer leans back in his armchair.

"Don't," I warn him. This nickname is reserved for my parents.

"I'll stop if you come over and give me a kiss."

I want a lot more than that, but also want to chat. There's something masochistic in the way we arrange our dates every other day, "establishing boundaries," as we call it, "taking it slow," we say as we starve for each other on the evenings we spend separately so that sex becomes a marathon.

"What's with the new construction in East Ayana? Guys said a restaurant." I sit sideways on the desk and lean over, teasing him with a peek at my cleavage. His gaze flickers down then up.

"It is."

"Wow, not a talker today?"

His eyes are too mischievous. He's in the mood to play, but there's nothing more I love than getting him all worked up.

"The restaurant is not on Main Street," I say, trying to pry the info out of him, "tucked away instead, small. No one knows much about it. Why?"

"Because it's meant for one person. Though I'm sure everyone will enjoy it."

I cock my brow in curiosity. After a minute, I burst with impatience. "Are you gonna tell me or is it some conspiracy or another elite kid's project?"

He shakes his head with a smile. "Your impatience is gonna ruin a lot of surprises in your life, wild thing."

"My life?"

"That place. Yes. It's a present for you."

I gape at him. "For me?" I produce an amused chuckle. "A restaurant, seriously?"

Archer's smile grows wider as he nods, his gaze so arrogant yet beautiful that I want to sit on his face.

A restaurant for me—what a crazy and unnecessary thing. But then, billionaires have their own quirks, I guess. I don't need a restaurant. I'd rather have that chef who—

"Wait." My heart starts beating wildly. "What kind of restaurant?"

Archer laughs through his nose. "Are there many options?"

I raise my brows.

"My girlfriend's favorite food."

Oh.

My.

God.

My jaw drops in shock.

"Thai food, of course," Archer says proudly.

I make a squeaking sound because I've never gotten presents from guys before, and definitely not a freaking restaurant.

"A chef and several guys who worked street food stalls in Bangkok are moving to Zion."

I want to melt onto the floor and orgasm while he tells me more.

"So you'll have an entire crew who can make a menu of

anything you want. And if you want to splash green curry around like you did last time"—his eyebrow cocks, reminding me of that failed date—"we can go real wild."

The desire to jump him and kiss the hell out of him is so strong that I have to restrain myself when I get off the desk and start taking slow steps toward him. "Thank you," I say coyly.

"Come here and kiss me," Archer orders softly.

I sashay around the desk and lean with my hands on his thighs.

He leans over for a kiss, but I pull away. He frowns. I smile.

"On the lips?" I tease him. "Or…"

There's a tell when Archer is horny—when his thigh muscles tighten just barely noticeably under my palms.

There's a tell when he's amused—his chest shakes a tiny bit with a suppressed chuckle.

I'll know all his tells soon.

Right now, my boyfriend is gonna get the royal treatment. From his queen, obviously.

"Your lips are your best part, wild thing," he murmurs when I kiss him softly, teasing the seam of his mouth with my tongue.

"Yeah? What's yours?"

"Down there." He catches my lower lip between his lips and sucks on it.

"Corlo, shut the blinds, lock the door," I say loudly, push Archer's legs wider apart, and go down on my knees.

I unzip his jeans and push them down, reeling in his eagerness when he helps me.

When Archer used to be cocky, he acted like he was doing a favor, offering his body. Now that he is comfortable with me, he's so eager to play, it's empowering.

I pull his cock out like I'm unwrapping a present, teasing him with the slowness. Then do my favorite thing—make love to his beautiful erection, licking its length, stroking his bare hips, squeezing his balls the way he likes it, motivated by the quiet grunts and sighs that escape him as his hands sift through my hair.

He lifts his hips off the chair, wanting to push into my mouth, and I suck on his tip, then take as much of him into my mouth as I can. I'm gonna make it so good for him. I'm gonna suck him until he begs for release. I'm gonna—

He explodes into my mouth so suddenly that I jerk in surprise but don't let go until I lick him clean, his grunts quieting, and he throws his head back onto the chair with a heavy exhale, closing his eyes.

Wow. What happened to the patient Archer?

His grin is his approval when I tuck him back into his jeans and zip him up, then slide up, planting a kiss on his cheek.

"Thank you," he says, though this was my thanks to him. "Come here." He tugs me onto his lap, but I resist.

"Um, I have to do some work."

"Seriously?" He tucks a wild strand of my hair behind my ear, and I melt at his gentleness.

"Yeah. But we're still on for dinner tonight, right?"

I can get anything I want from him at any time. It's amazing how far we've come.

"Uh-huh. Dinner and a movie." His smile is way too

sexy, and I'm already anticipating the dinner scenario and the movie that we'll never finish. We never do.

There's a knock at the door.

"Guess we are done right on time." I chuckle.

Whoever's knocking, they'll see his flushed face—the king of Zion is more relaxed than ever.

I open the door to see Margot's grim expression. She can't stand me, I know. And right now, I'm pretty sure she'll hate me even more.

Slowly, locking my stare with hers to make sure she gets the point, I wipe my lower lip with my thumb, then my forefinger, then lick it for emphasis.

"We're all done," I drawl with a smile as I walk away.

## 27

---

## KAT

ZION IS GLOOMY AS IF SOMEONE HAS TURNED OFF THE LIGHT switch. Heavy clouds hang over the island, swallowing its green peak, yet it's hot and muggy.

I resurface, wiping my face with my palms, salty water on my lips, and look around.

It's seven in the morning, and I'm taking my usual swim in the ocean. A Taekwondo group is hay-ing away in the distance. I think I see Cece there. What is she gonna fight on Zion? Mental health issues?

There's a small figure just to the side of the group, repeating every exercise—Sonny Little. He's Ayana's kid now, happy to be here yet restless and with no direction, which should be sorted out with some schooling. I wonder how many kids like this are at Port Mrei and the Ashlands, homeless, hungry, growing up amongst the Savages, becoming the lost generation of Port Mrei.

The ocean water is warm, but the weather's been chang-ing. There are rain showers almost every other day. But the clouds don't always clear out like they do throughout the sunny months. Instead, overcast skies hang above the island, sinking lower day by day.

I walk out onto the beach and watch the slick speedboat pull up to one of the docks. A black silhouette jumps off —Raven.

I see him every now and then as he leaves for Port Mrei or comes back. I've learned his schedule, and now that I see him stomp across the beach, I have an idea, and when I get to the office an hour later, I send Archer a text.

**Me: I want to go to Port Mrei.**

His blinds are pulled up, and my cocky lover sits in his chair, feet on top of his desk as he drinks coffee and watches me. He checks his phone but doesn't respond.

Rolling my eyes, I walk into his office and give him a peck on the cheek. Yeah, we're dating the proper way.

"Finally. Good morning," he drawls, checking me up and down like he wants to learn my outfits by heart.

"Ohhh-kay." I take a seat on the chair across from his desk. "So, I've never been to Port Mrei, and I'd like to go."

He cocks his head. "We can take the security crew and go."

Jesus, really? Not a step without an army?

"I'd like to go with Raven."

Archer's eyes turn into slits. "Why?"

I shrug. "I'd like to see what he does there, where he goes, what people he meets."

"That's a no. I don't want you in the places he goes, let alone around the people he deals with."

Annoying. "Technically, I don't need permission. I was just informing you."

"Oh, I see." Archer stretches time by taking the slowest sip from his coffee cup. "Then technically, I don't need your permission to fly to the mainland to do whatever I want. I'll just inform you."

I rise from the chair. "We are not turning this into a controlled relationship, are we?"

His jaw tightens. "I'm only concerned for your safety."

"Raven seems fine."

"You are not Raven. No one is. The guy can see a fly approaching and slice it in the air with a knife before it gets within ten feet from him."

"I'm more than capable of taking care of myself."

"So you say, wild thing, but I don't want you in situations where you have to *take care of yourself*."

Archer's stubbornness only makes me more persistent. So the next day, I show up on the beach again. I'm wearing cargo pants, a tank, and boots, my hair tied in a bun at the back of my head, and sunglasses shading my eyes though it looks like it's about to drizzle.

I count minutes. At twelve sharp, Raven walks out onto the beach and heads for the docks.

"Hi!" I wave from the distance as I trot toward him.

He nods. Doesn't stop. Doesn't look away from me though.

"I'm coming with you to Port Mrei," I say as I start walking next to him, barely keeping up. He's taller than me, though not as tall as Archer, and he moves much faster without seemingly any effort.

"You are not."

If he could talk any less, I'd think he was mute.

"I want to go. I'll just hang around when you do what you do."

"Did Archer give clearance for this?"

"Since when does anyone need clearance to go to town?"

"That's a no then."

"So, let me get it straight," I say hurriedly as we approach the docks. "You can do favors for the elites, delivering whatever their illegal indulgences require, without Archer knowing, but taking me with you for a ride requires his approval?"

Yep, I've done my homework, collecting rumors here and there.

Raven turns slowly to face me, his lips twitching in what could be a smile. "Are you trying to blackmail me?"

"No, just wondering." I swallow hard.

There's a strange energy about this guy who can scare the hell of anyone without saying a word. And now, he's talked more than I've ever heard him talk, and his low voice is pleasant and in stark comparison with his steely stare. Like silk against a sharp razor.

"You are Archer's business," he says. "And I don't need problems."

"There won't be any. I can always go by myself and tell Archer you knew and refused to keep me company."

"You are playing, sweetheart."

Fuck. This makes me mad. I pull out my last card—the story Archer told me several days ago.

"Okay. If you take me, I'll throw in a good word for you to Maddy."

Nothing changes in his expression. God, even Archer has a wider range of emotions in his poker face. My dad probably does too.

"You stay close," he says suddenly, catching me by surprise, as we stop by the speedboat. "You do what I tell you. When I'm gone, you stay with a guard."

"Yes and yes and yes," I say, my heart pumping with excitement. So, he does have a soft spot for Maddy. What do you know?

Without looking, Raven stretches his hand toward me, and I stare at it in surprise until he lifts his indifferent gaze to me and motions with his eyes to the boat.

*Oh.*

I take his helping hand as I get in—out of politeness.

*Right.*

He's a gentleman with a Swiss Army knife in his pocket.

Who the hell is this guy?

I'm yet to find out, but one thing is for sure—I'm about to get the most exciting tour yet.

## 28

### KAT

Have you ever traveled to a small tourist town after pandemic and economic decline?

Have you been to third-world countries' small towns that have pretty ethnic facades, but three blocks from the main street, women smoke in doorways, selling themselves, teenagers offer drugs, jobless men sit on half-broken chairs, drink beer, and play cards while little kids run around in torn dirty clothes and play with empty tin cans?

Camden outside Philly? The outskirts of Tijuana? South Beach after Spring Break? Combine it all, add an ocean breeze, flowering trees, vague sounds of reggaeton, the smell of smokers and burnt rubber, excessive garbage that litters the streets, and occasional armed patrols.

Ta-da!

Welcome to Port Mrei!

The port is decent, despite the excessive armed guards' presence. Everything seems to be coated with salt—buildings, roads, piers, guards' clothes, and their grumpy attitudes.

I wait with two guards while Raven disappears into one of the warehouses. Excitement almost draws a happy squeal out of me. I now understand what Marlow meant by island fever. Being out of Ayana is refreshing.

We take a military jeep that has too many storage containers—for guns, I know that much, and a static mount, a turret—whoa—to secure an automatic weapon—jeez, intense—and do a drive around town.

One guard is driving. The other is in the back seat next to me.

In the front, Raven is silent like I offended him greatly, though somehow, out of everything I said, Maddy was the golden word.

"I think he has his eye on her," Archer said the other night.

"Maddy? Out of all people?"

"Uh-huh." Archer wiggled his eyebrows. "He doesn't have a chance."

Maybe not, but mentioning her to Raven worked magic.

As we ride through Port Mrei, the guard next to me gives me the shittiest tour of my lifetime.

"That's downtown," he says, lazily exhaling clouds of smoke, a cigarette squeezed between his thumb and forefinger. "That's where all the shops are."

No shit.

Downtown is decent. If you don't look closely, it could pass for a tourist town, minus the tourists. Most people are locals, riding bikes, scooters, and shabby trucks.

We take a turn and drive along the beach side, the locals scattered out on the boardwalk, homeless dogs and seagulls picking at garbage, shirtless kids playing soccer on the beach.

"Pelican Beach," the guard says.

I could deal without his comments. But I guess Raven is going the extra mile for me. That is, an extra mile through the town that vaguely reminds me of certain hoods in Bangkok.

The memories flood me as we keep zipping through the streets, taking me years back, to when I was younger, the day ahead long and full of adventures. Days seemed so much longer when I was a teen.

The guard points at something in the distance—what an effort—but I miss the story. I keep Raven in my peripheral. He's chain-smoking. The driver curses someone out, then pulls up at a shady garage and whistles. Another armed guy emerges from behind a tall concrete fence, passes him a package, then casts a long look at me over the sunglasses.

"Can we drive to the Ashlands?" I ask, but my words pass unnoticed.

I guess that's a no.

We stop at a street food stall, and the guard next to me jumps out, the line of people scooting back to let him in as he picks up plates of food and, without paying, brings them to the car.

"*Pupusas*," he explains, and the taste explodes in my mouth with local herbs, grease, and the flavors that are superior in street food to any Michelin restaurant.

We keep going but now run business errands, zooming

from one location to another, dropping off the package they just got and picking up a crate that the guy sets down at the back of the jeep, a crate wrapped in a tarp, one corner slightly hitched up to reveal a biohazard sticker.

I don't ask questions, but now I understand what Marlow said about Raven—he's not your regular dealer, considering he's the one who's in charge of weapon contracts on Zion.

Shady exchanges, shady neighborhoods, shady hand-shakes—I've seen it before, except Raven doesn't get out of the car even once.

The Jeep slows down, driving along another narrow back street when Raven speaks for the first time, "Pull over before we reach Coco Jumbo."

"Why?" the driver asks.

"Don't want to flash her around."

*Huh.*

When the Jeep stops, Raven pulls a handgun from under the seat and tucks it inside the waistband of his jeans, then reaches down to fix his jean cuffs—another gun, and the realization makes me perk up.

"Stay put," he says, his voice sharper this time as he and the guard from the back seat walk out onto the street.

The driver stays behind, *guarding* me or whatever the deal is. He props his booted foot against the dashboard and lights a cigarette.

"What's in Coco Jumbo?" I lean with my elbows on his seat.

"A meeting."

"With who?"

"Business."

"What kind of business that I can't go?"

He lazily puffs out the smoke and turns to look at me, then turns away. There's a seven-flame grenade tattoo on the inside of his forearm—Foreign Legion, impressive.

"What's your name?" I say, making sure he can hear friendliness in my voice as I lean forward onto his seat and snake my arms closer to his neck.

He slowly takes a drag and puffs out the smoke. "James."

"James. How about we take a stroll? I bet the guys are gonna take a while, and I wanna see more of Port Mrei."

"Not an option. We're staying here."

"Don't be a bore," I whine intentionally. If he hasn't heard about me, it'll come across as girlie.

"You've seen enough. Case closed, young lady. Chill."

And there it goes again. *Hello, rude ass, Foreign Legion or not.*

"I thought we could get along, James," I say with that cheesy doll voice that even Margot would be proud of.

He spits loudly through his teeth and doesn't acknowledge me, only tilts his head back against the headrest.

*Oh, sweetheart…*

I said I wouldn't do it again. To Archer, that is. But this guy is just begging for it. He could've been a gentleman, but he wasn't, and now I'm gonna be mean.

My arms are still wrapped around the base of his headrest, but I unclasp them, then swiftly loop them around his neck and squeeze.

"Night-night," I say when, seconds later, the guy is

slumped in his seat, his arm falling over the driver's door, letting the cigarette fall from his fingers onto the dirt.

I jump over the door and onto the ground.

"Behave yourself, James," I say, tapping the door with my palm, and head toward Coco Jumbo.

## 29

---

## KAT

COCO JUMBO IS A TAVERN JUST AROUND THE CORNER. A GROUP of decently dressed guys smoke outside and nod to me as I walk through the swinging front doors.

It's stuffy inside, the fans blowing around the flies. The smell of fried rice, roasted meats, and stale beer hangs heavy in the air. Reggaeton trickles quietly from the invisible speakers.

Over a dozen heads turn to me when I enter, everyone going quiet. I feel like I stepped into a vacuum, my steps too loud as I spy the bar counter and confidently walk toward it.

I don't know why Raven is so paranoid. No one will know me here. I don't have to acknowledge him. Thank you, cargo pants and my wild curls—I don't exactly look like one of the Ayana elites.

I approach the bar and ask for a glass of water.

"Just waiting for a friend," I say casually since I don't have money or whatever they use as currency in this place.

I pull my sunglasses up on top of my head and turn toward the two middle-aged dudes at the bar counter who stare at me way too eagerly.

*Easy, sweethearts.*

The short plump bartender in his fifties with long hair, tattoo sleeves, and a towel over his shoulder passes me a glass.

It must be the worst water I've had in my life, like it's been in someone's mouth already, but I take slow sips as I lean with my elbow on the counter and turn around, studying the place above the glass rim.

People are scattered over the tables, some with empty plates in front of them, others with beers, on tap—I'm guessing that swill they make locally.

I spot Raven and two other guys at one of the tables with beer bottles, an ashtray, a plate of unfinished food and dirty napkins.

The shitty tour-guide guard stands behind Raven as three local guys lounge at the next table, their guns in holsters on full display. Three more guys lean against the far-end wall, pistols on their duty belts.

*Holy shit.*

This is not a casual meeting with partners or employees.

I try to look nonchalant, slowly turning away, when a loud voice from that direction says, "Miss Ortiz! What a surprise!"

I stiffen. The tavern suddenly goes dead quiet. There's a creak of chairs as everyone shifts to look in my direction again. Not a word is spoken in the seconds that are full of tension. I can hear a fly zipping by.

The bartender clears his throat. The two dudes next to me are now gaping, and not in a friendly way.

I turn slowly to see the chubby man across from Raven slowly get up, and there's a distinctive sound, so familiar from the past—the sound of several gun triggers cocked.

Raven slowly gets up too, glaring at me.

The chubby man is wearing a cowboy hat. A golden tooth sparkles when he smiles. *At. Me.*

Several guys at the nearby tables hold their hands on their holsters. Staring. *At. Me.*

"Miss. Katura. Ortiz," the chubby man says exaggeratedly loudly with pauses like he's in awe. A cigar hangs between his fingers. "Will you not come over to say hello?" He takes a lazy step toward me and fixes his belt buckle, then spreads his arms like he expects a hug. "The First Lady of Zion. What an honor."

*Shit.* Only now do I understand Raven's warning.

The man approaches slowly, his eyes locked with mine, a permanent smile on his face.

"Mister…?" I say quietly.

"I go by Butcher." He presses his palm to his heart, bowing slightly. "These people, they really like nicknames."

So this is the mayor of Port Mrei, the thug, the enemy, the guy who's in charge of the less fortunates.

I quickly take in his gold watch, ironed clothes, cowboy boots, a strong smell of cologne, gem-studded rings on almost every finger, thick mustache, and inquisitive deeply-set eyes. Somehow, he looks friendly and approachable.

He walks toward me with his hand stretched out, palm up.

"Sir," I say with a smile, putting my hand in his for a shake.

He grips it, not letting it go, brings it up to his lips, and kisses it for a second, two, three—way too freaking long to be appropriate—his eyes on me the whole time. When he finally lets it go, his eyes narrow just a tiny fraction in silent laughter.

Now that Butcher is closer and touched me, I realize he's not chubby. He's muscled, in fact probably very strong, but with a slight beer pooch over his studded buckle.

"Will you join us for a drink?" he asks with extreme politeness, pointing to the table.

But Raven is already stepping around it. "I'm afraid Mr. Crone gave clear instructions for us to be back by a certain time."

I smile at Butcher as he knots his brows in fake disappointment.

"What a pity." Everything about his voice is theatrical and slightly mocking. "How is our Chancellor?"

The intentional pity in the voice is meant to anger—I know what he's doing.

"He's alright, thank you," I say softly.

"Mr. Crone is not afraid to let his beautiful lady roam around the island unprotected?" He accentuates the last word.

My phone rings in my pocket, but I don't take my eyes off Butcher, whose lips twitch just slightly. "Won't you pick it up?"

"It's alright," I say, "but we really do have to go."

"Will you send my regards to Mr. Crone? And my

condolences about his father." He fakes sadness. "Our Chancellor is such a busy man. Never has a minute to visit our wonderful town. Perhaps, we could do dinner at Ayana?"

He's playing. This guy has never been invited to Ayana. But that doesn't mean he hasn't been there.

O'Shea's words are so clear now. *Every service employee, every kid that washes the dishes at a restaurant, every cleaning lady…*

This guy is way smarter than he seems. Powerful men always are.

All the smells suddenly disappear—beer, old wood, food, cigar smoke. The only smell is danger. It's thick, hanging in the air.

"I'll stop by tomorrow." Raven's cold voice cuts through the silence. He motions to me with his head toward the door and takes a slow step to the side, his body too rigid.

*Thank you, Raven.*

"It was nice to meet you," I say, nodding to Butcher, whose smile doesn't falter a fraction of an inch, his eyes unblinking.

"Oh, yes, yes. Definitely."

Slowly, he locks his hands behind him and turns in his spot, watching us as we walk out.

As Raven and I walk through the tavern, the guard walks backward and doesn't turn until we are out the door. When we are outside, he spits on the ground. Raven lights a cigarette then pulls his phone out of his pocket and dials.

"I'm sorry." He exhales a cloud of smoke into the phone. "This wasn't supposed to happen. We're coming back."

He cuts the phone call when we approach the car. James, the Sleeping Beauty, glares at me, his nostrils flaring.

Yep, I fucked up.

The proof is a missed call from Archer and a text, **What's happening???**

Only when we reach the port and board the speedboat, no one saying a word to me like I just betrayed my own country, do I dial Archer.

"Are you alright?" he asks in a curt voice.

"Yes. Arch, listen, I'm sorry. I kinda—"

"We'll talk when you get back to Ayana," he cuts me off and hangs up.

I'm in trouble.

I know that as soon as I walk into Archer's office when we arrive at Ayana.

His gaze is cold, pinning me down as he slowly gets up from behind his desk and walks toward me.

"Listen," I try to explain, "it's all my fault. Raven had to do business, and I didn't listen, and—"

Archer passes me his phone.

Oh, shit.

It's a picture of Butcher kissing my hand, taken about twenty feet away from the bar counter at Coco Jumbo.

"Would you like to know what else he said in the message?" Archer asks coldly.

I swallow hard. Butcher sent a message?

"He said, *'Can't wait to have a closer acquaintance, Mr. Crone. You have fine taste in women.'*"

Shit. "Archer, I know you are mad at me. I know I messed up—"

"Kat, listen to me." He takes a step closer and takes my face between his palms, too gentle for the anger that's burning in his eyes. "When I ask you not to do certain things, it's not because I want to control you, but because I want you to be safe."

"I know." Shit.

"I don't want you to find yourself in a situation that jeopardizes your safety."

"I know."

"So next time, please, listen."

I just messed up royally, and this guy doesn't snap, doesn't even lecture. He strokes my freaking face with his thumbs.

Who is he? A saint?

I stand on tiptoes and kiss him once. "Sorry, babe." I kiss him again. "Won't happen again, I promise." I kiss him again. "I truly am sorry."

I keep kissing him even when he so obviously tries to suppress a smile and pull away from me. I fist his shirt and bring him back to me and kiss him again.

"Ssssso sorry." I kiss him again. "So-so-so-so sorry." Then again, until his lips break into a grin and he fists my hair, kissing me properly this time.

Forgiven.

God, I suddenly love groveling. I can so grovel to this man. Naked, wearing high heels, boots, or nothing, even cuffed to a bed.

"So sorry," I coo.

Archer is suspicious now. "You know what this is called? Kat's bullshit." He doesn't sound angry, and his grip in my hair softens. "You do what you want on the spur of the moment, then think it over afterward."

"So sorry," I repeat, leaning in for another kiss, but he pulls away.

"Stop fucking around." He's trying to be serious, but can't.

"Sorry."

"I warned you."

"So-so-so sorry."

"Another sorry," he says with a warning that I already look forward to, "and I'll have your legs pinned behind your ears on this very desk and my cock so deep in you that you'll forget how to breathe."

I slide my hand down Archer's torso, feeling him stepping into me, feeling him rub against me, his cock hard in his jeans.

"Promises, promises," I tease.

His hands on me tighten again.

"So, so sorry," I keep whispering, pushing his buttons, and smile as I kiss him.

He bucks his hips at me, pressing his hard bulge against me, then lets go and gently pushes me toward the desk. "You asked for it, kitten. Change of plans. I want you bent over this desk, pants and panties down to your knees. Now."

And I'm all about it when he orders, "Corlo, close the blinds, lock the doors."

Sorry not sorry.

# 30

## ARCHER

I'T'S MY BIRTHDAY. TWENTY-FIVE SEEMS OLD, BUT I'VE NEVER looked forward to an upcoming year like I do now.

I'm at the office early, before Kat. I deal with emails and chemistry charts, because my schedule is cleared this afternoon and tomorrow. Screw work. I deserve to celebrate myself, if only with some alone time with my wild thing.

Here she is—strolling into my office in a knee-length dress, her hair tied in a bun at the back of her head. She carries a plate with some crazy pastry in her hands, a single candle lit up as she sings, "Happy-birth-day-to-you," in that soft Marylin Monroe voice.

With a smile, I get up from my chair to blow out the candle and give her a kiss on the cheek.

"So appropriate," I murmur, noticing that the pastry is shaped and decorated like a DNA's double helix.

"Happy birthday, babe," Kat says with a broad smile.

I take the plate out of her hands and set it on the desk.

"I want my chain back," I say as seriously as I can.

Her expression changes to confusion. "Why?"

"I want it back, Kat." I kill my smile.

She looks almost lost, her eyes roaming my face, as she shakes her head slowly. "No."

"Kat?"

"Archer! What's happening?" Panic sweeps over her face. "Archer. Please, tell me it's not—"

Shit, I didn't mean to give her the wrong idea. So I walk to the desk and pull a present out of the drawer.

Yes, I've ordered a present for her.

What do they say? What can you possibly give the man who has everything?

Someone asked me once what it's like to be this rich. I don't know what it's like not to be. Being born wealthy is like having two legs. You take it for granted because it's never been different. When you lose one, that's when you realize how precious your two legs were.

Having money is like having food in the fridge—something matter-of-fact-ish. But what if you are lactose-intolerant? Diabetic. Or have heartburn. Or stomach cancer. That food won't make you happy.

Which brings me to this moment. I've been hungry for two years, just didn't realize it and couldn't figure out what the cure was.

Her.

Kat is the best present the universe could possibly give me, and if anything makes me truly happy it's the puzzled look on her face when I give her the small jewelry box.

"What is it?" She stares at it in confusion.

"A present for you. I told you that you can have my chain until I get you something worthy."

"Arch!" She looks at me with pity. "But it's *your* birthday. I should've given you something. Except—"

"Kat, look at me." The way she feels bad is endearing, though that's the last thing I wanted her to feel. "It's my birthday, and I want it to be special. Trust me, there are very few things that can make me feel that way. And you are definitely the one."

She opens the box and gasps, then bites her lip as she runs her forefinger along the gold chain with a Mother-of-Pearl pendant.

I study her face. "Want me to put it on?"

Kat is flustered. A smile flickers on her lips, and she bites her bottom lip when I go behind her, remove my chain, and put the necklace on.

She doesn't touch it, doesn't want to see it in the mirror, her gaze wandering all over the place as she turns slowly to face me.

"Kat, come on." I almost feel like I did something wrong.

"It's just… I've never gotten presents like this."

"This is nothing." I step closer and run my finger along the necklace, brushing her skin. "What would you like? Couture clothes? Designer bags? Diamonds in all colors?"

She laughs nervously and shakes her head. "Thank you," she whispers.

What I want for my birthday is her, all to myself.

"Dinner tonight, yeah?" she asks.

Right, dinner.

Marlow called yesterday and asked if I wanted to have dinner with him and Ty and Dani and Raylin. Kat apparently didn't mind, and I couldn't say no, though all I want is to spend more time with Kat.

"Yes. I wish it wasn't with Marlow and Raylin," I say now. Should've kept my mouth shut—Kat looks almost disappointed.

"Tsk. It'll be alright. And then we can do whatever you want. Deal?"

"Oh?" I pull back and duck my head to meet her eyes. "You sure you want to know what I want?"

I suck in my cheeks, giving her an intimidating stare— she offered, she's screwed, or she will be in many ways she can't even imagine. My cock hardens at the thought. I can certainly survive dinner with a couple of people if I get to go wild with her afterward.

Kat realizes what she said, stares for a moment like a wild cat caught off guard, then rolls her eyes.

There are many things I want to try with her, like the upside-down pose.

She frowned when I first mentioned it. "What's that?"

"That's when you stand on your head, full frontal, and I fuck you."

Her stare turned horrified. "Are you insane?"

I laughed in response. "I'm telling you. They say it's quite an experience. For women mostly."

"No." She shook her head so fast, I thought it rotated 360.

"You'd be surprised," I insisted, but she pushed me away and threw a pillow at me.

"No! Absolutely not! Not happening, Archer. I just had a visual, and circus sounds like a more respectable thing than what you're suggesting."

I'm sure the upside-down thing just flickered in her mind, and I notice her hesitation.

"No-no-no," I warn her. "Don't back away. You said whatever I want, right? It's my birthday."

She can't hide slight alarm. We've mostly done the usual routine, which, to be fair, I need every night and morning for weeks to tame my hunger for her.

"Okay," she gives in.

She's in for all sorts of fucking. And I can't wait to get over that dinner thing with Marlow so I can have her all to myself. Naked. Doing anything I want at my command.

We've been doing this dating thing for only several weeks, but every date is an all-night shenanigan that is nothing short of wild.

Right after Kat leaves, Droga calls me.

I grin—the fucker remembered the date.

"What's up, old man?"

We chat for a minute when I have an idea. "Hey, wanna grab Callie and the kid and come over to Marlow's for dinner tonight?"

I get an inarticulate sound in response.

"It's just Kat and me, Marlow, Ty, Dani, and Raylin. He wants to do dinner, and it would be nice if you stopped by."

Maybe, I'm rushing things.

"I'm not sure, Crone. Sorry, man."

*Right.*

I feel stupid for asking, disappointment momentarily marring my otherwise cheerful mood.

"No worries," I say.

"Have a good one, yeah?"

Margot calls on the in-office phone to congratulate me. Doesn't even bother showing up, which is unlike her.

Amir stops by and gives me a case with a blue fossilized mammoth tusk, which I stare at, startled—I actually got a present for my birthday.

The rest of the day is uneventful, mostly me zoning out with thoughts about my family. It's my first birthday when Dad didn't call me. Though his phone calls were always a courtesy, it still hurts.

Several cousins call and shout congratulations into the phone. Now that I'm officially a billionaire, more distant relatives are concerned about my well-being. Even those who haven't been on my radar for years saw the *Forbes* article that mentioned me and my father's death, so now my assistants have to filter through three times as many invasive phone calls.

Several of my dad's friends call. Courtesy calls, again—I answer with the same courtesy because networking is important.

I get a surprise call from Mr. Volkhonskiy, the president of the State Bank in Belarus, who my father was close friends with for as long as I can remember. He resides in the States now and came for my father's funeral, so I have a long conversation with him.

My email notifications light up with routine emails from Dad's former staff—my birthday is probably still on their scheduled emails. **From the White House staff**, they say in the signature lines.

There comes a blast from the past in the form of a text from Anna Reich.

**Happy Birthday, love!**

Really?

I don't bother replying since she didn't have the decency to show up to my father's funeral.

For the rest of the day, the phone is mostly silent. Kat is gone too early, getting ready for dinner, and I suddenly feel like canceling the dinner and just spending time with her, doing something ridiculously boring instead of wild sex. Drinking. Watching movies. Pulling out an old Monopoly game—not the Post-Change edition that they released recently, but the very first one—and spend hours nerding out.

It's early evening, and I finally leave the Center, get home, take a shower, and change.

Kat's shirt is hanging over the shelf by my bed. She complained that the maid puts her stuff away and then she has a hard time finding things, so the maid doesn't touch her things anymore. I emptied out a closet for her to use when she's at my place. I love order and cleanness, but the gray floors of Cliff Villa definitely look better with her clothes scattered over them. She doesn't have many clothes here, except panties, because the wild thing gets too excited and ruins them. Maybe we need to eliminate them from her wardrobe altogether.

The thought makes me laugh as I fix my hair in the mirror and walk out into the living room.

The villa's acquiring Kat's scent and looks like there's life in it, which is a strange thought because I've resided here for two years.

Alright. Just an hour at Marlow's place, and I'll snatch Kat away.

**Want me to pick you up?** I text Kat.

**Kat: It's okay. I'll see you at Marlow's!**

I leave the villa, jump on my bike, and zoom to Marlow's.

The memory his drunk episode and me and Kat breaking his coffee table brings a smile to my face as I ring the bell, and the door opens to reveal Kat.

God damn!

She looks great in cargo pants and tractor boots as well as in a mini-dress, like right now, paired with stilettos, but also in a bikini, naked—you name it, Kat rocks it.

She strikes a fashionable pose with a dazzling smile.

"Hey, you," she casually throws at me and steps aside to let me in.

"A kiss would be nice," I say, stepping inside, my eyes on her as I'm about to swoop her into my arms—I deserve more than a kiss on a day like this—when the sudden sound assaults my eardrums.

"HAPPY BIRTHDAY!"

It's a loud roar, so unexpected that I almost jump.

The music starts blasting as my eyes shift to a huge crowd of people in the living room who stare at me with smiles.

"Happy-birth-day-to-yoooooou—" they start chanting as they clap their hands, dozens of them.

I stand dumb-founded.

"Happy-birth-day-dear-Ar-cher—" they sing at the top of their lungs, and when the song is over, they erupt in cheers and whistling, the confetti suddenly shooting off from everywhere.

In seconds, the crowd surges toward me, hugs, arms, kisses, congratulations. But more than surprise, there's something else that keeps me silent—a fucking lump in my throat as I, for once, don't know what to say.

## 31

## KAT

I clap my hands in excitement like I'm the birthday girl here.

Over fifty people are attending, maybe sixty—I lost count. Even though Archer might hate it, he'll stick around at least for a hot second. I know Cece got him something special. His other friend, Qi Shan, did too. Dr. Hodges and his wife were delighted to attend. Everyone was getting ready for days, talking and discussing, like it's the biggest event in years.

Waiters, food, drinks, a DJ—check. *Thank you, Cece!* She's the queen of partying.

Raven and Bishop are here. Amir and several people from the lab that Archer works closely with. The elite group, over thirty of them. Bo showed up, and so did Maddy—it might be the first time I've seen her out.

Somehow, when Marlow and I sat down to make a list of a few people to invite for a small surprise party, there turned out to be quite a number who cared about Archer and would've been upset if they were left out.

So what started with ten close friends turned into fifteen, then twenty, and then Marlow gave up. "Well, let's just make a huge party like back in the old days, and if Archer doesn't like it, you'll take him home and make up in some other way."

"What if he gets angry at the whole idea?"

"So, he'll hang out for a minute and bounce. It's your job to curb his anger. You're about the only one who can."

"Just a reminder, you need to learn to curb your emotions."

Of course, Marlow got to listen to the drunk sobbing messages he sent to my phone instead of to Raylin's. He apologized, blushed, huffed and puffed, but sure was glad they didn't reach the intended recipient.

"Wanna tell me what that was about?" I asked.

He wouldn't. "That was a fucked up night. I topped myself, for sure."

"Yeah." I smile.

"I was… *V gavno.*" Shitfaced.

I laughed.

"Broke my coffee table that I paid a fortune for."

My stomach turned at the words. "Why, was it expensive?"

"It was from a club in New York where Red Hot Chili Peppers and Madonna and other stars first performed. Yeah, it's a fucking gem."

I didn't say a word. Seems like coffee tables are Archer and my thing.

Right now, Marlow looks happy and suave.

And Archer doesn't look mad. He seems startled. Lost, maybe? I can't gauge his reaction, except it's nothing like I've ever seen before. His poker face is shit right now. There's something vulnerable in the way he doesn't look at people for too long, rakes his fingers through his hair, scratches his eyebrow with a soft smile, again and again, so sexy in his black shirt with sleeves rolled up and jeans, yet suddenly so familiar—I'm one of the few who recognize his vulnerable state.

He hasn't really left the hallway yet, because everyone is crowding around, forming multiple lines, giving him a hug or a present, though the present table against the wall is already packed with towering boxes and packages of God-knows-what. What could Archer possibly want? Except just that, presents—it's the thought that counts.

And dozens of thoughts gather around him, joking, laughing, patting him on the back, kissing his cheeks—those lipstick smudges will drive him insane.

My eyes burn with tears. I hope Archer realizes that a lot of people care about him. If only he would let them close again.

Archer is overwhelmed. He doesn't show it but sucks in his cheeks. Good. That's the best kind of present—to feel human, loved and thought about.

I want to see more of him like this—among friends, at parties, or on a football field—God, I wish I could—or laughing with Droga like they are right now, or doing motorcycle tricks, or in an octagon, half naked and feral but safe.

I want to see all sides of him, knowing he's my guy.

My. Guy.

The words do something weird to my heart. It gets hard to breathe, and that goofy smile tugs at my lips.

The music goes quieter all around the villa, the sound of the microphone tapped cutting through the voices and laughter.

Marlow is slick like a runway star—hair tied in a bun at the back without a single hair out, sunglasses, a silk buttoned-down shirt, halfway open, necklaces dangling, tight jeans.

Wow.

He perches his sunglasses on his head, then jumps up onto the bar counter, a microphone in one hand, a cocktail glass in his other.

"Alright, you guys, attention!" he calls out, and everyone goes quiet and turns to face him. "We have our man here, Archer Crone."

Everyone turns toward Archer, forming a semi-circle, cheering and whistling.

"He's been in hiding for some time but rose like a phoenix from the ashes!" Marlow declares with pathos. "And decided to finally grace us with his presence. So if you were ever waiting for the second coming of Jesus, here it is, ladies and gentlemen."

The crowd woot-woots.

Archer shakes his head with a modest smile—he's cornered.

Margot puts her hand on his shoulder, and for once, I let it go. She's been with him from the beginning and through many ups and downs until I arrived. I can bear this minute of her closeness to him.

"I'm talking on behalf of at least a dozen people here who have known Archer for a long time," Marlow continues. "We really miss the times with you, man. When you changed all Deene official flags and insignia to 'Happy Birthday, Archer' and got suspended."

Twenty or so people explode with laughter. "Go, Crone!"

I raise my eyebrows. He did that?

Marlow grins. "And when you went streaking in the Deene student pool."

Cat whistles shoot across the living room.

Archer? Really?

"And when you—on purpose—crashed a Deene golf cart into Mrs. Helligarg's car because it was too old but she didn't have money to change it and you hated that she parked too close to your Aston Martin Vulcan"—more cheers sweep across the room—"yep, and so you ended up buying her a new car."

I don't know this guy, I swear, but he is grinning. God! Archer is grinning—we must've done something right tonight.

"And the time when you lined up all of the frat guys naked across the lawn in front of the dean's office and made them do the chicken dance."

"Oooohhhhhh!" There are booing sounds as Archer tilts his head back and closes his eyes in what looks like embarrassment.

"And we are all older and we'd like to think, wiser,"

Marlow goes on but in a more serious voice. "We've been through a lot, so maybe no streaking or shrooms—"

"Take Marlow's advice, because he doesn't use it!" someone shouts, and laughter echoes through the crowd.

"Shut up!" Marlow snaps with a grin. "But!" He spreads his arms like a showman. "Let's stay close. This is our home. It could've been much worse if you, Archer, didn't bring us here on that fateful Spring Break." The room goes really quiet now. He's right, but he hit a sensitive topic. "And we try to make the best of it. The only way it can be is if we keep tabs on each other. Love you, man!" He stabs his forefinger at Archer in the crowd. "Happy Birthday, Archer!"

## 32

### KAT

The villa erupts in cheers and whistles. I stand behind Archer at a distance and watch Margot kiss him on his cheek. She only gets this one chance. Another peck, and she'll be floating strangled in the pool later tonight.

The DJ turns up the music.

The waiters come out with appetizers and trays of drinks, and everyone disperses as Archer fights off several people, ruffles his hair, and looks around, searching.

He finally finds me in the crowd behind him, and I give him the warmest smile I have.

*My* Archer.

Everyone steps away from him as I approach.

"Happy Birthday," I say and kiss him on the lips. His cheeks are smudged with lipstick, but his lips are my domain. "You are not mad, are you?"

"Not at all. Thank you."

But he's struggling, even though it's unnoticeable to

anyone but me. He looks away, trying to smile, and I feel like there's a mist of tears in his eyes.

A little over a month with these people let me on a lot of secrets. Affairs, grudges, chronic depression, painkillers, drug and booze addiction, one suicidal attempt besides Archer, broken hearts, and mental breakdowns. I can only imagine what two years stranded on a resort can do. It's the size of a small town, but just like Marlow joked, money can't buy mental wellness.

But these people have bonds that go way back. The bonds from the times when they were happy and invincible, and those memories will never fade, not even after what the world endured after the Change.

Despite Archer's arguments, what he needs right now is friends and support.

I leave him talking to Cece. Plenty of people want a minute with the Chancellor. They miss him.

I spot Axavier, who looks slick in a designer tiger-print surf tank and leather pants, emanating excessive cologne, over-the-top hair products, immaculately lathered skin—he doesn't even know that he's giving himself away.

Being in the closet is a bitch.

"Babe, don't try so hard," I tell him.

"Try what?"

"Pretending like you're having a good time when all you do is steal glances in that direction." I nod toward Milan, Cece's stylist, his blue hair in stark contrast with his yellow pants and an unbuttoned vest over his bare torso. He looks calmer but edgy, throwing occasional glances across the room at Axavier.

"Why are you paranoid about coming out?" I ask. "These are your friends."

"I don't need to come out," he hisses under his breath. "I'm bi. Whatever."

"Exactly."

"Exactly. Some chicks are not into guys who swing both ways."

"Oooooh-ho-ho." I cough up a burst of low laughter. "Greedy, aren't we? You wanna swing both ways but wanna make sure you keep it all compartmentalized. Wow, dude. Good luck."

"I don't need luck."

"You'll need something soon. Judging by how antsy you are around Milan. What is he?" I pause in pretend thoughtfulness. "Plan B? Sidekick?" I smirk at Axavier rolling his eyes. "Tail-gating? Is that what this is?"

"Fuck off, Kat."

"Drinks! Drinks! Drinks!" Margot and one of her loyal Chihuahuas sashay toward us through the crowd with a tray of cocktails.

Shocking, considering there are waiters at the party and the Pink Medusa never lifts a finger to make anyone happy. Except Archer, if she had a chance.

But she's aiming right for me and Axavier.

"Snow in July," I murmur and fake a smile, for Archer's sake. Gotta keep this party fight-free.

"Axavier, sweetie!" Margot passes him a cocktail. "My special recipe."

She takes another drink and gives it to me too forcefully. I'm pretty sure she doesn't know any recipes except how to ruin someone's life.

"To Archer!" she cheers and shoves the empty tray to her friend.

Her girlfriend smiles at me, her gaze almost sincere with admiration when she says, "You look—"

"Like you fit in," Margot finishes with a snake smile. "In another life, you know."

"Jesus," Axavier murmurs.

"You look like a Malevich painting," I say sweetly, nodding at Margot's knee-length tube dress that's spotted with geometrical blocks.

She raises her eyebrows. "That's a big word for someone who thinks high art is graffiti in Bangkok hoods."

She'll die tonight, I promise.

She pulls out a phone, turns her back to us, and takes a selfie of all of us.

I don't bother looking at the screen. Instead, I step closer and lean over so no one hears the ugly side of my sense of humor intended for this precious creature.

"Marge," I say—she winces when I call her that, "why don't you take a selfie of your asshole and pass it around? Maybe you'll finally find a boyfriend."

"Is that how you found yours?"

"Archer prefers my face. But *you* are obviously struggling."

Mrgot fakes a laugh and swings her hips to the music beat as she walks off, throwing me one last glance so poisonous that the safety pin tucked into my dress—a habit that my mom taught me and an Eastern European thing against jinxing—would not have saved me. Or her. She needs to be careful or there'll be murder on the dance floor tonight.

"You two will never stop, huh?" Axavier says and downs the drink in one go.

"Whoa, slow down," I warn him, noticing another flick of his eyes in Milan's direction.

The cocktail is actually amazing. But I need to watch how much I drink. After all, it's Archer's party, and I'd rather make sure it all goes tip-top and he has the grandest time than get wasted and do something stupid.

My heart warms at the sight of Archer on the other side of the room making rounds and taking time talking to everyone. When he catches me staring now and then, locking his gaze with mine, my heart blooms like a freaking lotus on muddy water—strikingly and powerfully, my knees weak when he winks at me.

I thought that being officially together would give me peace. Instead, my feelings for him only grow stronger. I wake up thinking about him if he's not next to me, or I study him in his sleep if he is. I wait for the evenings to have together time, but the nights apart are excruciating.

Archer makes his way toward Marlow, who's sulking. Whatever is happening with him and Raylin, he won't talk to me. Like it's a secret.

As if on cue, Raylin's blond bob appears in front of me, her big eyes and full lips mesmerizing—it's impossible to get used to her beauty. She says hi, then laughs at Axavier's joke, her hand on his bicep intentionally too friendly. She does it a lot with everyone. But in moments she's alone, her smile disappears, her gaze focusing on nothing in particular as if she's lost.

Kai seems happy with Callie on his lap, smiling and constantly touching him—those two are inseparable. So are Ty and Dani. That group is the happiest—laughing, drinking, exchanging jokes, Ty dressed in all designer clothes, now that he got his funds back—he's back in his element.

Cece is drunk already and so humble, her hand wrapped around Bishop's bicep. Tattooed, a mountain of muscles, yet humble and gentlemanlike, Bishop definitely looks out of place.

The familiar pink hair flickers next to him as Margot steps in front of him and tries to block him from the rest of the group.

"Check this out," I say, nodding to Axavier, who's more interested in his own little drama.

"She's definitely *aware* of him." Axavier takes the cocktail which I barely touched out of my hand and downs it.

"She's good at bullying people she doesn't like."

Axavier laughs loudly. "I doubt that guy can be bullied. If anything, he can *take* her. Hard."

"Yeah, but she's a cunt—who wants that?"

And right away, there's a loud gasp, "Ohhh," as Margot purposefully dumps her drink on Bishop.

I watch, shocked. "Holy shit, does she not have a sense of decency? At least tonight?"

I turn to Axavier, but he doesn't notice what just happened. He's swaying, already drunk—how the hell did he get wasted so quickly?—and bluntly stares across the room at Milan.

The party is getting rowdy too quickly.

I walk up to Bishop. "Hey, Chase, let me get you cleaned up."

I pull him away and toward one of the bathrooms.

"Don't mind Margot," I tell him as I wipe his shirt with a handful of paper towels. "The girl feels entitled like she's the queen of the world."

"Yeah. She needs an attitude adjustment, to lay off Archer, and probably get laid."

I snort out a laugh, liking this guy even more. "I barely know you, Chase, but you might be a psychic. What did you say to earn Medusa's wrath?"

"She asked me what I preferred to drink. Cheap local beer or moonshine."

I snort, rolling my eyes. "Typical Margot."

"I said, I could tell her what I want my mouth on, but we'd have to be in a more private setting."

I laugh harder, finishing cleaning his shirt. Yeah, I like him.

"They're good people," I say, tossing the tissues in a trashcan. "Well, most of them. I think they're just too wary who they let in their circle."

"I'm not trying to be in their circle, sweetheart. The only reason I'm here is to see Archer finally happy."

"I know. But they"—I nod in the direction of the party—"are just like us, but with a golden shell around them. Once you crack it, they're more humble than you think."

Bishop fans his t-shirt, his muscles bulging through the fabric. "I can see that you already cracked Archer's shell."

"Right." I grin. "Margot though—hers is steel-reinforced

like a bank vault. She's curated her personality ever since she reached puberty. But trust me, she's not the hot shit she thinks she is."

Bishop opens the door for me, and the loud music thuds into our chests. Leaning over, he says. "Do you know what I used to do for a living?"

I know.

"Cracking others' shells." He winks at me again, and for a moment, I think that Margot doesn't deserve the attention of a guy like this, but hope that he teaches her a lesson anyway.

## 33

## ARCHER

Holy shit, the whole world is here, and surprisingly, it makes me feel loved.

Droga and I step out onto the pool terrace, grabbing some fresh air.

"Heard you went to town the other day," I tell him.

"Yeah, visited some friends. Candy at Venus Den."

"A courtesy visit?"

I know all about the Outcasts and Candy's girls back in the day. Also, her helping Droga when I was high as a kite and announced the manhunt on him.

"She said, rumor has it, Butcher had a guy on the inside, here at Ayana, part of your crew. And he went missing."

"No one went missing. Unless they are staff, which we don't exactly keep track of. Unless it's…" I pause, thinking about O'Shea and Cunningham. I told Droga about them.

"That's what I was thinking," he says, taking a swig of a beer. "Unless it's one of those guys you have held up."

Fuck. This is such a mess.

"I'm just giving you a heads up," he says. "Raven should talk to Candy. A lot of guys go through her place and spill things. You'd be surprised." He takes another sip of his beer and then shoulders me. "I don't wanna bother you with rumors or work stuff. Sorry, man."

"Is that all you went to Port Mrei for?"

"Got a new tattoo."

"Like you need more?"

He only shakes his head. "Callie designed it. It's private."

"What is it?"

"Don't be a perv, Crone."

"C'mon. Is it her name? On your dick? Wouldn't fit, I don't think."

Droga throws his head back. "Fuck off. But also… Got you this. It's nothing much, just memories." He gives me a wrapped package he's had tucked under his armpit for a while. "Didn't want anyone to see it in case you wanna keep it private."

"The hell?" I'm curious. I tear off the paper and see the back of a letter-size picture frame. Then flip it and—

"Holy shit, Droga," I exhale.

"Yep." He takes a sip, studying people around like a watchdog.

It's a picture of Droga, me, Marlow, and other frat guys standing in a row on a lawn, naked. A bet. A drunk night. A chicken dance. Talk about bad decisions…

"We fucking deleted this picture, Droga. All of us. We swore," I murmur, staring at the blast from the past as my lips stretch in a grin against my will. Some shameful things don't seem so bad years later. This is definitely not for the public eye, but holy crap.

"I don't remember swearing to anything," Droga says, innocently looking around.

"So you kept it."

"On my phone, yeah. There's plenty of candy for the eye. I might just give you a whole photo album of this stuff next year."

It's a full-on comeback, the walls that we built around us have crumbled, and Droga marches across the rubble toward me.

"Thanks, man," I whisper, not able to kill the grin.

"Have fun, yeah?" He slaps me on the back and walks off and I walk back inside.

Marlow is leaning on the bar stand, scowling across the room. I follow his gaze—Raylin is laughing about something Axavier is whispering in her ear, her hand on his shoulder.

I could tell him that Axavier plays for the opposite team, but it's not my secret to spill.

Marlow needs to grow a pair. It's surprising, considering Marlow is a lady's man, but not tonight, not with Raylin, drowning his bravery in a glass. It's familiar and makes me smile. Unlike me, he's a soft drunk, turning into a teddy bear with a wild streak as the liquor makes its way into his system. The famous streaking episode from Deene that everyone credits me for was Marlow's dare after a bottle of rum we shared.

"What's up, buddy?" I clink my glass to his as he drops

his head back and exhales like he's weighed down by some existential problem.

"Nothing, man. Life. Complicated."

"It can be. Life or chicks?" A smile tugs at my lips as I nudge him. "Maybe you should slow down on booze, then go talk to her and take all of her attention."

"Who?" The fucker is playing dumb, not even meeting my eyes, then he changes the topic. "It's your birthday, dude. If you're bored, we can change up the scene. What do you feel like doing?"

"My hot assistant." I see Kat in the crowd of people across the room. She looks gorgeous and watches me with a playful smile. "Who happens to be my girlfriend."

A quick laugh escapes Marlow. "Lucky bastard."

"I am. Thanks for this." I motion around. Celebrations lost their meaning to me a long time ago, but this, for the first time in many months, feels like family.

"Nah. It's all Kat."

My heart tightens at the thought.

If I didn't know Kat, I would've picked her from the crowd, hit on her, done a whole lotta filthy stuff to her in my mind, and then probably talked her into coming over to my place and doing it there.

The thought stuns me. I thought she wasn't quite my type when I first saw her. Now, looking at her, I realize she's perfect, so different from anyone I ever met but easily fitting with the crowd of the posh elites, or with the security guys at the Diggs, or the Outcasts on the Eastside. It's a gift she's not aware of, the one I didn't spot right away.

I slowly make my way to her, and she watches, her body

scandalously sexy in the red minidress and sparkly high-heeled boots.

God, I fucking love red.

"Hey, birthday boy," she says with a smile that I love.

I'm falling for her so fast that it makes my head spin. Feelings are not my forte. Anger or extreme affection—I can't control them. The first has become familiar. The latter…

"You're too serious for the number of drinks you've had," Kat says, studying me.

"Are you counting?"

"Yes."

That's a surprise. "Why?"

"Just want to make sure you're okay."

"I'm fine. But after you promised alone time, this dress feels almost disrespectful."

Now, she looks worried.

I tongue my cheek. "It's my birthday, and I was looking forward to you naked. Instead, you have a zillion people and are staying as far away from me as possible."

She bites her lip, batting her lashes at me. These eyes, makeup, lipstick, long legs, and hourglass figure make me feel almost bitter that I'm not yet showing everyone that she's mine.

"I wanted to give you time with everyone," she says apologetically. "They've missed you. You might not realize it, but they talk about you, the old times, and how you all used to be. They forgot what it's like to have you as a friend. Trust me, many of them want you back."

The sincerity in her soft voice does that familiar thing to

my heart where it pumps as if trying to break out of my chest and latch onto her. I haven't heard words like these in a while and appreciate them.

Someone comes up from behind me, snakes his arms around my neck, and weighs down on me.

"There you are, birthday bitch." It's Qi Shan. "Dude, so good to finally hang out," he says, his rum breath grazing my face.

Kat lifts her brows in a silent, "I told you so."

I immediately feel bad for making Kat doubt herself when I really appreciate her effort to reconcile me with the old crew. So when Qi Shan leaves me alone, I step closer to her and put my hand on her waist, gloating at the glances that start darting in our direction.

"I'm teasing you, wild thing," I say softly. "One, you look drop-dead gorgeous, and I haven't taken my eyes off you since I stepped into this villa. Two, I have this urge to punch the guys who openly stare at you."

"Archer! They are—"

"Shhh, I know." I know I don't need to worry or be jealous. "Three, thank you for the party. It means a lot. It's a slow comeback to normalcy."

I kiss her softly on the cheek, feeling her body lean into mine.

"Four"—she wraps her arms around my neck, and the feeling is back—like there's no one in this world but her and me. "You will absolutely see me naked tonight. I didn't want to smother you with my attention in front of everyone. But..." Her eyes drop to my lips. "I can, if that's okay with you."

I want her lips on me. I don't even mind her deep-red lipstick on my face, despite the fact that I might look like the Joker.

"Since when do you need permission to smother your boyfriend?" Our faces inch closer until our noses touch, her scent and the smell of her Cool Water perfume erasing any other scent around.

"Are you worried about the lipstick?" I swear, this woman can read my thoughts. "It's a stain."

"Meaning?"

"Meaning the lipstick stains my lips, and then I wipe it off." She kisses me, gently sucking on my bottom lip. "I know you don't like lipstick. So there, that's the trick. Now, can I kiss you in front of everyone?"

"If you don't, I'll start groping you right here so that no one has any doubt—"

She shuts me up with a deep kiss that makes my arm wrap around her waist and pull her closer as I lean into her, bending her backward.

A wolf whistle spears through the music and an "Aww!"

We don't pay attention, kissing in front of everyone. Someone walks by, leaning over to us and shouting through the music, "Yeah, Katura! Show him!"

And she laughs into my mouth, then buries her face in my neck. I expect her to pull away, instead, she starts swinging her hips to the music, nudging me to follow.

We dance. That's the second time this year. Both with her. I have so many firsts with this girl that I feel like I've been cooped up my entire life. We all partied like animals back at Deene, but Kat brings with her a different kind of party.

"And now we're dancing," she says and brings her smile to my lips again, teasing me with soft kisses.

"You keep grinding against me like this, and we'll have to step out for more than just dancing."

"I'm up for anything as long as it's with you."

"Well, you are getting me hard in public."

"Oooh, now you know how I feel when you slip those filthy messages to me in the office. At least you don't have to walk around in wet underwear." She presses harder against me, and, yeah, now she totally feels my mood down there.

I slide one hand down to her butt and squeeze it. Her hands rake into my hair as she closes her eyes and nuzzles my cheek. I try to smile but my heart thuds at the thought of everyone seeing me like this—lost in my feelings, in her.

I catch sight of Droga splayed on the couch, legs wide open, Callie perched on his lap as she chats with Dani. He winks at me as he takes a sip of his drink.

There's a commotion by the pool, and everyone turns their head to see Axavier on the floor.

Kat makes an attempt to move in that direction, but I stop her and hold her in my arms. "They'll deal with it."

Someone tries to get Axavier up, except he's too drunk to stand, and he laughs, jerking on the floor like an epileptic.

Cece's stylist gets on his knees next to him, and then there are gaping stares and O-faces, because Axavier holds Milan by his hand, not letting him get away, then starts stroking his face with his other hand and pulls him down for a kiss.

Everyone looks shocked, but the music keeps blasting and the party keeps going.

I bury my face in Kat's neck, licking it and making her giggle.

"Why does it feel like everyone is spiraling out of control tonight?" she asks, her hands getting more insistent as they roam my body.

I laugh. "You mean, for once, it's not you and I?"

I notice Raven leaning on the wall, scanning the hall like he's a bouncer. He's always watching. He cocks his head, his eyes narrowing—Maddy is several feet away from him chatting with a girl. It's the first time I've seen her out mingling.

She starts walking toward the terrace. Raven follows, only to stop where she just stood and bend over to pick something up—her wrist bracelet. He sticks it in his pocket and walks in the opposite direction.

Raven is observant, but right now, he looks like a stalker.

"Archer, we need to talk." Someone taps me on the shoulder, and I swear, I'll punch him for interrupting this perfect moment.

It's Marlow. His phone is in his hand, and his gaze is anything but drunk. "Check your phone."

"Dude, not now," I snap.

"Archer, check your phone," he insists. "Then tell me what to do."

Kat looks worried as I dig in my pocket, checking my phone.

Four missed calls from Slate.

Several messages.

My eyes widen as I read them—fuuuck…

"I have to leave," I tell Kat.

"I'm coming with you," she says right away. "Can I? I'm not staying here without you."

I nod, my eyes fixed on the message on the screen.

"What is it now?" she asks.

I can't lie, and I can't suppress the nasty feeling inside me—something always goes wrong on this island.

"O'Shea is dead."

# 34

## KAT

Blood.

O'Shea's lifeless body.

An eerie feeling at the hollow sound of multiple foot-steps against the concrete floor as me, Archer, Marlow, Raven, Bishop, and several security guys walk into the holding cell and stare at the body on the floor.

"How?" Archer asks coldly.

One of the security guys rubs his neck, looking apologetic. "There's no way Cunningham could do this unless he had someone on the inside."

Cunningham is gone—that's the harsher news. We should've kept an eye on *him* instead of O'Shea.

Archer exhales loudly, tilting his head back. "Fucking great. Our entire security team is jeopardized. How the fuck—"

He doesn't finish, only ruffles his hair.

The security guy shifts uneasily. "We've announced a search and are sending a team to Port Mrei to do a sweep.

Another team is on the cameras, studying every second of footage to see if Cunningham slipped out through the checkpoints."

Bishop shakes his head. "If he was smart enough to escape, he's smart enough to get away unnoticed—in a disguise, in a work trucks, a bus, anything."

"I'll have a talk with Butcher," Raven says, his voice cold and indifferent as he leans with his shoulder against the wall and smokes. "Ninety-nine percent chance he had something to do with it. But he won't admit it. Still, he needs to know we're on it."

"Apparently we are not," Archer snaps, turning around and searching for Slate. "Okay. We are activating all the cameras on Ayana. Twenty-four seven. No objections. All the inactive cameras across Zion—same thing, including the Eastside, since there's no one there and it's a haven for squatters. Slate, get me two more security guards. One at Katura's house, the other one following her twenty-four-seven."

I want to object, but arguing seems like adding fuel to the fire.

I stare at O'Shea. His head is turned unnaturally—his neck has been snapped. That's cold. Considering that this was done by a supposed friend, it's brutal. Only one thing makes a person do ruthless things to friends—money.

"We should get on a video call with Mr. Ortiz," says Marlow.

Archer pulls out his phone and starts typing, the beeping of the incoming messages interrupting now and then.

"A meeting with Mr. Ortiz in fifteen at the Center. My office," he says.

So much for his birthday celebration.

I feel like I failed at yet another thing to make him happy.

## 35

---

## KAT

THE NEXT DAY, O'SHEA'S BODY IS MOVED TO THE PORT MREI mortuary. An island-wide search for Cunningham is announced, and a reward is offered. He won't have a place to hide unless he has allies, and that's the biggest problem.

After a meeting with my dad last night, Archer and I went to Cliff Villa. Talked for hours. Then had sex, twice, impatiently, but none of the "whatever you want" I promised. We just needed a release and each other.

Something's coming our way. There are eyes everywhere, and I made the stupid mistake of venturing to Port Mrei like freaking Tinker Bell into a lion's den. I almost wonder if Cunningham's escape had something to do with it. Was it Butcher's message?

The security guards outside Archer's villa didn't exactly evoke a romantic setting last night either.

"Do you think we are in danger, Arch?" I asked him as we lay in his bed before dawn, exhausted and grim, his arm around me, my fingers stroking his skin—the only thing that brought me reassurance that we'd be fine.

"You are with me, wild thing. I'm always right here. We'll be fine."

No one is fine. Slate now follows me everywhere—Archer gave up his most trusted guy who's been with him since Deene, and now has two other guys who escort him everywhere. For all we know, Cunningham could still be at Ayana.

We gather in Archer's office early in the morning.

"Security went through the cameras," Marlow reports, "but a lot of people go in and out of Ayana every day. Their badges get scanned, but there are simply too many time-stamps to track to catch one fraud. If Cunningham has connections, he could've left Zion already. Considering, people are smuggled in and out."

Archer's jaw tightens. "Is everyone just gonna bring it up every time we talk and do nothing?"

"What do you want to do?" Marlow asks grimly. "Change guards? Hire new port management?"

"Yes and yes. Every time you change employees, it takes time for them to settle in before they are comfortable enough to break the rules."

Raven stirs. "They don't need to be comfortable. There's already a well-oiled process in place, and Butcher is running it."

Our heads turn to him.

Archer's eyes flash with anger. "Are you saying you knew about it all this time and didn't say anything?"

"Archer, I'd be stupid if I oversaw export and import in Port Mrei and didn't know the unwanted details. I do business with the thugs and the gangs, and yes, Butcher, too. We might not discuss it with him, but I know plenty of what's happening. There's always compromise and leverage."

"Leverage."

"Yes, leverage." His voice is low and slow-paced but with that edge that leaves invisible cuts on your brain. He's not afraid to lay out the truth. "If you want to change how Port Mrei has operated in the last two years, one, get a completely new security and surveillance team—that's over two hundred people. Two, eliminate Butcher and his crew —that's several hundred people, and by eliminate, I mean, gone from Zion. That's the only way you can change the already existing power dynamics. This part is quite impossible—Butcher won't give up without a fight. And last but not least, find Milena Tsariuk so you don't have the entire world invested in this place. Does the above sound like something we wanna take on right now? Let me know."

Silence hangs in the air again. Archer stares down at his desk, his gaze too tense. Marlow's eyes are covered by his hand. Raven is the only one who is unfazed by what he just said.

No one has suggestions because the only way to sort out what's happening is to change everything around. He's right. My dad said as much.

Raven speaks again. "You don't need my opinion right now, Archer, but I'll give one anyway. This island has been operating in Ayana versus Port Mrei mode for some time. Tsariuk's business brought too many undesirables and has been weakening Zion's security for a while. There are mechanisms in motion, not the good kind, and it's only a matter of time before everything blows up."

Archer pinches the bridge of his nose. "So what do you suggest?"

"Move the Center elsewhere."

Archer snorts in contempt. "It's impossible right now. The main problem is that there are too many people at Ayana who've made it their home."

"Precisely. So there's another option—wait and see. And while we are waiting, we should get ready for the worst."

"Which is?"

"That eventually, even the security won't keep the Savages and Butcher's people from trying to claim what they think belongs to them—complete control of the port, Zion's economy, and, the cherry on top—Ayana."

This was supposed to be Archer's day off. But O'Shea's incident already changed that. Cunningham is like a spider that disappeared in our bedroom. The security disaster feels like imminent doom approaching. And Archer is on edge—I can see it when he pours himself a drink in his office and sits for an hour staring at the wall.

It's evening, and Archer tells me he has a conference call. I go home, Slate by my side, which makes me feel like I'm in some spy movie.

"This is awkward," I say to him.

"What is?"

"You really gonna follow me everywhere?"

"That's my job."

"Like I said. Awkward."

"Why?"

I laugh, then remember that Slate has been with Archer since Deene. Some people live surrounded by security at all times.

It starts raining before I even reach my bungalow. The sky darkens. I can hear the stormy ocean in the distance.

I don't know how long Archer will take with his meetings, but I want to be with him tonight.

My phone beeps, and my eyes widen when I see the name.

**Margot: I hate to rain on your parade, sweetie, but…**

There's a picture attached.

It's Archer in a green shirt, jeans, leather jacket, and sunglasses, and some girl in a designer dress, her blond hair in a high ponytail. His arm is around her waist as she leans on him. There's a private jet behind them.

**Margot: Anna Reich is in town.**

My heart gives out a heavy thud.

Archer's ex is here?

I zoom in on the picture and notice little things. How pretty she is. Polished. Everything about her—clothes, jewelry, makeup—screams money. But I also notice Archer's hair, which is shorter than it is right now. And the sky is cloudy but sunny.

The picture is old—the realization makes me exhale in relief, but the fact that he didn't say anything about his ex coming makes anxiety pull at my nerves.

Of course, he doesn't pick up his phone when I call.

I can do this. I can totally keep my cool, right?

I text Margot.

**Me: What do I care?**

**Margot: Oh, I don't know. Just stay away from his villa tonight.**

What. The. Hell?

I text Archer to call me back, but half an hour on pins and needles with no response from him makes me angry.

Does he really have a meeting? why doesn't he pick up?

"Fuck this," I murmur to myself, walk out, and head to Cliff Villa, not paying attention to Slate, who shadows me. Even Slate irritates me. It's drizzling and getting dark already. At night, he'll spook me every time I'll hear his footsteps behind me.

I storm to Cliff Villa, but the door is locked. It's a bad sign—Archer never locks the door. I punch in the code and walk in.

The unfamiliar pop music trickles through the speakers. The sweet perfume in the air makes a shiver run down my spine. So does the scent of body powder and the wine bottle and two wine glasses on Archer's coffee table no one's allowed to touch. A woman's fashionable jacket hangs over the couch arm.

The hair on the back of my neck stands on end.

I want to go to the bedroom but I'm afraid to see something I won't be able to unsee.

"Archer?" I try to sound calm, but my voice doesn't come out so haughty.

"Oh, hi, there!"

The chirpy voice turns me around, and I see slick blond hair, a cocked brow, and a wide lip-gloss smile.

But it's her body that makes my stomach turn—slim and flawless, wrapped only in a towel...

## 36

### KAT

I hate women whose hobby is fucking others' happiness. Not men's, no. Their hobby revolves around destroying other women's moods and confidence.

Margot is like this. But I think she only does it because she's a miserable bitch.

This one—I study the girl who looks like she just stepped off a beauty magazine—is a professional life-wrecker. Her smile tells a story of dozens of fucked-up girls who dared to stay in her way. I know this type—she'll make it her mission to ruin any female who dares to look better than her.

"Who are you?" I ask though I know the answer.

She shouldn't be here. There's no reason for her to be in my man's house wrapped in a fucking towel.

Yet, she is.

"Who are *you*?" She studies me up and down with poisonous contempt, though I'm sure if she's friends with the Pink Medusa, she knows about me already.

"Archer's girlfriend," I say.

"Oh, right, the flavor of the month."

*Bitch.*

Keeping cool is getting harder by the second.

"You have to leave," I say, my blood starting to boil. I pick up my phone and call Archer again. No response. Only a message.

**Archer: I'm in the middle of something. I'll call you back.**

The girl's perfect lips stretch in a smile like she knows she's getting under my skin. "Archer's at a meeting. He won't pick up random calls unless it's someone important."

Her smile grows bigger as she walks to the couch and fishes a phone out of her purse, then dials and presses it to her ear.

"Oh, hi!" she chirps, her unblinking gaze on me like that of a snake. Gracefully, she lowers her ass on the couch arm and crosses one bare leg over the other like she's posing for a magazine cover.

I wouldn't believe she was actually talking to Archer if her phone didn't light up, letting me know someone answered.

My stomach churns. He answered? *Her* call?

"Guess who's here?" she asks. "Yeah, she is… Not impressed, no…"

Her gaze glides up and down my figure, and I really hate the feeling of wanting to slap her around.

"See you soon. Byyyyeeee!" She hangs up and tosses the phone on the couch, then leans back on one arm. "So, can I help you, sweetie?"

I could drag her out. I could throw her in the pool. I could choke her out. But I promised Archer that I'd practice patience and wouldn't overreact. So I do the only thing that will keep that blonde creature in one piece for now—turn around and leave.

I'm mad and need to clear my head. The first idea that comes to mind is swimming. It's dark, but I don't care. Nature and water are the best therapy. So is exercise.

I stomp toward the main road that goes downhill to the boardwalk, disregarding someone calling my name.

*Flavor of the month.*

I should've wrapped her blond hair around my fist and dunked her into that fancy stone toilet bowl in Archer's bathroom.

I can't get the bath towel out of my mind. I am jealous, no denying it. No girl would walk around a guy's house naked if she didn't think she had a chance with him.

*I'm in the middle of something. I'll call you back.*

I reach the beach in no time and start pulling off my tank as I walk, stumbling on the sand. My shorts come off next. I hear the muffled sound of the heavy footsteps behind me but don't care that Slate will see me in my underwear and bra.

The ocean is dark and uneasy, but I need to transfer my anger into it.

The sound of an ATV approaching with a spotlight doesn't stop me.

"Miss! It's too dangerous to go in," a guard shouts.

He exchanges words with Slate, but I ignore them,

walking up to the water. It's warm, splashing wildly at my feet—the ocean is stormy.

"Miss! The rip current is too strong!" the guard shouts again.

I raise my middle finger in the air as I walk along the yellow light from the ATV on the black water and dive in, cutting the wave.

The warm wet darkness envelopes me. I reemerge and start swimming in slow powerful strokes.

I need to stop thinking. Thinking so much it spins my brain and makes me reckless at the thought of another girl at Archer's villa. But that was the promise I gave him— being patient. So I blow off steam here, trying to focus on the water and the waves that splash into my face, but unable to think of anything but him. Always *him*.

I don't look back to see if the guard left. I keep swimming, mindlessly swinging my arms, cutting another wave, and gliding underwater when I feel I'm losing my breath.

I slow and still for a moment, but the water keeps carrying me.

Shit.

I turn and start swimming back toward the shore, but the tide pulls me in a different direction.

My limbs are tense with burning pain at the effort to swim.

*Relax*, I tell myself and lean back, trying to stay on my back above the water, letting the tide take me far away from the shore.

My heart is racing but I try to make as little movement as possible.

I'm so good about gauging danger, just not when I'm distracted by anger.

A nasty feeling grows inside me. The realization that hits me is heavier than the pull of the powerful mass of water.

I swam right into the rip current.

## 37

## ARCHER

ANNA REICH.

The name lights up on my phone, but I don't pick up.

Strange how people who once were important in your life don't mean anything anymore. I don't feel the slightest excitement about seeing my ex. I know why she's here. She wants a piece of the action, now that my fortune tripled after my dad's death. What girl doesn't dream of marrying a billionaire?

Fuck her.

I need to talk to Kat before she gets the wrong idea. Kat's mind is like hydrogen near a lit match.

My phone flashes with Slate's name—he only calls me in emergency scenarios.

"Yes," I say calmly.

"Mr. Crone. It's about Miss Ortiz."

I frown. "Yes?" She probably ran away from him.

"Sorry, sir. She went swimming, despite one of the guards trying to stop her."

Swimming? In this weather? "And?"

"She didn't come back."

Dread washes over me with such force that my fingers gripping the phone turn white. In a second, I'm on my feet and rushing through the door. "Where?"

"Main beach. Pier 12 mark."

"Turn on the shore spotlights!" I snap as I run to my bike. "Emergency sirens on! Guards on jets in the water. Now! Every person available! Have a Waverunner ready for me!"

The memory of my mom and Adam never coming back from a car ride flash like a giant warning sign in my mind as I jump on the Streetfighter and fire up the engine.

*Fucking Kat! Hold on, baby!*

That's when the emergency alert for her vitals goes off on my phone. Her heart rate is 170. Fuck!

I reach the boardwalk in less than a minute, drop the bike, and run across the beach.

I dial Bishop. *Pick up! Pick up!* He's lived on this island for years and knows it by heart. Plus, he's a surfer.

The sound of the beach sirens is so abrupt and loud that it feels like the end of the world. The spotlights come on like an explosion of light and start sweeping over the coastal area, revealing a dozen guards, some of them darting across the beach toward the piers, others firing up jet skis and Waverunners.

I run up to one of the guards who already has one ready for me.

Bishop finally picks up. "Hey, Archer."

"Bishop! I need info! The tide on the west side of Zion,

what is it? Direction of the rip current. Distance from the shore. Fast!"

You can tell Bishop has military training because there are no unnecessary questions as he spits out the info, and without saying goodbye, I hang up and jump on the jet ski.

The siren goes quiet after the emergency announcement. Spotlights shine on the water, illuminating the wild waves that crash at the shore from the darkness. A dozen jet skis and Waverunners cut the breaks, mine among them.

Someone shouts at me from the pier, "We didn't locate her yet, sir," the voice muffled by the deafening sound of the ocean.

"How long ago did she go in?" The water splashes my shoes as I struggle to veer against the crashing waves.

"Twenty minutes or so!"

"Call the patrol along the shore half a mile north!" I yell. "Tell them to search the beach in the direction of Ayana!"

I rev up the motor, cranking it to the max, and start cutting the waves heading north.

"Kat!" I roar, though I know it's useless. Even if she's floating above the water, we won't hear her from afar.

My heart beats like a thousand drums. My mind is reeling. My eyes squint against the splashing water and the bright glow of the waves under the strobe lights from the security towers as I crash through a wave after wave after wave.

*Dammit, Kat!*

She's a wild one. She's fucking thunder. She's the storm that doesn't give a shit about others when it sends bolts of fury. She laughs in the face of danger, and right now, I can't fucking stand it. I used to be careless. I gave it up for the protection of this island. That's what I see in Kat—she is a brighter version of myself before the Change.

And that's the problem. Fearlessness can be destructive.

"Kaaaat!" I roar, my heart pounding so fast that I am afraid I will have a heart attack.

I keep going north, in the direction of the rip current like Bishop said. By now, she could be as far as a hundred yards away. Rip currents won't pull you under but can exhaust you, and if she pulls out of it, she might be swept under by the waves.

Other guards on jet skis are spread out through the waters along the beach, but I'm the farthest one north of the pier marker where she went in.

The farther from the beach I go, the darker it gets. I stop the jet ski, silence it, and listen as I bob on the water, the waves loud and high.

"Kaaaat!" I roar, ripping my vocal cords.

I can only see twenty or so feet ahead. I turn on the motor, spin the jet ski around to search the radius, then fire up north for another twenty yards or so, cut the engine, and shout Kat's name again.

Dante wrote about the nine circles of hell.

I'd say, there are only two.

The first one is the dark moments in your own life. It's your personal hell, inverted, consuming you with self-pity or self-loathing, leaving you empty. Whatever it is, it's you against the world.

The second and much worse one is when you realize you've lost a loved one. It's a different type of horror. Being in a world that's empty of your loved ones is unbearable. You lose direction. It's not you against the world—the world simply doesn't make sense anymore. I felt it after I lost Mom and Adam.

And as I repeat the cycle over and over again—ride, search, stop, shout Kat's name, listen, closing my eyes so I can hear better for any minuscule signs of life in the vast roaring ocean—I feel like I'm in the second circle of hell again.

Despair rips my vocal cords as I shout Kat's name and slam the handlebar in frustration when I hear a voice.

Hers.

Meek and coming from only twenty or so feet away.

"Kaaaat!" I roar, then listen, latching on to the sound.

I idle the jet ski in that direction, then wiggle it to illuminate the dark surface of the ocean.

And then I see her.

"Kat! Hold on!" I shout as I see an arm shoot up above the surface.

I idle closer, then kill the motor, catch her hands, and pull her up. She fumbles, water dripping everywhere, as I set her in front of me.

She's in her underwear and bra, panting, wiping her face with her palms as we rock on the waves.

"Wild girl," I murmur in relief, trying to press her toward me but she pushes me away.

"I'm fine," she blurts, then smoothes her hair. Her beautiful body is hunched and suddenly seems so weak that it breaks my heart.

"Come here," I say, pulling her toward me, but she pushes me away again.

"I'm fine."

God dammit!

I almost lost her. Almost lost my mind. I want to cradle her in my arms, but she's in her feisty mood.

I wipe the salt water from my face.

She's a hundred yards away from the fucking shore in the worst possible weather. Any other time, I would've yelled at her. But that's not how I feel right now.

Anger and frustration slowly pull back, giving way to a different feeling—gratitude. For her being alive. For the relief that her snappy remarks bring because she's okay. If Kat's snappy, she's fine. The day Mom and Adam didn't come back flickers in my mind again, and my heart squeezes so tightly I can barely breathe at the sight of her.

Without another word, I find a flare in the storage compartment and shoot it in the air, the night sky above us lighting up red, then shed my shirt and help Kat put it on.

"Get behind me," I order, and she obeys, not looking at me.

Slowly, I ride up closer to the shore and toward Ayana.

Jet skis fly toward us. Slate is one of the first ones, and he radios the news, the speaker at the watch tower announcing the end of the search.

I motion toward my yacht. "Go ahead to the *Empress* and make sure it's open," I order Slate, then pull Kat's hands and wrap them around me, melting at the feeling of her instantly sagging against me from behind.

"Hold on tightly, Kat. And, please, don't argue."

## 38

## ARCHER

I TURN ON THE LIGHTS IN THE MAIN LOUNGE OF THE YACHT and sit Kat down on the couch.

She awkwardly looks around, and though I'd rather be in my villa, my yacht is a better idea—she can't run from this place and no one can walk in and interrupt us.

I bring a towel and hand it to Kat, then get down on my knees in front of her and sit back on my heels.

Kat is quite a sight in her black lace panties and bra, her hair smoothed into a long tail that she squeezes with a towel, her movements edgy but slow. I should be jealous that Slate saw her dressed like this, but I only feel relief that she's safe.

Coughing now and then, sniffling, her shoulders hunched, she still looks gorgeous. How is that even possible?

With a smile, I wipe a drop of water from her chin. "You are crazy, wild thing."

"You are a liar," she bites back.

*Ouch.*

"I don't like that word."

I reach out to stroke her face to calm her, but she slaps my hand away.

"Fuck off," she snaps quietly.

"No, thank you." I cock my head at her—she's angry about something. "Now explain what happened, because something obviously did."

She purses her lips angrily.

"Come on," I insist.

"You know,"—her eyes are etched with bitterness when she looks at me and smirks—"the level of radiation in our blood, the children, the future generations—we are all fucked. Not this island. Noooooo." She makes a theatrical frowning face. "But the ones on the mainland are. Our genes are fucked. We develop cancer and die."

What's this about? "No one is gonna die here, Kat. We have medicine. The children are gonna be fine."

"Yeah. The rich ones." She snorts and looks away.

"Kat, stop," I say slightly irritated with her weaseling around. "We have the formula. The world is gonna be fine. It's not about the world right now. What's up? Tell me."

She casts her eyes down at the towel in her hands. "You are always fine, Archer. Aren't you?"

I don't like this. I take her hands in mine. "Kat, don't dance around. We've been here before. You are angry and want to say hurtful things. Before you do and feel bad about it later, tell me *why*. What's up?"

She bites her lip. "Are you sleeping with her?"

*What?*

She raises her gaze. "Are you fucking Anna?"

I tilt my head back and close my eyes, blowing air through my puffed lips.

Unbelievable.

A year or so ago, I would've had a different reaction. I would've probably been fucking Anna if she came to Zion, yeah. But a year ago seems like a different life.

I open my eyes to meet Kat's expectant gaze. "Why would you ask that?"

"It's a yes-or-no question, Archer."

"No." I shake my head. "Why would you ask me that?"

"But I'm not like her."

"Thank God!"

"But… You'd take her back if she asked?"

"What?" My eyes almost fall out of my sockets. "I haven't seen her in two years, and I have no desire to. But that's the wrong question. You are the only person who—"

My phone vibrates in my pocket. I pull it out—yeah, what do you know—Anna Reich.

I wouldn't have picked up any other time. But guess what? Something isn't right.

"Long time no see," I say into the phone.

Kat cuts me a glare and tries to get up, but I push her down and keep my hand on her thigh, stroking it, then put Anna on speaker.

"Archie!" Anna squeals too enthusiastically. I've forgotten how irritating her voice can be. "Where are you, sweets? Are you avoiding me?"

"Sweets," Kat murmurs with an intentionally crooked smile.

"Yes," I answer. "If you didn't get the clue yet."

Kat sucks in her cheeks and casts her eyes down. I like her jealousy, just not when she rushes to her death because of it.

"What are you doing on Zion, doll face?" I coo, imitating Anna.

Kat mimics, "Doll face."

Cute. I purse my lips, trying not to grin.

"Where are you, Archie? I've been looking forward to seeing you."

"You didn't come to my father's funeral. So, that's hard to believe."

"I was—Oh, Archie! Tsk, you know how it is. I flew in to surprise you. How about a little reunion?"

"I am with my girlfriend. What's up, Anna? We can chat tomorrow, though you could've told me everything over the phone and not bothered coming to Zion."

"Girlfriend? Oh, my." She's overdoing it now. I'm sure Margot had a chat with her and poured all her poison into the info.

Kat tenses up and lifts her chin at the words. I take in her arched eyebrows, beautiful lips, curled in a smirk she can't hide, the dangerous twinkle in her eyes—she's really fucking cute when she's jealous.

And I'm really annoyed that Anna is taking up too much of my time from Kat. "I'm sure you know I have a girlfriend. Though the fact that you came anyway means someone didn't give you the news the right way." Fucking Margot.

"Your girlfriend was looking for you."

"Where?"

"At Cliff Villa."

There it is.

I look up at Kat, who rolls her eyes.

"What are you doing at my villa, doll face?" I say with as much sweet poison in my voice as Anna's. I should've known she'd try something like this.

"I'm staying here, no? I thought we'd have a good time. Remember the good old times?"

Now I get it—Kat met Anna Reich.

It makes me angry that Anna got to meet her before I could warn Kat. And angry that Anna assumes she has any tie with me still, in fact, fucking furious that she's playing games with Kat.

"Did you get a lobotomy, doll face?"

"What?"

"Listen to me." I take a second to curb my momentary anger. "You have no business in my life. Not personal, not work. Im not sure what you were looking for when you flew here. Wanna have fun—go for it. Go hang out with the others, have a little vacation. You can stay with Margot or get your own suite, but I need you to leave my villa right away. My girlfriend will be back soon, and she's feisty."

I smile when Kat shows me the middle finger, chased by a glare. I show her two fingers and wiggle them, chasing it with a wink.

"She's really possessive," I carry on, my eyes locked with Kat. "Mad about me. Knows martial arts. I'm not sure how you are still in one piece after running into her at my villa. Kinda a miracle, really."

Kat's stare is murderous, and my smile turns into a grin.

"Honestly, I'm glad you are fine," I keep going, hearing Anna's huffing on the other end. She doesn't take rejection well. "Because my lovely girlfriend, well, she is too into me. She doesn't let women close. So if she didn't smash your face into that coffee table, you are lucky. God, Anna." I exhale heavily, dramatizing. "You really *are* lucky. Kat has this violent streak." Kat hisses something at me and tries to get up, but I only grin and hold her down. "You didn't touch the coffee table, by the way, did you? It's her favorite. She goes nuts if anyone so much as sets a finger on it."

"I am sitting by it as we speak," Anna says bitterly. "I just set my drink on it. Oopsie!" I would've killed her myself right now. "Is that a problem?"

"Well…" I pause for emphasis, locking my eyes with Kat again. "My girlfriend likes to fuck on it. As well as on that couch you are sitting on. Ssssso…"

I hear the sudden movement—Anna jumping off that couch like it's hot. Kat sucks in her cheeks, hiding a smile.

"So, doll face, do yourself a favor and get out of my place, like, now. You don't want Katura Ortiz coming back. It won't end well. Security won't help you—she's friends with all of them. *I* won't help you." I pause and grin at Kat, who's still trying to hold back a smile. "After being at my villa, you see her anywhere at Ayana—run. My girl is a loose cannon."

Without waiting for a reply, I hang up and dial Slate.

"Slate, do me a favor. Anna Reich, remember her? Yeah, she's at my villa, obviously lost. I need you to go there and make sure she vacates it as soon as possible. If she refuses, you can drag her out of there. You have my permission. She's trespassing."

I toss the phone onto the couch and gaze at Kat.

"Hide your claws, wild thing."

She casts her gaze down.

The yacht living room is quiet. The sound of the splashing waves seeps through the open terrace doors as I study Kat.

"Did she insinuate something?" I ask. "Because I haven't seen her yet. And to be honest, I couldn't care less. I won't. So, spill."

Kat's expression softens, a cute pout on her lips that I want to kiss and lick until she purrs in satisfaction. She has no idea what she's in for once we sort this out.

She still doesn't look at me. "What am I supposed to think when I walk into my boyfriend's villa and his ex walks out wrapped only in a towel?"

I cock an eyebrow. Anna has balls. Desperate, for sure. She came with a plan. "And?"

Kat's eyes snap up at me. "And what?"

"What happened? What did she say?"

"Nothing really. Not like I want to talk to your fuck girls."

I hold back a chuckle. "Wow. Since when do I have fuck girls?" I can't help teasing her. "So you got jealous, huh? Really-really jealous?"

I smile as I reach to stroke her face, and this time, she lets me. My kitten got mad about another woman, and it's fucking hot. I like seeing her so possessive.

"And you almost drowned because you got jealous," I

say softly.

She holds my gaze for the longest time then blurts out a quiet, "Maybe."

"Maybe," I echo, feeling so fucking in love that it rips me apart. "You are in my head, Kat. I can't think of anyone else. Since I met you, I can't even fathom having any other girl next to me except you. And you still think that I would do something like this to you?"

She casts her eyes down at her hands, and I take her chin between my fingers to make her look at me.

"You need to know that there's only one woman in my life. That's you. Everyone else is off-limits. That goes the other way around." I raise my eyebrows. "Got it?"

She nods.

"I need you to know that you are more important to me than any other person on this island, Kat. I'd never jeopardize what we have."

She nods, her expression finally softening. I can't stay away from her anymore, so I lean in and kiss her softly on the lips, no tongue.

"But here's the thing, Kat. We had an agreement, yeah? You get angry—you come to me."

"I called you. You were busy." She sounds guilty.

"And you got impatient. And broke the rules. And put security in emergency mode. And scared a lot of people. Most of all, me."

She bites her lip. "You want me to apologize?"

"No. If anything ever happens to you, I'll send the entire army of mercenaries to your rescue. But—"

She peeks at me from under her eyebrows. "But?"

"I need to blow off steam. And tonight, I'm gonna do it my way."

I let the words hang in the air between us as I get up and walk to the doors to close them, then turn on the music, walk back, and hold out my hand. "Come with me."

Kat takes it and follows me to the master bathroom. It's a giant space with a shower stall, several sinks, a bidé, and a big tub up the steps in the corner.

Kat tries to look angry but I see her glancing around in curiosity.

"We're not going anywhere tonight," I say as I turn on the shower and wait for the water to get just the right temperature. "We are spending as much time on this yacht as needed to figure out what you and I need to figure out."

I turn to meet her defiant gaze.

"You have nowhere to run, wild thing. Tonight, you're all mine. And you'll take everything I give you. Understood?" I take a step closer, my body already tingling with anticipation. "Let's get you naked first."

## 39

---

## KAT

I could've drowned, but that's the trick with rip currents—you have to let go and stop resisting, and eventually, if you still have strength when it kicks you out into the open sea, you swim back to shore.

The rip current that I really need to avoid but it's too late now is Archer.

I feel fine. I got a little scared. What I have a problem with is holding back my feelings.

Archer gently unclasps my bra and pulls it off, then goes down on his knees and pulls down my panties. The gesture is so innocent, yet I feel like he's readying me for some ritual. He wants to fuck? I'm in. I need to recharge.

He strips and leads me to the shower by my hand.

The warm water feels nice after being stranded in the colder salt water of the current. But instead of getting it on, Archer turns me around, my back toward him, and under the warm shower stream, starts unbraiding my hair.

I close my eyes and smile. He's gotten to like it—letting my hair loose. My whole body tingles at the sensation of him tugging at my braids and raking his fingers through my wet hair. And then he starts massaging my scalp. The fruity scent spreads in the shower as I realize he is shampooing my hair.

My body tenses at the sensation. What guy *does* that?

"Feels good, kitten?" he murmurs.

"Yes," I say, feeling awkward letting him do that but melting at his touch.

"I need to clean you up and make you relax."

My body gets heavy with want at the words. He lathers the shampoo into my hair, then runs his hands along the thick mass of it down my back, then his foamy hands slide up along my shoulders and turn me around.

This guys—his dark eyes and wet hair falling into his face, making him look messy and hot and sexy as the water shoots off his shoulders and droplets of it cascade down his body—never ceases to amaze me.

I look down and see his erection. My beautiful guy is hard, which makes me smile with satisfaction. He's always hard. Hard to read. Hard to resist. Hard overall.

I spasm in my lower belly at the sight, wrap my hand around his erection, and start stroking it.

"Slow down," he orders softly as he runs his hands down my arms, tracing their movement with his eyes.

I keep stroking him, then slide my hand lower to cup his balls. His lips tighten, and I squeeze his balls harder, massaging them.

He brings his soaped hands to my breasts and strokes them in soft circular motions. My nipples harden under his touch. I arch into his hands and start stroking him faster.

"Slow down," he repeats, not looking at me but studying my breasts, his gentle touch so erotic that I want to whimper with the need to have him inside me. The erection that I so patiently work on needs to be closer to where I throb with need.

"Kitten." He looks sharply at me as he runs his hands along my waist. "Slow. Down," he breathes out quietly but with warning, a tiny smile on his lips.

He doesn't want to come? Fine.

His hands slide along my hips, and one makes its way between my legs and rubs my pussy.

I push myself into it. If it's a slow game of seduction, I'm in, as long as he delivers at the end. But it's hard to keep the slow pace when he's naked and so close.

Archer lets go, takes me by my shoulders, and gently tilts my head under the stream, washing off the shampoo, my body heavy from his soothing touch. When we're finished, he leads me out and starts drying me with a towel.

"How are you feeling?" he asks.

"Fine."

"I'm serious, Kat."

"Well, now that you are serious, I think I feel great, actually."

"Hungry?"

"Seriously?"

I stare at him as he gets on his knees and wipes my legs.

This is the sexiest thing I've seen. His face is on the level with my bare pussy, and his expression is too indifferent when he dries my legs, then slides the towel up to my junction.

"I will be hungry if we play around," I tease him.

I'm wet. Really freaking wet.

A smile tugs at his lips as he gets up and rubs the towel between my legs as he stares at me.

"That towel won't help," I breathe out, wanting to jump him.

"Just want to make sure you are—"

"Fuckable?"

He cocks a brow. "What I have in mind will take a lot of energy."

"If you don't fuck me right now, I'll choke you out, and you'll wake up with your cock in my pussy. Does that sound like a lack of energy?"

"Tempting. But save that script for another time."

He wraps the towel around me, letting me hold it, then warps one around his waist and leads me out and into the open-concept kitchen in the main lounge.

He takes his time making hot tea for me, throwing mysterious glances at me now and then as he searches the cupboards for a cup and sugar.

I sit at the kitchen island and brood. Any other time, we would've been all over each other by now, in fact, on the second round already. Maybe, he's punishing me.

Archer doesn't say much as he brings a cup of hot tea to me, sits down, and watches me drink it, studying me like he's trying to figure something out.

I do feel much better after drinking it. My hair is drying, turning into a curly mess. There's no arrogance in Archer's gaze, but there is want and something else that I can't figure out. Caution? What exactly does he want?

"I want you to let go tonight. With me. All the way," he says quietly.

*All the way* confuses me.

"I need you to forget that you constantly have to be in charge and aware of what you're doing."

My brain screams to resist because he shouldn't get what he wants as a way of punishing me. But my pussy whispers, "Why not?" And that's it, I'm dizzy with curiosity. He wants to do the upside-down thing? I'm in. *Whatever you want.* Sure.

He shifts, trying to read me—I know him so well.

"Let me fuck you the way I've wanted for the longest time," he says so calmly that it scares me just a little bit. "You can't handle it—you let me know. You tell me to stop, we stop. Trust is important."

"And you know what it is?"

"If you want, you'll have your turn with me whenever you wish. Tonight is my night."

*His* night—I still try to figure out what it means. We've never appropriated our time together before.

"If it's your pride talking," he continues, "don't let it pull the breaks. Let yourself go for once. Deal?"

His voice is so soft and without a hint of pressure that I hear myself say, "Deal."

He rises from the table. "Then lose the towel, wild thing. Bare yourself and come with me."

I halt for a moment, wondering if he might have some psycho plans for me. He notices.

"You are too afraid to let go, Kat. Like it will diminish you in some way—"

"Stop talking," I whisper, drop the towel, and take a step toward him.

## 40

### ARCHER

I LEAD KAT TO THE MASTER BEDROOM AND THE GIANT RED bean bag, in stark contrast with the beige-white interior. I've always hated this thing, but the color seems appropriate now, and I can't think of a more handy thing for what I'm planning.

"It's called a love sack," I say. "I like both words. And I'd love the sight of you on it."

Kat stands in front of me naked, her gaze slightly hesitant though she tries to project confidence by arching her brow.

I go around her slowly, place my hands on her waist, and kiss her shoulder. "I want you to bend over its back part, knees on the seat."

She's beautiful, her hair full of heavy and messy curls— Kat unwound. I think that's my favorite look on her.

I give her a gentle nudge, and she kneels on the seat and leans with her forearms on its back.

She turns to look at me, her dark eyes glistening in the

lamplight, the view so perfect I want this picture—her leaning on the bean bag, her ass sticking out at me as she's finally submitting to me.

The view is enough to make my dick harden under my towel, and I drop it. Kat's eyes drop to check me out, and I slowly stroke myself. The knowledge that she finally trusts me and is willing to do what I ask burns me with anticipation.

I walk toward the nightstand and retrieve some silk lace from the drawer. My yacht is full of sex toys that I've never used and won't. They've made rounds during the hard parties a long time ago. But the lace has never been used.

"Hands together behind you," I say and wrap the silk around Kat's wrists, tying her hands. "Up and over," I instruct her, and she obeys. "More," I say and cup her pussy from behind, nudging her, smiling at the feel of her slickness against my palm—my kitten is already wet.

I nudge her until she's hanging over the bean bag, knees off the seat, her head the perfect distance from the floor.

"Perfect," I say, giving her ass cheeks a stroke, her skin breaking out in goosebumps right away.

"Are we doing some crazy S&M thing?" she asks timidly.

"Not at all." I walk around the bean bag to stand in front of her, her face level with my cock. "We are just doing things my way, kitten."

I lower myself to my knees and push her unruly hair out of her face.

Her eyes are blazing. There's doubt in them, then a flicker of humor as I pull her hair back and to one side, letting it hang loose. There's mistrust in them, too, as I kiss her softly on the lips, giving her just enough tongue to tease her.

"I'm not as crazy as you think," I say, rising to my feet, and take my hard cock in my hand. "I just want to order you around, kitten. And I want you to enjoy it."

I stroke myself leisurely. Kat's gaze flickers between my erection and my eyes, then back to my cock. The sight of her restrained and willing to go with whatever I choose is exhilarating. I can't spend another minute without being inside her, and oh, there are a few options tonight.

I hold my dick in my hand as I step close to her. "Lick," I order softly.

She takes an exquisite taste of me, running her tongue from where my fist holds my cock up to the tip. When she's not in a hurry, she's delicious in the way she works and takes me in. I don't want a simple BJ. Now that I know what she's like, I want her to make love to my cock like she did that one time at my crib. Her full lips glide deliciously along my shaft, then the tip, licking off pre-cum, then back down. I cup my balls and push them toward her. She licks, and licks, sucking on the sensitive loose skin right under the shaft, making me growl.

"Just like that, kitten. Perfect," I encourage her, manipulating my cock and giving her the parts I want her to work on.

Maybe all the other girls were doing it wrong all along. Kat is curious about sex in the best way. Usually, in charge or feisty, just not tonight.

Right now, her tongue explores the texture of my cock,

licks every inch of it, sucks on the tip, and darts into the slit, making my knees weak at the sensation.

I wish I could have her hands on it, or cupping my balls, or sliding up and down my thighs. But this is perfect, making me tense and ready. Her eyes flicker up at me, the compliance in them sending me over the edge.

Kat stops licking and puckers her beautiful lips just lightly, planting little kisses on my length.

Holy hell, could anything be more erotic?

She looks up to meet my gaze and takes the tip between her lips, sucks it gently, then kisses it, then licks the rim.

I stare wide-eyed. I've had more blowjobs in my life than I can count—basic, elaborate, professional, lousy, fantastic quickies. I've had it all. Or so I thought. But this—her—is a new level of artistry.

Her tongue places little licks along my hard length, and I move my cock around to guide her.

"Open your mouth, stick your tongue out."

She obeys, and I rub the tip of my cock on her tongue, enjoying the sight of her at my full command.

"Suck," I say, stroking her cheek, and her mouth wraps around my cockhead. "Fuck, kitten," I grunt, knowing that I won't last as long as I want to. The first time, that is.

I let her suck me off for some time, then pull out and gently rub my cock on her lips before I feed it to her again.

"You are so fucking good," I exhale, my balls heavy, my cock throbbing for release as I thrust deeper into her mouth.

"I'm gonna fuck your mouth now, kitten. Relax, okay?"

I let go of my cock and thrust slowly first as I push her hair off her face and gather it at the back of her head, tightening my grip. I push harder in her mouth, faster, holding her head in place. She makes little noises, choking slightly.

"Relax," I whisper as I pick up the pace.

Her mouth is my prisoner, and so is the rest of her tonight. I've wanted this for the longest time. And the view is electrifying—Kat's hands tied behind her back and her mouth full of my cock as I fuck away.

My knees bend as I try to accommodate myself inside her, getting deeper but making sure she is not too uncomfortable.

My hips snap forward.

My fingers anchor in her hair, the thick curls I want to braid and unbraid and play with endlessly.

I fuck her mouth with absolutely zero finesse.

"Ssso good," I murmur, picking up speed. "Take it all, kitten," I whisper, stuffing myself inside her.

I come with a growl, blowing into her so powerfully that my weakened legs shake.

"Fuck," I hiss, easing myself out of her mouth. I let go of her hair, letting it spill down the sides of her face, then take my cock in my hand. "Lick it clean, kitten." She does. "More."

Her licking calms my cock. It's getting the loving it's been wanting. And I get what I want—her, following every whim of mine.

Satisfied, I go down to my knees, palm her face, and kiss her.

She tastes like me, her tongue slow and weak after I've worked her.

"You alright?" I ask.

She licks her lips, her eyes watery. "Yeah."

"I was right again," I murmur into her mouth, planting little kisses on it.

"About?"

"Your mouth is beautiful."

"I know."

"Full of my cock."

Kat always tries to dominate. She's always aware of what's happening and what I'm doing to her, even when she's high on orgasm. But I want to see her disarmed and beautiful in that pure feminine way.

"Let's take care of you, wild thing."

I go behind her and take a moment to enjoy the view of her bare butt. I give it a stroke with my fingers, her body twitching at the touch as she can't see what I'm doing. I go down on my knees behind her, the bean bag sinking under my weight. Who would've known that a giant bean bag is the best sex prop?

Bracing my hands on each side of Kat's body, I lean over and flick my tongue between her legs, giving her pussy a tiny lick.

She gasps.

"You like that?"

Of course, she likes that. I repeat the motion. Then again.

She's slick with juices that drip down her thighs—my wild thing got all turned on from being fucked in her mouth. Good.

I push her thighs apart. "Open your legs for me, kitten. More. Like that. Perfect."

Her toes barely touch the seat, her butt is so high up that her pussy looks like an exotic flower, and I'm about to eat the fuck out of it.

I tease her pussy lips apart with my fingers and let my tongue do the work.

We've done this before, but it's peculiar how sex acquires a different energy when it's laced with feelings.

I'm not playing with her tonight. There's nothing to prove to each other. I don't want to trick her or tease her. I want her to lose herself as I fuck her. I want her helpless with need and desperate for my attention. I want to drive her over the edge so hard that she learns to let go every time in the future.

I lick her thoroughly, working her sex, rubbing my tongue on her swollen clit, once in a while doing a long swipe from front to back all the way up to her tailbone.

Kat makes an inarticulate sound, a mewl that turns into a sexy sob. She's so responsive that it's not a job to lick her pussy but a pleasure, her sexual need and eager response edging me, making my dick swell again.

"Faster," she exhales.

There she is, ordering. Right now, I listen. The louder her moans get, the more desperate I get with the need to have my dick inside her again.

She cries out when she comes, so needy, so beautiful, her pussy dripping on my tongue as she pushes it in my face.

"Round two will be a duet," I inform her with a smile, pushing to my feet.

I lean with my knees onto the bean bag, pull her a little lower down, and bring my cock to her entrance. She's still lost in her orgasm, but I don't give her time to recover when I drive hard inside her.

She cries out.

"Right there," I grunt in relief as I thrust inside her again and right away set the tempo.

ARCHER THRUSTS IN AND OUT OF ME WITH LONG, DRAWN-OUT, rhythmical strokes.

My pussy is on fire. He didn't give me a break, going from fucking my mouth, then licking me meticulously, tastefully, like he was doing it for him, not for me. And while I was still high on orgasm, he entered me with one hard thrust, making my toes curl in pleasure.

"Right there," he exhales as he pumps into me.

My shoulders are getting slightly stiff from the position I'm in, but my head hangs low, and it's making me dizzy and even more disoriented as I swim in the sensations.

My butt is up in the air like I'm an offering. I'm so wet, drenched, in fact, that Archer is moving effortlessly inside me. My orgasm subsides, but his hardness inside me starts another wave of pleasure.

Just then, his hands spread my butt cheeks, and his finger swipes the moisture to my back entrance and starts massaging it.

I've always been afraid to let go with men. With Archer, even more so. Mistrust, pride—yeah, I know my faults, they all play a role. Archer and I have taken a big step ahead, but there's always caution. We fuck wildly, but it's a power game, always is.

But something is missing in his gaze tonight. There's no cockiness. Since our love language is sex, he's using it to make me let go.

I want to wiggle away from his finger. It's somewhere it's not supposed to touch. I want to tell him to stop, but it feels surprisingly good, too good. My pride is hissing at me in warning, but his finger sends a jolt of pleasure as it presses harder, sinking deeper into me, making every thought in my head dissipate.

His cock stimulates my pussy, and his finger stimulates something that shouldn't even be an option, yet starts triggering another wave of pleasure.

I moan so loudly that I should be ashamed but am not.

"You like that?" His voice is teasing yet warm.

"Yes," I whisper and nudge my butt up against his finger. "Fuck." A sob escapes me, and my eyes roll to the back of my head.

"That's right, kitten." His voice is muffled as all I sense is his cock filling me up and his finger on that untapped pleasure button.

The man is a pro at everything. He was right. He reads my body like a freaking book. His finger on my back entrance pushes just a tiny bit more inside, the feeling odd but the pleasure from it overriding anything else I've ever felt in sex.

"Archer," I almost sob, losing my mind.

"Yes, kitten." He thrusts and thrusts and rubs me, his hands palming and spreading my cheeks, making me feel so good I want to whimper. And I do, melting into the bean bag, a boneless mass that wants to be fucked and used.

I cry out when the orgasm sweeps through me like an explosion, making every part of me tense, melting every cell in my body.

I don't want him to stop. I just want him to fuck me endlessly. But he pulls out gently, unties my hands, and helps me up.

"Come here."

I've never heard him talk so gently during sex. He was supposed to take, yet this feels like he intends on giving me every shade of pleasure there is.

I stumble off the bean bag, dizzy and disoriented. Archer chuckles and holds me by my waist to steady me, then picks me up in his arms and carries me to bed.

My body is happy and lax. I stretch on the bed, enjoying the feel of Archer's body when he gets on top of me, his hard cock rubbing against my thigh.

"You didn't come," I murmur in realization.

"No." There's that mischievous sparkle in his eyes as he pushes damp strands of my hair off my face. "Not yet, kitten." Oh! "We're finally coming up to the main course. I've wanted to have you that way for some time. And I want you to enjoy it."

Wait, what the hell is the main course?

"What way?" I frown, my brain too slow to dissect the words.

His hand gently strokes my thigh, then slides to the junction between my legs.

Again?

Until I realize it's slipping farther to where his fingers were just minutes ago, to my back entrance.

"This way, kitten," he whispers and, before I can object, kisses me.

His tongue slowly strokes into my mouth, making me dizzy again. His finger massages my back entrance and doesn't feel too intrusive anymore, now that I know how it can make me feel.

Yet, slight panic makes my heartbeat spike.

"Arch." I'm not sure about this.

"Kitten, I want you to try it. You might find out it's your favorite thing."

I bite my lip, but his gaze is slightly disappointed like I'm denying him something that should be shared.

"Will it hurt?" I ask with hesitation.

"It might. A little. If it's too much, we'll stop. I'll be very careful."

I nod. His soft kiss on my lips is reassurance. He gets up and walks to the bathroom and comes back with a little bottle.

"It's lube oil," he explains, noticing my eyes dart to the bottle.

"So you've used it?"

"Nope. This yacht has seen many things but not that."

He leans with one knee on the bed, his beautiful cock erect. How can you not love this body, taut muscles, and dark hair falling in messy strands onto his face? If I were a guy, I would've probably turned gay with him.

He pours some of the liquid in his hand and smears it over his cock, his eyes locking with mine.

I don't know why my heart is beating like I'm losing my virginity.

Oh, wait…

Suddenly, it clicks. I've never done it before, and Archer knows that. *That*'s his point. He wants something from me that no one else got.

That's the switch I need.

He's back on top of me and slides his cock against my slit, teasing me, as our eyes lock in the realization that he is my first, in this way. I'm not losing anything, I realize, I'm sharing myself with him. And my heart flutters in anticipation and nervousness when he presses his tip against my back entrance and pushes in gently, then stops.

"Kitten, relax," he whispers. His gaze fixed on my face evaluates my reaction. "Relax, baby."

*Oh, maaaan.*

That's the first time he's used that word. It catches me off guard, turns me on beyond belief, and when his fingers start gently stroking between my legs, I want him, his cock, inside me, any way he chooses.

I push against him, signaling for him to carry on, and he pushes in again.

"Don't be nervous. It'll feel good," he whispers.

This feels weird and hot and special because I have zero experience in this department. But all I want is to feel.

I lift my head to kiss Archer, welcoming all of him,

his mouth, his fingers, his cock stretching me, the burning increasing. He's thrusting inside me in tiny increments, and though it hurts a little, the sensation of him filling me up *there* slowly unwraps a different sense of pleasure in the place I never thought it could come from.

"That's it, kitten."

It feels good, surprisingly good. He feels gigantic, slowly and carefully thrusting in deeper.

"How are we doing? Good?"

His whisper drives me insane.

Then his fingers slide into my pussy.

"Ah!" I can't help my loud exhale. Him filling me up in two places creates an unusual pleasurable pressure that starts expanding like it's too big to stay inside me.

"You okay?" Archer murmurs.

His face is flushed. He might be more nervous than I am. Too careful. Too slow. But he keeps moving.

"Oh, fuck," I exhale again as he thrusts inside me. It's too good, and I want more of it, faster, harder.

"Too much?"

"No," I whimper.

He talks like he's giving, not taking, and it makes all the difference. This is a new level of intimacy.

"Feels good?"

"Yeah." I breathe out. "Yeah." I moan because it gets harder to hold that overwhelming pleasure inside. "Yeah…"

I'm trying to stay focused but I can't. All I do is feel.

"Close your eyes," he says, and I do and start free-falling into a pit of ecstasy. "Let me know if I need to slow down. Tell me what feels good."

His voice does. It's so soft and considerate and yet so fucking sexy like he knows he's getting me somewhere wonderful I've never been before.

"Faster," I whisper.

Archer increases his pace in both places. "Like that?"

My legs wrap around his back as I try to get more of him, greedy and needy.

He kisses me.

Fuuuuck.

It's a trinity.

Thrust. Thrust. Thrust.

His cock. His fingers. His tongue.

The thought that he's in three places at once dissipates just like his mouth that's not on me anymore, his whispers enveloping me, "There, kitten. You are doing so good."

Every inch of him penetrates me, opening me up and fanning the fire inside me.

I fall.

I fly.

I'm tense.

I'm falling apart.

I'm hard.

And I'm boneless.

I can't explain it—the heat spilling through my body, the giant wave of pleasure carrying me away as I cry out, again and again, as a full-body orgasm wracks my every cell.

I've never experienced an orgasm like this—endless, not subsiding but carrying on where I want to go harder and faster and let him rip me apart completely just to prolong this.

My brain is mushy, only registering a soft whisper in my ear, "Third time's a charm."

A soft chuckle.

A harder thrust.

"Just a little longer, kitten. Fuck..."

And then Archer grunts so loudly that it sounds almost animal-like as a hot sensation fills me from the inside.

I would've laughed if I wasn't on cloud nine or, to be more exact, somewhere over the moon. Spaced out. Floating. Lost. My body is weightless despite the slight soreness in that particular spot and then emptiness when Archer slides out of me and sags on top of me.

We are sweaty and breathing hard, wrapped around each other. I want to kiss him but can't find the energy to move. Instead, Archer bathes me with slow lazy kisses—on my neck, face, and shoulders, as if he's done something wrong and is apologizing.

And all I can do is lie there, reveling in his touch, feeling amazing and grateful. Is this heaven?

## 42

## KAT

I'M SPLAYED ON THE BED, STARING AT THE CEILING, reconsidering everything I know about sex so far.

I can barely move, let alone walk when Archer asks me something about the bath then pads away. The sound of rushing water comes from the bathroom. After a while, he comes back.

"Come here."

He leans on the bed, slides one arm under my thighs, another under my back, and picks me up like he has all the energy in the world while I just tilt my head onto his shoulder.

The giant tub in the bathroom looks like an ice cream with a big foamy peak over it.

"You need to rest," he says and takes the two steps up to the tub, then lowers us both into the water, which is not too hot, just perfect. Everything is perfect. This guy is a dream, and I might be the luckiest girl alive.

I gather my hair and tie it in a messy bun on top of my

head, my arms so heavy like every bone in my body was liquified.

Archer pulls me down into his arms, my back against his chest, and splashes warm water onto my arms as I tilt my head back to rest against his shoulder.

"It's so nice," I murmur.

For a while, it's just that—silence, hands caressing each other, my fingers feeling the texture of his knees, raised on each side of me. His hands trail to my breasts, caressing them and playing with my nipples, his fingertips making them hard and my skin tingle with want.

"You are getting me all worked up again," I say, too sleepy and lazy to react, though it's erotic as hell.

"I just like your breasts. I can lick these puppies until you come, you know."

A laugh escapes me. "I can't come from you just doing that." He doesn't respond, and it gets me all confused. Wait… "I mean…" I turn my head to meet his smiling eyes.

"Got you curious, kitten? Curiosity killed the cat."

"You mean, no tricks?"

"I didn't say no tricks. I said I can make you come by kissing your tits. Correction, I can do that with only my mouth touching you. How about that?"

"You can't."

"Wanna bet?"

"Not tonight?" I plead.

"No, kitten. You are tired."

"Yeah, I'm exhausted."

"I'm sorry, kitten. I didn't mean to be too rough."

Sorry?

I turn my head to meet his gaze again. "I liked it. A lot."
I love everything he does.

"What's a lot? On a scale from one to ten."

"Eleven," I blurt out.

Archer chuckles. "That's not how the scale works."

"See? So good, my brain can't count anymore."

He wraps his arms around me, and I study his eyes for a moment, his too-serious smile, his overly discerning gaze. I've finally gotten the biggest revelation about Archer—when he lets go, he can be a very gentle man. Whoa.

"What?" he asks softly, nuzzling me—the gesture so tender that it makes my heart flutter. Every day, he tops everything he's done before.

"What did you do to Archer Crone?"

He burst laughing, his chest shaking against my back. "Gave him a day off."

I smile. "Good. He was kind of an asshole at times."

Archer laughs again.

I did that—made him happy for a moment.

Gently, he pushes my head down, trying to playfully dunk me in the water, and I laugh, fighting him off, then catch his arms and hold them around me.

"I like when you laugh," I say quietly.

And just like that, we go still, wrapped in each other, in the silence that's slightly uncomfortable.

Because we rarely do this, feelings.

Because my heart beats loudly.

And because in a moment, I feel Archer's lips press into my hair, planting a little kiss on my temple.

I cover his hands with mine to tighten his embrace, my

heart tightening impossibly with it, my eyes blurry with tears.

"Love you," I breathe out barely audibly.

*Ahhh, damn.*

I hope he didn't hear.

My breath hitches, and my chest gets heavy with slow powerful thuds of my heart.

He was an assignment. A job. And an escape.

Now, I want to get lost with him. *In* him.

Because now, he's my world.

## 43

## ARCHER

IT'S BEEN ONLY FIVE OR SIX HOURS SINCE WE WENT TO BED, BUT it's dawn, and I lay in bed wide awake.

Kat is making this cute breathing sound. Her arm is over my chest, her leg over my hips, her thigh pressing against my erection. Nothing tops this, the feeling of her wrapped around me.

Since when has cuddling become better than sex?

Old age, that's what's up.

Last night was perfect. That moment in the tub when we held each other was the sweetest I've ever had with anyone.

*Sweet.*

Am I getting soft in the heart? Yeah. Fuck it. I'll be cheesy for her if it makes her happy.

She *was* happy. Her eyelids were drooping when I got her out of the tub, a vague smile on her face, her hair a beautiful mess with curls dropping onto her face. Can anyone be this fucking hot after almost drowning, then taking it in all her holes?

This woman—I swear—will outlive me. Especially if I keep fucking her like a maniac.

My wild thing was beautiful last night. Cum-buzzed and barely standing when I dried her off with a towel. She didn't say a word, only played with my hair when I did so, and buried her face in my chest when I carried her to bed.

"You need to sleep," I murmured, covering us with a sheet and hugging her tight against me, her leg immediately going over my hips like she wanted to lock me in place.

I closed my eyes and remembered the words that slipped out of her mouth.

Two little words, barely audible.

*Love you.*

Just a whisper, but that's all I needed to hear.

And now I am wide awake. It's dawn, but I won't be able to sleep anymore, those words still flickering in my head and making a home there.

Finally, I attempt to move away, but Kat murmurs something incoherent as she latches onto me tighter.

This—morning, silence, waves lapping at the hull, seagulls outside the window, this carelessness of existence—almost seems like before the Change. And she is the cause of it.

Carefully, I lift her arm off me.

"I'll be right back," I say softly and watch her, splayed face down on the bed, for another moment before I walk out.

The ocean is so calm that it's unbelievable that last night it was stormy and almost killed Kat. But that's my wild thing. She is the female Poseidon, creating all kinds of havoc.

The warm breeze feels good against my skin as I scan the ocean. There—the little ripples in the distance and the darker shapes popping here and there above the water—used to be my mom's favorite sight on vacation. Whales.

I hurry back to the bedroom. Kat is cocooned into the sheet, her face barely visible, her hair a giant mess splayed on the pillow.

"Kat." I shake her. She murmurs and shifts away, but I pull her toward me. "Kat, come on. Wanna show you something."

Her sleepy squinting eyes are almost murderous, the frown so cute that I laugh when she finally sits up on the bed like a ninja.

"It better be a miracle," she grunts as I help her off the bed and nudge her out the door.

And I follow.

My dick follows.

My body follows.

My mind.

I want all of her. And I want to show her the most precious moments that don't seem like much but have connections to my past. Right now, she's the only one I can share them with.

I've never been romantic, but fuck me if this doesn't feel perfect—Kat wrapped in my arms, her thick curls tickling my chest as we stand on the main deck of the yacht in the soft glow of the rising sun that's still behind Zion.

"There, see?" I show her a whale sliding out of the water. "Another one." I point in a different direction.

Kat is awake now. I tilt my head to have a better look at her expression. Her beautiful lips are parted in that precious look of wonder that I've gotten to know so well.

I pull the sheet from around her, then cover her front and press her closer to me, her bare back tight against my front.

"Enjoying the morning?" she murmurs, nudging her butt against my crotch. My dick can't handle her teasing very well and stirs in curiosity.

"Yeah," I exhale with a smile as I pull her hair back, baring her neck, and plant little kisses on her skin.

She's an eager, naughty thing. Her sexual energy matches mine. Her hand snakes behind her, between us, and palms my erection through the fabric of my boxers.

"Wanna go back to bed?" I whisper, licking her earlobe.

She drops the sheet and drags it behind her between her fingers as she sashays through the terrace doors and toward the bedroom, swinging her hips.

I don't hurry, enjoying the view of Kat's body in front of me.

She drops the sheet as she nears the bed, crawls on it on all fours, then leans onto her forearms, burying her face in the sheets.

Her ass sticks up in the air for me.

Fuck.

I kneel on the bed, take the offering in my hands, and slide my cock inside her.

"Kat…" I can't help but call out her name. "Fuck, kitten."

She feels so good, her morning pussy wet and hot for me.

"Breakfast," she murmurs.

I grin like a clown as I fuck her with no hurry.

"Breakfast is the most important meal of the day," I say.

It used to be whiskey, now it's Kat's pussy.

My habits have changed for the better.

And as I fuck her slowly, I wonder if I'll ever have enough. If I'll ever stop wanting her so much, even after I had it all.

## 44

---

## KAT

164 FEET. FIVE STATEROOMS. MAIN LEVEL FULL-BEAM MASTER —"That's where you lost your back-door virginity," Archer adds with a proud grin. A full bar. An extended beach club with a pool, a hot tub, and a bridge deck. Cream and beige interior with stainless steel. Birds-of-paradise themed art and authentic, white peacock freaking feathers. Conference room, too?

"You kidding me," I whisper and touch every surface Archer points to just to make sure it's real.

The yacht looked like an apartment last night. Now, it looks like a floating mansion.

Archer is giving me a tour. It's extraordinary. We go up to the top deck with *al fresco dining*—Jonshu would've choked from amusement at my extensive vocabulary—then take the stairs down to the lower level and the transom. Archer is telling me about the *Empress* like he's doing a sales pitch, a permanent half-smile on his face, his eyes studying me like he's trying to figure out which part of the description will finally give me an orgasm.

I'm sure none of his friends were impressed before. Those guys are born on yachts and in chateaus with platinum Amex's in their mouths.

Me, I'm easy to impress.

"So this is my little girl," Archer concludes the tour.

"Little girl? You serious?" I roll my eyes at him.

"Dad used to have one twice this size parked in Monaco."

In his boxers, barefoot, without having taken his usual shower first thing in the morning, Archer looks so homey that the sight warms my heart. Especially when he stands rubbing the insole of his one foot on the arch of the other, his hair full of cowlicks, so endearingly messy next to the slick *serpeggiante* freaking *marble*.

I'm in his buttoned-up white shirt I pulled from his closet, but I feel like royalty following him around. It's not the people that create a sense of class and division, but objects mostly. This is unnecessary yet mesmerizing and elegant luxury.

"Does this place come with any good food in stock?" I joke, famished by now.

Archer leads me to the kitchen—yep, bigger than my current bungalow, though I didn't pay attention yesterday.

He pulls out bottles of juice from the fridge, then rummages in the cupboards and turns toward me with an apologetic look on his face and a bottle in his hand.

"Almond milk for pancakes? Possible? These are the

only things in the cupboard. I don't think this kitchen has ever been used."

"That's what's on the menu?" I ask.

"Unless you want MDMA. Found a bottle." He grins, and I burst out in laughter.

Eventually, he gives up the search. "Okay, so I'm gonna impress you and make you pancakes. Works?"

"Impress me," I say theatrically as he motions to the kitchen island and I take a seat.

I highly doubt he'll pull this off, but I wanna see him try.

And I watch him.

And I watch some more.

I can watch him endlessly.

The terrace doors of the lounge are open to the middle deck, letting in a fresh breeze. The water lapping at the hull makes for a special soundtrack, and I prop my head with my palm as I dreamily study Archer next to the *induction* freaking *stove with a touch display*. Seriously, this place will turn me into a material girl.

Archer makes this sound that I've never heard before, and I prick my ears in curiosity.

Whoa.

He's humming a song under his breath. I grin but don't say anything—it's my doing, thank you very much. He's all mine. Those strong arms, stirring the pancake batter like he's never touched a bowl before. That sculpted body. Those freaking boxers with little waves on them—I thought patterned fabric was a taboo in his wardrobe. That hair that he blows off his face as he obviously struggles, the counter already a mess, the frying pan sizzling on high heat as he shakes off several scoops of batter into it.

He's adorable—a word that I would've never used to describe Archer Crone in my wildest dreams several months ago.

Except now, things are different.

And also, this very minute, I feel like I'm gonna drop dead from starvation if he continues playing the chef.

The burning smell floats through the air, so I finally jump off the stool and walk up to him.

"I got it. Sit down," I order, nudging him away as he wipes his cheek with his forearms, already smudged with batter.

Yup, the pancakes are burnt.

I'll never tell anyone Archer Crone is a crappy cook. He's a talented quarterback and fighter. Wins motorcycle races and has a pilot's license. He's a wizard in organic chemistry and DNA chains. He's my Tony Stark. But pancakes are a mystery to him. Go figure this guy.

Ten minutes later, we sit at the kitchen island and eat perfect pancakes.

"We might have those for lunch too," I say.

Archer chokes on a piece. "I already called Slate. He's bringing some of your clothes in a minute. As well as restaurant delivery until tomorrow."

"We're staying till tomorrow?"

"At least."

"And your work?'

"I called April and canceled my meetings."

I narrow my eyes at him in suspicion.

"I do have a conference call with Amir and others tomorrow night, but I might make it from here."

I don't even hide my grin. A whole day with Archer feels like the best present. The weather feels like it too, giving the rare sunshine amid the gray clouds.

Archer's phone beeps, and I eye it suspiciously. He only glances at it.

"Food and clothes." He winks and walks out, and I follow him onto the deck and wave to Slate downstairs as he unloads the goodies and leaves.

I put my bikini bottoms on and walk out onto the deck again to suntan. Archer swims in the pool, and I squeal when he walks up to me and shakes his head like a dog, splashing water on my hot skin.

"Heeeey," I protest. He only grins and straightens, his broad form casting shade over me. "You're blocking the view."

He rubs himself. "You prefer the ocean over my sexy body? Rude."

And just to punish me, he flings himself right next to me, then shifts to place his wet head on my belly.

"Tyrant," I murmur with a grin, then close my eyes and slide my hand to stroke his hair.

Lunch is from Tapas and tastes better than ever. Must be the ocean air.

I can't stop studying Archer. The way he moves—so relaxed unlike any other time before. The way he smiles like he has no worry in the world.

We walk out onto the deck in the afternoon and stand by the railing, studying Ayana in the distance.

I love this place. But there's this constant feeling that something is going to ruin this happy moment, like we're only given so much to enjoy. It's eerie, unexplainable, invading my mind at the happiest of times.

"You're unusually quiet," Archer finally says.

"I was thinking that… You know, every time I feel like things are great with us, something bad happens."

"Kat." Archer's voice is a reproach. "You can't think like that. Nothing will happen. Everything is great. Or is there something you wanna tell me?"

It's my turn to give him a reproachful look. "It's just…" I turn away to study the peaceful ocean that literally yesterday was a storm. "Bad things occasionally happen when I think everything is great."

There's a moment of silence, and then Archer says, "What happened in Thailand?"

# 45

# KAT

My head snaps in his direction. "Who told you?"

"Your dad."

"Huh." I look away, not knowing why my dad did it or why Archer brings it up now.

"You don't have to talk about it if you're not comfortable."

I think it over. "It's okay, really. You know—"

I've thought about what happened there many times. My perspective changed over the years, after I started sleeping with men and seeing shit happening with other women.

"I was young and reckless," I say. "Doing stupid stuff in Bangkok, because my dad was always at work, and my babysitter didn't care. And, honestly, I had the best time of my life. The best friends. I delivered drugs, you know, when I was a teen. My friend, the lady-boy, Jonshu, talked me into it. I was making cash. Pennies, really, considering how much they paid actual runners for it. But for me, at fourteen, and for the next two years, it was huge. I was a rebel, so proud of myself."

I snort. Being an adult and realizing the danger and consequences of what I did back then makes my toes curl. We only laugh about a notorious past when we didn't get caught or punished.

"I wanted to be like those bad-ass agents, like my dad and uncle, the guys with guns in bulletproof vests who saved the good people and put the bad guys in jail. Except I started on the wrong side of the law."

I pause, smiling at how naive I was, only several years ago, yet an eternity between then and now.

"My dad took me to plenty of undercover operations when my babysitters weren't available. I used to sit in hotel rooms with the special op guys and eat ice cream when they brought in sex workers, "pussy dancers," and snitches. It was all like a movie to me. Except no movies show the pretty wild stuff I saw in Thailand. My dad tried to shield me from a lot of it, but he also wanted to make sure I knew some serious things. I felt I could do something too, you know. So when one of the special ops, dressed like a street hawker, talked to me one day on the street, I thought it would be cool to help. 'Don't tell your dad,' he said. I didn't. I felt like a spy."

"That's wrong," Archer says.

"Yeah, I would punch that guy in the face right now if he did that to another teen. But hell, what did I know back then? So they took me to one of their locations. They gave me a script. I thought I was being freaking cool, you know. Sixteen. Undercover. I was sent out with four girls to a dirty convenience store to meet the guys the agents were tracking. The whole thing was already setup with one of the girls, a recruiter. The targets took us in a van to some dingy club, into a basement. Sex trafficking was a dangerous word. Not that I really knew what it meant. *Really* understood it, you know." I pause, remembering. "And then they told us to strip naked…"

Only now do I look at Archer. His gaze on me is unblinking. His jaw is clenched. I know him so well by now that I can tell he's tense.

"So we stripped down to nothing. In front of the four tatted guys, one of whom I knew from running the drugs."

Archer flinches.

"I was never shy about my body. Not even when I was sixteen. I think I was feeling on a mission or something. But it felt disturbing doing it in a room with four men, and the whole time I kept thinking, 'It wasn't supposed to go this way.'"

I chuckle, but there's no humor in Archer's eyes, his lips pressed tightly together. I look away, studying the peaceful ocean. It feels like a relief to tell this story while surrounded by nature.

"One of the guys walked up to me and started undoing his belt."

Archer inhales sharply through his nose.

"He said, 'If you can handle all four of us, you can stay in Bangkok and work the streets. If not, you are off to Cambodia.' And Cambodia, I found out later, meant that you were kept in some room, drugged, half-conscious, serving anyone who came in."

Silence is heavy around us. I didn't mean to make this day so dark. But Archer asked. And I want him to know this part of my past.

I feel suddenly vulnerable. More than that very night when Dad stormed into the op quarters and broke the captain's face, then punched someone else, then took out a gun and threatened the entire team until they calmed him. My eyes burn with tears from the emotions that suddenly wash over me.

"The words that the thug said that night—they acquired their true meaning only later, years later, after the Change, after witnessing how easily humans can turn into beasts. When Kai finally told me what happened to Olivia—the short version, and I don't want to know the long one—I thought about that night in Thailand, and I knew... I fucking knew..."

I hold my breath, fighting back tears.

"Something really terrible *didn't* happen that night." I let out an exhale. "But knowing what was about to happen, what humans are capable of, being older and somewhat wiser now, I know what my dad felt all those years since we left Thailand. Why he still freezes when I bring it up. I think that's the worst part of PTSD—reliving the past, over and over, reconstructing it, creating multiple outcomes, some better, others much worse, spinning the horrible possibilities in your mind, the fucked-up fractal art of your past memories."

Archer shifts, steps behind me, and wraps his arms around my waist, pulling me tight against him. I bite my lip, trying to suppress a sob and take a deep breath.

"I know *what* would've happened a minute later if the team didn't break in the door and snatch me and the other girls away. They wrapped me in blanket, just like the other girls." I inhale and exhale deeply. "You know what I said, Arch?"

I swallow. It's the stupidest and most naive thing anyone could ever say.

"I asked them if we got the bad guys."

Tears burn my eyes, but I'm not a bit embarrassed about my feelings. Years after that night, I finally realized that I could've been broken forever.

Silence sinks around us as Archer holds me in his arms and presses his cheek to mine. Right now, I feel safe, though even the sunshine doesn't reach the nasty feeling in the pit of my stomach at the memories.

"I was so stupid, wasn't I?" I whisper through tears that finally run down my cheeks.

Archer only hugs me tighter. "You are the bravest person I know, Kat."

"Just hold me a little longer," I whisper.

He buries his face in the crook of my neck, and I close my eyes, wondering if the world finally went mad, because Archer Crone is not the Archer Crone I used to know.

Finally, I turn in his arms.

He brings his hands to my face and wipes my tears with his thumbs. I've never wanted him to see me cry. But that's not the first time I'm turning into a puddle in front of him. This should feel embarrassing, but there's not an ounce of judgment in his eyes.

"You are amazing, you know that?" he says with unusual softness.

God, his beautiful lips just need to be endlessly kissed. Especially when he smiles like this.

I chuckle through tears. "You smile way too often lately, Mr. Chancellor. It's suspicious."

He laughs, and I adore his laughter, too. "I like to keep you on your toes, Miss Ortiz. Alright. We need to change your mood. I like your smile too. Wanna do something you've never done before?"

His gaze is too playful when he pulls me in for a kiss.

## 46

---

## ARCHER

JUST WHEN I THINK I KNOW KAT WELL, SHE PULLS ANOTHER trick out of her sleeve, another story.

Shit.

My girl is a fucking soldier with a fascinating mind and an amazing attitude.

I kiss her deeply, pressing her as hard to my chest as I can. Physical contact can override the mental process, and here she is, her beautiful eyes smiling as she pulls away.

I want to see her eyes widen in surprise again. I love watching her excitement. It's contagious. Nothing much has excited me lately, but watching her is like seeing Old Faithful erupt, even though it shoots up in the air every hour of every day.

"Wanna swim naked in the ocean?" she offers.

I grin. "You are a loose cannon, aren't you?"

Kat is just my type of explosive. She throws her head back, laughing, knowing I'm thinking about it now.

"What do you know about sharks, wild thing?"

Her eyes widen in surprise.

There. I did it again, and I'm so fucking proud of it.

A minute later, she is changing into an orange bikini, and I watch her through the slit of the open door to the bedroom, like a creepy fucking schoolboy. I can't get enough of her beautiful body.

Another minute later, I hold her by her hand as we hurry, grabbing and kissing, downstairs to the jet ski docked at the yacht. And as I start the engine, she does a war cry as we zoom across the sparkling water toward the south beach and caves.

This little trip is nothing extraordinary, but when we step onto the sandy pebbled beach by the southern caves, the memories of my family vacations softly tiptoe into my mind.

I used to be happy here.

I used to have a family years ago.

I explain to Kat that there're a lot of sharks in the waters around, tell her they lose teeth.

"You are messing with me right now, right?" She snorts with disbelief.

Her mistrust makes me laugh. "No, I'm not. Tons of shark teeth wash ashore, lost among the pebbles and shell fragments. Come here."

I get down on my knees in the shallow waters and scoop up a handful of sand and pebbles, then sift through them.

Kat stands above me with her hands on her hips, watching in suspicion.

"We used to do this with sift trays, but you don't have to," I tell her. "The teeth are usually black."

"Bullshit."

I laugh again, I know how this all sounds. "I'm serious. They take on the minerals from the sediment and acquire dark colors. But if they're relevantly new, they can be white." I sift through the wet sand and pebbles with my fingers, then drop the remains in the water and grab another handful. "They vary in size from a speck to several inches long, but those are rare. The lower teeth are pointy, but the top ones are somewhat triangular."

I tell her all I know about sharks and then stumble upon a tooth. "There!" I show it to her, only a little black, polished, triangular-shaped object, half an inch long. "That's small, though."

She studies it with suspicion. "Can I keep it?"

"Sure."

She tucks it in her bikini top, then sinks onto her knees next to me and starts sifting through pebbles.

Twenty minutes of frustration later, Kat squeals and flashes a half-an-inch-long shark tooth with pride on her face.

I find another tooth, this time a bigger one, and while Kat sifts through the sand, I leave it where it is, slightly buried in the wet sand, and go around her.

"Move," I say, and she moves a foot further, then finds it, her eyes glistening with delight, her excited squeal lacing with the distant sound of the waves crashing against the cave walls.

I can't stop looking at her. She's the sexiest woman I know, yet when I see her crouched on her knees like she is right now, a little frown on her face from being focused as she's hunting for shark teeth, I want to cuddle up with her and never let her go farther than a foot away.

Okay, okay, this shark teeth hunt thing might've been a mistake. Kat takes everything with exaggerated enthusiasm.

The wild thing is so into it that she spends an hour looking for the damn teeth.

I give up and sit on the beach, enjoying the sun that's so rare these days and the view of her.

She eventually joins me, a smile on her face, her skin glistening from water. I watch the horizon and Kat studies the shark teeth in her hand, asking me all sorts of questions.

"I'm keeping all of these," she says, closing her hand into a fist.

She's gotten one that's an inch-and-a-half long and multiple smaller ones. The girl doesn't care about luxury but treats shark teeth like the biggest treasure. Go figure.

"That's the point," I tell her. "I used to collect them. We first came here for someone's birthday, about fourteen years or so ago, with Dad's friends. Adam, my brother, and I spent two days wandering along this side of the coast gathering shark teeth. We were obsessed. Got a whole tin of them but missed the cake party." I stretch my hand toward her. "I'll keep them for you," I say as she carefully transfers them into my palm, and I put them in the velcro pocket of my shorts.

"Are those sharks?" she asks, shielding her eyes with her palm and studying something in the water on the horizon.

"Could be."

"Do they attack?"

"Sometimes. Are you scared now?"

"Nah." She wrinkles her nose.

"I didn't think so. You can probably pick one up by its fin or tail if it gets too close to you and flick it off to the other side of the ocean."

"You bet I can."

We both laugh. I pull her in for a kiss, and soon, our wet bodies are grinding, me fucking her carelessly, a big wave washing up to our waists, her blurting, "My shark teeth!" as she squirms around my cock and tries to reach for my board shorts.

"They're fine," I grunt, and our moans, tanned skin, and salty water make for the best day ever.

When I'm ready, I pull out and cum all over her belly.

"You've been baptized beach style, wild thing," I say, and she bursts into laughter, her naked body shaking as she rolls in the sand, getting dirty brown streaks all over her until I pick her up and carry her into the ocean.

## 47

# ARCHER

I'VE ARRANGED WITH AMIR TO HAVE THE CONFERENCE CALL from the yacht the next day. I haven't had a vacation in forever. Spending time with Kat makes me realize that I needed time to rethink what I'm doing next, my state of affairs, Gen-Alpha. Her…

We spend the evening having dinner, listening to music, and drinking wine, which, surprisingly, Kat has a taste for.

Kat is tipsy and smiley—the way I like her. Her gestures are careless as she half-lies on the couch in the main lounge, next to the open windows, and puts her feet on my lap. I like that too, and she's a bit too tipsy to notice that I start rubbing them.

We share stories from our past, which makes me feel closer to her.

"I caught my parents having sex when I was ten," she says. "My dad just came home from overseas. I watched them through a crack in the door. Didn't understand a thing, you know, but it was exciting."

"Already a nymphomaniac," I say with a chuckle.

"Stop."

"I used to spy on my parents dancing. In the living room," I say.

"My parents danced all the time."

"Yeah. That's one of my favorite memories about our family. Mom was the only woman Dad danced with. Even at official events, functions, and all that government jazz. The other women who came later, after her—he just fucked them, kept them around just because. No one ever replaced her."

I suddenly feel nostalgic and have an urge to bring back the memories that I never shared with anyone until now. So I go to the music system and put on the song that reminds me of the good old times but also everything I lost. Except this time, I can handle it with Kat next to me.

"Oh!" she exclaims when the song comes on. "'One Of These Nights' by the Eagles."

I grin, approach the couch, and stretch my hand to her. "A dance?"

She hops onto her feet, a grin on her face as she comes into my arms.

It's old rock.

It's memories.

It's someone to share them with.

It's the sense that even when we lose the ones we love, we find those who can fill in the gap.

Kat feels perfect in my arms. Warmth envelops my heart when she lifts her face and asks, "What was she like? Your mom?"

I wish Mom got to know this beautiful girl.

"Soft. Kind. Loving. Yours?"

"Strong-headed. Pushy." She smiles and adds, "Loving."

We both laugh.

"Sounds like you, wild thing."

"Believe it or not, Dad is kind and soft."

"Shut up. Mr. Ortiz?"

"I'm telling you. His work is one thing. When he was with her or me, he turned into a big teddy bear. I guess opposites attract."

The song changes to "Dreams" by Fleetwood Mac. I pick Kat up in my arms, and she wraps her beautiful legs around my waist. We kiss slowly. And dance. And have more wine later. And talk for hours. I've never been romantic, but that changed when this wild thing stormed into my life and took my heart prisoner.

The next day we sleep in almost until noon.

My phone beeps annoyingly several times in a row—Marlow. I hesitate for a moment before I finally pick up.

"I'm off today," I say, peeling a strand of Kat's hair off my neck as she rubs her face on my chest and sleepily looks up.

"Just thought you'd want to hear an update about Cunningham," he says.

"I don't want to hear about Cunningham today," I say.

But Kat is wide awake in a second, wiggling her fingers and asking for my phone, so I reluctantly put Marlow on speaker.

"Spill. Fast," I say.

"A team did a sweep across Ayana. Nothing suspicious. They checked all the empty bungalows and villas. The resort in on twenty-four-seven surveillance. They went through town. Nothing. Raven talked to Butcher. Nothing, obviously. A landscaping truck exited Ayana the night of Cunningham's escape. He could've been in it, but the owners didn't crack. That's the only way. Unless he swam around half of the island, which is impossible."

"Right." I couldn't care less, but Kat seems satisfied with being kept in the loop.

"Coffee?" I ask her when the conversation is over.

I put on my boxers and pad to the kitchen, noticing pieces of our clothes on the floor from yesterday.

The espresso machine is the only kitchen appliance I'm good with. Thank God for Slate who delivered the food this morning and left it in the fridge.

I make a cup for myself and am making one for Kat when I hear her voice.

"Arch! This is an emergency!"

Her voice from the bedroom is slightly whiny. But I know that overtone—she's horny.

Smiling, I walk in that direction and lean on the door-frame with a coffee in my hand.

My smile grows into a grin. The emergency is my kitten, splayed on the sheets naked, her little paw between her legs.

"Can you take care of this?" She's so shamelessly sexed-up in all her lustful greedy glory.

She's my favorite emergency. My favorite girl. My favorite human. And *this* is my favorite job.

I push off the doorway and slowly walk up to the bed, taking sips of coffee and admiring the view.

"Kitten, you started the party without me. Show me what you want me to take care of."

Locking her gaze with mine, she drags her hands from her hips up, along her torso, over her full breasts that beg to be kissed, then back down.

"All of it, huh?"

Another sip of coffee doesn't keep me or my cock from getting all wound up.

"I got the sheets wet," she purrs, arching, seducing me with the sight of her body.

"Our sheets should be soaked." I set the coffee cup on the nightstand and slide next to her. "Your handyman is right here."

She crawls on top of me, warm and naked, licking coffee out of my mouth with her needy tongue.

My hand glides along her body, her hips, then cups her ass. Gently, I slide one of my fingers to her back entrance.

"Arch," she whispers and wiggles her butt away.

"Still too sensitive?" I murmur.

"Maybe." She bites her lip.

"Shy?"

"No."

Oh, hell yes, she is. She's blushing. I thought I loved her feistiness the most, but it's her occasional and rare shyness that gets my cock hard like an iron rod.

I slide my fingers between her legs and stroke her pussy. "So deliciously wet."

Now she rubs herself on me, but I pull my hand away

and push my leg between hers. "And rubbing your pussy on my leg. Let me see."

"See what?"

"Let me see you fuck my leg. You can play with me as you do so." My cock is so hard it needs attention.

I study her as she straddles my leg and starts rubbing herself on it slowly, her full perky breasts with hardened nipples keeping me hypnotized. She pulls down my boxers, just low enough below my balls, and starts stroking my erection.

"Remember we had a bet?" I say, flicking her nipples with my fingers and pushing my knee up against her soaked pussy.

"What bet?"

She doesn't even look at me, her eyes on my cock, her lips parted like she wants to swallow it. I'd like that. But now I have a different idea as I caress her breasts, and she pushes them at me.

"I make you come by kissing your breasts. I win, we try that upside-down position."

Her eyes fly up to meet mine. Her hand on my dick pauses. She stops moving. "No. Hell, no." She shakes her head almost with horror in her eyes which makes me laugh.

"Well, I guess it's a solo ride for you."

I push her hand away and nudge her to get off, then roll off the bed.

I pick up my coffee cup when something smacks the back of my head—a pillow—so hard it makes me stumble and splash coffee on my hand.

Gaping, I turn around and meet Kat's half-pouty-half-angry expression.

"You. Are. In. Trouble," I say, setting the cup back down. "I'm gonna upside down you right fucking now," I grunt, get on all fours on the bed, and slowly make my way toward her.

She backs away, but I grab her ankle and yank her toward me.

She squeals, fighting me off with a grin that I catch with my lips and eat out of her mouth like I need a meal. My hands squeeze her tits, making her moan.

"That's right, you little coward," I murmur, then duck my head to catch one of her nipples with my lips and suck on it. "Sssssuch a coward," I whisper, intending to tease her until she gives in.

"Okay-okay-okay. It's a bet."

I stop and lift my face to hers, my dick already burning in anticipation.

"One sec." I scurry off the bed, walk into the main lounge, and pluck one of the smaller peacock feathers out of a giant vase, then come back to the bedroom.

Kat is propped on her elbows, frowning at me. "Feather?"

"It's rare. White peafowl."

"What are you doing with a *rare white peafowl* feather?"

"You'll find out." I wink, slowly kneel on the bed, and crouch closer. "Apparently, you like all things antique and rare. So let's see how this works out."

"You said no touching, right?" She licks her lips with that familiar sparkle of anticipation in her eyes as she follows the tip of the feather that I run from her neck down her body and stop at her navel.

"I said my mouth on your breasts. Nothing about the props."

"Trickster!"

I give her a backward nod. "Now, push your breasts together for me."

She hesitates.

I cock my brow, warning her.

She lies down and pushes her tits together, the sight of them making me hard as a rock. I do a long swipe with my tongue from her belly button, up her torso, between her tightly pressed tits, then plant a kiss on one of her nipples, making her draw in a tiny sharp gasp, her belly jerking as she does so.

The tip of the feather is still on her navel when I look down. "Now open your legs for me." She does. "Wider." She widens them, bending her knees. "More, kitten. I want you as wide open as you can be."

She obeys, her thighs falling open to their utmost degree. If I didn't promise that my mouth would be on her tits, I would've already been tonguing her hot cunt right now.

"Perfect," I say, moving the feather down to her slit, its soft tip right away slick with her juices.

I turn to meet her gaze. Her eyelids are already hooded, her body arching with need as that feather strokes her pussy.

"Where were we..." I lean over to take her breast in my mouth, then let go with a loud sucking sound. "Real men use feathers to impress a girl, not flowers," I murmur. "Shall we start?"

The feather is in motion.

Soon, it will drive her crazy.

I fucking love winning bets.

## 48

### KAT

Who would've thought that a man like Archer could do more than take?

In the last two days, he gives. The heat. The tingling sensations on my skin. The kisses. Fucking me like his life depends on whether I come or not, in what way, and how many times.

The goddamn feather.

If I ever heard a story like this, I'd say it's degrading and plain freaking crazy.

Well, I didn't have any thoughts in my mind when I was mewling like a kitten, feeding Archer my breasts, and rolling my hips into that feather.

"Archer, more," I remember pleading, not sure what *more* stood for. More pressure. More orgasms. I was begging, that's for sure. I'll beg again to have more of him. All. Day. Long.

The two days we spend together, we talk more than

ever. Occasional phrases here and there. Small facts that slip off our tongues and let us deeper into each other.

"How did you get into chemistry?" I ask Archer. I never liked chemistry. The things we are not good at often fascinate us in others.

"Found a book in my aunt's library. She used to be a doctor. I liked the book, studied it. I was eight, so my family thought I was bullshitting around until I passed the O-level exam."

"At eight?"

"Yup. You might say that book paid for this island."

"And saved lives."

"Something like that."

"But that's not what you studied at Deene."

"No. I completed an advanced chemistry degree by the age of seventeen."

"Holy shit! Why go to college at all?"

"To feel normal. Parties. Football. I wanted to prove to myself I could be better than others at one more thing. And another. And one more."

"Overachiever, huh?"

"So are you. Just at different things."

"What's something you did that no one knows that you aren't proud of?"

Archer gives me a mischievous look. "Prying?"

"No. Just wonder what you are capable of."

"I slept with one of my father's mistresses when I was fifteen."

Maybe not that. "Gross."

"She slept with his best friend. And, to be fair, he was

with two escorts that night, and I was mad at him for many reasons."

I can see why Archer had a fucked-up attitude with women, growing up with a father who wasn't the best example of a family man.

"You?" Archer cocks his head.

"Well, I don't have raunchy stories like that. But... Remember I told you about the sheriff's son and his minions?"

"The one who tried to—"

"Yes..."

"You beat them up, right?" Archer smiles.

"Yeah. The charge was dismissed, but I was still angry. Knowing they could try to do it again. Or something worse."

I'm not proud of that night. But I'd like to think that I might've saved other girl who weren't as feisty as me and let men stomp over their pride.

"I drugged them," I confess.

"What?"

"Spiked their drinks at a party I snuck out to."

"You're good at sneaking into places."

"Yeah. Well, I had an agenda."

Archer opens his mouth to say something clever but changes his mind, waiting for me to continue.

"They had a cabin in the woods where they used to drink and bring girls. Club Thirty, they called it. Because they celebrated the number of girls they'd brought there by then."

"Jesus."

"Yeah, the girls' names were written all over like a fucking wall of shame. So they drank the spiked shit and passed out two hours later. All four of them. So I undressed them, placed their bodies wrapped in each other—I was creative, I'll tell you that—and took pictures. Many pictures. Suggestive ones."

Archer cocks a brow. "Creative, I'll give you that."

"I spread the pictures online the next day under a fake account, and the town was all about them."

"That's not that crazy of a punishment to rapists."

"No, not really. Embarrassing, true. Except one of them, Greg, had an adverse reaction to the drug I used. He ended up in a coma for a week."

"Oh, shit."

"I don't regret what I did. But if he didn't come out of the coma, I could've become a murderer."

There's silence between us, but it's not heavy. We are learning more about each other and what we are capable of.

"I used to do heavy drugs for a short while, after Droga's accident," Archer says in a quiet voice. "It was... a strange time. I overdosed once, went into the hospital. Exactly the same way it happened at the villa."

He meets my eyes and doesn't look away. It's the first time we've talked about *that* night. It's the first time he's admitted what happened.

"I guess we all have weaknesses," he says with an almost apologetic smile.

I nod. "I smoke pot occasionally. That's my vice." I smile broadly to ease the tension. "Although I tried some stuff back in Thailand. *Chocalee* or *Ya ba*. I tried that a few times.

It's methamphetamine mixed with caffeine. Strong like blow but a different high. That's my only drug experience."

"Microdosing, I still do it," Archer takes over this uneasy relay of confessions.

"I've heard about it. Used to be a Silicone Valley thing when it existed."

"Yeah. It's tiny amounts of LSD you take now and then. Helps you focus, makes things clear. It's hard to explain. It's like opening the brain cells that were never used before."

"You have too much responsibility with work."

"Yeah. It used to be. Now it's all about money. From the formula that we keep tweaking to adjust to the DNA mutation."

"Why not make the drug available through health insurance? Take it public?"

"It's about politics and Big Pharma. I brought it up with Dad several times, but he wouldn't have it. Me, I want out. I want to fuck off somewhere where every day doesn't remind me of the prison that this business keeps me in and the responsibility to those who are denied access to the basics."

"You are such a strong person, Arch, you can do anything," I say, and the words change his expression like he was just slapped in the face. His gaze on me is almost too intense. "What's wrong?" I ask, afraid I said something foolish again.

He shakes his head, his face softening into a smile. "Mom used to say my dad was the strongest man she knew. That he is—was—a politician, and it's a hard job. It's not always about doing good, but choosing the lesser of two evils. And that sometimes makes one a villain in others' eyes, regardless of what choice one makes. I don't want to be my dad, but I understand now how trying to balance high power can bring on others' hate."

"But power means taking care of others. If not, it becomes a dictatorship, and that's power laced with hate."

"Yeah. Some decisions are not up to me."

"Some things are. The town, Port Mrei. It used to be beautiful, Archer, wasn't it? Now it looks like a dump. Children live on the streets. You can change it."

"Why would I?"

"Because you can."

"How?"

"You have so many talented people around. And the new ones, the Outcasts. Ty is a landscape designer. Ya-Ya is a lawyer, and she used to work in the underprivileged sector and human resources. Everyone has talents. You utilize so many of them at the Center, but the Center is becoming that business giant that starts disregarding those who take care of the basics—the regular people."

"Do I know you?" I look up at Archer in surprise. He's smiling. "Since when do you care so much about Port Mrei?"

I shrug. "Well, if you make it your home, you have to, don't you? If it were my home, I would want every part of my home to be clean and well-off. If I were responsible for people, I'd want them to be happy. That's how the Golden Rule works."

"It *is* your home, Kat." His words make my heart flutter.

His eyes search mine for a yes. "I'd like it to be your home. Because that means you're here with me."

Archer reaches for my face and rubs his thumb on my cheek, and I manage the courage to smile. "I'd like that very much."

## 49

## ARCHER

IT'S EVENING. KAT LIES IN MY ARMS, OUR LIMBS TANGLED, bodies wrapped around each other as we watch the sun go down.

The two days we spent together feel magical, and I can't help but remember Droga's words: *She needs to know how you feel.*

"Kat, I need to tell you something," I say.

"Yeaaaah?" she purrs softly, her little paws stroking my bare chest, my skin humming at the touch.

"You are beautiful and amazing."

I don't smile as I say it, and she senses something else is coming. You can give her a sassy compliment, and she'll swallow it. You give her a gentle one, and she hides away, like a turtle in its shell.

It's so obvious now as she drops her gaze to my chest.

"Oh, no. I've seen that look before, when you pull away. Look at me, Kat."

"What's going on, Arch?" She's avoiding my eyes.

"Kat, look at me."

She looks up from under her eyebrows as if I'm playing a game.

"Bear with me for a minute, okay? I'm trying to tell you something."

I've spent countless hours thinking about her and me. There are not enough thoughts to describe how she makes me feel and how she's changed me in the last months without meaning to do so.

"I said before that you are important."

"I'd better be." She's still playing.

"That was an understatement, Kat."

"Okay." She laughs but keeps glancing away, returning her gaze to me as if in suspicion.

I tip her chin with my forefinger so she can't look away, her gaze shooting arrows through my heart that starts beating faster by the second.

"I'm in love with you, Kat."

My heart slams in my chest. Kat's smile fades. Her eyes widen as she loses the grip on how to project her confidence.

I've known this for a while. But it's a different story to lay my heart out for her. I've said these words before to others, but it's the first time I actually mean it. *Feel* it profoundly.

"You and I," I say as Kat blinks, trying to arrange her face into an expression that won't give away her vulnerability, "we don't talk about feelings. We fuck them out. But you need to know this."

I smile to ease the tension that makes my chest so tight it's hard to breathe.

I know Kat well. She'll need time to process it and accept it. It's okay with me. For the first time, I'm not asking for anything back. I just want to give her the confidence of knowing that I'm in for whatever life throws our way, as long as she's next to me.

"I want you to know that you always have me." Looking into her eyes while I pour my heart out is weakening, like being on my knees. "Whatever you need, I'll be there for you. No matter how cold you think I am or how arrogant I come across or selfish, you are the most important person in my life."

I brush my thumb against her cheek, feeling her lean just a fraction of an inch into it, her lips parting. Her eyes don't leave mine, but her breathing increases, and her chest heaves.

Words hit her fast and hard, like sex. And just like the first time, she's trying to hide her reaction, retracting behind that armor she's built, telling herself she's a one-woman army and she doesn't need a man by her side.

*It's okay, wild thing.*

"You don't have to say anything, Kat. I just wanted you to hear it. You are my brave wild thing, the craziest and most intense person I know. You make me happy." She bites her lip, and *this* sign I know well—she's emotional. "When I came back from the mainland, I wasn't any better off than the night you found me on the floor of my villa. I felt like shit. Mostly because of what you said that night and me thinking that you despised me like everyone else."

"Archer, I never did. I don't. I was—"

"Shhhh. I know, Kat, I know. You were angry. And you weren't entirely wrong." I push a strand of her wild hair behind her ear. God, have I ever loved curls so much! "But I'm trying to change the way I treat people. I'm trying to be the man my mom"—I swallow a lump in my throat, remembering Mom's words—"once wanted me to be. And be the man that you have fewer reasons to be angry at. I want to be the man you turn to at your worst moments and the one you share your best ones with. I guess, I just want all of you. And there I am—a selfish prick again."

I laugh through the heavy feelings that tighten my chest, and she bites her smile, her eyes misted with tears.

"This is it," I say. "Us. I'll make the best of it. Just trust me, wild thing, and stick around. Because I want to give you the entire world on a platter. That's the least you deserve."

I won't lose her. I can't. And I'm scared that at some point, I might fuck it up. Or someone else will. There's that pendulum again—feeling blessed for having someone you love and feeling scared that it might not last.

I just laid the truth out, and it feels liberating but might be scaring Kat off. So I don't let her simmer in doubt but kiss her softly, trying to gauge her feelings by the way she kisses me back.

She's awkward at first—I'm more gentle than I want to show. We let the feelings out without words. My lips brush against hers as I revel at her gentle touch. Her fingertips stroke my arm, their touch soft like that of a feather, which is not something Kat does often and therefore even more special.

For some time, it's just soft kisses, then us slowly sliding each other's clothes off. Me tugging down her panties. Her brushing her hands on my hips. Me planting little kisses on her shoulder. Her little gasps as I do so like she's never been touched like this before. Our bodies inching closer. Me shifting on top of her, then slowly sliding inside her and thrusting in the slowest rhythm, accompanied by the soft lapping of the waves against the hull and the sunset glow painting her body gold.

I want to say this is lovemaking, I'm pretty sure that's what it is when we slowly fuck through sunset and, for the first time in my life, I don't chase an orgasm, just dissolve in the feeling of being inside her, filling her up in deep slow thrusts, taking her mouth like I'm savoring the first taste, catching her little moans and gasps.

"I'm close," she whispers.

"Come, kitten," I murmur into her neck, feeling my own orgasm building up. "Like that, yeah…" Her moans get louder. "Yeah? Good?"

She comes beautifully. Fuck, this girl's orgasm is an artwork.

"I love being inside of you, kitten. So fucking hot. Your… Fuck…"

I explode suddenly, pushing one more time as I empty into her, and we lie in the twilight for some time, almost falling asleep.

It's dark when we finally get up, and I say, "I'm taking a

shower," and slap her lightly on her sweet ass to ease the tension of what I said minutes ago.

I stand under the shower for some time, letting the water wash off the emotions.

My phone on the sink counter goes off with the high-pitched beep alert that's connected to Kat's bracelet. She's either playing with herself again or dancing.

The phone beeps again.

Then again.

I get out of the shower, throw on a pair of board shorts, and check my phone.

What the hell?

"Kat?" I walk out into the bedroom, but it's all quiet, so I pad into the lounge. "What are you up to, crazy girl?" I ruffle my wet hair as I continue toward the open terrace doors. "Kitty-kitty-kitty," I tease.

It's dark outside, and suddenly, a thought flickers in my mind—what if she fell overboard?

The phone beeps again, and now, my heart is thudding.

There's a strange smell in the air. Something different. Something that doesn't belong here or pristine Ayana. It's... foreign.

I slow down as I step out onto the middle of the dark deck.

"Kat?" I say louder, and the sound in response is a whimper from the dark behind me.

I turn and see Kat's silhouette in the corner, dark and hidden by the shadows.

"Wild thing—"

She steps out—no, she's *pushed* out by someone else who holds her from behind, his hand covering her mouth.

"Mr. Crone, a feisty little thing you got here," the raspy low voice says, sending chills all the way to my core.

A dozen thoughts flicker in my mind all at once.

Who is he?

How?

He's not supposed to be here.

What the fuck is his fucking hand doing on Kat's mouth?

My stomach lurches. I register his bleeding nose before Kat's eyes widen at something behind me, and she struggles against his hand and makes an articulate sound in an attempt to scream.

There's a momentary soft sound of hurried footsteps behind me.

A rustling of clothes.

That pungent smell is suddenly too strong.

I start turning, but something collides with my head, searing me with sharp pain, and I sink into darkness.

# 50

## KAT

IT DOESN'T MATTER HOW MUCH YOU ARE TRAINED TO AVOID danger, nothing prepares you for a sudden assault from behind.

I open my eyes and blink, trying to adjust to the bright lightbulb above me.

It's the only thing hanging on a wire off a dark-gray ceiling.

It's cold, I'm on my side, my shoulder numb, my body unusually heavy, and my hands won't spread too far. There's a sound of metal clinking against a hard surface—handcuffs. I'm handcuffed and chained to something!

I close my eyes, trying to fight through the sharp pain in my head that almost makes me lose consciousness again. The smell of chloroform is still in my nostrils, strong and pungent. I manage all my strength and sit up, slowly blinking, trying to adjust to the light.

Archer's on the floor next to me. His strong body is clad only in board shorts and seems lifeless.

"Archer?"

It all slowly comes back to me through the haze in my brain. The thugs. The nasty hand over my mouth. Me head-butting one of them. Guns. *"Be quiet, or I'll hurt him."*

Then darkness.

Now I look at Archer's body on a concrete floor and try to shake the sight off like it's a bad dream.

"Archer," I whisper, then get on all fours and crawl toward him. "Archer!" I shake him.

There's blood in his hair—they hit him on his head, but as I shake him again, a grunt escapes him, and he moves.

I sit on my haunches and wait for him as he slowly comes to it, grunting, and rises to sit up. He stares at the handcuffs around his wrists, then the chain—both of them lead to the wall, attached to a metal hook—then at me.

"We were kidnapped," I say and look around.

Something is not right with my body—I feel sedated, weak. Chloroform won't do it, it's a short-term drug, and my body is numb like I've been lying here for hours.

I shiver, looking down—I'm wearing only a tank and shorts—then study my arms, then register a sharp prickle in my neck and touch it—swollen.

"Let me see," I tell Archer, gently taking his head and turning it so I can inspect him.

"We've been drugged," I say as I find a swollen syringe puncture on the side of his neck.

"Fuck," Archer grunts, then brings both hands to his hair and rubs it, hissing from pain. The metal chains rattle.

"We could've been out for hours. Or a day," I say.

"What the fuck is this?" He looks around.

"Give me a minute," I say and study our surroundings.

We're in a forty-by-forty concrete room, musty and lacking oxygen. The concrete floor has damp spots in the corners and the seams. My bare feet are freezing.

"We are underground," I murmur.

There's nothing on the walls, only a light bulb hanging off the center of the ceiling, lighting the room with a low glow.

No cameras. Good. So we're not being watched.

"These guys are not pros," I say, mostly to myself. "Whatever the reason for them taking us, we might be in transition. This"—I nod around—"is not planned out properly. If it were Butcher's job, we would be in a more secure place and under surveillance."

"You don't know what's outside."

"True. But there's no camera. No peephole in the door either. Strange. Look at the door." Wincing through pain, I get up and walk toward it, only to halt several feet before it —the chain is not long enough. "It's like it was brought from some other building. The gap under it—see?"

Archer grunts as he gets up, then leans with his hands on his thighs, moving his head slowly. "Butcher is not exactly a sophisticated guy."

"He's better than that, trust me. Considering it's you, he would've made sure he had better surveillance. Unless he's hired some thugs and they are laying low for now before they take us to him."

I might be wrong, but that's the first step in assessing a situation—creating the most logical scenario and going from there.

I look down at the cuffs. They are not sophisticated but old, rusty, bulky things with a half-inch keyhole.

"I got this."

*Fuckers. Try this with someone else, morons.*

Archer straightens up and studies me with curiosity as I lift the hem of my tank and unpin a safety pin.

"Why do you have that there?" he asks.

"Old Eastern-European superstition from jinxing. Mom used to pin safety pins on half of my shirts. I still do it. They come handy in camping or rolling joints."

I smile as I carefully insert the pin into the keyhole, feeling for the latch.

The loud sound of rusty hinges from somewhere above makes me freeze like a deer in headlights. Two pairs of heavy footsteps make a descending sound, approaching on the other side of the door.

"Shit," I murmur, fist the pin in my hand, and retreat farther from the door as a precaution.

Archer balls his hands into fists.

"Archer, don't do anything reckless, please. They might be armed."

They fucking are.

The door opens slowly, and the first thing I see is the barrel of a gun as two men walk in, guns raised at us.

I hold my breath and study the two thugs, not sure if they're the same ones who took us.

They're both shorter than Archer but a bit taller than me. One of them has a swollen nose. *Hello, fucker.*

"The king of the hill," the other one rasps and laughs as

he gives Archer an up-and-down look. I recognize the voice.

Archer's chain rattles as he takes a step closer.

"Settle down," the thug barks.

The two are in their fifties, in plaid shirts, jeans, and boots, unshaved faces and sunbaked rough skin. The unclean stench coming from them is nauseating.

The one wearing a baseball hat sucks his teeth and walks up to Archer. "Settle down, boy," he growls, the gun too loose in his hand, the safety on.

My heartbeat spikes.

The next movement is so sudden that my brain doesn't process it fast enough, keeping me in a stupor for seconds.

Archer throws a sharp punch at the guy in front of him, sending him to the floor, the gun flying into the farthest corner, then starts kicking him.

The loud sound of a gunshot from the other guy deafens us, the room so small that my ears ring.

Adrenalin makes my heart pump like mad when I throw myself at the guy and start punching him.

He's much bigger than me. That's the truth about smaller people—they can fight but they can't wrestle a much bigger opponent. And as I punch the hell out of the guy, he latches on to my thigh and squeezes as hard as he can, sharp pain piercing my flesh as a scream tears from my throat.

"I'll shoot 'er! I'll shoot 'er! Step back, fucker!" the other guy shouts as the one underneath me throws me off him.

Before I can catch him, he crouches toward the door. I

lunge at him only to be yanked back, the metal cuffs cutting into my wrists and twisting me around.

Archer has his hands up in the air, eyes blazing with hate.

The two guys are on the ground, in the farthest corner we can't reach, panting and pointing their guns at us.

"Fucking bitch," one guy rasps, sending me a murderous stare, and spits blood on the ground.

Archer and I take slow steps back.

If they could, they would've shot us. But they didn't, not even when they were being beat up. That's how I know that they are not the executioners, they're hired.

The guy whose baseball hat is lying on the ground is bald, his face completely bloodied when he gets up, gun cocked at Archer.

"On ye' knees," he rasps, wiping his nose with the back of his hand.

"Fuck you." Archer spits at his feet.

The thug's chuckle is a nasty sound, with a gurgling that comes deep from his lungs and turns into a coughing fit. When he calms down, that nasty sparkle in his eyes is back. "Wanna trade ye' island fo' this pretty thing ove' here? Daddy can afford it, no?"

Archer's jaw tightens. "I'll cut off your balls and let you heal," he says in a sharp voice I've never heard before, "then drop you off on the mainland, in a prison, so they can play with you, you fucking degenerate."

The guy's face darkens as he shifts his angry stare at me and nods in my direction, licking his bloodied lips. "How 'bou' we take this pretty 'un to play?"

Not a chance. "Fuck you," I hiss, ready to claw and bite and kick with everything I've got.

But Archer shifts. Slowly, he sinks to his knees, hands still up in the air.

*Fuck, baby.*

I'm his weak spot, and he just let them know.

"Thought as much," the thug coughs out. "You"—he waves the gun at me—"on ye' knees, too."

Reluctantly, I do as told. And then I scream when the fucker swings his foot and kicks Archer in the face, sending him onto his back. He spits loudly on the floor and leaves, taking his buddy with him, the sound of a heavy metal bolt drowning the hissing that comes from Archer.

"Archer, baby." I crawl toward him and help him sit up. "I'll fucking kill them next time. Let's kill them," I keep murmuring as if I can heal Archer's bleeding nose. "Let me see."

I lift his face up toward the light, pick up the hem of my shirt, and carefully wipe away the blood around his nose that's starting to swell, then run my fingers along the bridge.

"Not broken," I say, inspecting it. "You okay?"

"Yeah."

With my teeth, I tear a piece of fabric off my shirt, then make two small patches and roll them. "Hold still," I tell Archer and insert them into his nasal cavities to stop the bleeding.

His hands take mine in his as he looks around at the dark splatters of blood on the concrete.

"They are not pros. And they didn't take us for themselves," he says.

"I know. One of the guns was a Grach. I've seen those on the charts when Dad used to teach me different kinds of arms. It's Soviet. Americans don't use them, so they must've come from Eastern Europe."

"We need to get out," I say, and then remember that we were going to do just that before the thugs came. "The safety pin!"

I had it in my hand when the guys came in. But Archer attacked them so suddenly that I joined on instinct.

Frantically, I look around the floor, then see the pin by the door. Crawling on all fours, I'm only several feet away when I jerk hard against the chains.

"Fuck!" I panic.

I lie down flat on my side and stretch one foot toward the pin, swiping right past it.

"Shit. It's stuck in a crevice in the concrete."

Archer is next to me. "Let me try." He does the same, wiggling his toes to coax the pin out of the crevice, but it doesn't work. "It could be done if one of the hands was free."

Archer shifts to stand on his knees before me then sits back on his heels and takes my face between his palms.

"What do you know about dislocating joints?"

# 51

## KAT

My stomach turns.

*What the…?*

I want to scream in frustration but take a deep breath instead, calming my nerves.

"It's painful and… Well, technically I know how to do it. I've seen it done before in the prison escape seminar my uncle watched with his buddies."

"So it works."

"Yeah… I mean."

"You need to do it, Kat."

Momentary horror washes over me. Me? Right now?

"Kat, sweetheart, listen to me."

Archer shifts closer to me, our knees touching, and grabs my hands.

I feel weak, though this is not the time to be a coward. I've trained for so many scenarios like this. In theory. Adrenalin is my weapon. I don't usually panic, but the thought of hurting myself is heavy.

"I can handle anything they do to me," Archer says, his eyes searching mine. I can't read him, though his voice is consoling. "But they probably won't dare. I'm their main trading card. But you, Kat—if they touch you, I won't be able to forgive myself. You hear me?"

I nod absently, trying to gain courage.

Right, I have to think about myself.

"So we need to get out of here as soon as possible," he says. "We have to. There's no other way."

He looks down as he massages my hands with his. Being hurt by others is always part of a scenario like this, but not deliberately inflicting pain on myself.

Slowly, Archer wraps my hands around his left one.

"I'll need my right one. And I can't do this to myself. You'll have to. You are a pro, wild thing."

A nervous chuckle escapes both of us—he wants me to do this to *him*.

I exhale, pulling my hands away from him, and smooth my hair. The thought of hurting him is even more atrocious.

"Kat, baby, look at me." He grabs my hands again, chains rattling in warning.

I meet his eyes. "Archer, it's very painful. Not as bad as bones being broken, but still."

"Kat, listen." He inhales and exhales slowly, trying to control his breathing and summoning his courage as I keep his gaze, not letting him look away. He is determined. "We have to do this, okay?"

His right hand presses mine onto his left one and around his wrist and thumb like he knows exactly what has to be done.

"There's no choice."

He keeps talking as I admire my beautiful guy who puts his trust in me—me, who came her to spy on him.

"So, let's take time and think it through. I can handle pain, trust me," Archer says.

I don't need to think it through. His voice is so calming that it grounds me, loading me with determination.

"I've had plenty of injuries before, a concussion, broken bones, and all that stuff. I can handle whatever—Aaaaaaaarhh!"

The roar that escapes him is less than subtle as in one powerful pressure movement I dislocate his joint and yank the metal toward me as he jerks his hand away, freeing it.

On instinct, he grabs his hand with the other one, but I yank it toward me and push on his joint to pop it back in place.

"Sorry, sorry, sorry, babe," I start murmuring, holding his injured hand in mine, rubbing it as he tries to pull it away. "Sorry."

Tears mist his widened eyes as he yanks his hand out of mine and lifts it in front of his face, staring in shock.

His eyes are wider than quarters, teeth biting his bottom lips as he grunts, closing his eyes to get through pulsating pain that I know—in theory—will subside within seconds.

I try to smile to reassure him. "So-so-so sorry, babe. I had to take you by surprise."

But in a second, he takes my head between his hands and shuts me up with a kiss.

"Fuck, you are savage," he murmurs, looking at me like

I've blessed him. He pulls away and massages his hand, checking it again and again.

In a moment, he crawls toward the door as far as the chain allows him. I watch with anticipation. His arms are outstretched, the fingers of the left hand clawing at the floor as he—

Reaches the crevice in the concrete.

*Fuck yes!*

My heart starts pounding.

His fingers dig out the pin, and he leans back, lifting his face with an exhale. "Got it."

I shift toward him right away. "Let me see."

I take the pin from his fingers so carefully like it's a magical spindle, then place his other cuffed hand on my lap and twist the cuff to position the keyhole so I can work it.

I know what I'm doing but still pray in my mind as I gently swipe the pin inside the keyhole once, twice, thrice. I pick up the little latch inside the lock and push on it, my heart giving out a loud thud when it clicks and the cuff falls apart, freeing Archer's hand.

"You are brilliant," he blurts, rubbing his wrist and kissing me on the cheek.

This time, I cheer as I set my cuffed wrists on my lap and work the locks until both hands are free.

"Whew!" I exhale, grinning, meeting Archer's gaze that says, "You are a star."

He yanks me toward him, burying his face in my neck.

"Kitten, your smell, fuck," he murmurs, his tongue licking up my skin.

It's adrenalin. It makes you lose perspective on the situation. But this is only the first step. We both know it.

So I push Archer away. "Arch!" I hiss, trying to hide a smile. "Jesus, you are such a psycho. We need to get out."

"Right." He rakes his hair. His nose is swollen. He's a brutal sight. "We need to plan this carefully," he says, and I'm ready, so ready to fight with him through this mess.

## 52

# ARCHER

K<small>AT SITS ON HER HAUNCHES ON THE FLOOR BY THE WALL</small> across from the door. Her handcuffs are open but wrapped around her wrists.

I stand behind the door, waiting. It might take hours, but we're ready. My nose swells, but I pull out the cloths— the bleeding has stopped.

Not even an hour goes by when we hear a heavy latch somewhere above us, then two sets of heavy footsteps approaching down the steps.

I lock eyes with Kat and nod, blood pulsating between my ears.

She nods back.

The bolt on the other side of the door is unlatched, and the door opens slowly.

I swing it open in one fast motion, duck, and slam into the first body. He hits the second one. All three of us fall onto the ground, grunts mixing with the thudding of my punches that I throw mercilessly like I'm at Carnage.

I hear Kat's quick footsteps and her loud voice, "Don't fucking move! Freeze!"

I pull back, panting, crawling away as I stare at what's in front of me—the same two guys, on the ground. One reaches for the gun he dropped, but I snatch it and point it at him.

One thug grunts, curled up on the concrete. The other stares at me in shock.

Kat's behind me, with a gun, and I rise, slowly backing away, and motion to both of them. "Get in."

They don't walk, they crawl, fucking imbeciles. They're inside the room when I swing my foot at one guy's head with a kick that's enough to send him "night-night" for some time. I send another kick to the other guy's jaw, and he slumps onto the floor.

Kat's gaze is full of amazement. Only a girl like her can appreciate brutal necessity like this.

We cuff the guys, rip one of their shirts and gag them, then take their radios.

"Ready?" I ask.

Kat shifts both hands on her gun and nods. "So ready."

God, I love this woman. Shorts, tank top, barefoot, and with a gun—it's my new kinky fantasy.

We are getting the fuck out of here. I latch the door behind us, dump the radios, and we creep up the dim stairs, lit by a bulb, and pause by what looks like a trap door at the top of the stairs.

"We are underground," Kat whispers.

"Yeah."

There are muffled voices outside. I flip the switch by the door, and we sink into darkness.

Slowly, like a thief, I push up on the door, opening it just an inch.

It's not much brighter outside—night, I realize, which means it's either the same night we were taken or probably a day later. The voices are quite far away, coming from about forty feet where there's a glow of a fire.

I lift the door another inch or so.

"There are two people," I whisper. "No, three. I don't see guns, but I'm sure they have them." I scan the area around as much as I can without lifting the trap door higher. "A truck parked to the right," I say, even though Kat is right next to me, squinting through the opening.

"Barracks or tents to the left," she whispers. "This is not Port Mrei, is it?"

"Hard to say. We could be in a backyard. Shh." I listen for some time, but there's no noise around. "Doesn't sound like the town though."

"There are only three of them but might be many more in those barracks or sheds or whatever those are," Kat says. "We'll have to move fast."

"Yes. We only get several seconds before they can grab their guns."

"So. Shooting or fighting?"

"If we shoot and there are more of them, we're fucked. If we fight, we have to do it fast and run."

"Right."

I'd never thought it'd come down to this in my life.

More so, that I'd be in a situation like this with a woman. But what a woman!

I look at Kat, gauging her state, but she looks like she was born for situations like this.

"I'll take the two on the left," I say. "You take the one on the right." I calculate the course of actions in my head. "We have several seconds to emerge before they realize we're not their buddies. Tell me when you are ready."

She exhales loudly through her mouth, then leans over, confusing me for a second before I realize she's giving me a peck on my cheek.

"Ready," she whispers.

"Okay, slowly."

I hold the trap door above me as we start crawling out onto the dusty ground.

My eyes are on the thugs who chat and drink by the fire and don't notice us. Not even when we are out of the bunker and I slowly close the door. Not when we take careful steps through the darkness toward them.

Only when one of them turns his head in our direction, I bark, "Now!" And Kat and I dart toward them.

We reach them before they find their guns. I smash one in the face with the handle of my gun with a force that sends him sagging onto the ground, then slam into the other one, who trips on the fire pit, falls, and I smash his head several times before his low grunt quiets.

I spin around to see Kat sitting on her haunches next to the third guy, lifeless on the ground, a vague smile on her face.

"C'mon." I motion toward the darkness behind the barracks.

"Hey!" the voice, coming from the distance, makes us halt. "Hey, you!"

"Go!" I snap, grabbing Kat's hand, and dart for the shadows when a gunshot pierces the air.

"Fuck, fuck, fuck," Kat pants behind me as we run around the building. "Motherf—" Kat yelps.

"You okay?" I drag her along a wooden wall, through some bushes.

"Stepped on something."

More voices come from the fire pit. A sound of a radio beep, the another one.

"Trey!"

"Radio the Dice crew!"

"Search the premises!"

A dog barks in the distance, its barking picked up by a second one, then another, then suddenly the whole goddamn place comes alive.

There are no fences or property divisions. We crawl from one shed to another one. Then a tent. Then trip on old cardboard boxes. Step in a pile of oozing trash. Slip on the garbage-slimed dirt. Then cross some dirt path. Notice the bonfires ahead. Veer away behind another dark building.

"Fucking Ashlands," I murmur, scanning the semi-dark and piles of garbage.

Something squeaks under my feet—rats, this fucking place has rats!

The heat is overwhelming. The air is thick with nause-ating scents that don't belong to the Zion I know. The shadows are the darkest shade of black, the rest of the area hazy with smoke that swims through the dim air.

No, this place is not dead. It's alive like no other, but with the worst of humankind.

There's a sound of an engine starting, then another approaching from the distance. I yank Kat behind one of the shacks and halt. There are shadows in the dark alcove of a dilapidated shed in front of us. They're moving around, but not coming out, though I have a feeling they watch us. The stench here is stronger—human waste, cooked food, unclean clothes.

Suddenly, a bright light sweeps across the low roofs of the barracks—spotlights.

"Fuck, they're searching for us," I say, pulling Kat down to sit behind the shack with our backs to it.

The truck stops right behind the building that hides us. We can't move, can't go anywhere. All we can do is wait.

"We're in trouble," I tell Kat, and we turn our heads to look at each other.

It starts drizzling. The drops of water feel good on my bloodied hot face, and I want to laugh darkly, because Kat might've been right—she and I are cursed.

I take the gun with my left hand and find Kat's hand in the dark, lacing my fingers with hers.

"Someone will notice we're missing," she says.

I pray that we survive this. Of all the things I can lose— my career, my wealth, the island—she's the one I don't want to carry on without.

"Yes, they will," I say, trying to sound more hopeful than I actually am.

## 53

### MADDY

I'VE GOTTEN USED TO CHATS WITH CALLIE AND KAI, EVENINGS with Ty and Dani, and even Marlow, who I've gotten to know better. Bo is fully recovered, but we only see him in the evenings when we gather at someone's bungalow for dinner, a rare occasion for me, because I try to get more night shifts, any shifts. Work is my therapy and my escape.

I say *we* because we still feel like the Outcasts from the Eastside, though most of us settled quite comfortably into Ayana life. Comfort is a tricky word, especially after the two-year hostility between the Eastside and Westside. But Archer handled it well.

"He is a changed man, trust me," Ty said one day.

Everything has changed, indeed, since we all moved to Ayana. I like it but am not sure it won't ruin me in the long run. The Eastside was perfect. Isolated. Ayana is a boiling pot waiting to spill over.

Callie's face is glowing as she sits in one of our rooms at the medical ward and talks about Kai. That's all they talk about—each other. No one else exists when they're together. It's love like theirs that makes one believe in soulmates.

When she brings up the story of how she drew Kai's full-sized portrait, I laugh and glance at Sonny Little, who sits on the examination table, his feet dangling—he's way too young for stories like this.

Sonny is chewing on his favorite potato chips. I'm doing yet another check-up. The kid has never been to a doctor, so he's curiously studying my hands every time I touch him like I'm invading his personal space.

We still haven't located his parents and don't know how old he is. Archer did DNA testing and studied his biological marks, determining Sonny's age to be nine or ten. The kid seems happy, though he refuses to get a haircut, and his dark hair is still down to his shoulders and messy as ever.

Callie's phone beeps.

"Kai," she says, and her face lights up like she just got a present. "Hey, you," she answers.

But her smile drops right away, and eyes snap up at me. "What do you mean?" She puts Kai on speaker.

"Archer and Katura are missing," Kai repeats in a tense voice.

"How do you know?" Callie asks.

"Archer was supposed to have a meeting. He never responded. So Slate went to the yacht to check on them. They're gone. We don't know for how long. Their cell phones are there. Their Ayana bracelets are cut off, no way to track them."

That's what people don't understand. No money or

security guards can protect them forever if someone wants to hurt them. I know that better than anyone.

"Can't you track them on the cameras?" Callie asks.

"They must've been taken out by boat," Kai replies and exhales loudly into the phone. "Shit. They sent a team to Port Mrei. Raven went to talk to the mayor. But they suspect him anyway. And there's no way to track every street and house in town. They are about to send a swat team with all the guards who are off-duty."

"But it's a big town. They'll never be able to locate every basement and holding place."

"They could, but… It'll take time."

"Ashlands," Sonny butts in, his mouth full of potato chips.

Callie frowns. "The Ashlands?"

Kai's voice comes in again. "Could be. But there's nowhere to hide there."

"There' bunkers," Sonny says indifferently, chewing.

"What bunkers?" Kai snaps.

"Where the' keep guns an' all."

I exchange startled glances with Callie. "How do you know?"

"I liv' there fo' some time. Know places," he announces with pride like we're talking about a game.

"Little," Kai says with urgency. "Would you be able to show those places on a map?"

Sonny shrugs. "Wha's a map?"

"I'll be right there," Kai blurts and cuts the call.

Only five minutes pass before there are loud footsteps in the hallway, then the door opens to reveal Raven.

Uh-oh. This guy…

The first time I saw him, his eyes hypnotized me.

The second time, he gave me an uneasy flashback from my past.

When he came to the medical ward with bruises after the fight at Carnage, we didn't say much to each other. Sometimes, all you need to tell you there's something different about a person is a strange shiver down your spine at the touch, an unusual sensation in your heart when he speaks to you, the fingers with missing phalanges too gentle when they wrap around your wrist as you try to touch his old scars, the soft "Don't," and the tingling on your skin at the contact, too prolonged for two strangers who've never spoken before.

Raven's gaze is on me as soon as he steps into the room, followed by Kai.

I shake off the thoughts, the memories, and the strange excitement at seeing him again.

I take a slow step to shield Sonny. I don't need to make abrupt movements or say things loudly—Raven notices every little detail, like a predator. Something in me wants to get under his skin, see what makes him tick, what's behind this reserved man everyone is too cautious about. His power is scary but contagious, reminding me of the past and the men I used to be around.

"I need the kid." Raven tells me in that soft deep voice that doesn't fit his almost cruelly cold expression. He's talking to me, not Callie, who's in charge of the kid, like I'm the boy's mother, then gives Sonny a backward nod. "You're coming with us."

He's in my domain now, and I know how to handle men like this—everything with him has to be a respectful negotiation.

So, I shake my head. "No, he's not," I say calmly.

Raven's eyes probe into me with almost surgical precision, a humorous sparkle in them like he just heard something ridiculous that surprised and intrigued him.

He takes a step closer. The smile on his lips doesn't reach his eyes when he says quietly, "He's coming with us."

I match his emotionless smile. "You learn how to talk to a child, you get to talk to one. Otherwise, you have to go through me."

A quiet, "Huh," escapes him.

It feels like it's just him and me in the room, a silent duel, but I won't budge unless he's nice. "Maybe, you should *ask* him if he wants to go."

"I will," Sonny says eagerly from behind me. He's fascinated with everything, including new people, though he doesn't yet know who to trust.

Raven only cocks a brow at me as if saying, "See? I win."

"Maddy." Kai steps from behind him. "Can we please take Sonny? He'll be fine. I'll take care of him. But he might help. *Really* help." His gaze is so warm—it's impossible to say no to Kai. "Please," he mouths and kneads his brows in a plea.

Sometimes, that's all one needs to resolve a conflict—a request, permission, and an ounce of understanding. Raven doesn't get that. He moves like a dark shadow used to people stepping aside when he makes his way through.

"I'm coming with you," I say and turn my back to Raven, then sit down on my haunches in front of Sonny. "You don't have to, kiddo, if you don't feel comfortable."

Sonny's eyes shift upward and behind me. I know who he's looking at, and it's uncanny—the kid is not afraid but curious about Raven when he shrugs his bony shoulders and pushes his long hair off his forehead. "Yeah. I don' min'."

I feel Raven's gaze on me all the way to the Center. He's on a sports bike behind our golf cart, as if on purpose so he can watch me.

I grew up amidst danger. I was taught to get used to it, accept it, and make friends with those who might hurt me one day. I've changed my ways since then, but Raven reminds me of where I come from. Maybe that's the reason I feel excitement when he's around.

We walk into the Center and to the surveillance part. I've only been here when we came back from the Eastside, and the fact that there are so many eyes and so many screens showing every part of Zion makes me uneasy. I close my eyes for a second, swallowing hard when I turn to see Raven's cold stare burrowing into me.

I feel goosebumps on my skin, yet I have a hard time looking away.

"Okay," Kai says, setting Sonny down at a big screen and kneeling next to him as the rest of us stand behind him. Raven's next to me, our shoulders almost touching like he's doing it on purpose. "Give us the Ashlands." The surveillance guy next to Sonny moves the mouse and clicks, zooming in on an aerial view of Port Mrei and the vast polka-dotted area next to it. "Do you recognize any part of it from this far?"

Sunny shakes his head. "Wha's this?"

Kai motions with his finger to the surveillance guy. "Closer, much closer, on any area, so he can see the landscape and structures."

The surveillance guy does what he's told.

Kai turns to look at Sonny. "Better? Do you recognize any of the tents?"

Sonny turns his head and then bends his entire body like he's trying to read an upside-down picture, then does it the other way.

"I don'," he murmurs almost apologetically and then turns around to look at Raven—Raven! Of all people!

Raven gives a backward nod. "Bring out a drone."

We all turn to look at Raven.

So does the surveillance guard. "How many? And where do you want them? East? West? Port Mrei entrance?" he asks with no surprise as he picks up his phone and dials someone.

"One, for now. Night vision model," says Raven, his arms crossed at his chest as if he's the boss here. "Start with the road from Port Mrei, bring it lower to the ground but high enough so no one can reach it. It'll be easier for the kid to orient himself."

The surveillance guy does as he's told, and in a minute, Sonny stabs the screen with his finger. "Turn left. Behin' the broken shed, there's a trap door."

Kai marks it on the paper map in front of him.

In a minute, Sonny stabs the screen again. "Under the

big ol' tent with a wind bird, there's a door tha' goes down under."

He points out two more places like this, and we all stare in shock.

Just then, the screen goes dark.

"What happened?" Kai blurts out.

"Someone must've knocked it out," the surveillance guy says, makes a phone call, then announces, "Signal lost."

That's when Raven says quietly, his voice low but etched with danger, "Send a dozen more drones to scout the area. Get every surveillance guy on it. I'm staying here with the kid. Call Marlow, Bishop, and get the head of security. We need to send the swat team to the Ashlands. Now."

## 54

---

## ARCHER

GOD, HOW I NEVER WANTED TO SEE THIS PLACE. BUT HERE WE are, the Ashlands, the den of Savages. The rain makes everything even worse, lifting off the putrid smells into the air.

It's nighttime, but the shantytown teems with life. Barracks, makeshift tents, fire pits—who knows what happens in the darkest pits of this hell... Those fires never die, not even during rains and storms. Warming, cooking, burning remains...

There are muffled voices everywhere. A freaking baby is crying in one of the dirty nests that make up this God-awful place. That's humanity—carrying on even in the worst places.

I'm trying to figure out what our next move is. We are half-naked, barefoot, with two guns but in hostile territory and chased by maniacs. Shadows creep here and there. There are glints of bonfires in the distance. In places like this, one never knows who is an enemy or just a bystander.

Someone might rat us out with just one shout. Someone might mess with us just for fun.

Kat and I sit with our backs against the wooden boards of someone's shack and wait for a chance—for what, I'm not sure, hopefully, to get out of this fucking place, though this might be way harder than escaping the underground prison cell.

The group of thugs behind our building doesn't move. A scooter pulls up to them, then storms off. We can't come out or move yet. We might have to wait it out.

For a place that doesn't have electricity, for the middle of the night or whatever time it is, this place is set in a soft hazy glow—fires, smoke, dust. My eyes have adjusted to semi-darkness. Kat's eyes wander around, assessing, her expression too calm, considering the situation we're in.

She sounds almost dreamy when she whispers, "Remember you said once, 'We don't do anything but fuck?'"

"Yeah. We did way more than that."

"We danced."

"We danced," I echo with a smile.

"Now we've been kidnapped, we beat the guys up, and are hunted in the filthiest pits of this island. You jinxed us, Archer. I wish we weren't doing *that* much. We always get carried away, huh?"

I chuckle but don't like that it sounds like it's my fault. "I never wanted to put you in danger, Kat. You know that, right?"

We've been through highs and lows that top most relationships I know, but this is the cherry on the cake.

"I have a feeling it's my fault," she says quietly.

"What? No. Absolutely not. We'll make it," I reassure her. "I don't have a choice. I can't lose you."

"Well, if you lose me, who will keep you on your toes?"

"True."

"Arch." Her whisper suddenly drops the cheerfulness.

"Yes, kitten." I close my eyes. I wish we were back on the yacht, fucking, dancing, cuddling, watching the sunset —any scenario where I usually call her that.

"You know how you told me I'm important to you? Back on the yacht?"

"That's a serious conversation for someone who doesn't like talking about feelings. And we are in deep shit right now."

Yet her voice grounds me. It used to get under my skin. Now, it's the one thing that makes me feel alive, as long as it's next to me.

"I love you," she says.

I turn to look at her, but she's staring ahead into darkness.

This is the most awkward moment to confess. But then, it's my wild thing, always taking me by surprise.

I take in her messy hair that looks like a giant nest that I love to pieces, her serious face, her beautiful profile, the slope of her shoulders, that bronze skin that I love feeling against mine, her bare feet that probably hurt as much as mine after running on pebbles, trash, and whatnot. She holds a gun between her raised knees, and the sight of her is so brutal and beautiful that it takes my breath away.

She finally turns to me. "What?" Her smile is too shy.

I shake my head. I'm so in love. And anger spikes in me at the thought that I couldn't keep her safe.

"I wish we were back on the yacht," I say.

"Well... If there's one person I'd ever be willing to go through this shit with, it's you, Archer."

"Yeah?"

"Yeah."

She's perfect.

She's the one.

I'll build a fucking chapel at Ayana to lay my claim on her.

"*Ma-yá ka-ra-lé-va*," I say, smiling.

She bites her lip.

"Arch, about those words... They don't mean what I told you they did."

She thinks she's tricked me. Little does she know that I've relied more on the internet and dictionaries than on people my whole life.

"Kat, you *are* my queen."

She's startled. "Wh— How long have you known?"

God, I love catching her by surprise. "Back then I didn't trust a word you said."

"And now?" She's looking at me like she's pleading for the right answer.

There's a commotion behind the shack, an angry fight, then radios beeping, making us shut up, then it quiets down again.

I stretch my hand and push a wet curl out of Kat's face. "I hope we can trust each other with everything," I finally answer.

"I do," she blurts faster than she can think of a more sassy answer. "I trust you, Arch."

This conversation is in the wrong place and time, but something tugs at my chest—a tiny prickly thought that all this may end badly, and I just want another minute with her, even if it's in the stinky slums, behind some dumpy hut.

"Would you like a gold tiara as a present, my queen?" I ask her, tilting my head back, feeling raindrops tickle my face, and smile, though my chest clenches impossibly tight. I wish I'd told her so much more—how amazing she is, how much she means to me.

"Nah. Boring." She chuckles.

"A gown from white peafowls' feathers?"

"Is that one of your innuendoes again? No, thank you. Though I do like feathers in a different context."

"A diamond-encrusted gun?"

"That's a thought."

I snort. "I was joking, Kat."

"Tsk. Tease."

"Seriously? You'd like that?"

"Sure. A Brownells. Or a Smith&Wesson. Can I have my name spelled out in gold on it?"

"Which one? Katura, wild thing, or kitten?"

She bursts into a muffled chuckle.

"Kat," I whisper and have to take a deep breath because the sudden eerie feeling is uneasy—what if things go terribly wrong tonight? "If there's a chance…" I don't finish. I can't. The thought that I can lose her starts clawing at my heart in the most painful way. "I just need a kiss, one more kiss."

She leans over right away like she's thinking the same, feeling the same, her lips pressing to mine and her hand cupping my cheek in the sweetest kiss.

"I love you," she exhales.

I swear, when we get out of here, I'll take her as far away from all this mess as possible, even if it means giving up everything I've worked on in the last years.

The distant sound of the Ayana emergency alarm snaps both our heads in that direction.

"Finally," I breathe out in sudden relief, and we pull away from each other. It's only a matter of minutes before the guards reach the Ashlands, if they figure out where we are. Only now do I realize we don't have our bracelets on.

"Shit, they might go to Port Mrei," I say.

"If they're smart, they'll come here too," Kat argues.

But then there's the sound of heavy footsteps.

"Over here!" someone barks right behind the shack we are hiding at.

"Run!" I snap at Kat, and we both dart in the opposite direction from the voices.

"They're here!" a shout follows, then the sound of heavy footsteps chasing us.

We jump over some garbage piles.

Someone whistles.

"There! There! Get 'em!"

A dark shadow tries to intercept us, but I slam into it and keep running, Kat at my side.

We can't outrun them, not barefoot. The rain hardens,

and in a moment, it's pouring, the water running down my face, blinding me.

Someone shoots in our direction, I pull Kat left, behind a big tent and a fire with a group of people around.

There's a round of gunshots and a loud explosion, lighting the air with an orange glow and sparks.

"What the fuck?" I exhale, panting, slowing down as Kat and I crouch behind another tent. How many are there? "They are not supposed to bomb the freaking place."

"It's a riot, Archer. It's not the guards. It's the Savages."

I peek from behind the building. "It looks like a gasoline drum explosion. Jesus…"

"There!" She pulls me toward a darker path between wood shacks.

"Freeze!" someone barks behind us, but we're not stopping.

"Get 'em!"

"Right there!"

A shot pierces the air.

How the hell do they have so many guns?

Someone slams into me, and I roll onto the ground, losing my gun.

"Archer!" Kat yells.

I jump up and throat-punch a guy. Someone punches me in the shoulder, and I turn and start punching his face.

I break free and stumble toward Kat, who points a gun behind me, her voice full of worry when she says. "Archer, there's a giant group of them coming."

Shadows stream toward us.

"Run!" I yell.

"What?"

"Run, Kat. I'll cover you. Run to the shore. There's a camera there, the surveillance team will see you. Run! I'll distract them!"

And I throw myself at the approaching crowd, punching away, roaring as I try to draw their attention.

## 55

## KAT

Archer roars as he sends blow after vicious blow into one thug, then another, a myriad of them running like insects toward us.

"Go!" Archer yells without looking.

It startles me.

Of all the things he could've said, sending me away was the worst call. The fact that he thinks I'd ever leave him makes me feel hurt, then angry.

Someone pulls me by my hair so roughly that a scream escapes me and my scalp feels like it's sets on fire.

The anger in me explodes.

"Aaaaargh!" I roar from pain and rage.

I twist around immediately and slam the person to the ground, jump up, and kick him viciously with my heel.

My limbs are heavy, my feet shredded, my knuckles bloodied.

One thug.

Then another.

Then I hear many more voices behind me. I turn but don't see Archer.

"Archer!" I scream, but the only thing visible is a snake ball of bodies farther away from where Archer was.

*No-no-no!*

My nerves are jangling, my brain is on fire, my heart racing. I've never been so sure about anything as right now —there's not a chance of me leaving Archer behind.

I stumble and run toward the mess, my eyes on the pile of bodies, Archer buried under them.

I can't see him, can't hear him. My heart thuds like it will explode in a second. All sounds mix together—my heavy breathing, the whispering rain, the grunts, and the thudding of kicks and punches.

I'll never leave Archer! Even if it'll leave me bloodied and bruised. Even if the worst comes for me afterward.

I can't.

Not a fucking chance in this motherfucking world!

If he's being dragged to hell, I'm going there to get him. He's mine. And these people—

I roar in anger like an animal and shoot the gun in the air, then point it at the human mess. I've never shot at actual people, but that's about to change.

I shoot at the thugs one by one as I approach.

Torso shot.

Torso shot.

One more.

Another one.

I could've shot them in the head. Even in the dark, I'd still hit where I aim. The fact that I'm shooting at real people doesn't bother me, not when those animals are hurting *my* Archer.

A couple of thugs fall with screams and several scatter away like spiders. But several more are kicking at Archer. They must be high or drunk, immune to the sound of gunshots. Even the ones who went down start scrambling toward the group again. I can't shoot the ones close to Archer for fear of hitting him, so I aim at the ones farther away.

Someone slams into me, sending me to the ground, but before I get up, I kick at the body that flung at me, sending it to the ground too.

Another one rushes to me. It's dark, but I know danger when I see it. It doesn't have to have a face. I swing my foot, slamming it on the side of the face I can't see, a grunt escaping it.

In seconds, I pick up the gun from the mud and jump to my feet.

"Wanna play, little girl?"

A voice behind me whips me around, putting me face to face with an old thug baring his crooked teeth in a slimy smile. He grabs my throat with a steel claw, cutting off my breathing.

Without hesitation, I knee him in the balls, and when his hand slips down, I hit the moron who was taking his time sweet-talking right in the plexus. He's paralyzed, a guttural sound escaping from him, as I smash the butt of my gun in his face, sending him to the ground like a log.

"I'm a woman, motherfucker. Have a problem?"

I dash toward the thugs that are on Archer.

He's on the ground, but still fighting them off, one thug wrestling him, while others send kicks aimlessly—the beasts don't even care if they hurt each other.

I grab one by the hair, press the gun to his back, and pull the trigger, but a hollow sound follows.

"Fuck!" I toss the gun aside and throw him at another guy.

Someone grabs me from behind, strangling me, lifting me off the ground. I hold on to his arms around my neck and kick with both feet at another one who rushes toward me.

There is no end to them. More are coming. I'm thrown onto the ground. A kick in my gut leaves me breathless for a moment. Another one makes me dizzy, then another when I try to get up but fall down.

We lost.

The two of us.

I kick back in a last attempt to get back on my feet.

"Archer," I cry, knowing that he lost too, that he can't get back up, but wanting one more time to hear his voice.

## 56

# ARCHER

THROUGH THE MUD AND THE SLUSH AND THE KICKS AND THE punches—I'm on the ground, wrestling and fighting in reflex by now, just trying to keep going—I suddenly hear Kat's voice, my name.

She didn't leave! She's somewhere near, and by the sound of it, in pain.

I snap back to life, kicking someone's leg from under them. I roar and start punching away, pushing up, then surging forward through a mass of bodies, my fists slippery from pouring rain and blood as I punch into flesh.

Gunfire erupts only twenty or so feet away, and the thugs duck and halt, their circle around me loosening.

"Everyone freeze!" someone commands.

Another round of shots go off.

I raise my head, wobbling on my feet. About a dozen shadows in uniforms and night vision goggles are approaching like a wall, and I frantically search for Kat.

The thugs start retreating slowly, crouching away, and I

find her sitting on the ground and run to her.

"We're fine, fine," I murmur, checking her face and helping her get up.

Her hair is wet, she's a mess, the side of her face bloodied, but she grabs my head and kisses me on the lips, salty wetness mixing with my blood gushing through my cut lip.

There are more of us to fight off the fucking Savages, but a sudden shot pierces the air, and one of the guards goes down.

The mercenaries have seen every shade of brutality in war zones. But they rarely see a riot of fucked-up drunk and high nothing-to-lose low-lives who crave blood and violence. That's why riots are unstoppable. You never understand why the rioters hurt their own, but it's simple—an animalistic reflex, driven by adrenalin. Violence is contagious and tends to turn off the most basic human instincts —reason and self-preservation. Biological reflexes are the strongest in humans. We are, in essence, animals. Throw in intoxication, and we become killing machines.

A deafening bang and a bright orange explosion assault my eardrums and eyes. Dirt showers us head to toe, sending us all crouching. It's not a bomb but a gas tank or something, lighting up the Ashlands with a hellish glare and sending a heat wave in our direction.

Several guards are on the ground. The others start shooting point-blank at the figures now clearly visible against the giant orange glow.

The tents catch on fire.

Wails echo through the dark.

More shadows come as bullets start whining all

around us.

My feet are raw from stepping on trash and stones, but I hiss through pain and hold Kat tight next to me as I yell, "We gotta start moving!"

The loudspeakers on the Western side of the Ashlands go off. An army of guards is closing in from the West, pushing all the thugs in our direction. Some thugs might surrender, but the ones running—*fuck*—are running toward us…

"We have to go!" a familiar voice yells.

I fucking know that voice!

My eyes widen at the silhouette clad in the guards' uniform and a bullet-proof vest, marching toward us with a gun in his hand and a fucking grin. "What's up, bro? Got a bit tossed around?"

"Kai!" Kat squeals.

Fucking Droga!

My breath hitches in my throat as I can't believe my eyes, my lips stretching in a smile.

"Stop gawking and start moving," he commands.

"Move toward the eastern shore!" a guard yells. "Cover the front and the back! Move! Move! Move!"

A shadow runs toward me, and Droga intercepts him mid-way, smashing him with a gun.

The guards have no mercy, firing repeatedly at the shadows.

"Fucker," Droga hisses as he kicks another thug away, then takes a spot next to me, shielding me.

"What are you doing here, Droga? You got lost?" I tease him, still in disbelief he's here.

"Nah. Was passing by, heard someone whining, 'Droooo-gaaa,'" his voice turns all pathetic, "'co-o-o-o-me sa-a-a-a-a-ve me.'"

Laughter escapes me, and it's the most ridiculous moment—me grinning as bullets rain all around us.

There's a familiar humming in the air, and only now do I notice a drone, then another, but they are shot down immediately.

We are moving slowly but steadily, like a small column, away from the fire and into the darkness.

Places like this shouldn't exist. I never suspected there'd be so many people in these slums. And so many of them are angry and reckless, the guards sending a shadow after shadow to the ground as the darkness echoes with moans of pain.

There are several guards ahead of us, weapons raised. Several others are behind, covering us.

Another shot in our direction jerks one of the guards, and he sends a round of shots in response.

A radio crackles. "Forty-two, come in."

"Got them," one guard blurts into the radio. "Moving toward the shore."

"Boats are at the location," comes the reply.

"Copy."

There are fewer structures here, the landscape bare even though it's hard to see. There's a desert of nothingness ahead, the sound of the waves crashing against the rocks louder.

It's easier to breathe, except for the smoke that hovers above the ground like fog. Fuck, we almost made it out.

We crouch in the dark, the guards' flashlights off, but the little green lights on their night visions indicate they know where we're going.

God, there's a reason I stayed away from this fucking dump.

I crouch closer to Kat and take her hand. She squeezes it hard. Droga is on the other side of me, looking around, though here, outside the Ashlands, away from the fire pits, it's harder to see.

"Almost there," a guard's voice blurts into a radio.

"Copy."

We've made it! The sound of the waves has never been more beautiful.

Automatic gunshots assault us, bullets whistling at our feet, and send a rain of dirt and pebbles at us.

"Cover!" the guards shout, but a gang of more than a dozen rush at us from nowhere.

The guards shoot, but a body slams into me, sending me down. I kick and slam my fist into whatever tried to attack me, then jump onto my feet and kick another shadow.

Droga is on someone and sends the thug to the ground, then turns to look at me. "You okay?"

A dark silhouette ten feet away from him approaches fast. I don't need the light to see it's holding a gun, pointing at Droga.

"Droga!" I shout, reach him in several wide strides, and slam into him right as the shot goes off.

The impact of both of us falling to the ground is painful, piercing me in several places at once.

"Aaaargh!" Kat's roars, then comes the sound of

someone being kicked, a moan, angry, "Fucker." That's Kat.

God, this woman is perfection.

I try to get up, but I'm dizzy.

"Dude, you okay?" Droga's voice is near or above me, I can't tell. I try to get up but end up on all fours.

"Move! Move!" the guards yell.

"Yeah…" I make another attempt but fall down right away. Something's not right.

Kat and Droga are on me.

"Archer, baby…"

There's a flashlight in Droga's hand. "Fuck."

"What?" I try to get up and succeed this time, but the sudden sharp pain in my ribs is nauseating.

"You got shot," Droga says. "Fuck-fuck-fuck! I have a bulletproof vest!" he shouts. "What the fuck, bro?"

"Archer, you'll be fine," Kat murmurs with a strange desperation in her voice.

I'm fine, aren't I? I'm fine.

But there's that searing pain again, and suddenly, it's hard to breathe.

"Fuck, I…"

I wanna bend over like I can fold into the pain to make it go away, but doing so hurts even more.

"He's shot. Fuck, Kai, he's shot." Kat pulls her tank top over her head, leaving her only in her bikini, and tries to tie it around my ribs, then rips it in half and finally manages to secure it around my wound.

"I'm fine," I grunt, taking a deep breath and flinching at the pain somewhere in my abdomen. Callie didn't shoot me months ago, so now a fucking Savage did.

"Fuck," Kai exhales, swinging my arm around his neck. "Let's move. Quick!"

The explosion is so sudden that it sends all of us to the ground again, showering us with dirt and pebbles.

For a moment, there's only buzzing in my ears, the rest of the sounds muffled. I move my jaw to crack my ears, then shake my head.

"You alright?" The voice is muffled, but I recognize it—Droga's.

"Where's Kat?" I stumble onto my feet, the pain in my chest so sharp that I almost pass out but manage to stand.

"She's right over there," he says, panting. "Get her out of here!" he shouts to a guard.

"Archer!" Kat is fifty or so feet away, sandwiched in-between several guards who keep shooting around.

"Go with them!" I yell. "We're coming!"

But there's another explosion, right between us, and Droga drags me away, into the darkness.

A guard follows with his back to us, shooting at whatever he can see in his night vision. "Move North! They blocked the way to the shore!" he yells. "We have to go around!"

I can barely stand but feel Droga's arm around my back, my arm suddenly around his neck—I think I blacked out for a second.

"Move, Crone. Move. We have to move," he murmurs, breathing heavily, both of us stumbling on rocks, gunshots piercing the air.

I know that's not the proper way to the shore. We are on the rocky part that ends on cliffs at the ocean. This is not right. But our access to the beach where the boats are is cut off.

"Moving toward the caves," the guard blurts into the radio. A gunshot pierces the air and he yelps. "Fuck! Fuckers!" He sends a round of shots toward the Ashlands.

It smells like seaweed. The dark ground is now in contrast with the lighter sky—we're on the cliff tops, an open target here, and the only place to hide is the caves down below.

"I'm injured. Fuck," the guard curses. "Move toward the caves," he orders. "I'll cover you. Don't come out until we come get you." Then he blurts into the radio, "Thirty-two. Injured. The subjects are moving into the caves. Access to shore blocked. Send reinforcement."

Droga nudges me to move faster. "We have to hide in the caves."

"Where's Kat?" I can't see much with rain trickling into my eyes. It might be blood, I'm not sure anymore.

"She's with the guards heading toward the boats. She'll be fine, Crone. But we need to hide."

The guard isn't behind us anymore. It's quiet. The rocky surface we are on is sloping down.

Only Droga knows where the hell we're going. I can't focus. Can't see much. Only feel his arm around me.

Droga fumbles with something and a circle of light appears on the ground—his flashlight. "Careful," he guides me.

There's a soft lapping of the water ahead of us, a sound of an explosion somewhere far in the distance, and occasional shots.

A gaping hole ahead signifies the arched entrance to one of the caves as we step into it, and the sounds start disappearing, eerie hollowness closing around us.

My feet step into the shallow water. I lose the footing and almost drop to my knees, but Droga's arms catch me.

"Fuck," he murmurs. "We need to stop here."

Just then, the sharp whistle of a bullet zips through the air.

We duck.

"They're following. Fuck, Crone, move."

The water rises as we walk forward, the flashlight showing the monstrous cave around us.

"How far do we go?" I ask.

Droga turns around, shining the flashlight onto the ceiling and the slimy walls. "We can't go back. And we can't stay in this cave."

"Why?" The water is only up to our thighs.

"It's high tide. The entrance will be blocked soon." His voice bounces in echoes between the walls. "This cave is not tall enough. It'll fill up with water in a matter of an hour."

I push Droga away and lean on a rock that protrudes out of the water. It's slimy, cold, and I feel like pressing my forehead to it to cool down my burning head and manage my strength. A short break is all I need. The pain is so sharp that I feel like my body is cut in half.

"Droga, go ahead. I'll wait here."

"Crone, get your shit together." His strong hand jerks me up, and I meet his worried gaze. "We can't go back. Savages are waiting at the entrance. But if we stay here, we drown."

381

## 57

## KAT

A GUARD HELPS ME INTO ONE OF THE THREE SPEEDBOATS parked at the shore. Several guards stand in the position farther away, pointing guns in the direction of the Ashlands and occasionally firing.

My body aches. I have multiple cuts and bruises, and my feet are shredded, but I feel alive like never before.

The guard who helped me motions to the others. "Let's roll!"

Panic sluices over me. "Wait! Wait! We're waiting for Archer and Kai!"

"We're leaving a boat with several men to wait for them," he says, not looking at me. "We need to get you back to safety."

"You kidding me?" I shout. "I'm not going anywhere until I see them get in the boat!"

I start crawling out of the boat but his rough hand on my arm stops me.

"We're getting you to safety and sending reinforcement. We can't stay here."

"Not a fucking chance!" I snap at him and jump off the boat into the water, the bare soles of my feet on fire. So is the rest of my body, but I don't care. I'm not leaving Archer behind.

"Miss!"

I stumble out of the water and onto the shore when strong arms catch me from behind. "Get back."

"Let go!" I snarl and slam my head back only to find nothing.

The arms suddenly toss me forward and into the water.

When I stand up, dripping, the guard stands in front of me, his hands outstretched like I'm a psycho who needs to be sedated. "I'm sorry, miss. We follow orders. There's nothing you can do. Professionals are doing the job. They'll get the targets."

*The targets.*

Motherfucker!

"Please, get back in the boat," he says, taking slow steps through the water toward me.

"Does Kai have a radio? Droga?"

The guard picks up his radio. "Update on Mr. Crone? Come in?"

It's still raining. The shots still echo in the distance—that could be Archer!

"Update on Mr. Crone?" he repeats.

My heart pounds harder for several seconds of silence when the radio crackles and Kai's voice comes in.

"It's Droga. We're in the caves. Entrance blocked. Crone is injured."

My heart leaps in despair when he comes in again.

"Send a team to the northern Devil's Caverns entrance. There's a high tide. We only have an hour."

But the guard is already pushing me back into the boat, and another one starts the engine.

"Cover us!" he shouts as the boat shoots off the shore, then picks up the radio again. "Heading to the Eastside, Devil's Caverns."

## 58

## ARCHER

THE WATER IS UP TO OUR CHESTS ALREADY AS WE STRUGGLE TO walk from one cavern to another.

Kat's cloth is washed away, the water keeping my wound open, a bad thing, but I can't have negative thoughts right now. Water makes it easier to move, supporting my weight.

Droga gives an update to a guard on the radio, then tosses the radio away. He loses his bulletproof jacket and lets it sink into the water. The gun goes next. Then the duty belt. He holds the flashlight between his teeth, and in this moment, I know that he's a much stronger man than I am.

He motions to go forward. "Keep up, Crone."

"Right behind you," I hiss through pain, on the verge of passing out. My confidence is gone as I can feel my strength draining into the water. "How do you know where to go?"

"I don't."

"Great."

Droga snorts as we move along the wall of one cavern,

through a narrower arch, to another, much bigger. The light from his flashlight bounces off the walls, water all around us, dripping from above, the shadows dancing like ghosts.

"We could stay here, no? Until the tide goes down again?" I ask.

I need to rest, stop moving, and close my eyes for a minute. Everything's blurry. I can only see an outline of Droga's upper body against the halo of light bouncing here and there.

"We could, but we would be swimming. Which is tough to do for several hours. With your wound—impossible. So move your ass, Crone."

I do, pushing through pain.

"I've been here before," Droga says, either to calm me or distract me. We keep pushing forward, the water already at our shoulders. "Ty knows these caves by heart. He drew a map for me once. When I was hiding from you."

He snorts.

"Right," I murmur.

"Now I'm hiding *you* in here. The irony, huh?"

He turns around and positions the light below his face, which illuminates it like a fucking scull mask.

A chuckle escapes me, which resonates with another burst of pain.

"If I die here in your arms, Droga, that would be just the cherry on the cake."

"I don't need a fucking cherry, Crone. Move. Don't talk."

The lowest I ever felt in my life was when I got the news about the crash that killed my brother and Mom.

The angriest I ever felt was the day I found out Droga had Callie in his room all night after the Block Party, and the whole campus was cheering.

The strongest I ever felt was after the Change, when we went through death toll records, grieved about the lost families, then set up Gen-Alpha and realized that Zion saved us and now was our home, and I could protect the ones who got lucky. Even if that meant establishing strict rules and not taking shit from anyone.

The most on top of the world I felt—not when I got my formula approved by the FDA that put it on the list of top five gene therapy medications, which put me in the top ten *Forbes Thirty Under Thirty*. Not even when the most powerful leaders from the Middle East, Asia, and the US flew to Zion for a short and very discreet meeting to discuss the investments into the drug.

No.

We always think it's the grand events that are the best, when, in fact, it's the small things that make us the happiest.

The most euphoric moment in my life was when Droga and I won that street bike race in Camden. None of our Deene friends were there. No one in Camden knew who we were. We raced the street pros and won, the two of us cutting the finish line. Didn't matter—Droga or me—we fucking beat them and celebrated like whackjobs. I remember cheering with him with beers on a dirt pullout on some deserted highway out of town, roaring at the top of our lungs and laughing madly, feeling high on the win like no drug has ever made me feel.

The happiest I've ever been? Before meeting Kat? Before our reconciliation? Before the two days on the yacht? When Droga and I did the cross-country trip through Mexico. It wasn't a day, but an entire trip, with all its brawls with the local mules, and that drunk night at a roadside cantina when I threw up like a motherfucker, and a detour to Baja where we swam with the local fishermen.

Droga has been in more important moments in my life than anyone else.

And now this, stuck with him in the caves where we might drown.

We are swimming by now, or, to be precise, floating along the sides of the caverns, holding on to the walls. Droga turns to check on me now and then, saying things to keep me coherent, the flashlight between his teeth or in his hand.

We swim into a smaller cave and stop.

I'm not sure how long we've been in the caves but too long for an open wound to be in the water. My body feels heavy like it's made out of lead. I'm following on instinct, without realizing how many caves we swam through, except the one we're in is small, the water only two feet or so below the ceiling.

Droga turns to look at me.

"How are you?"

I breathe in tiny increments, the pain so sharp, spider-webbing through my torso that I can't take deeper breaths. I think I answer, but everything is dizzy. Something blocks my nostrils, and I gasp, choking on water.

"Crone-Crone-Crone! Look at me!"

Floating, still registering the stone wall I'm clinging to, I open my eyes.

Droga's face is in front of me, only inches away. "You with me?"

I nod.

*Not for long.*

"Droga, if we get out of here, I'll build you and Callie a fucking Taj Mahal."

He spits out water. "Taj Mahal is a mausoleum, Crone."

"Fuck. I know that. My bad." I close my eyes, feeling dizzy, losing my grip. "I'll build you a palace."

"I don't like palaces."

"Right. I forgot. You like huts and shitty outside shower stalls."

I chuckle but then hold my breath in excruciating pain. He doesn't know that he's in my will. If something happens to me, he and Callie will be richer than God.

"Archer, you are not fucking dying, okay?" It's the first time in years he'd called me by my name. "Not on my watch. I don't have any family left but Callie and you. So toughen up, fucker. If you don't make it, Kat will kill me."

Kat, my wild thing—I so fucking wish she were here. Not in danger. Just next to me.

Droga and Kat—the two people who went through shit because of me and still stuck around and now have to go through hell again.

And that's when I hear Droga's voice again. "I got your back, bro."

Fucking tears well up in my eyes.

"I'm sorry, Droga. I fucked up so many things for you."

"Stop whining, Crone."

I'm not whining, just want to leave a few good words behind.

"You brought me to this island," he says, bobbing in the water in front of me. "It's fate or whatever you wanna call it. And I'm not letting you go. You are too important to me, yeah? Always have been. But I'm not a psycho like you. So my methods of dragging you through hell are a bit different than yours."

I smile inwardly, clenching my jaw in pain so tightly, I feel like my teeth are sinking into my jawbone.

"Okay, pay attention," he says. "Right now, you'll have to do the best you can, because we'll have to dive."

His words pulsate through the dark, and my mushy brain can't process them.

A sharp slap on my face jostles me awake.

"Crone! Stay with me!" he barks.

"So loving," I murmur and finally do smile.

"Crone, just hold on for several minutes. We need to do this, yeah?"

I think I nod, but my eyelids are heavy.

"Okay." Droga's voice is coming in and out like there's a bad connection. "On three, you hold your breath and do your best to push through the water. I'll guide you. But you need to stay awake for this," he says, his voice drowning out. "Crone! Open your eyes!"

He slaps me again on the face.

I try to focus.

"We only need to get under this one passage. They're waiting for us, yeah? Kat and the guards." He motions somewhere but I don't see anything but his face. "Take a deep breath?" Summoning all my strength, I do as he tells me. "One. Two. Three."

He pulls me down, underwater, and forward.

His strong hand is the only thing I feel. I follow him like seaweed, trying to stay focused, fighting through the water. My head is spinning. The feel of water warping around me is comforting, except, this time, I don't want comforting darkness. I want light. Her. I want to see Kat again.

And that's when I finally slip into darkness.

# 59

## KAT

THE HOLLOWNESS OF THE DEVIL'S CAVERNS IS TOO EERIE AS WE softly rock on a speedboat in the center of it.

The strobe lights point at one of the walls, dark murky water lapping at the slimy stone. One of the guards talks on the walkie, the beeping of the radio and his voice echoing through the large hollow dark dome of the cave. I feel like I'm in someone's giant mouth, and I never liked horror movies.

I stare at the brown patch of water, lit up by the light, murky amongst the blackness around.

And I wait.

And wait.

My heartbeat seems to slow down, my body so tense I can't move.

I stare at that brown patch of water like it's the most beautiful thing I've seen.

That's when the first bubbles come to the surface.

"There!" I jump up to my feet.

"Throttle closer," a guard orders.

There's a bigger bubble, something moves underwater, then Kai and Archer's heads appear above it, Kai's sharp gasping echoing through the cave.

"They made it!" I shout, then my stomach lurches, because Archer's eyes are closed, his face is motionless, his head tilted backward onto Droga's shoulder.

"He's out!" Droga shouts. "Take him. He needs CPR. Fast!"

Archer is lifted out of the water and splayed on the bottom of the boat.

"I can—"

"Move away!" the guard barks at me before I can offer to do CPR.

I know how!

I scramble to the side on all fours to give room to the guard, barely noticing the other one helping Kai, who falls into the boat, breathing heavily, then crawls toward Archer.

Archer's body is etched with cuts and bruises, so much worse than when he was at Carnage during that fight with Kai.

And blood. There's more blood seeping out of the wound below his ribs, the cloth I tied gone.

The guard starts chest compressions, then leans in and gives him mouth-to-mouth.

Archer chokes and spits out water.

"Archer!" I crawl closer to him, lift his head and help him to half-sit up as the guard blurts something into the radio, the engine roars, and we shoot out of the cave into the open sea.

I kneel before Archer. "You're alright. You'll be fine. Just stay with me," I murmur. "Shirt!" I shout to the guys. "Someone give me a shirt!"

Kai pulls his over his head and tosses it to me, wet.

"A dry one!" I bark.

A security guy strips his, and I tear it with my teeth and make a bandage around Archer's torso, then use the rest to tuck under it and create more pressure on the wound, pressing on it with my hand.

"You are doing great, baby. So great. Stay with me, yeah?"

We ride like we are in a powerboat race. The boat zips around the east and south sides of Zion.

"Archer?" I cup his face with my free hand.

"Yes, kitten?"

He responds!

"I love you, baby."

But he's quiet, his eyes drooping.

"Baby, please, talk to me."

He doesn't.

"Archer, just listen to my voice and stay with me."

He's not responding.

"Please, baby. Don't do this to me. I need you."

His eyes are closed, and I don't know if that's because he's hurting or lost consciousness. A lump in my throat makes it hard to talk, but I lean over and stroke his face as if he can hear.

"There are so many things I never told you, baby," I murmur.

The guards and Kai can probably hear me, but I don't

care. Everything suddenly seems alive—the roaring of the boat engine, the rain slashing at my face, the waves crashing at the hull, the bumps as we cut the waves, the wind ripping my hair across my face—everything but my beautiful man.

There's nothing I can do but tell Archer everything I've always wanted to but was too afraid.

"I never told you how much I love your hands on me. Or the way you smile when I say silly things."

I chuckle.

"Your smell. Your taste."

*Everything about you.*

"The way you call me kitten. I love it."

I shift to curl up next to him, keeping my hand pressed tightly against his wound. His skin is too cold when I press my lips to his bare shoulder. I breathe out as if I can warm it with my breath.

"I never said the right things, or the important ones, the ones I keep to myself because I'm too afraid to let them out. Afraid that if I say them out loud, I'll lose you, or share you with others."

I bury my face in his cold and damp neck, trying to catch his scent that's barely there, overshadowed by the smell of musty seawater.

"I love our breakfasts."

I stay quiet for a moment, trying to hear his breathing. He *is* breathing.

"I've never had a breakfast with a guy. Or two in one morning."

I chuckle but feel tears well up.

"I miss you when you are not around. It's hell. It started a long time ago. That's what made me angry—that we kept our distance, and I couldn't handle it well. I was angry at myself for feeling that way. Now I'm angry that I never told you those things before. Because I'm a coward."

I sniffle, swallowing tears.

"I'll do the upside-down thing, Arch. I promise. First thing. Yeah?" I chuckle through tears. "Just stay with me, baby."

Archer's bleeding through the bandage. I can't lose him. He's my hero. He shielded Droga. He jeopardized his life for me. This man deserves a fucking medal. And to be happy.

"I love you so much, Archer," I whisper, my lips so close to his face, and I kiss him, his nose, his eyes, as if I can share my strength with him. "Stay with me, please."

A barely audible grunt escapes his mouth, then he whispers, "I had to almost die for you to tell me all this?"

I raise my head to see his eyes half-open.

And I laugh through tears and pray. I'm not a religious person, but in the worst moments, we all pray. To something. Someone. For a better outcome. For another chance.

I kiss his face, again and again, letting my tears fall onto him, hoping that we make it to just another day together, even though I want an eternity with him.

# 60

## KAT

ARCHER IS IN THE MEDICAL CENTER, SEDATED, CLEANED UP, and all taken care of. He has a through wound—Dr. Hodges' words bring tears to my eyes.

"Fucker has nine lives, like a cat," Kai jokes.

Archer is lucky. I am even more so—I have him back. Besides losing a lot of blood, he'll be fine and will sleep for the next twenty-four hours.

It's early morning, and I go to my place. Slate follows me and stays at the door. Ayana is still in emergency mode. Security is on high alert. I clean up and change and go back to the medical ward and spend the day and night in Archer's room.

The next day, I call Dad and give him an update, telling him everything in detail. It's hard to gauge his reaction, but his jaw is clenched.

"I need to talk to Marlow, Raven, Bishop, and the rest of the team," he says grimly.

I can't quite figure out my feelings about what happened in the Ashlands and tell Dad about it.

"I might've killed people," I say quietly, trying to come to terms with the thought. "I didn't think about anything in that moment but the fact that they could do something horrible to Archer. They were... I just went off, I guess."

"Kit-Kat, listen to me." I know Dad will work the same therapy technique they used on him during undercover work. "Those who didn't have the intention to hurt you stayed away. Those who had other intentions attacked, and there's nothing wrong with self-defense. That's what it was. Remember the shooting in the mountains right after the Change? If that man didn't hesitate instead of following his moral compass that didn't get the memo about the Change, his wife and daughter would've been alive. So would he. You did what you had to do."

I nod, quiet and still puzzled. "You know what bothers me the most, though?"

He doesn't ask. He's my therapist right now.

"That I don't feel bad about having hurt those people."

There, I got it off my chest. I would've shot the entire Ashlands and Port Mrei to protect Archer. The thought that I could've hesitated with horrible consequences makes me shiver with horror.

"You did great, Kat. You are safe. So is Archer. I suppose there's personal security all over you two now," Dad says.

We sit in silence for a moment, and I feel like I'm finally letting go of the thoughts about that awful night in the Ashlands.

"Here's the thing though," Dad finally says. "Archer is not the most important person to Butcher."

I snort at his ridiculous words. "What do you mean?"

"That guy Raven is."

"What?"

"Without Raven, Butcher will have Port Mrei, the port itself, the access to everything that comes in and out of Zion. He'll have the power to cut Ayana off. That's why I want to talk to everyone and Raven in particular. And soon."

It's a heavy thought, and we agree to discuss it with Archer when he recovers.

There's one more thing left on my list before I go back to the hospital. Threats are not my thing, but it looks like I need to teach someone a lesson.

Twenty minutes later, I knock at Margot's villa.

She opens the door in a blue jumpsuit and golden high heels, one brow arched, one hand on her hip. The girl probably sleeps with heels on, or maybe was born in them. I've tried to talk myself out of this, but bitchslapping is the least she deserves.

My polite smile is definitely an acting masterpiece. "Can I come in for a moment?"

With Archer in the medical ward, a dozen reasons run through Margot's pink head about why I'm here.

I scan her villa as I walk into the living room. Pink and gold are her favorite colors, not surprising, considering she was probably born from two gold bars having sex in a vault of a Swiss Bank.

"What do you want?" she asks curtly but with a trace of curiosity in her voice.

I don't have time or the desire to study her Barbie house, but I do listen carefully—she is alone. Good. That's all I need.

"I told you to leave me alone, yeah?" I turn around to face her.

She rolls her eyes too theatrically, walks past me, and flings herself on the couch, a magazine in her hands. "I don't have time for nonsense." She flips a page loudly. "If you came to sort out your insecurities, leave."

"I don't like nonsense, Margot."

Her arrogance only makes it easier to do what I came here for.

"You pushed it too far this time. Made me angry. Messed with Archer and me."

She tears her eyes off the magazine and cocks her head at me with an obvious irritation that makes my blood boil.

"I almost drowned because of your stupid pranks." I talk slowly, taking pleasure in intimidating her. "Archer and I ended up on the *Empress*, where we had a grand time, thank you very much. But also, that's where we got kidnapped, and Archer almost died."

"Ugh. Spare me your sappy stories. It's not my fault you are a looney."

"No, I suppose not."

"Get lost, Katura."

"In a second. I need you to turn around for me."

She frowns, giving me the most disgusted look I've ever

seen. God, this girl could be pretty if she weren't such a cunt.

"Did you lose your mind?" she snaps.

I walk up to her and nudge her shoulder. "We can do it the easy way or the hard way. Turn around." I push her lightly.

"What the fuck!" She slaps my hand like it's dirty.

"Fine. Your choice. I asked nicely."

She's so confused that she doesn't even fight when I lunge at her. Granted, the fastest this chick ever moved was probably through a Chanel shop. Her self-defense instincts are non-existent.

I push and move her as she starts fighting back, trying to slap and scratch me, but she has no chance.

"What the fuck! You—"

I get behind her and wrestle her down onto the couch.

She sounds like a mouse.

"You are a screamer, Margot. But no one can hear you," I say, chuckling, as I finally have her face down on the couch pillow. She keeps screaming and thrashing under my weight, but I straddle her and kill her attempts to scratch me. She's probably more concerned about her manicure than what I'm about to do.

I press my palm hard on her back, pushing her into the couch. "You either hold still or I'll hurt you."

"Get the fuck off me, bitch!" she squeals, but her thrashing subsides. She knows she has no chance.

I slide my left hand into her pink hair, fisting it. "I said, hold still, or I'll cut you."

She's panting. Sobbing? Jesus, girl, where did all that

sass go? After what she pulled off, she needs a real fucking lesson.

"You know," I say calmly, tightening my grip on her hair, "I always hated your pink hair."

And I pull the scissors out of my back pocket.

## 61

## KAT

I never really got to touch Archer the way I want to. Now that he's asleep, I stand by his hospital bed and run my fingers through his hair, study his face, his powerful form under the hospital sheet, and glide my hand along his torso.

God, I hate hospitals.

I forget myself until I hear his low voice. "Are you fucking around or looking for trouble?"

It's so quiet and unexpected that I freeze like a possum, lifting my eyes to meet his, half-open, studying me.

"Hey." Tears spring to my eyes at the sight of him awake, my heartbeat spiking. I wish I could hug him, straddle him, squeeze him. But he might still be too fragile.

"Hey, wild thing." He smiles. Smiles!

A kiss is the only thing I can offer for now. Then I kneel on the floor by the bed so he doesn't have to lift his head to look at me and take his hand in both of mine, resting my chin on the mattress. "How are you feeling?"

"Fine," he says, his voice stronger than I expected as he studies me. "Your hair looks like a nest."

I blush—I've slept here for hours.

"My favorite nest," he says, chuckling.

"Asshole," I murmur as I try to tame my curls.

He sits up, grunting, leaning on his good arm.

"You shouldn't move!" I protest.

"Come here." Weakly, he pats the mattress next to him.

Carefully, I crawl onto his bed, prop myself on my elbow, and lean in to give him a proper kiss.

His mouth takes mine with urgency like he wasn't just sedated for hours.

"Whoa, mister, so full of energy," I murmur, my heart so full of love for him that it feels too big for my chest.

"Missed you." He kisses me again. "I woke up once before. You were sleeping in the armchair."

"I was?"

I kiss him again when the knock makes us pull apart.

Slate's giant form appears in the doorway. "Boss." He grins—Jesus, does he ever? "How are you feeling?"

"Fantastic," Archer responds, wrapping his arm around my shoulders and pulling me closer.

Maddy comes to check on him, then another nurse.

"Kai was here while I went home to take a shower," I say, my hand absently stroking his chest clad in a blue hospital shift. Archer looks incredibly humble in a hospital bed. "Also Marlow, Ty, Axavier. Bishop stopped by. Margot." I hide an evil chuckle. "She has a new haircut."

"What?"

"A pixie. Looks cute."

Archer frowns. "She hates short hair."

"Not anymore."

Her new haircut doesn't bring me as much joy as the memory of her shrieks while I was cutting her hair like I was taking her life away.

*Bitch.*

We talk for almost an hour and can't stop touching each other. We had to be kidnapped by thugs, beaten up, and go through bullets and explosions to get here. I'm not surprised. Nothing about us is mundane since we met. And as we talk, I steal more touches and breathe him in like a total creeper.

The sun sets, sinking the room into dimness.

Archer's kisses get a little too insistent, and I love it. We're back in our own little bubble, if only for a short while. There's security outside the door, outside the hospital, and at our houses. I feel somewhat safe outside, but next to Archer—well, I could go through the best and the worst with him. Except this one-on-one time is becoming my favorite. God, what happened to Kat-on-the-go?

I run my forefinger along his split brow and still-swollen nose.

"You have all these wounds. They give you an edge," I say, trying to sound playful.

"An edge?" His lips curl in a smirk.

"Yeah. I like that."

"My edge?"

"You."

"*You* are my edge, Kat. You are the sharpest edge, and I never wanna lose you."

He mimics me, running his fingertips along my slightly bruised jaw, then gently turns my head to the side and brushes his fingers along the bruises on my neck. Then pulls me in and kisses me.

His lips are way too insistent for a person who just got shot. My hand slides under the blanket, tracing the cotton fabric of Archer's gown until I reach his bare leg and slide my hand back up. He shifts, spreading his legs and opening up for me.

"Now I get the appeal of skirts," I murmur into his mouth as my hand reaches his privates, surprised to find him hard. I don't mean to get him all stirred up but can't help it either. "Such easy access," I whisper as I gently stroke his cock under the shift, making him grunt. I swear, no sedatives will ever defeat Archer's erection. Nothing will ever stop me from wanting him in the most inappropriate times.

"I need a little therapy," he says. "Get on top of me, kitten."

I stop. "Archer, maybe you should take it easy, I can just go down—"

"Nuh-huh. I want you. You started it. Get on my cock, kitten."

I get off the bed and shimmy out of my pants and panties in seconds, then unwrap his body from the blanket, lift the gown, and straddle him.

"Tell me if anything hurts," I say and slowly sink onto him, grunting at the pleasure of him filling me up.

"There you are," he whispers, closing his eyes and tilting his head back.

Sex is Archer's food, diet, drug, exercise, and, judging by how he already rolls his hips just a tiny bit to thrust deeper inside me, pushing through pain—his medication.

I lean over and kiss him, rubbing against him, trying to mind his ribs and other body parts that might hurt. But he apparently doesn't. His hands lift my shirt and yank the bra up, freeing my breasts and cupping them with his usual hunger.

I moan, riding him. This will be a quick fix until he gets a little more stable.

There's a knock at the door, but we don't stop. Another one, more insistent.

"Hold on!" I shout. "We're having sex!"

"So subtle," he murmurs into my mouth, and I feel him tense under me. He needs some attention right now. So I disregard my own needs and increase the tempo, fucking him rhythmically until he comes and sags against the bed like he just ran a marathon.

Clothes back on, sheets in place, I pass him a glass of water and walk to open the door for Dr. Hodges, whose smile is way too humorous for what I just yelled as I rode Archer.

"Sorry," I say, embarrassed.

Doc promises to let Archer go home in a couple of days, but only if I agree to get a live-in nurse and watch him day and night at least for a couple of days.

"Tsk," I say disappointed.

Doc gives me an apologetic look. "Too much?"

"You should've said two weeks. Then I'd have him all to myself for longer."

Laughing, he leaves, and I'm about to text Droga to come and give me a break for an hour or so. Archer doesn't need that much supervision, but suddenly, the whole world wants to be next to him. Freaking Axavier suggested that all of us move to Cliff Ville to take care of Archer. What is this, high school?

"He's not crippled," I said, regretting it right away because Axavier seemed almost hurt at the words.

Right now, I can't stand to spend even a minute without Archer. "So, listen, I'll go to my place and get a computer. We could watch a movie or something. If you can't sleep, that is. Or whatever you want. Tell me."

"Come here." Archer pats the spot next to him, and there I am again, lying next to him, stroking his face like we are cheesy Romeo and Juliette who found out they got to Heaven and now have all the time in the world for each other.

"I said some things on the yacht, but I'm not sure you heard me. *Really* heard me."

"I heard you, Arch," I say, his fingers playing with my hair giving me goosebumps.

"I am head over heels in love with you, Kat."

My heart flutters. But I'm not scared of the words this time.

"Before Cece's birthday, I was already falling for you, Kat, fast and hard. I tried to rationalize my feelings, fight them, but it didn't work."

His confession is too open, but it also makes my heart beat so loudly that if Archer's phone was in the room, his vital tracker for me would've exploded.

"I've never felt like this before," he says. "Never wanted anyone like I wanted you. I've never felt as happy as I was with you. I've never been as low as I was when you said those words the night of Cece's birthday. I wanted to stay away so I could think clearly. But that seemed harder when you weren't around and all I wanted was to be with you."

Feelings overwhelm me, but I keep my eyes locked with his as he speaks.

"I've never shared my dreams with anyone, Kat, but you are part of them now. Before, I dreamed of conquering the world, but I can send the world to hell if you tell me you don't care about it."

"You did conquer the world last time I checked."

He pushes the hair out of my face. I melt when he touches me like this.

"That's not what I mean, Kat. Things are changing. Ayana and Zion are not what they used to be. There will be more attacks. But this entire island means nothing to me if there's a threat of losing you, Kat. I can't."

I don't understand. "What are you saying?"

"That if you say the word, we can leave. We can go anywhere. Peru. Iceland. I have houses in Sydney and São Paulo. Where would you like to go?"

"You're not serious…"

"You'd better have more trust in me. Take your pick. We can leave for good. I'll never jeopardize your safety."

"I don't care where I am. As long as it's with you, Archer."

His smile is more of a reflex. He let go. I can tell by the

way he looks at me, his eyes glazed over with emotions, and he doesn't hide them.

"You are the most amazing person I've ever met, Arch," I say. It's not a compliment, it's the truth, and it's my turn to man the hell up and tell him how much he means to me. "The strongest too. This island needs you. No, don't roll your eyes at me. I'm not saying this because it uses you and your resources. But because you have the power to make it the best it can be. Not just Ayana, but Port Mrei. And the Ashlands. Especially, the Ashlands."

His jaw tightens at the word. There have been security searches in the Ashlands, cleaning sweeps, and arrests. Ayana has its cameras on at all times, because now our safety is jeopardized, and it will only get worse before it gets better.

"You know," I say, "they say that a country is not judged by how it treats its citizens but by how it handles its prisoners. There are a lot of people who need help with turning their lives around. You saw that."

"Look at you, Mother Theresa."

I narrow my eyes at him as I slowly say, "I've never met anyone I enjoyed choking out so much. I might try it again—"

He lunges at me too quickly, considering his injuries, but I don't fight back when he wrestles me into his chest in a playful choke hold. But then his hold loosens. He doesn't let me go, just holds me. His other arm wraps around my back, and he buries his face in my hair.

There's silence. We can exchange words and insults and

cocky remarks, but it's the silence between us that's the most meaningful.

I finally break it. "I might be hot-tempered occasionally. And irrational. But I'm crazy about you, and sometimes I go overboard when I think I might lose you."

"You won't."

"You are the one who's saved millions around the world. Me, I would sacrifice that entire world for you, Archer. The world depends on you. Because if you are in danger—I'll set it on fire." I try to swallow a lump in my throat. "I want to always be by your side."

I sniffle, trying to hold back tears.

"I love you, beautiful," he says softly. "I love your body, and your crazy mind, and your free spirit. You push my buttons, get under my skin, and you make me the happiest guy on earth. The day you choked me out, I knew you were the only woman who could take my breath away."

I chuckle, but my chest tightens, and my eyes burn at the thought of how much I love him. Love, the scariest word, now grips my heart in the tightest chokehold.

"I love you too," I whisper.

"What was that, you little coward?" He pulls away to look at me.

I blush. I've said the words before, felt them inside me for weeks, repeated them in my head over and over again, and whispered them on the boat when I thought he might die. Yet, saying them to his face is different. It feels like everything inside me surges while the world around stays the same.

*Jesus, Kat, keep it together.*

But I haven't been together since I met this man.

"You are the most fascinating man I've met. I think I knew I'd be in love with you before I even met you, when I studied your file before coming to Zion." I smile into his chest, then peek at him. Archer is smiling, his gaze never leaving me. "Does it sound strange?"

"Sounds like you, kitten."

I laugh, hiding my face in his chest again, then raise my eyes at him. "I love when you call me that."

"I know." He taps my nose with his forefinger, and my heart warms at the gesture.

"This is awkward," I whisper, shy at this display of affection.

"I'll bring the usual Archer back in just a minute."

"I'm not used to this. You like this. Us."

"We won't do it often, I promise."

We both laugh. We must be the weirdest, fucked up, emotionally repressed people out there.

I smile, rubbing my chin on his chest, keeping my gaze locked with his. "I love you."

"I love you more, wild thing." He smiles.

"Nah. I love you more."

"You know it's not a competition."

"It's not. You are right." And I can't help grinning. "But I'd like to point out—"

He shuts me up with a kiss, his hand at the back of my head gently fisting my hair.

I had a valid point, I promise. But Archer knows my weak spots. And he just invaded one of them with his gorgeous mouth.

## 62

## ARCHER

I'M IN THE HOSPITAL FOR THREE LONG DAYS. DURING THAT time, Kat doesn't leave my side.

"I want you to ride my face," I say to her one night, obviously getting better since I'm horny as hell and mad that I still have to abide by Doc's rules.

Kat blushes, laughs, then rolls her eyes.

"I'm serious." I watch her lick her lips and realize we've never done that yet. I point my forefinger at my face. "Now."

She darts to the door to lock it and comes back so fast that I want to laugh.

Some girls are enthusiastic about shopping with their boyfriends, cooking, and watching movies or whatnot. My girl is enthusiastic about my tongue. Can't blame her. I ace everything. Maybe, besides making pancakes and shooting guns. But then, my girl likes my tongue and kills it at making pancakes and shooting guns. Occasionally, God creates perfect matches. Don't hate.

On day four, I fight with Doc and leave for Cliff Villa. There's a day-nurse from Port Mrei there. Alma cooks and glows like a Christmas tree at the sight of me and Kat. Kat and I watch movies and fall asleep cuddling in my bed, *our* bed.

Two weeks of sex and sleep and dinners together. One could call it a vacation. But also two weeks of reports about the Ashlands at war with Zion security. The area has been raided several times. Several bunkers with weapons were uncovered. But everyone knows that's not all of it. How many of those exist?

Port Mrei lies low. Raven and his security team went to meet with Butcher, who denied any involvement—another bad sign since he's in charge and waits for an opportunity to strike.

There are a lot of changes to come.

And day fifteen of me back from the hospital ward starts with three agendas.

Agenda #1:

This morning, Cliff Villa echoes with Kat's loud cries as she falls onto the bed and scrambles on all fours to get away from me.

"Screw this!" she snaps at me.

I sink onto my knees, shaking with laughter.

We did the upside-down thing. *Tried*, to be correct.

Kat was doing a headstand. I held her legs and spread them open, wrapping them around my hips. Gotta say—the view of her pussy from above was out of this world, and I didn't hesitate to lean over and lick her. That the proper way of eating out.

Too bad the logistics didn't quite work afterward. I slid my cock into her for a hot second and tried to fuck. She wobbled, then cursed when I slid out and tried to suppress a chuckle at the ridiculousness of it all. She finally broke free from me and fell onto the bed like an acrobat on a mat.

"You are crazy!" she shouts, her face beet-red, as she sits up right away, pissed like a wasp in a rattled nest.

"You are a beginner," I reason, still shaking with laughter.

If ridiculousness can even be appealing in a sex scenario, there's no other person I'd have it with than my wild thing.

"You are crazy," Kat hisses as she gets off the bed, throwing a pillow at me to shut me up.

"Katura Ortiz, have you met yourself? Come on," I tease her. "One more try."

"Not a chance!" She snatches her clothes from the floor. "It's… It's ridiculous. I can't believe I went along with this nonsense."

I lunge at her but she yanks her hand away, pointing her forefinger at me. "Don't. I'm done here. Gonna take a shower. And—" She whips around, her hand on her waist, the other still pointing a forefinger at me, her expression dangerous. My naked warrior is up to something, and I cock my head, leaning back on my elbows and admiring her. "Since I agreed to your upside-down endeavor…" She pauses with a warning that hangs in the air for a moment.

I fold my arms behind my head, stretching on the bed and giving her a full view of my naked body, hoping she'll come back for more exercise.

"You didn't *agree*," I argue. "You lost a bet. And made a promise once again, on the boat ride." I grin. "You promised a whole bunch of things, so you can't back away, kitten. I almost died, remember?"

I'm so working her right now and love that feistiness in her glare-slash-batting-her-lashes.

"Archer Crone, don't give me this 'injured pigeon' act. You turned out fine. But since I go along with a lot of your crazy ideas, I want to try something with you, too."

"Oh, I'm all ears."

She can't possibly suggest anything I won't be willing to try or anything that can surprise me—

"Pegging," she blurts out, tilting her chin as if in a dare.

"Excuse me?" My jaw drops in shock.

There's that shit grin on her face as she catches my shocked stare.

"You are pushing it," I argue. Not a fucking chance!

"Oh, yeah?" She turns around slowly, taking her sweet bare ass toward the bathroom, and I can tell by the seductive swing of her hips that she's messing with me.

Not fucking happening. "Kat! Not a chance!" I sit up, still processing what she just said.

"Oh, yeah?" She doesn't turn around as she approaches the wall slab to turn into the bathroom. "Com-pro-mise," she sings as she disappears into the bathroom.

"Kat! Come here, now!"

I don't like those crazy ideas, considering my girlfriend is capable of choking me out and doing God knows what in the meantime. We need boundaries here, rules. I'm— Fuck! I'm more than a little fucking uneasy.

"Kat!"

She doesn't come back, and her shit grin flickers in my mind again. Annoyed, I get up and stomp toward the bathroom. "You are so in trouble. The fuck you get these ideas from? Axavier? That guy, I swear…"

My cock is still hard, and Kat needs a proper spanking, plus the clear message that there are certain things I refuse to compromise on, including…

Pegging, seriously?

But we'll discuss it while I fuck her.

Because when her pussy is filled with my cock, she's a lot more agreeable.

# 63

---

## ARCHER

Agenda #2 is probably the most important meeting since the one when Gen-Alpha medication was approved by the FDA.

Seven board members and I are discussing the possibility of taking Gen-Alpha public, which is a huge deal, not only for the board members and investors but also for the people affected by radiation. An IPO will ensure the availability of the drug through health insurance.

I take the time to dress up and enjoy Kat studying my attire like I'm a model. I've always been more or less calm even before the most important meetings. Now, if it all fails, I know I have something to come back home to—her. I'll always have her, and the thought makes me feel invincible.

"You know," I say, sharing yet another secret thought. There's a lot of this between us lately. "I used to get jealous when I saw Droga and Callie back at Deene staring all gooey-eyed at each other. I'm a selfish asshole, that was the only reason I lured her away from him. I was afraid to lose my best friend, and did anyway." I walk up to her and pull her into me. "But if anyone ever tried to pull something like that with you and take you away from me… I swear, Kat, I would rip their hearts out and put them on a stake on public display like they did in medieval times."

"Mr. Chancellor, ever the romantic."

"I can never lose you, Kat." I bow my head to press my forehead to hers.

"You know what? If anyone tried to steal you away from me, I'd do much worse. There are those interrogation techniques they used at Chinese prison camps during—"

"Wild thing." I press my forefinger to her lips, silencing her. "This was supposed to be romantic."

She shakes her head, laughing. "I'm joking."

She pulls back and fixes my suit jacket. "Looking gorgeous," she says, stretching her hand toward my face, her forefinger about to tap my nose. I clutch my teeth at it, making her squeal, then pick her up, and throw her over my shoulder. My wound is not fully healed yet, making me wince with pain, but I can't help messing with her.

While Kat whales and threatens and claws at my ass, I carry her to the front door, then set her down and give her a kiss.

"Slate is outside, but lock the door. There's a new code on it."

"What is it?"

"0525"

"Why?"

"The day you washed ashore Zion."

Kat's smile flickers on and off—she gets shy instantly in

moments like this—then she whispers, "I love you so much."

I'll never tire of hearing this. My heart does a "back willie," "front willie," and "burnout" all at once.

"What was that?" I smile, wanting her to say it louder. She's still in practice mode when she says things like this and shies away right after.

"Love you, bye!" she blurts and shuts the door in my face, making me laugh as I walk toward my bike.

I get to the Center when a message beeps on my phone.

**Kat: You are great, baby. You are powerful. You are the strongest person I know. You'll make it happen!**

And then another text comes.

**Kat: I love you so much.**

I stare at the screen. No one has talked to me like this in the longest time. Not even my dad. The fact that I have someone who tells me these simple words means the world. Kat and I used to feed off each other's arrogance. It was a double-edged sword. Now we are sharing each other's strengths.

I text back.

**Me: Katura Ortiz, did I tell you that you are amazing?**

**Kat: What was that?**

*Brat.*

I grin, typing, **I love you.** Then send another text, **There's a present for you in the closet for tonight.**

Presents make her smile, and I want to see all the shades of her smiles.

Droga sent me a text the other day.

**She's worth waking up to.**

And a picture: me asleep in my hospital bed, hooked up to the IV and heart monitor. Kat is next to me in her clothes on top of my sheet, halfway over me like she always is, her hand on my chest. I know she's asleep in the picture but totally invading my hospital bed.

That picture beats all the ones before. Soon, I'll need a photo album for us. These pictures are getting cuter by the day.

There's a knock at the door, and Amir pops in. "Are you ready?"

His eyes don't leave me as we approach the door of the conference room.

"Just so you know"—he places his hand on my shoulder —"despite what my father's opinion is, or others, I am with you a hundred percent, Archer. You have my support."

There are quite a number of people lately who support me. The feeling is new, and though most people take it for granted, I feel extremely grateful.

## 64

### ARCHER

"How did it go?"

Kat meets me at the door when I come back to the villa after the meeting, and I'm momentarily distracted by the sight of her. Her hair is loose and styled to one side. Her makeup is done. Jesus fucking Christ, I thought I was getting a wild thing, but she occasionally transforms into this sexy bombshell and takes my breath away.

I can see she's on pins and needles.

"Great," I answer, and she throws herself at me and wraps her arms around my neck. "The meeting was a little intense, but I think we're on the right track with Gen-Alpha."

But I don't want to think about that right now, because we have agenda #3.

Tonight is the opening of Kat's Thai food restaurant. It's called Bangkok. Kat is super excited about this simple name and even more so about the big party with half of Ayana attending.

I lose my suit and change into jeans and a black dress shirt.

Kat disappears in her closet and comes out wearing the red Givenchy dress I bought her. The gold chains secured over her shoulders hold the loose red fabric that cascades down her front but leaves the sides and the back bare, ties around her waist, and hangs loosely down to her calves with a side slit.

She's sin incarnate. I'm speechless. She stands on her tiptoes and turns around, showing herself off as she bats her eyelashes at me.

I want to fuck her against the wall, bang the shit out of her, screw our brains out until we're sweaty and panting and naked on some surface of this house we still haven't fucked on—there're only a few options left.

If only she wasn't obsessed with Thai food so much...

But I think I found my new kink—fawning over my girl and spoiling her.

I walk into my closet and get the small jewelry box from a drawer.

"The final touch," I tell her when I emerge and see her already in her high heels.

The present is the Icon Cushion Cut Yellow Diamond pendant and earrings from Graff. I'm not an expert, but Cece drools over Graff's diamond craftsmanship.

"Archer," Kat whispers as I help her put them on.

"Come here." I lead her to the full-length mirror in her closet and stand behind her, admiring the view.

"How much did it cost?" she asks.

"Does it matter?"

"I'm just curious."

"Well, it was either that or a brand new car, but you can't drive at Ayana."

She whips around in my arms. "What?" She's impressed—checkmark. "And it, what"—she carefully touches the necklace with her fingertips—"just sits around my neck?"

"Yeah, wild thing. It just sits there and enjoys the privilege. Until you get a pearl necklace."

She swats me away with a grin.

Kat never asks for anything, and I want to spoil her endlessly. I have the money to impress her, but I want to do so much more—show her the world. I just had to know she'd choose me over the rest of the world. And she did, a few times, risking her life doing that.

"You look amazing," I say.

"Someone said I look the best in my birthday suit." She smiles. "In fact, most of Ayana knows that."

We both laugh. We let go. This is the new *us*.

We walk out into the living room, and she pauses by the painting. "Now that I think about it, I match. Look!"

She strikes a pose against the gray wall, her dress a bright splash of red.

"Makes sense." I nod. "Red is my favorite color."

"I thought it was gray."

"Nah, red."

"Since when?"

"Since I met you."

She laughs again happily. She loves compliments. And I love her laughter. Also, the color red. It's the color of danger, but also seduction, and—as per my own philosophy—uniqueness. That's Kat.

"Let's walk," she says as we leave Cliff Villa.

She looks around at Slate and the other guard, who follow us at a slight distance. "You think we can outrun them?"

See?

"Stop." I shake my head with a smile.

"We should carry weapons."

"You have bodyguards for that. Though I gotta admit, you are excellent with guns."

"Yeah, well, shooting ranges, simulation rooms, paintball. Hey! I can be your bodyguard!" She laughs again and slides her arm around my waist.

I swing my arm around her bare shoulder as we walk. My wild thing is more excited about danger than she should be. Adrenalin junkie—I didn't fully understand the concept until her. I didn't know or understand many things until her. There's my life before her. And then there's *her*. She's the most gorgeous woman who's ever walked the earth, the most sneaky and brave. My beautiful spy. My personal Nikita.

Feelings suddenly overwhelm me and I feel… Fuck, I feel proud walking next to her.

Whoa, ladies and gentlemen! The king is officially on his knees.

"So what's the plan after the restaurant?" she asks.

"Easy there. We didn't even make it to the party yet. And it's *your* first party."

"Yeah, well…"

"Do I hear hesitation?"

"You don't. I just want to spend more time with you."

I grin, tightening my arm around her shoulders as we walk. "We don't have to stay long. My place after that."

"I was hoping for it."

"Actually, I want you at my place every night. And day. And morning."

She lifts her face to look at me.

She's already at Cliff Villa most of the time, but occasionally goes back to her bungalow, and in those hours, Cliff Villa feels empty.

"I want you to move in with me," I say.

She narrows her eyes at me as if checking if I'm bluffing. "Are you sure you can handle it?"

"I should be asking *you* that."

"Arch, I'll drive you insane. I like decorations and all sorts of things on the walls." This is not rejection, because her voice is way too excited, and so is her grin.

"I'll compromise."

"And plants."

"Deal."

"And shelves and pictures of us." She's pushing it.

"Sure."

"And a dog."

"That's a no."

"Archer!" She laughs anyway.

"By the way, I have another present for you."

"You'll spoil me rotten."

"I intend to."

"What is it?"

"It's a surprise for after the party. But I'll give you a hint. It says, 'kitten' on it."

Kat halts, pulling me to a stop, and frowns for a moment, then her eyes widen. "You did not…" Her mouth falls open.

I laugh loudly. "Yep."

"Kitten? Seriously? I was joking, Arch!" She frowns. "Nah. Did you really?"

"Well, *I* wasn't joking."

I did get her the gun she wanted. Yep, encrusted with white diamonds and red rubies, because, well, red is her color. And yes, it says 'kitten' in gold-plated letters. And yes, this woman makes me do silly things.

"Archer!" She swings her arms around my neck. "You're so fucked up! I love it!"

We both laugh loudly, our chests shaking against each other.

She pulls back right away, her eyes wide in excitement. "Can we go home real quick to look at it?"

"No."

"Just a quick peek! Please-please-please?"

I know her theatrics by now. "Shh, no. It's your restaurant opening night."

She wrinkles her nose in disappointment, but I can tell she's happy. We stand under a street light for a moment, our eyes not leaving each other, and she says the one thing I'd never expect from Kat:

"Maybe we should've done a small romantic dinner tonight instead. Just you and I."

I brush my thumb against her cheek, and she leans into

427

it, her eyes fluttering closed just for a moment.

We have a lot of people and friends waiting for us, but the fact that she always chooses me makes my heart melt. This affectionate sparkle in her eyes will soon change into a mischievous one, but the way she looks at me right now is meant only for me. Her feelings shine through her eyes so powerfully that they assault me like a tsunami wave. I'm the only one who knows that Kat—Kat in love.

I smile and kiss her temple.

"They are waiting," I say softly. "Shall we?"

And we start walking.

In a moment, Kat will return to that flirty-sassy self that she shows others.

I'm the only one who gets to see all sides of her. It's a privilege.

Kat is the madness that keeps me on my toes but lets me finally sleep peacefully at night when she's in my arms.

She is the serpent that constantly seduces me with crazy ideas and the sweetest apple I bite into, learning something new every day, even if it leads me to ruin.

She *is* my ruin, wrecking me with her passion at night. And she rebuilds my strength every day, when she looks softly into my eyes and says, "You are the strongest man I know." Not the richest, not the smartest, but the strongest.

With her, I feel I can part oceans and move mountains. And I'll do it for her in the blink of an eye.

She is the softest silk and the sharpest dagger. Ukrainian, Puerto Rican, and the whole world in between. A world so diverse that it makes my head spin.

Yet, when she snuggles up to me at night, I can hold that entire world in my arms.

She *is* a queen. *My* queen.

There's a thought I've entertained for some time. I just need to make sure she's ready for it. She will be, soon.

*Katura Crone.*

I smile to myself.

Sounds abrasive, just like her.

Perfect.

# EPILOGUE
## RAVEN

ONE THING I STAYED AWAY FROM FOR THE LONGEST TIME WAS parties. I have no interest in large gatherings, flattering, and forced politeness.

But there's a change of heart lately. It's a girl. Not just any girl, but the most good-hearted and liked girl on this island, Maddy.

Maddy, Maddy, Maddy.

She's a mystery. I can't explain it yet, but she's drawing me in. She doesn't know that I'm watching her closely.

Bangkok is booming with music and laughter, laced with the smell of whiskey and spices. Half of Ayana is at the grand opening of the restaurant Archer build for his girlfriend.

He's chatting with Kai Droga and Ty Reyes, winking at Katura across the room. They survived the Ashlands—this is a post-victory high.

I lean on a statue of a sitting Buddha by the small inside waterfall amidst the bamboo trees as I watch everyone.

Our precious island is in its happy bubble again. This place is like a trampoline, shooting you high on serotonin, then bringing you low, and you are lucky if you don't miss and land on a hard surface, breaking your bones.

Archer has had more extremes than anyone else, and look at him—smiling, drinking, celebrating, not realizing that what happened in the Ashlands is crumbs compared to the war that will soon break out on Zion. It's only a matter of time.

The rowdy crowd goes through a line of buffet food, chats and drinks. Soon, they'll be dancing, and there'll be more drama. Hence, me usually staying away from parties.

Except there's one person who finally showed up on the social scene—Maddy.

I saw her come in an hour ago, wearing a light blue summer dress and white sneakers, her hair loose. She's the only reason I'm here. I like to keep tabs on people who interest me, and she's become the number one on my list.

It's an hour of me doing just that—staying away from everyone, watching, sipping whiskey, and watching some more.

I eventually lose sight of her for a minute, then find her in the crowd with Marlow. The two make their way with cocktails in their hands toward the other side of the water-fall where I stand, close enough for me to hear their conversations.

Katura stalks toward them with a plate in her hand. She looks gorgeous, right up Archer's alley—I've seen his girls before, though knowing Katura's background, his choice surprises me.

Katura pushes the plate into Marlow's chest. "There. That's *Kua Kling* and is super hot, for daredevils."

"I said I wanna try."

"I warned you. You might hurt yourself."

"I like living dangerously," Marlow responds, takes the plate, then says something in Russian, and Kat bursts out laughing.

They look around, like they're sharing a secret, then blurt, "Sorry," to Maddy.

"You're fine. I have to go anyway."

Maddy sets her cocktail down on the waterfall edge, pulls a hair tie from her clutch, and fixes her loose hair into a bun—I know she's going to work the night shift at the medical ward. She's always working. It's admirable. She's a loner like me, too.

What I see next gives me goosebumps.

Kat blurts something in Russian to Marlow again, and they both burst out laughing.

Maddy stands with her back to them as she fixes her hair and visibly tries really hard not to laugh. She purses her full lips and bites the bottom one. And no, not because Kat's laughter is contagious... The next time Kat says something in Russian, Maddy's lips twitch in another smile.

My skin is thick as a python's, cut, bruised, and weathered. But there are goosebumps...

Maddy, the Good Doer, huh? Who would've thought that the good girl of Zion has a secret no one saw coming?

I realize now what drew me to her in the first place—something hiding under her calmness and confidence, the dark past that can relate to the devil in me.

Maddy says goodbyes and leaves the restaurant, and my heart thuds so hard that even Carnage fights don't compare to the amount of adrenalin that pumps through my veins when I follow.

Catching dangerous lies, finding out deep secrets, and learning others' weaknesses is my hobby. There's something unsettling in seeing little cracks on perfect surfaces, but inevitably, you touch them, and scratch them to see how deep they go.

Flaws are human nature. The Bible is not a manual on how to fight them but an encyclopedia on the wide range of human imperfections. You didn't know you were a sinner? Go to church, they'll open your eyes. Feeling happy? Open the holy scripture, it'll let you know that you don't have redemption.

Who knew that perfect Maddy has a crack?

I follow her in the dark for some time, then, making sure no one is around, I call her name.

She turns in surprise, but unlike others in my presence, especially at night, there's no unease in her eyes, not even a tiny bit, never has been—that's what startled me about her in the first place.

Her gaze acquires the intensity of someone too attracted to danger. It's unusual and amusing—a girl, not afraid. It makes me want to push her farther, see what makes her afraid, which part of me will scare her if she ever got to know me better, and she will, soon—the anger that lashes out when someone gets too deep into my own cracks, or the number of people I've hurt, or the scars all over my body that tell monstrous stories.

"How are you?" I ask, stepping out of the shadows and slowly approaching her, coming close, closer yet, too close, testing her, my chest almost against hers as I step into her, which would've made any other person take a step back.

But she doesn't budge, never does.

*Interesting. Alright.*

I take a tiny step back, giving her room.

"I'm good, Raven, how are you?"

What's unusual is the subtle but obvious assertiveness in her tone. It has an edge that's never there when she's around others. *Sweet soft-spoken Maddy,* as Archer said. It's her sweetness I crave and that very tiny edge that I want to dig deeper into, peel off her outer layer to see what's underneath it.

When she's alone with me, which only happened on a few occasions, I heard that dare in her voice. There's no sweetness in it. Maybe, sexiness. A slight shift to a different personality, the one she hides from everyone else.

"I'm great," I say.

The tension between us is palpable as we stand in front of each other like predator and prey, and I like it. She always looks me straight in the eyes as if challenging me. It surprises me and turns me on. I like that too.

"What makes this evening great?" she asks, that dare in her voice again.

*You. Or what I'm going to do to you.* She'll find out soon enough.

"I watched you in the restaurant, Maddy."

She blinks slowly and nods. "You did." Not a question —sweet Maddy is too perceptive.

"Wondered what you were laughing about with Katura and Marlow."

Her poker face is great. "Just a joke."

I stretch my hand toward her face, waiting for her to pull back, but she doesn't, doesn't even acknowledge it, her eyes locked with mine the whole time. I brush my finger along a loose strand of her hair. Her eyes widen just a tiny bit at the touch, but even this overly inappropriate gesture doesn't make her flinch or pull away.

*Huh.*

"A joke," I echo, cocking my head as I study her. "Except, they spoke Russian."

My finger inches down the side of her face, her neck, sliding along her smooth bare skin and to her shoulder, stopping at the strap of her dress.

I shift my eyes to meet her gaze again.

Hers is blazing. But not with fear, realization—she got caught, she knows that, and I'm the worst person to know her secret. Also, the best one to keep it. For a price, of course. It will come with heavy consequences. Doom is inevitable. I've felt it for months. But if I'm going down, I'm taking everything I can from life. She'll be my last meal.

I let a smile out to play when I say intentionally calm and soft, almost in a whisper, sensing her tension, "Do you want to tell me how you know Russian?" Then calmly add, *"Maddy?"*

Letting her secret out spikes the anticipation that makes every cell in my body come alive—she'll be mine.

"Or should I call you Milena Tsariuk?"

If you're craving more of **Ruthless Paradise**, I have great news!
A Russian mafia princess/ the most dangerous guy on Zion who falls madly in love with her/ a hurricane/ another kidnapping/ a vicious war between Ayana and Port Mrei— are you ready for **RAVEN (Book #5)?**

## ALSO BY THIS AUTHOR:

RUTHLESS PARADISE SERIES:

BOOK 1: **OUTCAST**
BOOK 1.5: **ANGEL, MINE** (NOVELLA)
BOOK 2: **PETAL**
BOOK 3: **CHANCELLOR**
BOOK 4: **WILD THING**
BOOK 5: **RAVEN**

STANDALONE NOVELS:

**BROOKLYN CUPID**

Printed in Great Britain
by Amazon